MEG'S MOMENT

By

Amy Johnson

World Castle Publishing
http://www.worldcastlepublishing.com

This is a work of fiction. Names, characters, places, and incidents are products of the author's imagination or are used fictitiously and are not to be construed as real. Any resemblance to actual events, locations, organizations, or person, living or dead, is entirely coincidental.

World Castle Publishing
Pensacola, Florida

Copyright © Amy Johnson 2011
ISBN: 9781937593247
Library of Congress Catalogue Number 2011937352

First Edition World Castle Publishing October 1, 2011
http://www.worldcastlepublishing.com

Cover: Karen Fuller
Editor: Beth Price

Dedication

For Josh, Zach, Ashley and Tyler. My inspiration and my world.

Amy Johnson

Chapter One

"Passion or comfort? That is the question. Which is more important in a relationship?" asked Megan Malone, domestic Goddess, column author, mommy to two Golden Retrievers and one defiant gold fish. Megan was seated at her weekly 'What's the Topic' luncheon with the girls at their usual table in the 'Usual Place', a trendy soup and salad joint in the middle of town.

"Clarification?" asked Josie who was infinitely 25, blonde this week and dressed in leather from head to toe.

"Ok. Would you rather be with someone who you are absolutely comfortable with where you don't have to put up a front and pretend? Someone who knows you better than you know yourself and knows exactly what you want and like. Or would you rather be with someone who sucks your breath away with a look, looks at you like you're lunch, then scoops you up and devours you sexually until you forget your own name," Megan clarified.

"This for you personally or for the column?" Stacy inquired. Stacy was the most logical and sensible of the girls. She was 30 years old, lived in a sensible home on a sensible street, drives a sensible car and has been married for five years to a sensible man. Nothing wrong with any of that except sometimes, sensible is boring. And in Stacy's case, boring and predictable could quite possibly describe her from cradle to grave.

"What?" Meg asked a little preoccupied.

"The question. Is it for you personally or for the column?"

"Oh!" Meg faked surprise bringing her hand to her chest and making her eyes wide. "For the column of course. I'm perfectly happy in my marriage," she lied.

5

"Who you trying to convince honey?" asked the always observant Mickey. Mickey was a therapist's wet dream. He's a bi-polar transvestite who had living a double life down to a fine art. You see Mickey was a bit confused. Sometimes he wanted to be a boy in which case he dressed like one and went by his birth name Michael. Other times he wanted to be a girl, a diva really, and dressed in drag usually cramming his size 13 foot in stiletto heels. While in drag he went by Mikayla. Since most of the time he wore jeans and a T-shirt the girls just called him Mickey and he tended to bounce back and forth from Michael to Mikayla at random. Today he was just Mickey styling in his skinny jeans and pink T-shirt that had the word 'Princess' blazed across the chest.

"Ignore him. He's just looking for some scandal," Ali said giving Mickey a stern look.

"I don't have to look for it honey child. I am a walking scandal. Scandal makes life fun. What you need is a little more scandal and a lot less drab. Ok-ay," He high-fived the other women at the table while Ali kicked him under the table. Ali was the newlywed. We hate her. She was totally in love with her new hubby and never let an opportunity pass to let the world know. Sometimes we wanted to smash her in the head with a rolling pin but mostly we just love her and were happy that one of us finally found the real thing. Ok so we envied the hell out of her. Sometimes.

"Can we just get back to the original question please?" a frustrated Meg asked.

"Passion or Comfort?"

"Passion! Absolutely! Life is too short to spend your time in bed with a mechanical robot stuck in missionary position. I for one need a little variety. A little spice," reported Josie.

"Well that's one way of looking at it. I mean we all know that the reason you can't make it to a third date with anyone is because you're a spoiled princess pain in the ass. But if you look at it that way it appears that you replace them instead of you getting dumped. Optimism works for you babe," Mickey took a long pull on his lemonade and opened his mouth to start on her again but stopped when Ali kicked him under the table again. Josie eyed him with narrow slits that if looks could kill would have spontaneously combusted his head right then and there.

"Well I for one vote for comfort," Stacy began. "We all know that passion fizzles after a while and I would take comfort and continuity over passion anytime. Love isn't always excitement and sizzle. It's hard work and when the passion is gone the important thing is that you have something left. Something that will stand the test of time. Like comfort. With yourself and with your partner," Meg nodded and Josie and Mickey both rolled their eyes.

"Boring." Mickey and Josie both said in unison.

"No not boring. Sensible. Realistic," Stacy defended.

Another eye roll.

"What do you think Ali?" Stacy asked hoping for a little support.

"Well" Ali sat her diet coke on the table and played with the straw. "I think you can have both. Look at Bill and me. We've been married 2 years now and we are completely comfortable with each other. We are set in our routines and habits and sure life is fairly predictable but just a look can set our souls on fire and make our stomachs do flips. We have comfort by day but at night we can set the sheets on fire, and usually do. It's like once naked we turn into animals and the passion drips off of us like sweat. Why just last night…"

"Boring," Mickey and Josie interrupted.

"Why is it boring? Are you saying true love is boring?"

"No. True love isn't boring when we're in it. But since we're not, we don't want to hear about it. So like I said Boring," Josie waved her hand at Ali as if to erase the matter.

"You're just jealous!" Ali responded with narrowed eyes.

"Hah! Jealous of what?" Josie demanded with an incredulous look on her face.

"How bout of the fact that while you'll be at home tonight with cucumber slices on your eyes to get rid of those hideous bags, I'll be at home in the arms of my prince who loves me so thoroughly and deeply that I sleep so pleased and relaxed that I don't end up with a big zit on my forehead caused from the stress and loneliness of being a shallow tramp like you," Everyone gaped openmouthed at Ali who picked up her diet coke, took a long swig and innocently shrugged her shoulders. Meanwhile Josie had the metal napkin holder examining her forehead and searching for imaginary bags under her liquid brown eyes. "Bitch," she muttered, then jumped from the booth in a mad dash to the bathroom with her menu covering her face.

Ali gave a sweet smile and asked the group "What?" All innocence and sincerity.

"That was mean," Megan began. "You know how she gets about wrinkles and bags and stuff. Ever since she hit thirty it's been one constant nose dive. We all need to be sensitive to that."

"She started it!" Ali exclaimed.

"She deserved it!" agreed Stacy.

"Back to the question guys. Mickey?" Megan asked attempting to change the subject.

"Passion! All the way Babe. When the passions gone it's over. Sianora Sweetheart. Time to move on. If you don't the other person will. Passion is the name of the game girlfriend." Mickey gestured for the waiter and asked for a refill of lemon-aide.

"That's so typical of a man." Stacy began. "All they're interested in is sex, sex, sex. I bet if you asked ten men on the street without their wives present they would all agree with Mickey. It's so freaking shallow and… and…."

Mickey interrupted with obvious disgust. "Do I look like a man today? Hello. I am wearing my pink 'princess' shirt and pink suede sneakers." He stretched one long leg out, swung it around and plunked his size 13 on the table. "Now I never come to lunch with the girls as Michael. So all opinions expressed here are the sole beliefs of the vivacious Mikayla. And furthermore, Josie is all woman and she agrees with me. And once the new wears off Ali's marriage she'll feel the same. And Stacy…well Stacy wouldn't know passion if it crawled up her leg and bit her on her g-spot." He removed his foot from the table, took a sip, swallowed and continued. "You see I'm a realist, I know when to hold 'em and I know when to fold 'em. When you shake up the bottle and there's no fizz left. It's time to chunk it and shop for a new one."

"That's ridiculous!" Stacy started but stopped when she saw Megan nodding her head in agreement with Mickey.

Megan sat her glass of tea down and looked at Stacy. "He might have a point Stacy, I mean what happens in a lot of marriages when men and sometimes women hit middle age and have a mid-life crisis? They grow tired of comfort and search for passion. Sometimes in sports cars or motorcycles or more commonly younger, hotter mates. It's like he said. When the passion goes flat, the shopping begins. Maybe passion is the name of the game."

Stacy stared incredulously at Megan, Ali seemed to ponder it and Mickey gave a palms up gesture followed by a satisfied grin. Josie rushed back to the table, took her seat and asked breathlessly "What did I miss?"

"Apparently that zit on your chin," Ali muttered and Josie gave her a look of horror, grabbed her menu and made a mad dash back to the bathroom. When an elderly lady at a nearby table cast a concerned look their way, Ali simply waved her hand and said "The runs. Poor thing."

Everyone was staring at her with maternal glares and she held up two fingers and said. "Last time. I swear. I'll be good from now on. Scouts honor."

A half hour later the gang had disbanded to go back to their jobs with the exception of Josie who made emergency appointments for a facial and massage. "What about work?" Megan had asked her as she closed her cell phone after making appointments.

"I'll just call in sick," She replied.

Mickey never letting an opportunity pass to get in a dig told her, "You'd have better luck if you called in ugly, honey."

Josie burst into to tears, grabbed her purse threw a twenty on the table and flew out of there.

***

On the drive home Megan pondered their discussion and her eyes stung with tears. She hadn't ever realized she wasn't happy until today. She'd been content in her little routines and a marriage that was comfortable. From the outside looking in she had it all. Her husband Ted ran a successful photography studio and made a comfortable middle class income. When they got married ten years ago they purchased a small tidy house less than a mile from her parent's home. In the early months of her marriage her and Ted had done crazy things like wallpaper the bathroom in the nude and there was one time when they were painting the bedroom where they threw paint on each other playfully and ended up making love on the drop cloth rolling around in lavender paint. Where had all that passion gone? What happened to them?

About a year after they took their vows, Megan had the whole homemaker thing down to an art and Ted's business was doing well, so Megan brought up the issue of raising a family. Ted resisted and Megan was so eager to please him that she decided she could wait, so instead she hinted around for a dog. When Ted said no to that too, she took matters into her own hands and bought herself a fish. She just needed someone or something to take care of or talk to while Ted was at work so she went to the pet store and bought herself a goldfish. She named him Spot and pretended he was a Golden Retriever. When Ted got home he made fun of her and her fish, told her she was stupid and that she needed to get a life. His words hurt her and his anger bothered her but it was the coldness in his eyes that really sent chills up her spine. It was the first time she'd ever crossed him and he didn't like the loss of control. But she stood her ground and Spot stayed. While Ted worked and she got bored she tried to teach the gold fish to throw the finger at Ted when he wasn't looking but since Spot only had fins and couldn't achieve the task she gave up. But somehow she knew that when Spot squished his little fish face to the glass and glared at Ted he was silently telling him to go to hell. She and Spot shared many secretive smiles on the matter. Then one day Ted came home with flowers and wine and apologized to Megan and she forgave him and Spot was no longer an issue.

After another two years of being the happy homemaker, Megan again got bored and tried to take a stand. She informed Ted of her plans to find a job. Again he said no and told her she wasn't good at anything but cooking and cleaning and that if she wanted to find a job she could look for a new husband while she was at it, so defeated once again she continued on as Ted's wife and Spots Mommy. Bored as hell and angry at herself. But once again Ted was sorry and she forgave him and as usual she tried to make do.

Life went on boring as hell until their fifth anniversary. Ted's business was booming and Megan had pretty much memorized every do it yourself program and completely redecorated the majority of the house but, she still couldn't find that contentment that she desperately needed. Spot was getting restless too and had expressed his need for a sibling so once again she brought up the issue of having a family over a candlelit dinner. Ted yelled and whined and pitched a fit and Megan became so angry that her and Spot moved in with her parents for a weekend. Her mother was not happy about having a fish for a grandchild but like all good grandmas she made him welcome and put a framed picture of him on the mantle. Spot seemed happy. But that Monday morning Ted showed up with two Golden Retriever puppies and said he'd think about having a family if she'd just go home. So she did and things were better. Spot had a brother and a sister and her parents had two more grandchildren to take pictures of. She had two adorable pups to teach how to throw the finger. Life was improving.

Then Megan entered a writing contest on the internet for a magazine. She won the contest and two thousand dollars. When the magazine called her back and asked her to write a weekly column for them she took the money and upgraded her computer. She accepted the offer and 'A Moment with Meg' was born. Although no one but her girlfriends knew she wrote it, she finally had something to do that brought her enjoyment. The girls started meeting weekly to discuss topics and she was stacking away a small nest egg on the side. She figured she could save the money to maybe hire a hit man to knock off Ted someday although she knew she could never do it. Control freak jerk that he was, she loved him.

So now here she was ten years into her marriage with a smart assed fish, two lazy pups and a marriage with no fizz left. "Megan Malone, this is your life," she thought to herself as she pulled into her driveway.

The first thing she did when she got in the house was call Josie. She was going to get some passion back in her marriage if she had to kill Ted to do it. It was there once. She'd just have to go shopping and buy an outfit that would wake the dead. And if anyone knew about shopping with a purpose, it was Josie. Josie answered on the third ring.

"Mmmmm?"

"Josie? It's Meg. Where are you?"

"Getting a massage. Sergio here is a miracle worker. He has magic hands," she lowered her voice, "and a killer package. He really knows how to relieve the tension." From above her Sergio smiled.

Megan needed a miracle. "Does he have any openings for today? I need some magic."

Megan heard Josie ask him in her sweet saucy voice reserved for getting what she wanted from a man. The fact that she was probably naked under a thin sheet on his table probably didn't hurt matters. They exchanged a few muffled words and Josie came back on the line. "Can you come down right now? He just had a cancellation."

Sure he did, Megan thought.

"I'm on my way. Gimme the address."

Fifteen minutes later she was in her bra and panties covered by a flimsy white sheet, listening to elevator music when Sergio walked in the door followed by Josie.

11

"You don't mind if I hang out do you?" Josie asked. Megan didn't respond.

She couldn't. She was engrossed in staring at this God who had just walked in the door wearing a snug pair of Levi's and a painted on shirt that hung on his muscles and perked up muscles in her body that she thought were dead. He had neatly cropped, black hair and the bluest eyes she'd ever seen. He was somewhere between 25 and 30 and the closest thing she'd ever seen to heaven on earth. His hands were large and masculine and in less than five minutes they'd be all over her. She silently racked her brain to remember if she was wearing pretty underwear that matched and hoped against her usual period panties and ugly bra held together with safety pins.

"Megan? Do you care if I hang around while you get your massage?" Josie repeated. Again Megan didn't respond.

While Sergio turned to wash his hands, Megan discreetly peeked under her sheet and Thanked God that she was wearing Victoria's Secret. She thanked Victoria too. Sergio turned around and smiled and Megan felt her body temperature increase by about a thousand degrees. She started praying. 'God don't let me do anything embarrassing like have an orgasm right here. I promise I'll be good. I'll call my mother every day, just please don't let me…'

"Megan!" Josie said loudly at the same time Sergio asked "Is this your first time?"

Holy Mary Mother of God! His voice was devastating. He sounded Columbian and his voice alone nearly sent her over the edge. Here she was lying nearly naked under a see thru sheet while this Columbian God stood before her preparing to send her body to places unknown with his magic hands. You couldn't cut the passion in the room with a chainsaw. Now if Josie would just get the hell out. What was she thinking? Passion or no passion she would never cheat on Ted. She'd just have to find this passion with Ted and…

"Megan?" Sergio and Josie both asked concerned. Megan snapped back to reality.

"Huh…Omigod, I'm so sorry. What did you say?" Megan asked.

"Are you okay Meg? You don't look so good. Maybe you should reschedule." Josie was saying. She walked over to Megan and put her hand over her forehead.

"Holy cow! You're burning up."

"No no... I'm fine," Megan persisted. Sergio and Josie didn't look convinced. Sergio stepped closer and cupped her cheek in his large hand. Megan lost her breath. Josie was right this man did have magic hands. Sergio said something and then Josie said something and Megan was pretty sure they were talking to her but she couldn't hear them because her body was on fire and when Josie pulled out her cell phone and threatened to call an ambulance and Sergio got his appointment book to reschedule Megan, she found her breath let out a deep sigh and said, "I don't need an ambulance Josie I'm fine. And I don't want to reschedule either."

Josie shut her phone and looked at Sergio who was looking from Josie to Megan like they were playing topless tennis.

"Well what the hell's wrong with you then" Josie asked.

"Nothing!"

"Are you sure?"

"Oh alright if you must know I was having an orgasm and I just need a minute to recover." Josie's mouth dropped open and Sergio raised a curious brow. "Jesus! It's been a really long time you know and then this Columbian God comes in with those...those magic hands and that ...that killer package and not to mention that body and...and..." Shit! Had she just said that out loud? '*God if you up there. Just take me now*' she thought. She closed her eyes and took a deep breath. When she opened them again, Sergio was still standing there examining his hands, a satisfied smile on his face. Josie stood beside him also examining his hands her mouth still open and her eyes huge.

"How come you never do that to me?" She demanded.

"I didn't do anything," Sergio protested.

"Well from now on I want what she got. For fifty bucks an hour it's the least you can do," Josie said still marveling at his hands.

"I don't know how I did it. I wish I did. I'd be charging a lot more than fifty bucks an hour if I did." Megan shrank back as far as she could in the bed. With any luck the ceiling fan would crash from the ceiling and put her out of her misery.

After a new set of sheets and an hour of pure ecstasy Megan handed Sergio a well-deserved hundred dollar bill and thanked him as he left the room. She stood to get dressed while Josie sat in the single wingback chair obviously still shell shocked from experiencing Megan's first orgasm of the New Millennium.

"Look in those drawers and see if there's a trash bag in one of them," Megan said.

Josie looked at her confused, "What for?"

From behind her sheet Megan shimmied off her pink panties and held them up to answer Josie's question. "Oh," Josie said and started looking through drawers. "Just put them in your purse Meg," Josie offered while rifling through the drawers.

Meg looked at her panties then her purse and shook her head. "No. There all…squishy." Josie continued her search.

"Well it's your squish. There's nothing in here except for some latex gloves."

"They'll work. Give me one." Josie handed it over and Megan stuffed her panties in it and tied a knot at the opening.

"It kind of looks like a deformed condom," Josie pointed out trying to choke back a chuckle.

"Well we should always practice safe sex right?" Megan added then finished dressing.

***

On the way to the car Megan felt loose and relaxed. She felt like a new woman. The kind of woman who had an orgasm on a massage table and would like to do it again. The kind of woman who would toss all of her period panties and ragged bras for sheer slinky Victoria's secret. She felt…passionate. Thank you Jesus and thank you Sergio. That man should have his name up in lights.

Josie however, didn't look quite as gleeful.

"What's the matter?" Megan asked a sulking Josie.

"I'm depressed."

"About what?"

Josie bit her lip and Megan thought she was fighting back tears. "About what Ali said. She's right you know. I'm going to be alone forever."

"No you won't. When you least expect it Mr. Right will waltz in and steal your heart."

Josie burst into tears. "What if it never happens?"

Oh Boy. In all the years Megan had known Josie she'd seen her cry over zits or an extra pound, wrinkles and a bad haircut. But never over a man. Or the lack of one. Megan patted her on the back and tried to comfort her. The sobs came harder. Megan used the only weapon in her arsenal. "You want to go shopping?"

"Shopping?" Josie perked up and all at once the tears ceased. "For shoes?"

"Sure."

"And handbags?"

"If you want." And I need you to make me look sexy and desirable Megan thought but decided to wait until Josie was in full shop mode before mentioning it.

"Where's your car?" Josie asked as perky and dry eyed as ever.

***

"Ok here's the deal," Megan said to Josie after they bought shoes and handbags. "I need you to help me find something that'll make me irresistible. Sexy but stunning. Slutty but elegant. Something that says, 'Come and get it big boy, but remember I'm a lady.'" Josie looked perplexed.

"Slutty and elegant?" Josie repeated. "I'm not sure that's possible." She began scanning the racks. "How about just slutty? I can do that. The elegant thing is more Ali's thing." She thought for a moment then added "I'll call her to help." Josie made the call told Ali it was an emergency and clicked off. "She's on her way. Let's start with the slutty first."

Ten minutes later Ali came barreling in the store breathless. "What's the matter?"

"Megan's having a crisis. She got a massage and had an orgasm and now she's walking around with her squishy panties stuffed in a rubber glove in her purse. I think she had an epiphany and now she needs an outfit that says 'do me big daddy' only she wants it to be elegant and ladylike and I don't know jack about elegance or being a lady. So we've been shopping for lingerie because you know, that's really kind of my area and we've got the 'do me' part done. Now we need your help on the ladylike part," Josie leaned a little closer to Ali. "And by the way she swears she's a five but trust me she couldn't squeeze those hips in a five if her life depended on it so when she's not looking we'll grab a seven and rip the tag off before she tries it on." She winked at Ali who was a cross between furious and amused.

"You called me about an emergency and I'm imagining all kinds of terrible things the whole way over and..." Ali turned to Megan. "You

15

had an orgasm?" Megan gave a weak smile and a nod. Ali's look softened.

Ali turned back to Josie. "Sergio?" Josie nodded. "That man is a legend," Ali muttered as she began eyeing the clothing racks.

"You know about Sergio?" Megan asked wondering why in the hell she was the only one who didn't.

"Of course. Every Tuesday at 4:00. Now let's get busy. We've got a lot of work to do."

Gee Thanks, Megan thought. "And by the way, I am a size five." Yeah right. Who was she kidding? She hadn't been a size five since third grade.

***

After what seemed like hours they finally decided on a simple red dress with a squared neckline and spaghetti straps that showed off Megan's long legs and round butt. Josie argued that it didn't show enough cleavage but Ali pointed out that Megan didn't have any cleavage to show off.

"Maybe if we duct taped her boobs together we could create some. I read about that in a modeling magazine. Models use it to enhance their bosoms. Supposedly it actually works," Josie offered enthusiastically.

"Well, it might work assuming you have some bosom to work with but in Megan's case we don't. Plus it would kind of do away with the whole elegance thing," Ali added.

"Yeah nothing says 'I'm a lady' like duct tape,'" Megan muttered. "And I do have boobs. They're just small. Anyways Ted used to say anything more than a mouth full is a waste."

Josie and Ali both shot her sympathetic looks. "He was just being kind," Ali said, her boobs jiggling as she laughed.

Winch, Megan thought. She had boobs and passion and Megan had neither.

"But you do have a great butt," Ali added.

Gee thanks. Too bad butt cleavage wasn't sexy.

"And gorgeous legs," Josie added. Yeah, nice legs leading to great butt cleavage topped off by enormous hips. Megan looked up toward heaven and asked God to zap her and get it over with. She closed her eyes and braced herself. Nothing happened. Shit.

"Who has great legs?" Mickey asked skidding to a stop. Megan turned around and Mickey took a step back. "You look bitchin' babe.

16

Totally hot! If I was Michael today I'd devour you." Mickey had changed since lunch and was wearing pink spandex running shorts and a white tank top with rhinestones spelling out the word 'Babe' against his chest. Definitely not Michael. No devouring today. Mickey took a step back and looked Megan up and down. He stopped at the top of her head and put his fist underneath his chin.

"The hair has got to go, honey. It looks…"

Megan ran a self-conscious hand through her long brown hair. "What's wrong with my hair? Ted loves my hair. He likes it long. He'll have a cow if I cut it." She thought for a minute than looked at Mickey. "And by the way, how'd you know we were here?"

"Ali called. And she's right, the hair ruins the look." Megan shot Ali the look of death.

"Oh, and congratulations on your orgasm. And don't forget about your squishy panties being in your purse. It could be embarrassing if you pulled them out at the wrong time like at church while searching for a tissue. Been there honey, it wasn't good." Everyone just stared at Mickey for a moment but shook themselves out of it. Anything was possible with Mickey. Anything! "So about the hair…" He began playing with it while Josie and Ali nodded their approval or shook their heads and made ick sounds.

Mickey took out his cell phone and called his hairdresser. He slammed his phone shut. "Damn! He's booked. Josie? How about yours?"

"I'm on it," She replied hurriedly and snapped her phone open.

"What's wrong with my hair?" Megan repeated but everyone ignored her. "Hello?" she called out as Josie spoke into her cell phone.

"We're on our way! ETA five minutes. Don't you dare put anyone else in that chair. Oh and by the way you might want to cover the chair with a towel. The last appointment I took her to she had an orgasm on the spot."

Megan looked up to God again. 'Please' she asked. Still no lightening strike or spontaneous combusting. Double Shit!

***

Megan sat in the blue salon chair on top of the towel that was placed there in case of accidental orgasm. Josie, Ali and Mickey were huddled with Gabe, Josie's hair dresser, in a strategic chat. Megan closed her eyes. If she was lucky a bus would crash into the window and kill her

17

dead on the spot. She braced herself for the impact. Nothing happened. When she opened her eyes she was face to face with quite possibly the sexiest man she'd ever seen in real life except for maybe Sergio.

Gabe was about 5'10 and solid. He had a face that was both menacing and angelic at the same time. His blonde hair was perfectly styled except for one stubborn strand that fell defiantly over his right eye. He had sea green eyes, startling white teeth, and cheekbones to die for. Megan squeezed her knees together and begged her pelvis to be good. She met his gaze and parted her lips to speak but before she got a syllable out he was already chopping away. Her long brown hair fell in long chunks from her head and again she closed her eyes this time thinking about jumping in front of the imaginary speeding bus.

After washing, and coloring and wrapping her head in foil, Gabe sauntered off to the back with Josie in tow. Mickey and Ali were flipping through magazines. Megan stared at her foil covered head in the mirror. Gabe said he'd be back in twenty minutes. Megan wondered if that was long enough to use the foil to contact aliens and ask them to abduct her. She'd probably have to endure anal probing but at least she wouldn't be embarrassed because she had nice butt cleavage.

Gabe returned and began taking her alien attracting aluminum away. He yanked and snipped and blow dried. Then shook his head, grunted, snipped some more, sprayed, and blow dried again. He smiled and Megan squeezed her knees together tighter. He dropped his hands said "viola" and handed her a mirror. She stared in the mirror in silence for a very long time. Her hair was blonde! And it looked like a cross between Meg Ryan and Cindy Lauper. If she hadn't been trying so hard to keep her hormones at bay she would've cried. It was short and choppy looking and it looked great but Ted was going to hate it. Her mother would probably have a heart attack. Spot would probably flip her the fin.

She took a steadying breath, her voice a little shaky and said "It looks…"

"Bitchin'," Mickey provided.

"Totally," Josie added.

"Hot," Ali contributed.

"My sentiments exactly," Megan said.

Gabe nodded and to Megan he said "That'll be two hundred bucks."

Chapter Two

After spending over four hundred and fifty bucks on her make over and another fifty at the grocery store Meg finally entered her house. Passion was expensive and if she was lucky she might have enough left to hire a good divorce attorney since Ted was probably going to kick her out and have her committed. She sat her bags on the kitchen counter and was greeted by Bitty and Bugs, her four legged children. They ran into the kitchen and stopped dead in their tracks. She bent down to love on them and they backed away. She called their names in her soft cooing voice and they took another two steps back.

"It's me guys. It's mommy. Don't I look pretty?" Guess not because they backed up further. She dug through her grocery bags until she located the doggy treats. She shook the package and both pups took a step forward. By the time she got the package open the dogs were in her lap. Dogs were so loyal. You could be Hannibal Lector, but as long as you had bacon flavored doggie treats they'll be your best friend. When the treats were gone so were the pups.

Megan went into the living room to deal with Spot. He came out of his pirate ship and before he could say or do anything she gave him the finger. He retreated back to his hideout and maybe it was just her imagination, but she could've sworn he was laughing at her. She dropped some food in his tank and went upstairs to hang up her dress. She looked in the mirror and sighed. What the heck had she been thinking? One orgasm and she'd flat lost her mind. And now she'd probably lose Ted. And the dogs would only love her when they were hungry. And she won't have enough money to pay for her divorce. Damn!

She started down the stairs when a horrible thought hit her. She'd cheated on Ted. She had an orgasm with another man. She was going to hell. That's probably why God had spared her today. She was asking the wrong person. She should have been looking down when she asked to be zapped. That's probably where people like her go. She took a deep breath and contemplated going to confession.

"Just calm down," she told herself. Maybe there's a clause in the bible designed for situations like this. A loophole so to speak. Stacy! She needed Stacy. Stacy was sensible. She never over-reacted to anything. She'd know what to do. Megan picked up the phone and called Stacy who answered the phone breathlessly.

"Stacy? It's Megan. Why are you out of breath?"

"I'm working out. Mickey just left. He told me everything. It sounds like you've had a very busy day."

"I need to talk to you. Can you come over?"

She must have heard the tears in Megan's voice because she said, "I'm on my way. Stay away from massage parlors and duct tape."

***

Twenty minutes later, Stacy came through the back door and gave Megan a once over. If she had anything to say about Megan's new look she kept it to herself.

Megan was crying over her cutting board that was stacked with vegetables.

"What's the matter?" Stacy asked grabbing a salad bowl and a knife.

"I cheated on Ted. I'm going to hell and my Mother is going to disown me." Megan relayed the whole story as her and Stacy prepared the vegetables for the salad. When Megan was done telling her story, Stacy cracked up in laughter. Megan started crying again.

"You didn't cheat on Ted, Megan. There has to be another person involved for that."

"There was! Sergio!"

"But there was no sex or kissing. There was no intent. You just…well it sounds like… maybe your hormones are just haywire. Cut yourself a break. It happens," Stacy said and Megan perked up.

"Has it happened to you?"

"Well no but…" Megan started crying again. "But I haven't met this Sergio yet. It could've happened to anyone."

"But it didn't. It happened to me and now Ted's going to divorce me and I'm going to be known around town as the 'Orgasma Queen'. People won't invite me to sit down for tea and they'll probably assign me my own pew at church and..."

Stacy tossed the vegetables into the bowl and took the knife from Megan's hand. As a matter of fact she should probably rid the house of all sharp objects. "Megan, look at it this way. Does Ted ever get any of those girlie magazines and retreat to the bathroom?"

"I uh I don't know. I've never seen them if he does."

"Well most men do and they uh... well they kind of have an...uh experience similar to what you had only theirs is on purpose. So, what if you found out that Ted did that every now and again? Would you consider that cheating on you?"

Megan tilted her head back and thought about it for a moment. "No." She finally said.

"Well then what you did is no different except that yours was an accident and his isn't. So I tell you what. Tomorrow after you've had time to cool off and calm down we'll search the house and see if we can find some of those magazines. If we do, then you're off the hook. If we don't then you can tell Ted and we'll go to confession and confess to your parents or pay whatever penance you think you need to. But you've had enough excitement for one day so let's worry about it tomorrow."

"You're right. We'll worry about it tomorrow." She covered the salad and placed it in the refrigerator. "I just hope we find some of those magazines."

'We will' Stacy thought *'because tomorrow I'm going to plant some here so you don't go crazy and leave me to raise Spot'.*

***

Stacy left after giving Megan a reassuring hug and Megan continued to make dinner. By 6:00, she had everything cooking and dashed upstairs avoiding mirrors to get decked out for her passionate evening with Ted. She took her red dress from the closet and laid it on the bed. She stared at it and tried to imagine what Ted would think. Would he find her irresistibly sexy and be so consumed by passion that he didn't notice her hair? Not a chance she decided.

Or maybe, Ted wouldn't be angry. Maybe he'd just leave her for another woman that was sane and didn't have unassisted orgasms...

She took her new shoes from the closet and sat them on the bed beside the dress.

Maybe if she put them on and ran down the stairs in the four inch heels, she would fall and hit her head and end up in the hospital and when Ted rushed to her side she could tell him that the hospital personnel cut her hair to examine the wound and he should feel very lucky she was alive. Yeah right!

She got out her new lingerie and tossed them on the bed as well. She wondered how well the material would hold up if she tried to strangle herself with the thong panties. Who was she kidding? She was screwed. She sat on the bed with her head in her hands. It was going to be a long night.

Bitty and Bugs slowly approached her bed and took their places at her feet. She petted their heads and they nuzzled her legs. "You still love me right?" The pups barked and jumped in her lap and began licking her face. She gave them both big hugs and shuffled them out of the room to get dressed. She was being silly. Ted would still love her too. The sight of her in that slinky red dress, those elegant shoes and her barely there lingerie was going to send him over the edge into a passionate frenzy and he was going to realize what a dope he'd been for taking her for granted. He'd make it his mission in life to make it up to her. And if he didn't she could use the heels of her new shoes to beat him to a bloody pulp.

***

By six thirty, she was dressed and ready to face Ted who should be home any minute. She put the pups outside, lit candles on the table and threw a Nora Jones CD in the stereo.

At 6:55 she heard Ted's car pull into the drive. She said a silent prayer that the ceiling would fall in and crush her like a pancake. She looked at the ceiling. Nothing happened so she went to the door to meet Ted. He was on his cell phone shouting impatiently at the person on the other end. Megan just stood there and looked at him, really looked at him for the first time in years. He still had a head full of blonde hair and his boyish smile. His eyes were a devastating light brown with little green specks around the irises that were now accented with little wrinkles around the corners that only made him look more handsome. His evenly tanned face sported a slight five o'clock shadow that gave him a rugged rustic appeal. His lean frame was in perfect form due to his obsessive nightly workouts in the basement. His firm, round butt was covered by perfectly creased jeans that bulged around his thighs and calves. He wore a white dress shirt unbuttoned at the neck and Italian loafers. If he stood at a distance and didn't open his mouth she could probably muster up an orgasm. She shivered at the thought. Two orgasms in one day would probably kill her or at least be grounds for a psych eval.

Ted started up the steps and paused at the front door, his cell phone still at his ear. Megan took a step forward, raised her chin and stuck out her chest. Ted dropped his phone. His gaze roamed from her recently chopped, and now blonde, hair to her newly painted toenails. He stood silently staring at Megan who was scanning the street for speeding buses or alien abductions. Finally their eyes met and Megan forgot to breathe. Ted brushed her cheek with the inside of his index finger then gently squeezed past her and sat in his chair. Megan stood motionless at the door her hand still on the doorknob. Ted was the first to speak.

"Where are the dogs?" Did she hear him right? After all the hell and humiliation she'd been through today to look sexy for him his first thought was the dogs.

"In the backyard and dinner is waiting in the kitchen." Without further explanation she strode to the kitchen and began putting ice in glasses and setting the food on the table. Ted joined her a few moments later and took his usual seat. He sat quietly, his napkin in his lap his gaze adverted to the floor. Megan was determined to let him speak first but he obviously had nothing to say so she broke the silence.

"It'll grow back Ted." He looked up still in a daze.

"Huh?"

"My hair!" She rolled her eyes up as if she could see her hair through her skull. "I know I should have asked you first but the hairdresser, he just started chopping and before I could speak…"

"You're hair looks nice." What? He liked it? Had aliens abducted Ted and replaced him with a new Ted who liked change and gave her compliments. She blinked several times and involuntarily raised her hand to the back of her neck.

"You like it?"

"It's… different but…Yeah I like it." He frowned. "Do you like it Meg?"

The words surprised her. He never cared what she thought or what she wanted, and because of that she hadn't even thought about whether she liked it. "Oh. I don't know, I guess so. I was so worried about what you would think that I hadn't even thought about it. I was afraid you would divorce me."

"What's for dinner?"

Hel-lo? Megan thought. Red dress, sexy shoes, slutty lingerie! What happened to ravish and devour. If she wasn't a strong Christian woman she'd stand on the table and flash him her butt cleavage. Instead she kept her dignity and said "Steak" in the perkiest voice she could muster.

They ate dinner in silence and when they were done Megan started clearing the dishes from the table to keep from bursting into tears. The only explanation for Ted's lack of attention was that he was secretly gay.

If he wasn't gay, then what was it? Was she fat? Did she have spinach in her teeth or a booger on the tip of her nose? She grabbed the toaster and squinted her eyes to see her reflection. Nope, aside from the hair she looked the same. She ran her eyes the length of her body checking for toilet paper stuck down her leg or imaginary cooties. Nothing! Instead what she saw was a thirty year old trim, well-toned body. Maybe Ted was just tired. And gay.

She finished the dishes and shut off all the lights and joined Ted in the living room. Ted was asleep in his chair, the remote control still in his left hand. She sunk onto the couch making more noise than necessary. Ted didn't budge. She picked up a magazine and flipped through the pages as loudly as she could. Ted remained in dreamland. Growing frustrated and agitated she rolled up the magazine and slapped the coffee table with it hard. Ted bolted up and looked around dropping his remote control.

"Fly," she explained and when he gave her a perplexed look she elaborated. "There was a fly on the coffee table. I killed it with the Better Homes and Gardens." He dismissed it and began looking for his remote control.

"I'll get it," she said and crossed the room, turning around so that her rear end was facing him and did her best Marilyn Monroe rendition of retrieving the fallen remote, giving him an ample view of her backside. She shimmied back up with more shake than necessary and handed the remote control to him.

He got out of the chair and gave it back. "Goodnight," he told her before taking the stairs two at a time. Megan let the dogs in and climbed the stairs to bed dragging her self-esteem behind her.

Chapter Three

She spent the next morning trying to forget the horrors of the previous day. She scrubbed the bathtub, gave the dogs a bath, and dealt with a defiant Spot while cleaning his bowl. She sifted through her email, and wrote her column for the week on 'Surviving a long distance relationship.' She figured she probably knew more about that than passion, since her and Ted lived in the same house but were distant as hell. They'd probably have a better marriage if he lived in Egypt. Or Columbia.

Columbia. Her thoughts strayed to Sergio. Now there's a passionate man. He reeked of passion from his beautiful head to his boot clad toes. She should have married Sergio.

Or Gabe.

What was she thinking? She loved Ted and she knew he loved her. He hadn't divorced her because of her hair. He may not have been jumping for joy when he saw the new her but he didn't run for the hills either. Maybe he was just in shock. Or gay. Or maybe she didn't look as good as she thought she did.

The phone rang. Stacy was on the other end.

"How'd it go last night?" Megan gave her the short version of the night's events.

"You can't be serious. That's it?" Stacy replied.

"Yep! And he skipped his workout last night and left an hour early for work this morning."

"You still want to search for magazines? Or are you OK with that now?"

"I still want to search but first I wanted to talk to you about getting into shape. You go to the gym right?"

"Yeah, four times a week. But Megan, that's not the problem. You look great."

"Maybe Ted doesn't think so," Megan said biting her bottom lip.

"Ted's an idiot. Look Meg; don't read too much into this. Maybe he had a rough day or he's just really tired…"

"Or maybe I'm too fat," Megan interrupted "or not fat enough or…" Oh boy. This was going to be a long day.

"Alright listen I'll pick you up on my way to workout. Be ready in about an hour. And Megan, there's going to be men there so try to control your uh…well you know," Stacy chuckled.

"Very funny!" Megan snapped then said, "I'll be ready."

***

By the time Stacy arrived, Megan was on the front steps raring to go. She had just devoured an entire Sara Lee Strawberry Cheesecake but since she ate it half frozen to save on time she decided the calories didn't count. Only calories at room temperature would damage your figure. She was almost positive she'd read that somewhere. Plus she needed fuel for jazzercise right?

Stacy had thrown a towel in the passenger seat of her Toyota Camry. Megan gave her a menacing grin, and sat on top of it. Stacy tried to hide her laughter.

"I didn't want to take any chances," Stacy explained.

"You're not my type," Megan retorted as she got in and buckled her seatbelt.

"Rough morning?" Stacy asked. Megan nodded.

"Cheesecake?" Stacy asked. Again Megan nodded.

"Strawberry Deluxe?"

"Yep."

"You save me any?"

"Well I was going to but then I read the expiration date and found that it had expired, so I was afraid it might poison you and I couldn't throw it out because the dogs might get into it, so I did the only thing I could to protect everyone involved."

"How humanitarian of you. Was it good?"

Delicious! "No, I had to hold my nose and force it in."

26

"Well you missed some." Stacy said gesturing to the piece of cheese covered crust on Megan's shirt just below her left breast. Megan scooped it off and handed it to Stacy who popped it in her mouth.

"Your right," Stacy said. "It tastes spoiled. Thanks for looking out for mankind by disposing of the rest of it."

When they got to the gym, Stacy parked her car and reached in the backseat to collect two bottles of water and a towel. They got out, locked up and entered the gym at a dead run.

"Why are we running?" Megan asked struggling to keep up.

"We're late. Adele hates it when people are late."

"Who's Adele?"

"My fitness instructor. She takes her job very seriously." They swung open the door and made it just in time for the warm up exercises. Megan took one look at Adele and knew she was in trouble.

Adele was somewhere between 40 and 50, about 5 foot tall and weighed about one hundred and fifty pounds of solid muscle. Her calves and biceps bulged, and her stomach sported a six pack. Her boob muscles were about as big as Megan's head and her voice was gruff and husky. She had her hair cropped close to her scalp and she shouted military like instructions over the loud music. Megan felt a sudden urge to salute, but quashed it when Adele wandered over their way.

"Who's this?" Adele asked Stacy.

"This is my friend, Megan." She gestured to Adele. "Megan, Adele." Megan nodded and stuck out her hand.

Adele didn't take it. Instead she looked Megan over from head to toe. "Turn around," she told Megan and Megan looked at Stacy who nodded at her impatiently. Megan turned around as Adele continued to size her up.

"Not bad," Adele began. "Butt looks Ok; legs are decent until you get to the thighs." In one fluent move Adele had her hands on Megan's hips pinching her sides. Megan blinked, too stunned to move. "These love handles are really unattractive dear. We've got to get rid of those." Adele moved on to Megan's arms pinching the skin on the underside. She shook her head sadly. "You're butts too boney, you've got chunky thighs, grotesque love handles and your arms are as skinny as pipe cleaners. You look like a bulimic Olive Oyl."

Megan stood there speechless debating whether she should walk out the door and tie herself to the train tracks or inhale another cheesecake.

Or maybe she should eat the cheesecake then tie herself to the train tracks. She wanted to cry. And bash Amazon Commando Woman in the head with a frozen cheesecake.

The music started pounding again and all the women obediently took their places behind their steppers. Adele began demonstrating moves and Megan tried to keep up. Stacy looked like she was taking a leisurely stroll through the park while Megan felt like she was climbing Mount Everest with a Volkswagen strapped to her back. Her breathing was ragged, her chest was on fire and her arms and legs felt like they weighed a thousand pounds each. And if that wasn't enough, the cheesecake she'd eaten earlier was gurgling around in her stomach like a dead weight. She was either gonna hurl cheesecake like the exorcist or drop dead on her stepper.

What the hell had she been thinking wanting to work out? The only working out she ever did was unbuttoning her pants after desert. This was torture. With her luck Ted would be ready for some passion tonight and she'd be in ICU. Shit!

"Ok ladies, warm up's over. Now let's get down to business," Adele commanded. The music changed to something with a lot of bass. What? That was a warm up? Oh God!

"Isn't this fun?" Stacy said her body not even glistened with sweat.

"Yeah. Loads," Megan managed. Not as much fun as slitting my wrists with a spoon.

About ten minutes into the workout, Adele ordered the ladies to pick up their weights. Each weight supposedly weighed five pounds. Yeah right!

Adele demonstrated the next exercise. She planted her feet firmly apart, brought one knee up and to the side while simultaneously bringing her weighted arm into a curl. It looked simple enough.

Megan took a deep breath planted her feet, brought her knee up, bent her arm to curl the weight, lost her balance, fell to the ground and smashed herself in the head with the weight. Little white spots danced before her eyes as she lay there, too tired to move, too embarrassed to get up. The music still blared and above her she saw the other women still working out. She closed her eyes and laid there lifting one weight in tune with Adele's counting. Finally Stacy saw her in the floor and shrieked. The music stopped, and when she opened her eyes Adele and half the class were standing over her. Adele leaned in close to her body.

"Get up," She ordered. Megan didn't even open her eyes.

"Can't."

"Why not?" Adele wanted to know.

"Because I think I'm dead." She heard Stacy chuckle.

"Don't be a wuss. You're holding up my class. Hurry up."

"Do you guys use a cleaning service here? Because if you don't you might want to check on retaining one, because this carpet smells awful."

"No," Stacy said. "That smell would be you." Megan grimaced.

"Fine lay there," A frustrated Adele growled. "Ladies back to your steppers."

"Can I get a pillow?" Megan asked just before the music came back on and the lights went off for Megan.

Megan awoke in a big, black, leather chair in what appeared to be an office. Her legs were propped on a large wooden desk and she had something very cold on her forehead. She heard a masculine voice conversing with Stacy and felt the wonderful chill from refrigerated air conditioning seep into her sweat soaked skin. As if she were afraid sudden movement would result in her head rolling off her neck she turned to the voices very slowly and opened her eyes.

Above her holding an ice pack to her head was a mountain of a man clothed only in spandex and sporting a single hoop earring in his left ear which was a stunning contrast to his sun bronzed skin. He had long, black hair held back in a tight ponytail and gobs of stiff hair curling about on his chest. He looked at her with a gentle smile and said, "Mrs. Malone? How are you feeling?"

"Huh?" was all she could manage. He handed the ice pack off to Stacy and positioned himself in front of her taking a seat on the desk.

"Mrs. Malone?" He tried again. The man was so big she had to tilt her head up further to see his face. Tilting her head hurt like hell, so she instead had a conversation with his crotch.

"Uh huh."

"My name is Tom Stratton. I own the gym. It seems as though you suffered an injury during your aerobics class. You apparently got knocked in the head with a weight and now you have a nasty bump on your forehead." *That would explain the ice*, Megan thought. "We were just discussing calling an ambulance. I would feel a lot better if you had a doctor check you out."

"Oh no. I'm fine. I just need a minute or so to get my bearings together," she told his crotch.

He sighed. "Stacy and I are going to take you to the emergency room. We need to make sure you don't have a concussion."

"I don't have a concussion. I wasn't knocked out. I fell asleep."

He raised one brow and the corners of his mouth tipped up. "During aerobics?"

"Yes."

"Isn't that kind of unusual?"

"No. I'm Narcoleptic. I can sleep anywhere. You know driving, scuba diving, mowing the grass, aerobics."

Tom looked at Stacy and then back at Megan. They were both trying to hide their amusement and be sympathetic. "Mrs. Malone, It's company policy that you be seen and it would really, really ease my mind if you were." He paused and placed his hand on her knee. Her skin prickled with goose bumps and she tried to contract her pelvic muscles. Please God no more embarrassing moments. Not a repeat of Sergio.

"It's not necessary." She swung her legs down from the desk, knocking his telephone off in the process. She stood on wobbly legs and struggled to balance herself. "I'm fine. See?" Just as the last word came from her mouth, her legs gave out and she flailed her arms to try to keep from falling again. In one swift move he had his arms around her waist preventing the fall. She hung there motionless.

"You're going to the hospital," he said and before she could open her mouth to protest he hurled her up into his arms and started to the door.

"No wait. I feel like I'm going to..."

"It's Ok Mrs. Malone. Just relax."

"No you don't understand. I think I'm going to..."

"Megan, shut up. He's right. You're going to the hospital," Stacy interrupted.

"But..." was all she could get out before the cheesecake she had eaten earlier forced its way out of her mouth and onto Tom's chest and Stacy's hair. "I think I'm gonna throw up," she finished.

After Tom and Stacy had cleaned themselves up and retrieved Megan from the chair once again, Tom carried Megan to his truck. "I can walk," she argued but Tom ignored her and once there buckled her in.

"I want to ride with Stacy," she protested. She was too embarrassed to ride with Tom. She'd knocked herself out at his gym, talked to his crotch, and barfed up an entire strawberry cheesecake on him. Humiliation was not a strong enough word to describe how she felt.

"No!" Stacy snapped. "I don't have passenger side air bags and I don't want puke in my car."

"Air bags?"

"Yeah, you're an accident waiting to happen. So go happen with him. I'll meet you there."

"Stace?" Megan said to Stacy's already departing back.

Tom patted her knee. "Don't worry, I'm not going to rape or murder you. I'm just going to get you to the hospital."

"I'd prefer the rape and murder," Megan said and closed her eyes.

The drive to the hospital was quiet. Tom hadn't said one word about her barfing on him nor had he been rude or demeaning. He just cleaned himself up, and treated her with the same careful concern he had before she got sick all over his shirt. He was probably afraid she'd sue the skin tight spandex off his butt.

She rolled her head towards the driver's side to take a better look at him. His profile was mesmerizing; strong jaw line, straight nose, almond shaped brown eyes. And those lips. Those full, full lips. She lowered her gaze to his bare muscular arms and the way his chest filled out his tank top. He was physical perfection. *I bet he's passionate,* she thought, and her mind wandered to how it would feel to have those eyes undressing her, those round lips on hers, those muscular arms caressing her… Her gaze found its way to his crotch and her mouth went dry. '*Stop it!*' She told herself. She glanced underneath her bottom in the seat.

"Did you lose something?" Tom inquired.

"No, I was seeing if you had a towel covering the seat?" If he thought that was weird, he didn't let his face show it. "What for?" was all he said.

"You don't want to know," Megan answered and rode the rest of the way squeezing her knees together and praying silent prayers.

After what seemed like an eternity at the hospital, the doctor confirmed that she had not suffered a concussion but she needed to take it easy the rest of the day. He wrote her a prescription for pain killers and Stacy drove her home. Stacy, being Stacy, was sweet enough to not bring up the whole ordeal. Stacy just walked her inside the house, fed the dogs and Spot, and left Megan on the couch with the remote control and cordless telephone. "Call me if you need anything," she told Megan before she left.

Megan now sat on the couch rotating the hospital ice pack to various sore joints and her injury. If she had the energy she'd run to the store and buy enough ice to fill her entire bathtub because every bone, muscle and joint in her body was on fire. Even her eyelashes hurt. And she barely made it past the warm up!

Spot stared at her from his bowl with an amused look on his face.

"Don't start with me or you'll be kitty food," she told the fish.

Her telephone rang and she reached to answer it moaning at the fire that shot through her joints. The caller was her mother. Her day went from bad to worse.

"Are you Ok?" Her mother asked, her voice thick with concern.

"Fine, why?"

"Well, Mildred's daughter, Kelly works out at some gym and she said that you were hit in the face with a weight bench and had to be carried out of the gym on a stretcher and rushed to the hospital."

"She exaggerates."

"So it's true?" She yelled for Megan's father, so she could tell him the news. "Why didn't you call your father and me? And why were you riding around town with a strange man? Were you going to the gym to impress this guy? Are you having an affair?" Megan imagined her mother clutching a rosary to her chest. "You know God frowns on adultery. What will people think? We'll have to move to another town and …"

"Mom!" Megan interrupted. "I wasn't riding around with a strange man. And I'm not having an affair."

"But Carol and Sandy were out walking their dogs when they saw you in a big green truck with a man with a pony tail. And why on earth would a man want a pony tail anyways…"

"Mom! He wasn't a strange man. He owns the gym and he was just taking me to the hospital."

"You shouldn't lie to your mother, Megan. Kelly said you went to the hospital on a stretcher. And you know better than to ride with strangers. You could've been raped and thrown in a ditch."

"I asked him to rape and murder me. The idea didn't appeal to him." Mom should be in Hail Mary mode by now.

"Megan? Are you taking drugs? Do you want me to make you an appointment for therapy? I'm going to call father Edmond to pray..."

"Mom, I have to go, there's a bus speeding by." She hit the off button on the phone before her mother could respond.

The phone rang again almost instantly. Figuring it to be her mother, she let the answering machine pick it up. It was Adele informing Megan she wasn't invited to any more of her aerobics classes. *"Oh Damn,"* Megan thought, like she was heartbroken over that. She should have Adele brought up on attempted murder charges because the woman had obviously tried to kill her this morning with the warm up exercises. The real workout was just to make sure she finished her off.

But Tom. Now he was something else entirely. Sweet, sexy, patient and gorgeous as hell, but modest about it. Even covered in strawberry puke he was still a magnificent sight. She would have to send him an "I'm sorry I dented your weight with my head and puked all over your luscious body" card. Did Hallmark make a card like that? She'd have to check. That was her last thought before dozing off into a dreamless, dead sleep.

Amy Johnson

Chapter Four

Megan awoke to the doorbell and put her pillow over her head. It was probably her mother with Father Edmond and the entire prayer team from church. They were probably here to exercise the demons that were obviously possessing her and making her do such horrible things like, riding around with gorgeous, strange men and carrying squishy panties in her purse.

The doorbell rang again.

Megan sighed, stretched, and began trying to think up her best lie. Dealing with her mother wasn't going to easy. She would probably go to hell for lying to her mother. And for committing adultery. Sort of. By the end of the week if her luck continued she'll probably have broken all 10 commandments and God would send the Grim Reaper himself to collect her butt and drag her to hell.

The damn doorbell rang again.

"I'm coming!" she yelled impatiently. "Hang on dammit!"

Megan hauled herself off of the couch and to the foyer. Pushing the curtain aside on the window, she looked out her heart almost stopped beating. It was Tom. He was standing there looking delicious in jeans and a t-shirt with his gym's logo on the front. His thick black hair hung loose on his shoulders. He looked like a little like Antonio Banderas and a lot like trouble.

Megan immediately began fluffing her hair and straightening her clothes. Satisfied that she looked like hell and had no time to do anything about it she opened the door.

"Hello Mr. Stratton," she said.

"Mrs. Malone."

"You can call me Megan."

"Okay. Megan. How are you feeling?" He was still standing on the porch and her manners finally kicked in so she gestured for him to come inside. He entered and she closed the door behind him.

"I'm fine. You didn't have to come all this way to check on me." He held up a small white bag with an RX symbol on it.

"I wanted to. Plus I have your prescription from the hospital." He paused. "May I take a seat?"

"Oh, of course," She gestured him to the couch where he handed her the bag. "Oh Tom, you didn't have to do this. I appreciate it but it wasn't necessary. What do I owe you for this?"

"Nothing. You were injured at my gym. It's the least I can do." When she opened her mouth to protest he waved her off and said, "I'll also make sure the hospital bill is paid for and you have a lifetime membership at the gym for free."

"Tom, I have insurance that'll cover the bill and I won't be returning to the gym."

He frowned and she continued, "I don't think I'm an exercise kind of person. Plus I've sort of been uninvited."

"By Stacy?"

"Adele." His frown returned. He was even sexy when he frowned. God help her. "She called and left a message that I was not invited to her classes anymore. I don't blame her. I screwed up her class and made a fool of myself. Even if she hadn't called, I'd be too embarrassed to go back."

"Don't worry about Adele. I'll take care of her. She has no right to treat you like that." Megan waved her hand in the air to dismiss the Adele issue. The last thing she needed right now was that woman pissed off at her. Adele would probably hunt her down and make her do pushups until her eyes bulged. She rubbed her eyes at the thought. Tom patted her knee and looked at her with concerned eyes.

"Is your head hurting?" he asked.

"Yeah, a little." She retrieved the ice pack from the table and held it to her head.

Her head did hurt but the ice wasn't for that. The ice was to cool her off from the heat that was burning through her from Tom's hand on her knee. Putting the ice pack directly on her crotch would probably be a telltale sign that he was making her hot, so she just held it to her head and tried ignore her stirring hormones.

Tom removed the medication from the bag and popped off the lid. "Maybe you should take one of these. It should dull the pain." He handed her a pill.

"Thank You."

"Where's your kitchen?" She looked at him, her expression blank. "Water. I'll get you a glass of water."

"Oh, through that door." Tom went to get the water and Megan watched his perfect backside leave the room, When she was sure he was gone she applied the ice pack to her crotch hoping to extinguish the burn there. He re-entered the room with a glass and sat down beside her, handing her the water.

"Thank you," she said after she swallowed the pill. He reached for the ice pack in her lap and lifted it back to her head. She stilled herself at his touch and their eyes met. Her heart was leaping out of her chest and she had to remind herself to breathe. She jerked her gaze over to Spot, who was watching with a sneer. Thank God he couldn't talk because he'd probably call her mother and tattle on Meg. Her Mom would probably try to have her fitted for a chastity belt.

"Megan?" Tom's voice pulled her out of her thoughts and back to his gaze.

They stayed looking at each other for a full minute, neither speaking, his hand still holding the ice pack to her head. He finally spoke. "Have you eaten?" She shook her head. "It said on the bottle not to take these on an empty stomach. We need to get some food in you." Great so she could puke on him again.

"I was just going to throw together a salad." She lied. She was really going to devour another cheesecake or something chocolate. Anything but salad.

"Why don't you lie down and I'll make you a salad. What do you want on it?"

Oh how about whip cream and you shirtless and...

"Oh that's okay. I've already taken up enough of your time..."

"Nonsense," he interrupted. "Now just relax, and let me feed you."

"I'll help. Or at least keep you company and show you where everything is." She stood and started to the kitchen. He fell into step behind her, placing his hand on the small of her back as if he was trying to steady her. Just friendly contact she told her hormones. Nothing to get excited about.

He went to the sink to wash his hands while Megan dug around in the refrigerator pulling out vegetables. He found the knife and cutting board in the dish drainer and began rummaging through the cupboards. He caught Megan watching him.

"Vegetable drainer?" he asked and she retrieved it for him and watched as he began putting the veggies in it. He had such masculine hands yet he seemed to move so gracefully in her kitchen. He moved the bowl to the sink, turned on the water, and reached for the sprayer.

"NO." Megan shouted just as he pushed the trigger on the sprayer that had been broken for over two years. Tom jumped back at her shriek while the sprayer shot around in the sink like a tornado drenching everything in its path with water. "It's broken," she said, "The lever thingy sticks and it gets water all over everything." Including Tom, in his tight shirt which now was stuck to his bulging chest outlining every hard muscle and curve.

"I see that." He flipped the water lever off and offered her a dish towel to dry her face with.

"I'm so sorry, Tom. First I puke on you and then this. If you were sane you'd get out of here quick before something else drastic happens."

"This isn't drastic, Megan." He closed the space between them. "It'll dry. Can I use your dryer?"

She nodded too embarrassed to speak. He grabbed the hem of his shirt and pulled it over his head, giving her an erotic view of his chiseled chest now glistening from the water. Megan took a step back and applied the ice pack to her crotch.

Tom grinned and held up his shirt.

"The dryer. Right." She led him into the pantry where he tossed his shirt in the dryer and hit start. He then went back to the kitchen and began preparing the vegetables.

Megan stood in the pantry contemplating the possibility of drowning herself in the washer. Convinced that her thighs were too big to fit in there, she rejoined him in the kitchen and sat down at the table casually letting the icepack find its way back to her crotch. Good Lord, she was losing it.

"...I wish I could change your mind about the gym," he was saying. "I'd love to see you come back."

"Maybe," she said. "But I think I'll stick to exercising at home where I can't make a complete ass out of myself." She closed her eyes as she remembered how stupid she probably looked when she knocked herself out. Gyms didn't have video cameras did they? If she saw herself on, 'World most bone head videos' someday, she'd have to drive her car off a cliff.

"It was just one of those things. Nothing major." Yeah right! "It's really Adele's fault. If she'd taught you correctly none of this would have ever happened. All you need is a good teacher."

"No, what I need is a miracle." He frowned, sat the knife on the counter and joined her at the table. He took her hand in his and rubbed it gently. "I'm a mess," she said.

"Tell you what. You come back to the gym and I'll train you personally." She shook her head but he continued. "You can drench me with water or puke on me whenever you please."

"Your sweet, but you heard Stacy; I'm an accident waiting to happen."

"So I'll wear a hard hat and up my insurance policy." She smiled and he added, "And I'll wear a cup." The thought of him in a hard hat made her dizzy. Or maybe it was his lack of shirt. Or the pain pills. Probably all of the above.

"Okay," she said finally. She'd tell him no later, when she could do it on the phone.

He smiled. "That's my girl." He removed his hand and went back to preparing the salad.

Had he just called her his girl? Maybe now would be a good time to tell him she was married to...what's his name? Oh yeah, Ted. She was a horrible wife. Give her an orgasm, a blow to the head and a muscled hunk shirtless in her kitchen and she couldn't even remember her husband's name. If she wasn't going to hell already she just got a first class ticket.

The sound of the front door closing drew her out of her thoughts and she half expected it to be the grim reaper. It was Ted. Close enough.

She heard him drop the keys on the coffee table and head downstairs to the basement. No 'honey I'm home' or nothing. Jerk. She bet Tom said 'Honey I'm home' when he went home. Probably wearing a hard hat and no shirt. She needed more ice. Thank God she was a woman and didn't have the equipment that showed arousal like a man did. Or like some men did. Ted should have an "Out of order" sign hung on his. God knows he never used it. With her anyways.

"Was that the door?" Tom asked.

"Huh?"

"Did someone just come in?"

"Oh, Yeah, That was Ted." The Jerk!

"Ted?"

"My…" Before she could finish Ted walked in the kitchen and began throwing ingredients on the counter for his protein shake as if having a half-naked man preparing a salad in his kitchen happened every day.

"What's for dinner?" Ted asked.

"Uh." Megan looked at Ted incredulously. He was worried about dinner? Hello! Earth to Ted, there's a strange man in the friggin' kitchen. "I don't really feel like cooking tonight. Maybe we'll just do sandwiches."

"I hate sandwiches Megan, you know that. I want…" He looked at Tom, "Who's he?"

"That's Tom." Megan supplied. Tom offered his hand.

"Oh," was all Ted said as he put the ingredients back, got water instead and started out of the room, like he was interrupting them. Megan felt a flood of anger.

"OH?" she yelled. Tom leaned against the fridge curious. "That's all you have to say is OH? You come home and find a man in our kitchen shirtless making a salad for your wife, who was knocked unconscious today by the way, and all you can freaking say is OH? Do you even wonder why he's not wearing a shirt or why his hair is wet?" She crossed the kitchen to Ted and poked him in the chest with her finger. "Huh? Do you?"

"Okay Megan? Why is his hair wet? Why is he missing his shirt?" His tone was sarcastic like there was no possibility there could be anything going on between her and Tom. Like just because he didn't desire her no one else would. Her blood boiled and she decided that the truth was too damn good for him. "Well?" he said.

Megan planted her hands on her hips and tilted her chin up. "I met Tom today and invited him over and we decided to skip the small talk and just get right to the sex." Tom raised his eyebrows and smiled. "So after he ravished me on the kitchen counter, we used the sprayer to hose it off and since you never fixed the damn thing it started shooting water like a geyser and got him all wet so we put his shirt in the dryer. Once I saw his luscious chest I got all hot and we were just about to get busy again when I suddenly got hungry, so Tom being the chiseled sweetheart that he is offered to make me a salad. We were just about to refuel and get after it when you came in and ruined the mood. You bastard!" She stood there waiting for him to get angry, to tell her what a tramp she was and order Tom out of his house but he did neither.

"Don't worry about dinner. I'll get takeout," was all he said and he went back to the basement. Megan stood there speechless blinking her eyes as if she wasn't sure she'd heard him right.

Tom also stood speechless still leaning on the refrigerator with his arms crossed over his chest, an amused smile dancing on his face, his eyes glittering.

"I'm so sorry Tom," Megan began, remembering Tom was still there. "I can't believe I just did that. You must think I'm a...a lunatic. I'm not usually like this. I don't know what's wrong with me." She buried her head in her hands praying that her head would explode. Tom joined her at the table again.

"It's probably the pain pills." Tom offered trying to hide his amusement. "I guess we should have taken that warning on the label more seriously. We should have fed you first." Yeah, like the label said 'if not taken with food you will temporarily lose every ounce of your sanity and make a total and complete ass out of yourself'. Megan kept her head buried and fought off tears of embarrassment.

"Megan?" Tom called out and took her hand in his again. "Megan, you've had a rough day. The day's events just caught up with you and you had to get it all out. It's fine. Really." She looked up at him. "In fact I'm flattered. I had no idea I was a chiseled sweetheart that got you hot. If it'll make you feel better, I'd be happy to ravish you on the counter. I would have done it earlier I just didn't know it was an option then." Megan gave a weak smile, Tom smiled too. "Feel better?" he asked.

She nodded, she did feel better. She just really hated Ted at the moment.

"Thank You," she said again, "for everything. You really are very sweet."

"So are you," he said still holding her hand. Their eyes met and for a moment Megan thought about letting him ravish her. Ted obviously didn't care. But she did and it would be wrong. So she'd do the right thing like she always did.

Tom's gaze fell to her lips and she felt heat shoot through her body. She needed that damn ice pack again. She finally broke her hand away and stood.

"You should go," she told him before she ran out of ice and morals and ravished him.

"Will you be Okay? I mean he's not going to do anything is he? Like hit you or…"

"Ted? Oh no. He never does anything." Literally! "I don't think he cares much anymore. He just kind of…exists." She went to the dryer to get his shirt, then rejoined him in the kitchen and handed it to him. He fished in his wallet for a business card and placed it in the palm of her hand, covering her hand with his.

"He doesn't deserve you," he said softly.

"I know," Megan said staring at their hands still touching.

"You call me if you need anything." Megan nodded still looking at their hands.

"Megan? Where are you honey? Yoo-hoo?" Megan felt her head begin to pound again. Her mother walked into the kitchen and caught site of the big, bare chested man, holding her daughter's hand with one hand and his shirt in the other and dropped the dish she was carrying. It looked like lasagna. Shit! Megan's favorite. Tom and Megan stood there frozen staring at her mother's shocked face and the mess on the floor. She released Tom's hand.

"Hi Mom," Megan answered as calmly as she could. "What brings you here?"

"I brought you dinner. I was worried about your head and…" she gestured at Tom.

"Oh Mom, this is Tom." Tom offered his hand and said hello. "He was just leaving. Right Tom?"

"Right. Call me if you need anything." Megan nodded and shoved him towards the door with her hip. She then turned to face her mother who was clutching the crucifix she always wore to her chest. "It's not what you think," Megan said.

"I don't know what to think, Megan. First the concussion, then you're riding around with a strange man, then I come here and your necking with another man."

"Okay stop right there. There was no concussion and there was only one man. Tom's the stranger from earlier and we weren't necking. God Mom, no one even says necking anymore. "

"Whatever!" her mother snapped. "Making out then, anyways then you make those comments about rape and murder and speeding buses and…your hair! What on earth did you do to your hair! It looks awful! It's blonde! You can't go to church with hair like that. What possessed you to go from your long pretty locks to this…" She waved her hands around in the air around Megan's head.

"I didn't cut it," Megan lied. "The people at the hospital did. They needed to examine my wound closer and they…" Her mother put her hands on her hips and narrowed her eyes. Megan tried again.

"Okay, the truth is these little green aliens came down and abducted me and…" Her mother's eyes grew even narrower now resembling tiny slits.

"Spot did it?" Megan tried and her mother threw her hands in the air and exhaled loudly. Megan winced and prepared for the worst.

"That's it Megan! I'm calling Father Edmond. You've obviously lost your mind. Divine Intervention might not even work. I've got to go to church. I'll probably lose my voice saying Hail Mary's and then I won't be able to lead the choir Sunday." She clutched her necklace again and looked at the ceiling. "Why me?" she asked the florescent lighting. "I used to have a normal daughter, well almost normal, she did bring me a fish for a grandchild but I could overlook that. Now she has affairs, and a trampy hairstyle and concussions…" She was still babbling to God as she left the kitchen and slammed the door shut.

Megan stood in the kitchen wondering who would be committed to the loony bin first. Her or her mother?

When she heard her mother's car door slam, she went to the silverware drawer, selected a fork and sat in the floor with her legs stretched out and began eating the lasagna her mother brought over. She may be going crazy, but even she wasn't crazy enough to let a perfectly good lasagna go to waste.

Amy Johnson

Chapter Five

After eating the lasagna off the floor, Megan sat next to the mess and cried. How could Ted have shown no emotion after she'd told him, what she and Tom had done? He cared more about his dinner than his wife's faithfulness. He was a jerk. An insensitive, selfish, scum-sucking, sack of shit. Tom was right! She was too good for him. She'd always been obedient, supportive, and faithful. And what had that gotten her? Sitting in the kitchen crying over a floor full of lasagna. Not to mention the fact that her mother probably hated her and her pets would probably disown her and choose to live with their father after he divorced her for...for what? She hadn't really done anything wrong. Maybe she should divorce him. All of this was his damn fault. If he'd shown her that he loved her and made her feel important or special she wouldn't have been sitting in the floor eating lasagna off the ceramic tile.

All she wanted was a little passion and pizzazz. Now she was probably going to get alone and abandoned. Maybe this would all blow over. She could smooth things over with Ted, and go back to being the bored, neglected housewife she'd been for so long.

The only problem with that was that before she never knew she was missing anything. Until that darn email she was happy with the monotony. Now she knew what she missing and she wanted it back. Problem was Ted obviously didn't.

Sure she could have a wild night with someone else, Tom came to mind immediately, but that wouldn't be right and more than likely it wouldn't last because she truly loved Ted. And she was certain that somewhere deep down he loved her too.

But if he loved her why hadn't he attempted to show her last night when she got all dressed up for him. And why didn't the site of Tom half dressed in the kitchen bother him. Even when she exploded at him and told him she and Tom had had sex on the counter, he showed no emotion and was only concerned with dinner.

What was wrong with her?

Just thinking about it made her cry more and when she realized how pathetic she was being; she picked herself up from the floor and called Josie.

"I called an emergency meeting," Josie said when she picked Megan up a half an hour later. "We're going to the 'Usual Place'. Everyone will be there except maybe Ali 'cause you know she's all in love and stuff and Bill is home tonight, so they might be cuddling or something mushy like that." Megan pounded her head softly on the passenger side window. Good for Ali, she thought.

"Anyways," Josie continued, "We can bash Ted all night and...oh by the way, your mother called my mother. She told her you're having an affair with some guy from the gym and that she thinks he hit you in the head with a weight because you cut your hair." Megan pounded her head harder.

"Great," she muttered.

"Oh that's not all, she thinks you're taking drugs. She said she's sending Father Edmond over to your house to talk you into going to rehab." Megan grimaced and groaned. "Oh but don't worry. I set the record straight." Oh boy! That's just what she needed. "I told Mom all about Sergio and the squishy panties. She agrees with me that at that particular moment you're karma got all screwed up and off balance and that once we get rid of the bad karma you'll be right back to normal. Mom's on the internet right now researching your predicament with a psychic. She said she'd call as soon as she knew something." Lovely, Megan's fate was in the hands of Aunt Cleo. "Anyways your Mom started talking real weird like she was talking in tongues or something and my Mom hung up on her. My mom said your mom needs therapy." Megan made a mental note to call a shrink and inquire about a family rate. "So, tell me more about Tom. He sounds like a total hunk. I'm thinking about joining the gym so I can scam on him."

"I thought your idea of weight loss was eating once a week."

"Oh, I'm not going to exercise. Duh! I'll just bounce around in a work out suit, maybe ask him to personally train me on the machines and stuff like that."

"Wouldn't it just be easier if I gave you his number?"

"No, men like challenges. I'll go in and play hard to get and I'll have him eating out of my hand."

"Josie," Megan said, "everyone knows you're not hard to get." Josie seemed to consider that for a moment her brows scrunched in concentration.

"You're right. Just give me his number then." Before Megan could respond they pulled up at the restaurant and Josie said, "Oh look Mickey and Stacy are already here."

***

"He's cheating on you!" Mickey said after Megan had relayed everything to the gang. Everyone was there including Ali. Ali might be a newlywed but she was always there when you needed her.

"Mickey! We don't know that, so don't upset her until we do," Ali growled to Mickey who had come straight from work and was dressed as Michael. But don't let the suit and tie fool you. He might be dressed like Michael, but it was definitely the sassy, Mikayla speaking.

"Well, then what do you think his problem is? I mean she confessed to an affair right there in the kitchen and he ordered takeout? That's not normal male behavior," Mickey said.

"But there was no affair, which means he had no reason to get upset," Stacy supplied.

"But he didn't know that," Ali began, "I mean what would your husband do if he walked in and saw a half dressed hunk in the kitchen with you? Affair or no affair, he still should have been angry or disturbed by it at least."

"Maybe he has a testosterone imbalance." Josie offered. "You know some kind of chemical imbalance that makes him act like a wuss or something." Everyone ignored her and cut her off before she had a chance to continue.

"I thought maybe he's gay," Megan said, and everyone turned to Mickey.

"What?" he said. "Just 'cause I'm gay sometimes doesn't mean I can spot 'em a mile away. I don't think he's gay. I could try to find out if you want me to but I personally think he's cheating."

"Which doesn't necessarily mean he can't be gay. He could be cheating on Meg with a guy." Just wonderful Megan thought. A man spends ten years with her and ends up gay. That's not the kind of testament she needed on her love resume.

"He's not gay," Stacy said. "And he may not be having an affair. This might just be the way he is."

"Let's not rule out the gay thing just yet," Josie argued. "I mean he works out all the time, and he loves that old car he has, and he never touches poor Megan." Megan shot her the mother of go to hell looks. "It's like he's...he's compensating for something you know like a little..."

"Josie! We don't want to hear about that," Stacy growled. "Lots of men stay in shape, or have hot rods. So what! It doesn't automatically mean they're gay or compensating."

Megan had had enough. "Look, does it really matter which of the two it is? I don't give a rat's behind if he's cheating with Sally or Steve. I just want to know if he is, so I can kill him and get it over with." Everyone stared wearily at Megan except for Ali who was removing all the knives and forks from the table just in case Megan got any ideas. Megan saw her and explained quickly, "Figuratively speaking of course."

"Of course," the gang said not very convincingly.

"Oh God, what am I going to do?" Megan cried, cradling her head in her hands. "I have to know. What if it's me?"

"It's not you honey. You're amazing. Everyone knows that. It's him. He's a jackass," Mickey said. The waitress came by for their drink orders. Everyone except Stacy and Megan ordered beers.

"Tequila, straight up," Stacy told the waitress.

The waitress was still standing there when Josie said, "I know! We can search the house and his office and find out for sure. Then if he is cheating, Megan can have a freebie with Tom. It won't count 'cause it'll cancel out with Ted's affair, and then maybe her karma will balance and she won't have orgasms by herself or puke on hunky guys." The waitress's interest in the conversation became intense.

"Make that a double!" Stacy told the waitress.

"Me too," Megan said.

"Scratch that last tequila," Josie said referring to Megan's drink, "She can't drink that," she lowered her voice, "She's taking drugs." The waitress looked at Megan who dropped her head onto the table with a loud clunk.

"Bring it anyway. I'll drink it," Stacy said.

"Now back to the real issue at hand. How do we find out if Ted's cheating?" Megan asked.

"Ask him," Stacy simply said. Sure that'll work.

"Yeah, just talk to him about how you feel and ask him how he feels, and see where it goes," Ali agreed.

"Like he'll admit anything. I still say we search the house and his office. Dig up some dirt. Then he can't deny anything," Josie said.

"What makes you think you'd find anything even if you did search. Ted's not stupid. If he's having an affair, he's not going to leave post it notes around his desk saying so," Ali said.

"True. But if he's cheating, we'll find something. Cell phone bills or condoms or phone numbers or maybe panties in his desk…" Mickey cut Josie off before Megan found a fork and lunged it at Josie's throat.

"I agree," Mickey began, "We can just take a look around. See if anything pops up. If nothing does great. But if something does, than when he denies it Megan can show him the proof and he'll have to tell the truth. Then we can call Tom." He turned his attention to Megan, "So is Tom seeing anybody?"

"Yes!" Josie answered. "He's seeing Megan and if Megan doesn't want him, I get dibs."

"You can't call dibs!"

"Can too."

"Can NOT"

Megan went back to banging her head while Stacy downed her drinks and Ali ordered more.

"Guys!" Ali shouted over Mickey and Josie. "If Megan doesn't want Tom, you guys can flip a quarter for him." They stopped arguing and Mickey pulled out a quarter. "I call tails," he said, throwing the quarter in the air.

"Figures," Josie said. Josie won the toss and that little problem was solved. Stacy feeling the alcohol now was the next to speak.

"Alright! Here's what I think," she said through slurred speech, "I think Megan is over reacting. Just because Ted isn't jumping for joy every time he sees her doesn't mean he's having an affair. He didn't freak out about Tom because he knows Megan well enough to know she would never cheat on him. He trusts her and he knew there had to be a perfectly logical explanation. And there was. Right Meg?" Megan nodded. Stacy turned to face Megan. "So I say you go home and talk with him and like Ali said, you tell him how you feel and what you need from him. You've been married ten years. He loves you." She put her hands flat on the table probably to steady herself from her spinning head.

"You got to give him the benefit of the doubt Meg," Ali said. "You guys just might be in a rut. Maybe all you need is a nice long talk." Yeah right Megan thought. What would Ali know about ruts? The ink on her marriage license probably wasn't even dry yet.

"I'll try it." Megan said. "But if that goes nowhere, I'm going to plan B."

"Which is?" Mickey asked.

"Tom," Josie supplied. "Right Meg? Tom is plan B huh?"

Megan rolled her eyes, "No! Plan B is the search."

"So Tom is plan C then. Okay I got it now," Josie said.

***

Later that night, when Megan was back home she went looking for Ted who was obviously not home. No note saying he'd be home shortly or telling her where he would be. She dumped her purse and jacket on the counter and went to check on her animals. The pups were outside chewing on Ted's favorite pair of running shoes. "Good pups!" she told them and left them to finish their task. Spot was hiding behind his treasure box again. She tried to lure him out so she could talk to him but he was smart enough to stay put, so she dropped some food in his bowl and sank onto the couch.

Ted had probably left her. She looked around the house and searched for his belongings. His tennis racquet, his trophies from high school, his autographed football, the stack of Sports Illustrated and Muscle Man magazines. Everything was still there where it always was. He hadn't left her. He'd just stepped out for something. Or someone.

Or maybe he thought she was crazy and feared for his life and left with only the clothes on his back. He could be at the funny farm now trying to get her admitted so he could come back later and retrieve his stuff. No. he wouldn't do that because who would cook his dinner then, or wash his clothes.

He was probably with his girlfriend. Or his boyfriend. She closed her eyes and tried to picture Ted with another man. She couldn't. Ted was too man-like to be gay. She thought of Mickey dressed like Michael.

He looked like a manly man too. And yet he was…What was he anyways? She made a mental note to ask him.

She picked up the phone to call Ted's cell phone. No answer. She tried the office and after four rings she heard Ted's deep voice on the answering machine. OK she told herself enough of this. She came home prepared to talk to him and he's was gone. Time to switch to plan B. She'd search the house. She called Josie to come help.

Josie showed up a half an hour later dressed to the nines in a red leather mini skirt that barely covered her butt, a matching red halter that did little to cover her bulging breasts and high heel boots that went up to her knees. Her blonde hair was pulled from her scalp and ratted into a sporadic mess of curls and her eyes were lined black with glitter eye shadow. She looked like Dominatrix Barbie with a bad hair do. Apparently she'd been on a date when she got Megan's call.

"Hot date?" Megan asked. Josie rolled her eyes and blew out a long sigh.

"I wish."

"Where's Mr. Wonderful now?"

"Outside in the car. I wasn't sure if you wanted me to invite him in."

"Sure. Go ahead." What the hell. Josie leaned out the door, stuck two fingers in her mouth and let out an ear splitting whistle. A moment later a figure stepped out of the car and started up the walk. Josie handled the introductions.

"Megan, this is Duff! Duff, Megan." Duff stood about six foot, and could only be described as scrawny. His hair was ratted, black and dirty and hung to the middle of his back. He wore all black leather and had piercings in every hole visible, and a thick black collar with silver spikes sticking out around his neck. A long chain hung from the collar and dangled around his waist. Dark sunglasses wrapped around his malnourished face.

"How's it hangin' babe?"

"Huh? Oh everything is hanging just fine thank you." She released his hand.

"Want me to kick his ass?"

"Huh?" Megan asked and Josie jumped into the conversation.

"Meg, I apprised Duff of the situation on the way over. He says he cheats on all of his girlfriends so he knows where to hide stuff. He can help us search." Duff smiled, gave a palms up gesture and planted an arm around Josie's shoulder. Megan blinked several times, wondering if Josie could be as clueless as she seemed.

"Josie, can I speak to you alone for a minute? In the kitchen?" Megan asked.

"Sure." Once in the kitchen Megan spoke in a very low voice.

"Josie, if he cheats on his girlfriends, why are you seeing him? And you do know him right? I mean he looks like he might...oh I don't know say gag and torture us or something." Josie placed her hand on Megan's shoulder and spoke sincerely.

"Meg, I'm not seeing him, we just went to a club. He's a musician!" Of course he was. "Anyway, we are just casual you know and he doesn't commit major crimes. Anymore."

"Anymore?" Megan should have called Stacy or Ali, they wouldn't show up with a Gene Simmons wannabe who spent his free time cheating on girlfriends and committing felonies. Of course they probably wouldn't help her prowl through Ted's stuff either.

"You know in his younger days he did some things, nothing major, just a little drugs, set a few fires. And there was the weapons charge but he swears he was set up on that."

"Josie, we really need to talk about your taste in men."

"Why?" Josie asked innocently. Could anyone be that clueless? Maybe all the blonde hair dye was seeping through to her brain and screwing up her neuro- transmitters.

"Never mind! Let's just get this over with," Megan muttered pushing her way past Josie back into the living room. Duff was standing there leaning in the doorway looking completely bored.

"So?" he asked. "Want me to kick his ass?"

"Not yet," Megan answered, wondering if this guy could fight his way out of a paper sack.

"So where do we start?" Josie asked excitedly. "This is so cool. Do you have any gloves?" Megan looked at her sideways. "You know so we don't leave fingerprints."

"It's my house, Josie. We don't need gloves."

"Well they always use them in the movies. You know they snap those latex gloves on and then crouch around in the shadows."

"You know I just ran out of latex gloves this morning. I used them all up on my last home invasion. I'll be sure to add them to the grocery list," Megan snapped.

"Well that just sucks! Here I was all excited to get my hands in some latex gloves and...."

"Latex turns you on?" Duff inquired.

"Totally!" Duff reached in his pocket and fished around.

"I got some love gloves. You can try them."

"Love gloves?" Josie asked, Megan rolled her eyes so far up in her head, she was sure she could see her hair follicles.

"You know condoms, rubbers." Duff handed them to Josie who snapped them open and began trying to pull them over her hands. Megan looked up and asked God to please take her NOW! Or at least take Josie.

"Well I guess these'll work. It's kind of hard to move my fingers but what the hell. It makes it more exciting don't you think Meg?"

"Sure Josie, whatever you say. You know when this is all done, I'm going to get you some therapy, or maybe a brain scan, you know make sure you still have one."

Josie laughed, "Of course I have one silly! The gloves were my idea remember?"

Megan contemplated throwing herself down the basement stairs.

"Let's start in the dark room. Ted knows I never go down there. If he's hiding something that would be the best place to put it."

"Oh God! I'm scared of the dark," Josie cried.

"I'll protect you, my little sex goddess," Duff consoled.

Great! That's all the world needs is those two contributing to the gene pool. Thank God for Special Ed.

"Josie, we'll turn the lights on. There are lights down there. It's just called a dark room because...Oh never mind," Megan muttered.

They went down to the basement to the section Ted had turned into his dark room. When he'd first started his business, he did a lot of work at home. Once he got the studio up and running he did less work in the basement but he did spend the major portion of his time at home down here and sometimes when Megan called him up for dinner he would tell her he was working. So chances were he still spent some time in there.

They passed his weights and workout machines. Josie crouched behind every piece hiding from imaginary people, her love gloved hands close to her body.

"He use all this stuff?" Duff asked.

"Obsessively," Megan answered.

"Remember my offer to kick his ass?"

"Yeah."

"Forget about it!"

Megan opened the door to the dark room, flipped on the lights and they peered in. There was lots of photo developing equipment covering the counters, vats of water in the sinks, and a shelf full of chemicals in the corner. Strung all the way across the room was a wire with metal clips that held a variety of photos for all to see.

Megan scanned them, seeing the pups, Ted's parents at their 50th anniversary party, a naked red head with very large breasts, a sunrise. Wait! A naked red head?

"Who's the babe?" Duff asked unclipping a photo of the mystery woman.

"I don't know," Megan answered, feeling her throat grow dry. "Probably a shoot from work." Yeah right! He shot weddings, birthdays, kids' sports teams and family portraits. This damn sure wasn't work. This was play!

"Here's one of her holding a baseball glove over her...you know," Josie said.

"Maybe she's a little league coach. You know he has a contract with the little league association," Megan growled.

"Ain't nothing little about those babies," Duff said pointing to the naked woman's humongous breasts.

"Let's look in these drawers," Megan said wanting to divert her attention anywhere else but at those pictures. There could be a very logical explanation for those pictures. Maybe Ted developed them for one of his friends. What friends? She reminded herself. Ted didn't have any friends.

"Meg?" Josie called out. "I think I found some pot."

"What?" Megan asked.

"Pot?" Duff called out. "Let me see." He took the bag from Josie, opened it, inhaled the familiar scent and smiled. "Yep! That's pot alright." He examined the green substance more clearly. "This here's some primo stuff babe. Wanna smoke some?"

"NO!" Megan shouted and snatched the bag away from Duff. "This is a drug free house. I have dogs and a fish upstairs. I have to be a role model." Megan tucked the bag in her pocket.

"You know Meg; a little dope might do that fish some good. He's too high strung. Maybe you should just sprinkle a little of that in his bowl. Chill him out a little."

"Josie! I will not get my fish stoned. Are you crazy?" Dumb question she realized even before the words left her lips. "Just keep looking!"

They kept looking around the dark room and Megan grew more and more grim as the search progressed. She was married to a man who had naked pictures strung across the room and stash of pot. She didn't even know Ted anymore and wasn't sure if she wanted to.

On the filing cabinet by the window was a picture of Megan and Ted right after they got married. They looked so young and happy. What the heck had happened?

Megan felt tears sting her eyes and fought them back. She would not cry. She would be strong and get to the bottom of this. Then she'd cry. She glanced at Ted's computer and tapped the mouse. The screen lit up and Megan went to Ted's inbox checking his email. Nothing there. They searched the rest of the dark room and found nothing else that proved Ted was a cheating dirt bag, which for some reason didn't ease Megan's mind.

"Let's go back upstairs. There's nothing else here," Megan said. As if she needed to find anything else. Her husband was a pervert pot smoker. Wasn't that enough?

Josie took her love gloves off and threw them in the kitchen trash. "Wanna search his office?"

"Yeah. I do. Lets…" The sound of the door stopped her dead in her tracks. Ted was home. The bastard! "We'll have to do it tomorrow night. I'll call you later," Megan whispered and ushered Dominatrix Josie and Duff out the back door.

"You gonna share the pot babe?" Duff asked. Megan pursed her lips and shook her head. "Just asking babe. No sense wasting some good bud." He finished on his way out the door.

Amy Johnson

Chapter Six

Megan stood in the kitchen waiting for Ted to come in so she could talk to him. She heard the door shut, then the familiar sound of his feet pounding down the stairs. A minute later she heard the basement door slam shut. Who in the hell did he think he was? If he thought he could weasel his way out of talking to her, he had another thing coming. He had some explaining to do. Like for instance why he had pictures of Miss January hanging in his dark room. And at what point he had become a pot head.

Slowly she made her way to the basement door and tapped lightly. He didn't answer. She took a deep breath and called his name in the sweetest voice she could muster. Again no answer.

"Ted! I know you're down there. Answer the door. We need to talk." Still no answer. "Ted!" she yelled. To hell with sweetness. "Open the door now!"

"Go away Meg. I don't want to talk. I'm busy."

"Oh really? Doing what? Drooling over Miss Little League?"

After a long pause Ted answered the door. "I don't know what you're talking about Meg."

"Really?" She lifted her chin and arched her eyebrows, then pushed her way past him, went down the stairs and picked up an antique camera he'd had for years. She turned it around in her hands like she'd never seen it before. Ted stood there silent his gaze following the camera. She threw the camera in the air and made a show of catching it at the last possible second. Ted lunged to catch it but she pulled it close to her chest, her eyes taunting him the whole time. She took a pitching stance, the camera in her throwing arm. "Know what I'm talking about now, Ted?"

"Megan, don't. That camera's worth a lot of money. My dad gave it to me." She mimicked a fake pitch letting the camera almost fall out of her hand.

"You're wasting time Ted. You're memory better come back soon or this camera's going out to left field."

"Megan, honey, please! I wanted to save that to pass down to our kids someday." Of all the things he could have said that was the wrong damn thing. She'd wanted kids for years and he'd been adamant about putting it off. Eventually she realized that he didn't want kids and she learned to deal with that. She had Spot and Bitty and Bug. But she would never get to experience their first days of school, or proms or graduations. "Meg! We can talk. Just give me the camera."

"Miss Naked Little League?" she said swinging the camera by its strap with Ted lunging for it each time it swung his way. "Now Ted!"

"Megan, you don't want to do this."

"Yeah! Actually I do."

"You're not like this Meg, your sweet and gentle…and…"

"What Ted? Obedient? Stupid?" She took another practice pitch. "Well not anymore I'm not. Now you have one more opportunity to tell me who she is and why you've got naked pictures of her in my house. I'll count to three."

"One."

"Meg, your mother called and she's really worried about you…"

"Two."

"--She thinks you might be taking drugs. We can get you help honey." Wrong answer Bud!

"Three!" Megan reared back and belted the camera towards the brick wall where it smashed into a million little pieces. Ted lunged to try and catch it, tripped over a barbell and landed flat on his face on the concrete floor.

"Look what you did! I hope you feel real good about yourself!" Ted said from the floor where he was wiping blood from his lip. "That camera was an heirloom."

"I do feel good Ted. Better than I have in years. And what good is an heirloom if you have no one to pass it on to." She turned to leave the basement then paused. "By the way, this is not over. You will sit down and talk to me about her and why you don't want kids, and lots of other stuff."

"And if I don't?"

"Then I guess I'll get plenty of pitching practice." And with that she stomped up the stairs and slammed the basement door shut.

Megan stood at the basement door for a few minutes breathing deeply and counting to ten. The old Megan would have been ashamed of herself for losing her temper and not acting dignified and calm. Well screw it! Dignity was overrated anyhow. The new Megan felt exhilarated and slightly liberated. That's right! The new Megan that had orgasms, and lusted after gym Gods and hunky hairdressers. That ate lasagna off the floor and cut and dyed her hair any way she damn well pleased and threw temper tantrums, and cameras and didn't care if her husband was lying in the floor with a bloody lip. She crossed her arms over her chest and snorted.

"Huh! Serves him right!" She told herself. Ted deserved whatever she felt like doing to him because he was a jerk.

A bleeding jerk who might need her help.

No! She told herself it's just a busted lip. No one ever died of a busted lip. She would not go down there and…ah hell. Damn her mother for raising her right. She filled a zip lock bag with ice and carried it to the basement door. With a loud sigh she opened the door and walked in. Ted was setting on his weight bench holding an old rag to his lip and talking on his cell phone. Abruptly, he ended his call and snapped the phone shut.

"Here," She said handing him the ice pack. "Sorry about your lip." He let the ice pack fall to the floor and said nothing. He didn't even move. Next time she'd drop a fifty pound block of dry ice on his head. The bastard!

***

Megan was channel surfing with the remote about an hour later when Ted finally came up from the basement. She was still steamed at him and hell bent on getting to the bottom of things. She decided to let him get settled and then she'd calmly, diplomatically bring up the issues of the naked woman and the marijuana. Then after that when she'd heard his explanations she'd talk to him about their marriage and how she wanted the pizzazz back. They'd have an adult conversation where both of their wants and needs would be expressed. Yeah right! She'd have better luck teaching the pups their ABC's.

Ted finally entered the room and sat in his chair. Megan surrendered the remote as a peace offering. His lip was swollen and his face was red but other than that he was plain old Ted. Quiet and calm as if he didn't have a care in the world. As if there were no drugs or X-rated pictures in the basement.

"Ted?"

"Yeah?"

"We need to talk."

"It's okay Meg. I accept your apology. Let's just forget about it." What the hell? Her apology? Was he friggin' nuts? She tried to squash her temper back down like she'd always done. She silently recited the serenity prayer. 'God grant me the serenity not to beat him over the head with a baseball bat. Amen!'

"I wasn't going to apologize."

"You weren't?" He frowned, "You broke my camera."

"You're lucky that's all I broke." He met her gaze then, she continued, "Now I want to know who 'Little Miss C Cups' is and no bullshit Ted. I want the truth."

"Fine. She's a client," he responded in his ever present calm baritone voice. "And by the way their D cups. Triple D's. So I guess that'd make her Little Miss D Cups."

Ok that was it! Call the coroner, Ted was gonna die!

Megan felt the heat penetrate her body and her muscles tighten. She felt like her ears were ringing and her eyes were on fire. Ten years of pent up feelings and emotions had now turned to rage! This was not going to be a pretty site.

She slowly got off the couch and went into the kitchen. When she returned she had a dish towel in her hand and she slowly, deliberately walked over to Spot's bowl and gently covered his bowl with the towel. Ted stared at her but didn't speak. Not until she'd sat back down, crossed her legs and picked up a magazine did he speak.

"What's with the towel?" He asked.

"I'm trying to be a role model for him but you're making it damn hard. Right now I'm experiencing some homicidal tendencies and I don't want Spot to watch me kill you." She never lifted her eyes from the magazine as she spoke in a flat, detached voice. "What with all the violence he sees on T.V and all I just don't really think it'll be good for him, so I covered his bowl. When he asks for his Daddy in the future, I'll just tell him you were poisoned or accidentally drowned or got shot." Ted's composure changed from relaxed and kicked back to shock and surprise.

"I'm sure it'll be hard on him and the pups. But I'll get them into therapy and what with your life insurance policy and all I think we'll survive." She yawned. "Oh look at the time. It's already eleven o'clock. Guess I'll hit the hay. Sweet dreams Ted." Megan rose from the couch and started towards the stairs.

"Her name is Tiffany." Megan stopped, her heart thudding against her chest. "And it's not what you think. She's just a friend." Yeah a naked friend. With Triple D's.

Naked Triple D's. And Megan had A cups. Life was so unfair.

"A friend?" Megan stood there for a moment trying to process his load of crap. Megan had friends. She didn't have pictures of them naked. Ali had never said 'Hey Meg, get a load of these babies. Wanna take a picture and hang it on the fridge where you'll see it every day?' She didn't have naked Mickey pictures.

"So how exactly did you happen to acquire these pictures of her?"

"I'm a photographer, Meg. It's what I do. I take pictures."

"Of naked women?"

"Well not usually, this was…uh kind of an accident."

"Oh, well why didn't you just say so? That explains everything." She returned to the couch her hands fisted and eyes narrowed. Sarcasm lay thick in her voice. "Let me guess you were at work, doing what you do and all of a sudden you accidentally stumble on to this naked woman who is accidentally posing in the studio. And you say gee, I should accidentally load my camera and snap a few accidental shots. Oh but wait you tell yourself, wouldn't it be even better is she accidentally posed with my sports props that I accidentally left lying around. Are you buying this load of garbage Ted? Because I sure as hell am not."

"Don't be ridiculous, Megan."

"Me ridiculous? Never. Uh huh. Not me." Her tone was so thick and full of anger she didn't even recognize it as her own voice. "Got any more accidents I should know about. You know; like if your clothes accidentally fell off and you tripped, and she was there to catch your fall and you were so grateful, that you accidentally had sex with her. Or maybe…"

61

"This conversation is over, Megan. You're acting like a child!" He turned his attention back to the T.V.

"You're right Ted. I'm acting like a child. And you know how children act. They throw temper tantrums and break things." She eyed his collection of stupid sports dolls with those hideous bobbing heads. "Expensive things. Things that mean a lot to people." She picked up Babe Ruth. "Yep, sometimes they break things that are priceless."

"Put it down Meg."

"Wasn't this guy a legend or something?" she said indicating the Babe Ruth doll in her hand. "Didn't he hit like a gazillion homeruns?"

"Yeah, Meg. He did. Look..."

"Well, he can chalk up another one 'cause this little guy is going out of the park."

"Look, Megan. I'll talk to you. I'll tell you about Tiffany. It's not what you think. Just put him down, stop breaking things and we'll talk." He rubbed his head with his hands and sighed.

"Does your head hurt Ted?"

"Yeah."

"Good! You want some Tylenol?" He looked at her sideways.

"Please." She returned Babe Ruth to the shelf.

Megan went to the kitchen and got Ted, the cheating dirt bag, a glass of water and something for his headache. While she was in the kitchen, she called Mickey.

He answered on the third ring his voice gruff from sleep.

"Mickey?"

"Yeah."

"Pick me up in about a half an hour. I'm ready to do that thing."

"What thing?"

"You know. What me, you and Josie talked about."

"Ted's office?"

"Yeah. So wear something appropriate for breaking and entering."

"Bitchin babe. I have just the outfit for it. It's camouflage with these little rhinestones and sequins..."

After cutting the connection with Mickey, she went back in the living room to deal with Ted. She handed him his water and the pills, he took them, sat the glass down, then crossed his arms over his chest and sighed. "Megan I know things..."

"Ted. I don't want to talk about it right now. Just go to bed, and tomorrow we can hash this out." He opened his mouth to protest but she talked over him. "It can wait till tomorrow. That way you won't have a headache and you'll have all night to think up a good lie. And please Ted, make it good. Don't just say the first thing that pops into your head. After ten years I deserve a better lie than 'It was an accident' or 'It's not what you think'." She laughed dryly. "At least try to be original, you know. Something that's not so cliché."

Ted's reaction to her words was utter confusion. He looked defeated, like he was trying to calculate the underlying meaning to her words. This was not the Megan he knew. The quiet, loyal, low maintenance woman, who met him at the door with a smile, and had dinner ready at six. The woman he'd married, never asked questions or threw things or spoke her mind. She was just there, loyal and obedient and quiet. Until now he assumed she'd always be. He wasn't so sure of that anymore.

"Megan?" He called out to her from the kitchen. When she didn't answer he went in there to find her scrubbing the floor where something had been spilled. "Meg?"

"What Ted?" she answered her gaze never leaving the floor where she was scrubbing the now dried and crusty remnants of her mother's lasagna from the tile.

He knelt down beside her and tilted her chin up so he could look her in the eyes.

"You're very beautiful," he told her. Try as she might, she couldn't help rolling her eyes at him in disgust.

"Go to bed Ted."

"I mean it. Maybe I don't always say it, but I've always seen it."

"Yeah, I'm sure you see it with Tiffany too." He shook his head and frowned.

"You've got the wrong idea about that."

"Whatever," she snapped. "Just go to bed, will ya? Leave me alone."

"Ok. I'll leave you alone." He took her hand. "I just want you to know, I've always loved you. That has never changed." Yeah right. Probably he loved Tiffany Triple D too.

She snorted in disbelief, "Well aren't I lucky? My husband loves me. Woohoo! I can hardly control my excitement. Now, leave me alone."

He searched her eyes for what seemed like an eternity, before finally releasing her hand and leaving the room. A moment later, Megan heard his footsteps going up the stairs, then the sound of running water in the bathroom.

She sat on the floor staring at the mess she'd been trying to clean up. Ted thought she was beautiful. He loved her. That's what she'd wanted right? She could probably follow him up those stairs and put a little passion back in their marriage. Now she had back a little of what she longed for. All she had to do was go get it. But it was too little too late. Now the thought of a passionate night with the man she once loved more than life itself made her want to throw up. All over her mother's left over lasagna, on the kitchen floor.

Chapter Seven

By twelve-thirty that night, Ted was sleeping like a baby, probably dreaming about Tiffany. Megan sat on her front porch steps waiting for Mickey to show up.

She had dressed in a black sweat suit, with black shoes and had a black Nike ball cap on backwards, her newly short hair sticking out the front. She'd loaded two flashlights, her purse and an old Polaroid camera in Ted's black gym bag and she clenched the keys to the studio in her hand. All she needed was Mickey and she was good to go.

Mickey was running late. And the later he got the more second thoughts she had. What she should do was wait until tomorrow, talk with Ted, and figure out where they went wrong and then develop a plan to fix it. Only that wouldn't happen, because he'd just lie to her and behave for a little while and once he was satisfied the coast was clear, he'd cheat again. And next time, he wouldn't be so careless about it.

Of course that theory only worked if he was cheating on her. Which, he had to be. Why else would he have naked pictures of his friend in the basement if he wasn't?

She'd have to divorce him. It would send her mother into a catholic frenzy but if he was having an affair, he had to go. She'd be alone. She blinked back a tear. She'd never been alone. She went straight from her parent's home to this house with Ted and even though they had a distant marriage, he was still there. A warm body to lie next to at night or share a meal with.

Megan saw headlights coming down the street and a moment later Mickey's car swung to a stop at the curb. She grabbed her bag, crawled in the front seat and rested the bag in her lap. She glanced back and saw Josie in the backseat.

"Ready?" Mickey asked.

"I guess. What took you so long?" Mickey pointed to the backseat with his thumb.

"I had to go get Josie. She'd a killed us if we hadn't brought her along."

Megan had a flashback to Josie prowling around the basement in her condom covered fingers and stifled a laugh.

"Where's Duff?" Megan asked.

"I sent him home. He's on probation. B&E would not be a good idea for him right now. He said if we do anymore after September he'd love to come along. His probation is up then." Megan rolled her eyes and bit her cheek to keep from lecturing Josie about her choices when it came to men.

"B&E?"

"Breaking and Entering?" Josie and Mickey both explained.

"Well technically," Megan began, "I don't think its breaking and entering, because I own the studio with Ted. So I think all we are doing is entering." She held up the keys to the studio. "With a key."

"So we won't be breaking anything?" Josie asked sounding way too disappointed.

"No."

"Well that just sucks. I even went out and bought some gloves." Josie leaned back in the seat and sighed. "My first B&E and I don't get to break anything. What a rip."

Megan and Mickey exchanged looks. He had an amused look on his face. He was certainly enjoying himself.

"Oh I know!" Josie shouted startling both Megan and Mickey. "We can give each other code names."

"Yeah like Larry, Curly and Mo," Megan said.

"No silly, like I'll be...Lolita." Josie eyed Megan and Mickey slowly. "Mickey can be Bond. James Bond." Mickey smiled. "And Meg, you can be...uh...Oh no I can't think of a name for you. Mickey?"

"Minds blank babe." Mickey answered.

Josie thought about it, "Mine too." Literally Megan thought. Good thing she had big boobs. At least God compensated for giving her an IQ of twelve.

"I don't need a name," Megan said flatly.

"Hey, we could be Charlie's Angels. What were their names?" Josie asked.

"The original ones or the new ones?" Mickey asked.

"Huh?"

"Well first there was the original series back in the seventies," Mickey explained to Josie. "And then they made a movie recently with a new cast. You haven't seen it?" Josie shook her head. "It's bitchin' babe. You gotta see it."

Megan banged her head on the passenger side window glass listening to Mickey and Josie talk about the Charlie's babes and their wicked outfits. The one thing about Josie and Mickey was that they seemed to be made from the same mold. They had the same personality and demeanor. If they could somehow share bodies, they'd be the perfect human form. With Mickey's intelligence and sense of humor and Josie's big boobs and model looks, they could do some serious damage. Of course they both did enough damage by themselves to keep Megan and the rest of the girls in a constant state of damage control.

Sitting in the car with them now made Megan think of the Wizard of Oz. If they were all going to see the Wizard right now, Mickey would ask for a killer set of knockers and a woman's shoe designer to keep him supplied in size 13's. Josie would naturally ask for a brain. And if she wasn't smart enough to ask herself, Mickey and Megan would make sure the request got through. And Megan, Megan would ask for the truth. For the truth about a man she'd spent ten years with, yet she felt like she didn't even know. And now sitting in this car she wasn't even sure she really wanted it. Loneliness wasn't appealing. In fact it scared her to death.

"Alright! We're here." Mickey announced as he cut the engine. "We just going to go on in?"

"Yep." Megan held out the key ring and began looking for the right key. She hadn't been to Ted's studio in years when he hadn't been there, so she had no idea which key fit the lock. When they got to the door she'd have to use the flashlight to see and start trying keys until she found the right one. They'd parked behind the studio and two parking lots over where the factory workers parked their cars for the graveyard shift. Hopefully Mickey's car would not be noticed.

"What if Ted wakes up and finds you MIA babe?"

"He won't," Megan answered briefly.

"Think he'll think something's up? Go out looking for you."

"He won't wake up." Either the words or her tone startled him because he stopped walking. Josie was digging in her purse and walked right into him sending them both lurching forward. It wasn't until then that the light from the parking lots was bright enough to take in their costumes.

"What do you mean he won't wake up? You kill him?"

"No. I dosed him. He'll sleep like a baby." She gave Josie a thorough once over. She might be clueless but when it came to fashion she was gifted. And creative.

"Dosed him? With what?" Mickey asked watching her closely through squinted eyes.

"Benadryl. I gave him three pills." Mickey stood rigid, his mouth open. "Don't worry," Megan explained quickly. "It won't kill him. It'll just knock him out."

"You sure?" From the sound of his voice he'd transformed into Michael. Responsible, reliable and cautious Michael. Too bad his clothes stated the absolute opposite.

"I'm positive." When he still didn't look convinced, she changed the subject. "And what's with the clothes. You don't look like cat burglars. You look like sex kittens."

"Divas," Mickey corrected. Once they got to the door and she felt covered from the entry way, she trained the flashlight on them. Mickey was wearing a tight camouflage mini skirt with a ripped hem that was decorated with rhinestones nestled together in haphazard patterns. His shirt was also camouflage and had the words U.S. Army sequined on the front. The wiry hair from his chest and arms stuck out everywhere. His bleach blonde hair was ratted and nestled a top a US Army visor and he wore combat boots which he'd embellished with spray paint and glitter to give them a camouflaged diva look. With his height and build he looked like G.I. Joe the drag queen drill sergeant in a circus side show.

Josie on the other hand had traded in her glitz and glamour look for an attempt at a gothic Marilyn Monroe. She wore a black bustier and short black leather shorts that covered a miniscule amount of her pretty little butt. Her legs were encased in black fishnet stockings that were ripped and torn-purposely Megan assumed- and thigh high vinyl boots with heels that added a good six inches to her five foot six frame. Her platinum blonde hair was arranged in a flawless bob and her makeup was black and flawless. Tough Marilyn Monroe may have been her inspiration; Marilyn Manson was the end result. And as usual she looked completely hot.

"I told you to wear something comfortable, something you could move in. You guys look like you should be trick or treating. Or better yet turning tricks," Megan said as she began trying the keys.

"Good. That's just the look we were going for," Mickey said admiring his get up.

"Yeah. I had to put together a special outfit for my first felony," Josie said, giddy with excitement. "Plus if we get busted and go to jail I want to look hot in my mug shots." She paused, pondered something. "You know if we get caught we could be on T.V. Maybe even Cops. They could do a special episode. You know Fabulous Fashion Felons or something like that. My Mom would shit a brick, if I wasn't dressed to the nines. She'd probably tape it and show it to all her friends and then..."

Megan continued trying keys doing her best to ignore Josie and her bulging cleavage. Mickey was holding the light for her while she tried the seventh key. The lock clicked and she swung the door open, and then slammed it shut again, covering her ears in a panic.

"What the hell was that?" Josie asked scurrying behind Mickey to hide.

"Sounds like an alarm," Mickey said, stating the obvious. Megan stood frozen staring at the door. When had Ted installed an alarm? And why? They'd never been broken in to. The studio was located in a nice neighborhood. There seemed to be no need for an alarm. Of course he did have a lot of expensive equipment.

"You know anything about alarms?" Megan asked. The question, of course, was aimed at Mickey but it was Josie who responded by pulling a small satin looking sash from her bustier and examining the tools.

"I used to date this guy once," She began and Megan and Mickey both rolled their eyes and shook their heads. "And he used to house sit for rich people when they were out of town, and he always had to...what do you call it? Circumvent their alarm systems. I watched him do it a few times. All you have to do is..."

Josie began to work on the alarm system with talk of 'demagnetizing the connection' and other terms that Megan knew nothing about. She just stood frozen in shock and disbelief as Josie matter of factly went through the how to's of disarming an alarm, all the while using the tools as expertly as a surgeon would a scalpel. You know for a woman with so little common sense she could surprise the hell out of you with some of the stuff she knew. This was evidence that she did have a brain, but maybe it was programmed on the wrong channel.

"…And that should do it." Josie tried the door and it was pure silence. No buzzing from the alarm. No ear scattering shriek. "See? Piece of cake."

"Uh Josie, this guy, where is he now?" Mickey asked.

"Jail. I don't know what for. He said it was a bum rap." And her IQ was back in the negatives. She must've burned what few cells she had disarming the alarm.

"Josie, you ditz," Megan snapped as they entered the office. "He's in jail because he wasn't house sitting for anyone. He broke into those houses and probably robbed them blind after he rolled you around in the sheets. Jeez!"

"You know him? I didn't think he was your type." She shrugged and pulled on her gloves. Megan began looking for sharp objects to impale herself on. The only person on earth more stupid than Josie was Mickey for bringing her. And beyond him was Megan for calling him. She knew better.

"No! Josie I don't know him. It just doesn't take a rocket scientist to figure out…You know what? Never mind! Just be quiet. You're giving me one hell of a headache. A migraine I think. It'll probably kill me. Or at least I hope it will." She rubbed her head and then looked up to God. She crossed herself and then began mumbling unintelligible babbles. Mickey and Josie looked at each other and then at Megan who was still having her own private conversation with God. Megan caught them staring and shivered.

"You see what you're doing to me? Now I'm acting like my mother. I'll probably start wearing pink curlers to the grocery store and polyester house coats. I need a life. I need some sanity. I need some serious therapy. I need…"

Josie, not being the patient subtle one, raised her hand and slapped Megan across the face causing her to lose her balance and trip over a tripod. She hit the ground with a thud and lay in the floor once again staring at the ceiling, a stunned look of disbelief on her face.

"You hit me!" Megan growled.

"I was saving you from a nervous breakdown. You need to snap out of it sister. You're giving me a headache." She inspected her manicure. "Now get up and let's see what we can find."

Jackson Westin lay crouched under the desk in the reception area. He'd cased this place for a week, and not a soul was ever around after seven. The one night he'd decided to make his move was the night 'The Insane Clown Posse' chose to break in. Just his freaking luck. He'd been so careful not to make a sound. Not to emit even a shred of light while he searched and these three yahoos came in and crashed the damn party. And with all the racket they were making he'd undoubtedly get caught.

At first he thought it was that scatter brained secretary Tiffany coming in to retrieve something she'd forgotten. Or that sleaze ball Ted Malone coming in to get it on with Tiffany. When he'd heard the alarm sputter and then shut off, he'd hidden, figuring they'd just go upstairs and get after it. That's when he'd simply slip out unnoticed, the same way he'd come in.

He heard a deep male voice and a faintly familiar female voice. Ted and Tiffany he thought. But then he heard another female voice and he had to choke back his surprise. Ted and two women? No way! Sure Ted was something with the ladies but two at a time? Not a chance. Hell, he didn't even know what to do with the one he had.

That thought made him hot with anger. All through middle school and high school Megan Johnson had been the object of Jack's desire with her simple beauty, her grace, her good girl image and enthusiastic attitude toward life. She was the one reason he went to school everyday. God knows it wasn't for the education, school wasn't his thing. Neither was dealing with authority. But he dealt with it anyway just to see her. To sit behind her in Math and daydream of her and him, exploring the unknown. Or to get a glimpse at that sweet crooked smile that made the blue in her eyes sparkle brighter than any star. Yes, she was the only education he wanted. And she never even noticed him. Sure she'd smile back or cast a shy wave to return his. But she never once spoke to him and probably didn't even know his name.

Then the summer before high school he went to his uncle's for the summer. He worked in his uncle's construction business and was supposed to be learning the ropes. He stayed so busy with work during the day and getting into trouble at night that he'd almost forgotten about

Megan. Almost. When he arrived home two weeks before school he barely resembled the boy he was when he'd left. He'd grown three inches and added thirty pounds of muscle to his scrawny frame. He looked like a man, broad shoulders, defined biceps, thick chest. The first day of school he'd turned the heads of the cheerleaders on campus. He strutted around, showing off his meat, like the campus was one big supermarket and he was the only beef cake display. He would have enjoyed the attention too if he hadn't seen her.

But there she was. In her short cheerleading get up, pom poms and all. Her hair had grown out and she'd... developed over the summer. She was beautiful before, but now her skin was a sun bronzed golden, her body had taken on the curves of womanhood, and her eyes were the bluest blue he'd ever seen. She was talking with the girls from the squad and she tilted her head back and laughed, her lips forming that crooked smile. And he fell in love all over again.

Only this time, she'd notice him. He'd approach her, and she'd talk to him. He'd make her laugh and she'd smile at him with that seductively wicked smile, her eyes melting him upon impact. His daydreams would no longer be dreams.

And then Ted Malone, all star quarter back, Mr. Homecoming King himself came up and swept her into his arms, lazily dropped her into the grass and toppled on her in a playful embrace. And she greeted him with that smile. Jack went back to the shadows again. Once again invisible. Unnoticed.

The thought of Ted Malone turned his stomach now just as much as it did then. He'd married Megan. Had some fairytale wedding. But it wasn't enough for him. Now he cheated on her and treated her like garbage. He hadn't any proof before now but he didn't need it. He'd seen Megan around town. She didn't recognize him of course but he'd never forgotten her. And she was just as beautiful now as she was then. Even more so. When he saw her and cast a smile her way, she still smiled back. That same crooked smile that stole his heart. Only now that sparkle in her eyes was gone.

Chapter Eight

"Help me up!" Megan growled and Mickey reached down and scooped her up.

She dusted the seat of her pants with her hands and fixed her eyes on Josie.

"Josie, if you ever do that again, I swear to God, I'll drop kick you so hard your boobs will deflate." She retrieved her flashlight from where it had fallen. "What the hell were you thinking anyways? You just don't go around slapping people."

"Well, you were irritating me! I had to do something. I chipped a nail, if it makes you feel any better." It did. Except that Megan felt the welt on her cheek where it had chipped.

"I'm irritating you? Are you serious? You are a constant irritation. Like hemorrhoids, only there's no cream called 'Preparation' Josie to relieve the burn."

"Well if it weren't for me we wouldn't have made it inside. I disarmed the alarm. And I'd rather be a hemorrhoid than a zit that just oozes and oozes green puss and nonsense babbles."

"Are you calling me a zit?"

"Are you calling me a hemorrhoid?"

"That's it, hold my flashlight Mickey. Lolita's going down." She shrugged out of her jacket. "Or better yet, give me back my flashlight. Maybe I can use it to knock some sense into her." Mickey held the flashlight over both of their heads.

"Ladies! As much as I'd like to a see a cat fight. Trashing Ted's studio is a bad idea. Let's get back to finding dirt on Ted." He handed Megan her flashlight back and gave her a stern look. "Plus Josie would kick your bony little butt and let me tell ya honey. It wouldn't be pretty."

"I'm pretty sure I can take her." Megan said her eyes still on Josie who was in a mock fighting stance.

"I used to date a guy," Josie began. "Who was a black belt in…well he was a black belt in something and he taught me some moves. So if I were you, I'd apologize real quick." Josie was flouncing around in front of Megan and it was all she could do to keep her eyes off Josie's jiggling boobs. If this went on much longer Josie would knock herself out and Megan could still claim victory.

"Dream on Lolita."

"Okay, I'm going to let it slide this time, but only because you used my code name. But one more comment and its light's out. Got it.?" Sure, whatever! All this time Megan had been thinking about speeding buses and alien abductions and all she really had to do was piss Josie off. Who knew? One thing was for sure. Josie was full of surprises. As long as Megan had known her- over 15 years- and the woman could still shock the hell out of her.

"We good?" Mickey asked tapping one humongous foot, his hands on his hips.

"Yeah," Megan and Josie both answered.

"Good let's get this show on the road. This thong is wreaking havoc on the twins."

Mickey adjusted his underwear from his crotch, turned on his flashlight and began searching for evidence that Ted was a lowlife cheating bastard.

***

"Shit!" Jack Westin muttered from his spot under the desk. These idiots were going to be here for a while. He couldn't see them and had no idea where they were or how he was going to get out unnoticed. He thought the studio had been filled with losers from the Ted Malone fan club but from the sounds of the conversation, they were with him on the Castrate Ted Malone quest. Maybe they should align forces and have a picnic after Ted was neutered.

He'd been tempted to hop out when the cat fight almost occurred. All he could see was a pair of perfect legs in fish net stockings, but he had a feeling that the body that belonged to those scandalous legs was worth going to jail for. But then the male with them had stopped it and he saw no point in going to jail if he wasn't going to get to see some girl on girl action.

One of the voices sounded vaguely familiar. He couldn't place it but he'd definitely heard it before. Soft and sugary with just a touch of venom. Dangerous combination. He'd bet his boots that the girl with the voice-hopefully the one in those fishnets- would be a lethal combination as well. He pictured her in a catholic girl get up, her back facing him, then she slowly turns around and calls his name in that sweet but deadly voice. He reaches for her and she faces him giving him that shy smile. Ah yes. That tempting, innocent crooked smile.

And where the hell had that come from. The last thing he needed to think about right now was Megan Malone. Although every fantasy he'd had since about age fifteen revolved around her and those ocean blue eyes, her hair long and full, mussed about from a wicked night of.... He began silently reciting the Gettysburg Address. Nothing could kill a fantasy or a hard on like Ole Honest Abe.

He heard the male voice holler at the other two to look at something. He snuck a peek and then quickly jerked his head back under the desk willing his mind to stop playing tricks on him. For that brief second, that small granule of time, he could have sworn that the girl with the hat was Megan Malone. He wanted it to be her more than anything, but then he wanted every girl to be her.

***

"What?" Megan whispered, joining Mickey at the reception desk with Josie close on her heels.

"Look at this." 'This' was a framed photograph of what appeared to be two lovers embracing in front of an ocean like backdrop. It was a beautiful photo that made Megan's eyes sting with tears. Not because of the dreamy look on the lovers' faces or the peaceful serenity of the ocean tide. Not even the intimate embrace or erotic heaviness of their eyes bothered her. What bothered her was that the awe stuck man in the photo was Ted. And the woman was Tiffany Triple D.

"Looks like we found Miss Little League," Josie muttered. "The slut. Check out her nose. I think it's had work." She squinted at the picture. "Yep that's definitely a nose job. When we find her and kick her narrow behind, remind me to get the name of her plastic surgeon. He's really good. Don't you think?" Megan snapped the picture from Josie and sat in the floor forcing herself not to cry. Ted had lied. Big flipping surprise. He'd said she was a client, a friend. He'd told her it wasn't what she thought, when it was exactly what she'd thought. Ted was a jerk. A liar, a cheat and a drug addict, with a swim suit model of a girlfriend on the side. The rat bastard. Tomorrow she'd call Sergio and tell him to clear his schedule. Ted was playing the field. Why shouldn't she?

Because she was raised better than that and her mother would kill her that's why. Plus she suffered from the Catholic Guilt Syndrome, which had been pounded into her head by her mother since before she could talk. The guilt would eat her up inside, and she'd be even more miserable than she was now.

"Where was this?"

"In her top desk drawer," Megan put it back. So Tiffany Triple D, Ted's friend was his secretary too. Convenient. She went back to Ted's desk to see what other depressing evidence she could find that would further confirm his indiscretions.

She was going to have to divorce him. No amount of love in the world could excuse his behavior. To hell with what her mother would think. To hell with Catholic guilt. And to hell with Ted. Her and Spot and the pups would move on and Ted and Tiffany could pump iron or each other or whatever tickled their home wrecking fancies. She was done being the stupid housewife.

She sat in Ted's chair and began rifling through his drawers. In the bottom drawer of his desk she found a bottle of Wild Turkey Whiskey. *When did Ted start drinking?* she thought. She fingered the cap off and took a long pull, letting the amber liquid go straight to her stomach. It burned like hell, but the burn felt good. It dulled the throb in her heart.

She trained her flashlight on the top of his desk. Everywhere she looked there were sports logos or team schedules. She shined the light on his desk calendar.

Then she took another swig of whiskey. September 16th, Tiffany's birthday. It was written in Ted's lazy scrawl in black ink. She searched the calendar for the January page. January 9th was blank. Her birthday and she didn't even rate it being sloppily recorded on his calendar. She'd given him ten years and three pets and she got a blank square.

Feeling the whiskey take hold, she grabbed a pen from his drawer and wrote 'Megan's birthday, you asshole!' in the appropriate spot, then slammed the pen back in his drawer.

"Hey guys, I got plane tickets over here," Josie hollered from Tiffany's desk.

"The drawer was locked but I jimmied it." She shoved a small flat piece of metal in her bra. Mickey looked at her in amazement.

"What else you got in there?" He pointed to her chest.

"Oh you know, a little of this, little of that." She adjusted her boobs and then turned to Megan who was squinting over the light from the flashlight. "Well, what do they say?"

"The tickets are to Las Vegas leaving on September 15th, returning September 19th. There's one for Ted and the other has Tiffany's name on it." Megan sank down in floor the leaning her back against Tiffany's desk. September 16th was that little bitch's birthday and Ted was taking her to Vegas. Last year for her birthday he'd taken her to the car wash. Mr. freaking romantic! She'd been all dreamy eyed at his muscular frame working the suds into her car. Now she wanted to work her foot in his crotch. My how things change.

"Mickey, give me my whiskey, and Josie go over there and jimmy the lock on Ted's desk." Mickey handed her the bottle reluctantly and Josie fished the metal tool out of her cleavage. Megan took a long swig of the whiskey then rested her head on her knees. She caught a small glare of metal from under Ted's desk and shined her light there.

"There's a man under Ted's desk," she said flatly. Then hysterically she shouted. "There's a man under Ted's desk." Mickey leaned over and looked, his lazy expression never changing, as if men hiding under desks after hours in office buildings was business as usual.

"Sure is," he said.

"A man?" Josie swung her head around. "Is he hot? Is he wearing a wedding band?"

The strange man crawled out from under the desk and put his hands out palms facing Megan.

"It's not what you think. I'm not a burglar. I'm a pri..." Mickey smacked him on the side of the head with the yellow pages and stood towering over him demanding he identify himself. The man look stunned and Megan wondered if it was the perfect view he had of Mickey's G-string or the blow from the yellow pages. Josie rushed to the man's side and flooded him with light from her flashlight.

"He is hot! Well except for that lump he's gonna have." She glared at Mickey. "Why'd you go and do that. Now his face is gonna be all purple and swollen. I find a perfectly good man and you thump him with a phone book."

"Josie, he's not a good man! He's a burglar. He broke in here, probably to steal stuff to sell to buy crack or something." The man stood to his full height and faced the gang. Megan took a step back, her eyes wide. "Hit him again Mickey before he shoots us or ties us up and rapes us," Megan said.

"Wait just a minute." Josie turned to the man. "Do you have a gun?" he shook his head no. "Are you going to rape us?" He shook his head no. "See, it's OK. He's not going to hurt anyone."

"And you believe him? What are you nuts? He's probably an ex-convict," Megan said. But she didn't believe it. He didn't look like a lowlife or a drug addict. He looked, delicious! Or maybe it was the poor lighting. Or the fact that her hormones had been on red alert lately. Probably it was just the whiskey. Like the old saying goes, the more you drink, the prettier they get.

"Want me to hit him again?" Mickey asked, now holding his mag-lite flashlight as a weapon. "This sucker'll crack his skull."

"Who are you and what are you doing here?" Megan asked, suddenly having to fight off a case of the drunken hiccups. How could she use a stern, scary voice with this man, when she had involuntary squeaks coming up her throat? She looked up to God and asked for a tornado to come and level the building. But with her damn luck, she'd probably land on Josie's boobs which would cushion the blow and save her life. Life was so unfair!

"My name is Jackson Westin and I'm a Private Detective." That was all he offered which wasn't enough for Megan. Josie seemed enthralled.

"A private detective. How sexy is that?" He smiled and gave a small shrug. "Oh man, your sex at first site rating just went way up. So do you have a detective kit? Can I..."

"Ignore her, she's an idiot."

"Hey!" Josie snapped. Megan waved her off and raised her voice to override her.

"You say you're a PI. Who do you work for?"

"Myself."

"Who hired you?"

"That's confidential."

"How'd you get in here?"

"Same as you." He leaned against the door jam, folded his arms across his chest and stared at her through amused eyes. She wanted to hit him with the whiskey bottle just to knock his attitude down a notch. Of course that I-don't-give-a-damn-little-lady attitude made him even sexier. God she needed a drink. Or a real orgasm. With an actual man this time. Preferably one she hadn't puked on.

"I used a key," She pointed out.

"So did I." He produced a small silver key and handed it to her. She looked at it and wondered how in the hell he'd gotten it. She had to steal hers from Ted, so what'd he do? Rub a magic lamp and make a wish?

"But I have a right to be here. I own this studio."

"Then why are you and your sidekicks, using flash lights. If you're supposed to be here, why don't you turn on the lights?"

"We're environmentalists. We're conserving energy by saving electricity."

"And the gloves?" Megan looked at Josie's hands and thanked God she wasn't wearing love gloves again. That would have been a bitch to try to explain.

"She has this scaly skin rash. Herpes of some kind I believe. It's really gross and very contagious. We probably have it to by now so if I were you I wouldn't touch any of us." He took a step toward her, trying to intimidate her she guessed. And damn it was working.

"And I'm the one asking the questions here Bud. So don't try pulling any fancy P.I. tricks or I'll have Mickey clock you again."

Megan turned around looking for Mickey to back her up but he was nowhere to be found. She yelled for him and he answered back, "In the can. Hey does Ted keep any Gold Bond here? The twins are getting a major rash babe. Sequined thongs and sensitive skin don't do too good together. No breathing room babe." Great the only man in the room who could beat this guy up and save her and Josie was in the bathroom suffering from jock itch caused by his panties. Megan was suddenly speechless so she grabbed the bottle and hit it again.

"Here's what I think," Jack began, "I think you're full of shit. If you owned this place you'd of already called the cops and we wouldn't be having this conversation." Megan glared at him debating whether she should down the rest of the bottle and hope for alcohol poisoning or hit him over the head with it for being such an arrogant asshole, with a killer body and orgasmic voice.

"Know what else I think?" he asked.

"Enlighten me."

"I think you need to switch careers. You suck as burglars."

"We do not!" Josie snapped. "We even have code names. I'm Lolita!"

"Maybe Lucy is more fitting. And she can be Ethel. And then there's Ru Paul in the bathroom." His smile widened. "Hell it was like watching an episode of I Love Lucy without the commercials. I especially liked the almost catfight. That could've earned you serious burglar in training points."

"You're an asshole," Megan said thinking about how dangerous he looked.

"So what's your point?" Jack said and Megan smiled that crooked smile and Jack fell in love again.

"My point is; you haven't told us squat. You haven't shown us any ID that proves you're a private detective; we don't know who hired you or what you're looking for. You somehow managed to get a key to this office and broke in. Then when we catch you, you try to give us burglary tips." She paused and slammed back some courage from the bottle. "And if you don't start giving me some straight answers, I'm gonna call the cops and have you arrested." Take that detective boy.

He looked her straight in the eye and took another step toward her. She tried to back up but hit the wall. She put her hand behind her back as if she could move the wall. Of course that didn't work so she froze. He came even closer. Megan swallowed hard and stuck her chin up to reach his glare. Pretty eyes she thought, for an asshole.

"Well Ethel," he said getting dangerously close now. "The pop quiz is over. I'm not answering anymore questions. Not until you do, that is." From where he was standing he could smell her hair. It smelled like…Tomato sauce? Then he saw what appeared to be a piece of pasta in her hair and he raised his hand and slowly plucked it out. She went very still until he placed the particle in her hand then she gave a shy smile and said, "Lasagna". He grinned and she stared back at him with those blue eyes you could just fall into and he knew he should have never touched her. He put his bad guy burglar scowl back on and said, "Well?"

"Call the cops Josie," Megan said defiantly.

"I wouldn't do that if I were you," Jack told Josie who was already cradling the phone to her ear.

"Do it Josie!"

"Not wise," Jack said his eyes never leaving Megan's.

"Why not? It sounds wise to me," Megan countered.

"Well it is her ass. Do what you want Josie."

"Wait, what did you say about my ass? Please don't say it's big, because if you do, I gotta tell you even though you're hot I will not hesitate to turn this into a slugfest." She cradled the phone receiver and moved to his side poking her finger into his arm. "You see? This is not a good week for my butt. I have PMS which means that time will be here any day, And when it's that time, I retain a lot of water and I get bloated which makes my…."

"Josie! Shut up! Too Much Info babe." Mickey said now smelling of medicated Gold Bond and looking a lot more relaxed. Then to Jack he said, "She's a little slow, you have to break it down for her." Josie was turning around in a circle checking out her butt and Megan took another swig on the bottle. Now God?

"Okay Lucy, here's the deal," Jack started finally removing his eyes from Megan. "You disarmed the alarm when you came in here tonight. You don't own this studio. That's B&E babe. Five to ten easy."

"Don't listen, Josie," Megan called. "He's just trying to scare you, you were with me and I have every right to be here." I think, she added silently. I mean it's OK to help your friend break into her husband's studio so that she can go through his things and gather evidence to make sure said husband is cheating so that said wife can divorce him and take half of said studio right? "My head hurts." She muttered.

"Actually you don't, this studio was recently sold to Anthony Malone. So unless you are Mrs. Anthony Malone, you are breaking and entering."

Megan stood there dumbfounded. What he was saying couldn't be right. Why would Ted sell his studio to his brother? Realization almost hit her before she thought of something else.

"And how do you know I'm not Mrs. Anthony Malone? Huh big Privates guy!" She hiccupped and then realized what she'd said but before she could recover it he was smiling that smile again. Sexy as hell. *So this is the guy Mom warned me about*, she thought. In the background Mickey and Josie winced, smelling disaster.

"I appreciate the compliment, I think. But to answer your question; Anthony Malone isn't married."

"Good point." She said around a hiccup. Then as the alcohol seemed to take its toll, she stumbled where she was standing and tried to regain

Amy Johnson

her footing. But it was Jack with his quick hands who grabbed her at the waist and steadied her. And what a big mistake that was. She felt so soft and lush underneath his fingertips and then he pictured her naked smiling up at him and he damn near lost his balance.

"Maybe you should sit down," He said and she said "No I'm fine!" but she left his hands around her waist so he let her stand just so that he could continue to touch her.

"So what we have here is a conundrum," Jack said. Josie screwed her face up and squinted at him so he added, "a problem." Megan let her head bang on the wall behind her and banged it again when she thought about how wonderful his hands felt on her. But he was a robber and that was bad so she squashed that thought quick. She locked her knees together and prayed to the Anti-Orgasm Gods.

"Not the way I see it," Mickey began. "See; Megan here will have a hell of better chance of explaining this whole thing to Ted, who will then explain it to his brother who will probably choose not to press charges." Megan caught the word probably and swallowed hard. "But you Mr. Magnum PI, you're gonna have a lot harder time explaining what you're doing here when you and I both know that even though you're a private investigator, it's still against the law to break into someone's office. Even cops can't do that without a search warrant and last time I checked PI's aren't issued search warrants just so they can snoop around and wish they were real cops. So…" Gee those episodes of Law & Order really do pay off.

"Well Actually I dated a cop once and …"

"Shut up Josie!" Mickey and Megan both yelled at her and she threw her lip in a pout and stalked across the room.

Jack still looked sly and sexier than sin, obviously unrattled by Mickey's wisdom. But he seemed to at least pretend to consider it and gave Megan his scumbag scowl and in a very deliberate voice he said, "Well ladies, maybe we can help each other then." Megan sighed and Jack said, "How bout this? I'll tell you what I'm doing here if you'll tell me what you're doing here and then we can compare notes."

"You first," Megan said.

"No, that won't work. You'll have to go first."

"Give me one reason why I should." Keep being an asshole she thought. At least it'll keep me out of hell for mentally undressing him and having some really nasty thoughts about…

82

"I was here first," He said flatly and Megan looked at Mickey for his opinion.

"He's got you there babe."

"Okay, but if you're just conning information out of me I'm making you take Josie with you. Now--"

"And that's bad?" Josie sulked. Everyone did a synchronized eye roll and Megan thought uh oh, I'm starting to like him again. Please go back to being an asshole.

"I'm, uh we're here because I think my scumbag husband is cheating on me with Tiffany Triple D." Jack looked confused so Josie jiggled her boobs at him and then he got it and turned his attention back to Megan. "So we searched the basement which doubles as his dark room and weight room and we found some stuff." She told him about the stuff they'd found and how she called a meeting and when Ted wouldn't talk about it she took matters into her own hands. "So I drugged Ted and called Mickey and…"

"Wait! Stop Lucy!" Jack said.

"I thought I was Lucy," Josie argued.

"Nope name switch, she's earned it." Josie started to protest but Jack ignored her.

"Say that slowly now. You drugged him?"

"Yeah!" she said then realized how bad it sounded and quickly explained, "With Benadryl, he'll live I swear. I think." She hiccupped. "Anyway so we came here to find hard evidence and then we found you." I'll give you some hard evidence he thought but reminded himself to focus. He had to admit though her drugging Ted did arouse him a little. Then he thought about her naked again and forgot to breathe.

"Ok I showed you mine, now show me yours." Megan said and Jack decided that he had to hear those words from her again. Only next time they would be on a bed, rolling under the sheets…

"Hello?" Megan called out and he jolted himself back to reality. A reality that consisted of her fully clothed, with lasagna in her hair and Cagney and Lacy watching. And he never wanted her more.

"Yeah spill it babe." And when Jack looked confused Josie said, "He calls everyone babe." And Jack gave Mickey a don't-you-dare-do-it-again look and Mickey picked up the yellow pages in one hand and the flash light in the other.

"Well I'd like to show you mine but, I'll have to plead the fifth. That information is confidential and shall remain that way. Sorry!" He looked at Mickey and added, "Babe".

"Hit him Mickey. Hit him hard," Megan said and then she said to Jack. "You are such a lying pompous asshole. I ought to call the…."

"Megan? Yoo-hoo? Meggie? Are you in there?"

"Oh shit. It's Mother Theresa. I'm out of here babe." Mickey was trying to cram himself under Ted's desk but abandoned it for the closet. Megan tried to focus on the banging of the door and not the banging in her head or her mother's shrieking voice as she tried to take a step and fell. Jack caught her from behind mid-fall and when she tried to struggle he held her tighter around the waist just as Josie answered the door and said. "Hey Mrs. J. What brings you here?"

Her mother stood completely still, clutching her purse in her right hand, her skin a pasty white and her jaw hanging wide open. She took in the sight of Megan bent over a desk with Jack behind her, both struggling for control and Josie in her fish nets and Lolita costume and she looked as if she might pass out. But God's speed was with her because it didn't take her long to recover. She walked right past Josie who was filing her manicure and looking bored, and went straight to Jack and Megan. She fixed her stare on Jack, who still appeared to be humping Megan, muttered a quick Hail Mary and pointed a small black device directly in his face.

"I demand you take your hands of my daughter. Right now Mister or I'll fire this entire can of Mace into your beady little eyes." She paused to read the label on the can and when she couldn't read it she held it close to Megan's eyes and said "What does that say dear?"

Megan rolled her eyes. '*Good thing I don't need a real rescue. I'd be dead because my mother forgot her glasses*', Megan thought.

"It says shake well, point and spray Mom." Her mother nodded and shook the can and regained her spraying stance with the look of a determined mother who wouldn't hesitate to empty the entire can to protect her daughter. The only flaw in her plan was that Megan would probably get just as much of the Mace in her face because Jack's face was right behind hers.

Jack let go of Megan and Megan lunged for the can of Mace, almost knocking her mother down in the process.

"Ma'am it's not what you think. I was…" Jack began.

But Megan's mom wasn't buying it and she repositioned her purse in her hand and in one swift motion she bashed Jack across the face with it and started yelling at him.

Josie winced and said, "There went the other side. You know he was hot when we first found him. Now he's starting to look like hell."

"Who in the heck do you think you are, young man? Putting your hands on my daughter like that? Why I ought to have you arrested." She belted Jack again with her purse and then she turned to her daughter who was trying to disappear into the wall. "And what about you Megan?" She whacked Megan with the purse. "Why, I ought to call your father. You know he couldn't sleep tonight because he has heart burn, but when I tell him what I just witnessed he's going to have heart attack." She swung her purse again and Jack stepped in front of Megan just in time to take the blow for her. Josie winced again and Megan tried to explain things to her mother but her mother silenced her with a glare. Mrs. J. sat down at Ted's desk.

"You know Megan we always wanted the best for you and just look how you've turned out. You've been seen consorting with three strange men this week and one of them hit you." Jack straightened and felt anger at the words 'hit you'. "And you cut your hair and then I find you in the kitchen with that man and there are condoms in your trash can." She paused and Megan looked genuinely perplexed. "I sanitized that counter by the way. You know I'll never be able to eat in that kitchen again. Oh God!" She clutched her chest. "I think I'm having a heart attack. Just take me now Lord, before Megan messes up my chances of getting to heaven." Megan rolled her eyes and thought I'm right there with you Mom. Lightening, tornadoes, speeding buses, I'm not picky.

"Mom!" Megan shouted but her mother was oblivious to anything she was saying.

"Oh Mrs. J., don't forget about Megan's orgasm at the massage parlor. It was awesome. I was there." Her mother's face went pale again and Megan threw a flashlight at Josie. "Should I not mention the porn flick?" Josie said shooting a 'what-you-gonna-do-about-it' look to Megan who shot her a 'your-dead look' in return. Jack watched them both hoping the cat fight might still be a possibility.

"Mom, she's joking about the porn." Megan's Mom looked like she was going to faint. Jack took a step closer to her and reached out a hand to steady her and she nailed him with the purse again.

"Don't touch me!" she shrieked. "First I catch you molesting my daughter and now you want to lay those filthy hands on me. I don't think so." She swung again but this time Josie stepped in and grabbed her purse away from her.

"He's had enough," Josie said.

Megan muttered, "We all have."

Megan tried to regroup. Ok first things first. Deal with Mom. She turned to her mother who was still looking very unstable.

"Mom! Get a grip. He wasn't molesting me. I fell and he caught me." Jack nodded and grinned and then thought about the mace just sitting there and took a step back. "And about the kitchen. What you saw was really very innocent."

"But there were condoms. Big ones."

Megan gave her a blank look and Josie hollered, "Oh those were mine." When Megan looked at Josie she said, "Remember I used them in the basement. I tossed them in the trash before I left."

"Oh my God! My daughter is making pornography in the basement." She crossed herself and Jack decided he really needed to visit that basement. And the kitchen.

"Mom, she used them for…never mind! Look, let's take this one thing at a time. First off, what are you doing here in the middle of the night Mom?"

"Well your dad had heartburn, so I was going to the store to get antacids, but then I thought you might have some so I went to your house and when no one answered the door I got worried so I used my key and went in through the kitchen and there was a wad of paper towels in the floor so I went to throw them away and then I found the condoms. Then I remembered that guy you were holding hands with in there earlier. You know the one that hit you?" Megan dropped her head in exasperation and Jack felt the anger again. "But then I remembered that nobody answered the door so I thought he might have kidnapped you so I sprayed the counter with sanitizer and went upstairs to check on you and I saw you in your bed so I went back to the kitchen and finished sanitizing the counter."

"So you thought I might be kidnapped but you sanitized the counter first. Thanks Mom!" Megan thought about jumping out the window.

"Well no honey, I just sprayed it. I wanted to give it some time to set."

86

"Oh. Well then I guess that's OK." Megan shook her head and took a deep breath. "So how did you end up here?"

"Well, when I only saw one body in the bed."

"Which was Ted," Megan pointed out.

"Well, I'm an old woman and I don't see well in the dark. You know if you hadn't of cut your hair…"

"Anyways you thought I was in bed and…"

"I still had to get the antacid so I was on my way to the Wal-Greens when I drove by here and saw lights, so I thought Ted might be here working late and I wanted to talk to him about your recent behavior." Her mother scowled and Megan frowned.

"My behavior. Right!" Didn't you get the memo? I'm thirty."

"So I pulled into the lot and started for the door when I thought I heard your voice so I shouted for you and then I saw that man molesting you…"

"I prefer the word rescuing," Jack said but her mother fixed him with a 'don't-mess-with-me-bud' stare and he shut up.

"OK, the rest we know." Megan seemed to relax a little. "Ok, here's what we'll do, Jack, go to the store and get my father some Rolaids, I will get my mother calmed down, bring the antacids here then Josie can take Mom home in Mom's car." Josie shot Megan a look she didn't even want to try to interpret. "Once you get Mom home, Josie, get her key and wait for me at the house and when Mickey drops me off he can take you home."

"I thought I was going home with Jack?" Josie said.

"Change of plans," Megan said.

Jack said "Thank God."

Josie jiggled her boobs at him as if saying 'your loss Bud' and then Mrs. J. lit into Josie about feminine behavior. "Well I'm not a lady." Josie began but before she could finish, Mrs. J. shushed everyone as if she heard a noise and then after a minute said, "Michael, get out of that closet right now young man."

"Who's Michael?" Jack asked and Mickey appeared in front of them laughing.

"It's a long story," Megan said.

Jack nodded and Mickey said "How'd you know I was in there?"

"I heard you snickering. You know it's not very polite to laugh at people behind their backs. You were raised bet..." Megan downed the last of the whiskey.

"Rolaids! Wal-Greens Now!" She told Jack and he obediently left to get them.

***

Fifteen minutes later her mother had antacids and a ride home. Mickey, Jack and Megan had reorganized the office to its original state- except for the empty Wild Turkey Bottle- which they decided to put in Tiffany's drawer and let her explain it to Ted.

"Your mother's quite a woman," Jack said.

"She's not too bad if you don't molest her daughter."

"I was trying to keep you from hurting yourself."

"That was a joke Magnum," Megan said. "You know for a detective you're kind of slow."

"Just tired." And I'm sitting so close to you that I smell the Whiskey on your breath and between that and the tomato sauce in your hair, I am so turned on that I don't have a lot of blood in my brain. Be still my heart.

"C'mon, Mickey, let's go!" She hollered out and then she stood and moved directly in front of Jack. "That was dirty what you did earlier you know. Not showing us yours." Jack thought about the things he wanted to show her but decided to keep those thoughts to himself. For now anyways.

"It's confidential. I can't share it with you."

"So you're a liar. And you break into people's houses or businesses and snoop. And you're a conman and you probably steal and gamble. Jeez, I need to hang with a better crowd. My mom's right, I'm earning the entire Johnson name a one way ticket to hell."

"Well at least I just lie, cheat and con. You're way more corrupted. I mean condoms in the kitchen, porn in the basement, drinking like a fish, massage orgasms." He grinned, happy to be sitting beside her and then she smiled. Uh-oh.

"Well my mother has a very active imagination. Don't believe anything that woman tells you."

"I'll be sure to decline my invite to Thanksgiving Dinner," Jack said.

"Right." Mickey filled the doorway after taking care of his twins again. "The prices a drag queen will pay for elegance," he said and Megan and Jack both shuddered.

"We ready?" she asked.

"After you babe."

"You know if you're going to continue your life of crime you might want to reconsider your choice of underwear," Jack told Mickey. He wanted to tell Megan that she should reconsider too and just go without but he remembered her mother's purse and bit his tongue.

***

It was after 3AM by the time Megan finally crawled into bed. After checking Ted's pulse to make sure the rodent was still breathing and letting the pups in she crawled into the bed in the guest room and tried to sleep. Mostly she just tossed and turned and loved on the pups. She was thinking about Ted and Tiffany and rubbing Bitty's belly when the pup let out a sad moan and Megan said, "I know, Daddy's a jerk and your Mommy neglects you to commit felonies and get felt up by robbers." She thought of Spot all alone down stairs and went to bring him to the guest room too. "Old fashioned quality time." She told them, then she frowned at the family she was never going to have. No babies, no soccer games or Easy Bake Ovens. No proud Daddy teaching his son how to ride a bike or his daughter how to dance.

That made her think of her dad and how he used to dance with her, her standing on his feet. How could she have had such an awesome father growing up and then marry someone like Ted, who didn't even play Daddy to the dogs or Spot.

And her Mother, bless her heart. She put everything she had into raising Megan and keeping a clean, organized home with these great hopes of spending her retirement spoiling her grandkids. Instead she had two four legged grandkids which she spoiled anyways and a fish that hides in his treasure box every time her Mother came to visit.

So now instead of grandchildren her Mother will probably be crushing up Prozac in her tea and stuffing Christmas stockings with doggie biscuits, rawhide bones, fake seaweed and fish food until she dies.

And then Megan realized that if she and Ted got divorced, she might not ever have kids and dogs don't live as long as people, she'd probably have to die alone.

She rolled over and her cheek fell right into drool from Bug's mouth and she wiped that off and remembered the pasta in her hair and eating lasagna off the floor. "Jeez. I'm a mess. No wonder Daddy's having an affair. I'd cheat on me too." She looked around the small tidy room and realized she bored the hell out of the pups and Spot because they were all crashed out.

And then there was Jack. Sexy in a reckless way but smart assed and smug as all get out. She wondered if he was passionate and then reminded herself that he committed felonies on a regular basis and was probably a con artist. She tried to picture herself with Jack, her cooking dinner in her apron, him sitting in the chair watching the ballgame shirtless with prison tattoos all over his body. She shuddered at the thought and then she pictured this mind blowing sex he might be capable of. Then that thought was crushed with one of her visiting him in prison and her Mother sanitizing every surface in the house. Yep that boy was bad freaking news. Sexy as sin, but definitely not worth selling her soul for.

She closed her eyes and thought about his hands on her waist and his dark brown eyes. And the way he seemed to look at her like she was the only person in the room. Then she envisioned the Johnny Cash tattoo on his chest from prison and decided that she'd take her chances in internet chat rooms before she'd think about going near Jack. It'd probably be less fulfilling but a hell of a lot safer.

After tossing and turning for about another hour she finally gave up and went to the kitchen. Johnson survival tip number one; when you're stressed, bake. That way you have food to ease the stress because desert always makes people happy and then once you eat all the food, you get fat and then you can stress over losing weight instead of the real stuff. Yes, repression is a highly regarded defense mechanism for the Johnson's. *Brownies*, Megan thought. Her mother would be so proud that she was using the kitchen for something other than sex. Hell double fudge pecan brownies were better than sex.

***

Across town, Jack Westin had trouble sleeping as well. Every thought he had drifted to Megan. He closed his eyes and pulled up her image standing in front of him, his hands on her waist, that innocent but determined look in her eyes. The sadness.

Somewhere between the cheerleading squad and happy homemaker her life had taken a turn for the worse. And she only knew the half of it. Ted was cheating on her but that was probably the least of her worries. And now Jack was stuck. He'd been hired to investigate Ted and he'd jumped at the opportunity just because he despised Ted and wanted nothing more than to see him brought to his knees. The only problem now was that he'd looked into Megan's eyes and seen the hurt and confusion, and he knew that what he had found would devastate her. Obviously she still loved Ted.

And why should he care anyway? She didn't even know who he was. They'd grown up in the same town, went to junior high and high school together and she didn't even recognize him. Of course it had been dark in Ted's studio last night and he was no longer the scrawny teenage geek he used to be. Not to mention the fact that she was drunk and thought he was a murderous burglar. Between the alcohol, the fear, and the proof that her husband was, in fact, an adulterous slime ball her brain probably wasn't firing on all eight cylinders. It was probably a miracle she recognized her own mother.

He had a brief memory of Mrs. Johnson's purse and involuntarily rubbed his head. That woman had a hell of a swing for an old woman. Thank God she hadn't had a bat.

He rubbed his eyes and tried to think of what to do. When he closed his eyes he saw Megan again, her hair a mess and that crooked smile and instantly his brain went back to mush. After all the torture he could bear, he finally abandoned sleep for a shower. His mind always worked better in the shower.

Amy Johnson

Chapter Nine

It was after seven when Ted woke up and strolled into the kitchen. He went directly to the cupboard that housed the medicine and fished out four Tylenol extra strength caplets. Megan was on her fourth batch of double fudge pecan brownies and humming mindlessly in tune with the radio. She kept her head focused on the mixing bowl and stirred the ingredients vigorously to keep from throwing the damn bowl at Ted, who upon arriving in the kitchen had not even given her a sideways glance or one single word. 'Good Morning' would be nice. Or maybe, 'How come you didn't come to bed last night?' She'd even settle for 'Hey Honey, I'm off to work so that I can sleep with Tiffany the Tits behind your back and sell the rest of our assets to my brother.' But instead she got cold silence. The bastard.

"Head hurt?" She asked trying to keep her voice light.

"Yeah!"

"Good." She'd meant to say that under her breath but hadn't succeeded. He gave her a confused look then washed the pills down with water.

"I feel like I've been kicked in the head," he said holding his hands to his temples.

"Don't give me any ideas," she muttered as she added the eggs to the bowl.

"Breakfast?" He asked tensely, expecting eggs and bacon and a protein shake.

"Nope." She added the pecans and continued stirring with more force than needed.

"Megan, make my damn breakfast. I'm going to take..." Before he got the rest of his words out she reached under the stove and pulled out a

93

skillet and flung it on the stove. It landed with a loud clatter and Ted winced from the noise. Good!

"Make it yourself," she snapped and added the vanilla to her brownie mixture.

"What?" The look on his face insinuated that she must be crazy to think he would make his own breakfast. "Meg, I don't have time for this. Make my..."

"Oh, what was I thinking?" she said. "Poor Ted, with his pounding head and busy schedule. I sure hope you can find time to shag Miss D Cups today. And while you're at it, have her make your damn breakfast!"

"You're nuts, Megan."

"You have no idea," she said and she grabbed the frying pan and tossed it in trash can. "Now, get out of my kitchen. I'm sure your little tramp doesn't like to be kept waiting."

"What the hell is wrong with you? I told you Tiffany is just a friend." He retrieved the pan from the trash and started to speak but something caught his eye. He grabbed the whisk from the counter where Megan had left it after beating the eggs for brownies and used the handle in to retrieve a condom from the trash can. He held it up to, and looked at Megan questionably as if expecting her to explain.

"Oh, that. Well that belongs to my friend. Keep digging. There's another one in there too." She moved to the refrigerator and got the butter to grease the brownie pan. Ted dropped the condom back in the garbage whisk and all.

"Megan, we need to talk."

"Sorry, no time." She pointed to the four pans of brownies on the counter.

"Megan!" this time he shouted and Megan blinked. He took a step towards her and grabbed her hands, then forced her to look at him. "We talk now." She stumbled and panic caught in her throat. He'd never hit her or even shown the tendency to do so but his grip on her wrists was tight and suddenly she thought she may have pushed him a little too far. She bit back the fear and stuck her chin out.

"What's to talk about Ted? You have a friend. I have a friend. Everybody's happy. You're friend has big tits and my friend has...well you saw the condom." When he didn't let go of her she added, "Now let me go before you're headache spreads to areas below your waist." He looked at her for a very long minute as the silence stretched and then he bent his head down. Megan closed her eyes and prepared for the blow, but he didn't head butt her.

He kissed her. A gentle, first date kind of kiss and then he released his grip on her and took a step back. He retrieved the frying pan and handed it to her.

"I'm gonna take a shower. Make my breakfast Megan," he said before walking out of the kitchen and heading up the stairs.

Megan stood there clutching the frying pan and staring into space. He'd kissed her. Now why in the hell had he done that? And to make matters worse he didn't give a damn about finding condoms in the trash can which would have infuriated any other man, especially when they'd found another man in the kitchen with their wife the night before.

She heard a loud clatter and then realized she'd dropped the frying pan, obviously forgetting she was holding it in the first place. Maybe her mother and Ted were right. She was losing it.

She had to talk to Ted. She'd explain the gym and Tom and the basement search and Josie's love gloves and how they ended up in the trash can. It would all make perfect sense and then Ted would tell her about Tiffany and the comical story about her naked pictures and Las Vegas and his Marijuana and they'd eat brownies and have a big laugh.

Yeah right! She wasn't even sure she believed her own ridiculous story much less his.

She looked in her cabinets for a bottle of Wild Turkey then remembered she didn't drink so there wouldn't be any. The thought of the whiskey made her sick to her stomach and she bolted upstairs to the bathroom fearing she'd throw up. Ted was in the shower and Megan barely made it to the toilet before she lost her mother's lasagna and half a bottle of whiskey in the bowl.

"Megan! I'm trying to take a shower." Ted said, sticking his head out from behind the shower curtain.

"Sorry. I'm sick!"

"Well be sick somewhere else for God's sake."

"I said I'm sick! Show some damn compassion!" she snapped.

"Get out of the bathroom!" Ted roared back.

"Fine!" she threw herself off the floor and went to the sink to wash her face, knocking over a jar of decorative marbles she kept on the lavatory next to a basket of scented soaps and a candle. The marbles flew everywhere, the jar broke and she heard Ted spew a long string of very explicit words that would have made any good strong Catholic run straight to the nearest confessional.

"Get Out!" he yelled and Megan almost started to cry. She was on her hands and knees trying to pick up the marbles and glass but then the tears started and all she could see were colorful blurs.

"But Ted, I have to pick up…"

"Out!" he yelled again, so she crawled out of the bathroom on all fours and slammed the door behind her and went back to the kitchen.

Back in the kitchen, Megan had traded her tears in for revenge and decided that instead of sitting around heart broken she'd just stick to her original plan. Find passion- no matter where it came from, as long as it wasn't Jack the burglar- and put it back in her life. Ted could take a hike along with his nineteen year old girl friend. Her mother could condemn her to hell for having an affair and if Spot and the pups turned on her, then so be it. This was Megan's moment and by God she was going grab it head on and enjoy the hell out of it. The screen door slammed and Megan ducked under the counter to hide from her mother. When she heard Josie's voice she stuck her head up to make sure it was her and then got up.

"Why were you under the counter?"

"Thought you were my mom." Josie chuckled.

"You look like hell. Have you even slept?" Megan looked down at herself, still wearing her felony clothes from last night. Her hair, a disheveled mess with probably more ingredients than just lasagna in it by now, she had the mother of all head aches and puke on her shirt sleeve. All passionate men feel free to step forward.

"No, I baked."

"All night?" Megan nodded and started to cry into Josie's cleavage. Josie patted her back and said, "Its Ok Megan, don't cry." When Megan had it a little more together she took a seat at the kitchen table with half a pan of brownies.

"Ok, I took off work today- I called in with PMS- so we'll spend the day together. Like when we were in high school." Megan shoved a brownie into her mouth.

"So what do you want to do today?" Josie asked perky as hell. "Massage?"

Megan shook her head 'No' remembering the last time.

"Shopping?"

96

Again Megan shook her head 'No' remembering she had no boobs, chunky thighs and above average butt cleavage.

"The Salon?" And when Megan shook her head again, Josie said, "Tell you what, you get cleaned up and think about it. We've got the Mustang, the MasterCard and all day. We'll do whatever you want."

"I have to finish my brownies," Megan said.

"I'll finish them. Just go get ready."

"You can't cook," Megan said looking at Josie incredulously.

"I'll figure it out. How hard can it be?" Megan had a fleeting thought about Josie catching the house on fire and the fire department coming out with their sexy passionate firemen, one of which could carry Megan from the burning flames and she thought 'What the hell' and told Josie what to do to finish the last batch.

"Oh by the way," she said on her way out of the kitchen, "That last batch is for Ted so feel free to spit in it."

Upstairs, Megan heard Ted turn off the water in the shower and figured by the time he finished shaving-which for some ridiculous reason he insisted on doing in the shower- she'd have about ten minutes to get the hell out of there before Ted emerged from the bathroom. She grabbed a t-shirt and jeans and got them on in record time, trying to hurry so she wouldn't risk running into him before her and Josie made it out the door. She had nothing to say to him right now and he was expecting breakfast.

She took the stairs two at a time on her way down with her shoes in her hands before she stopped dead in her tracks at the sound of her Mother's voice coming from the kitchen. She looked upstairs and thought about Ted and then at the kitchen door thinking about her mother and before she could decide which option sucked the least she heard Ted scream followed by a loud thud.

The next thing she knew the kitchen door swung open and smacked her in the face and through a haze she saw Josie and her mother scrambling up the stairs calling her name in panicked tones.

***

Megan woke up in a well-lit room with florescent lighting, white walls and an ice pack on her head. She looked around for Tom's crotch fearful she was reliving her unfortunate gym incident and when neither Tom nor his crotch appeared she reached the logical conclusion that she was in the hospital. Then Josie appeared with a stethoscope around her neck and Megan figured out that she was in Hell's hospital and Josie was the nurse. She closed her eyes telling herself that when she opened them again, she'd realize this was all a dream. And then she heard her mother's voice and preferred hell again, since she wasn't sure how she got here and her head hurt too bad to think up a lie her mother would believe.

"What happened?" Megan asked.

"We hit you with the door and knocked you out," Josie said while shoving the stethoscope down her cleavage.

"We?"

"Me and your Mom." She looked at Megan like 'Duh'. "Your Mom is here somewhere. I think she's talking to the doctor."

"Why on earth would you do that?" Megan asked.

"I'm trying to listen to my heartbeat," Josie said putting the ear piece in her ears.

"Not that, Josie. Why did y'all hit me with the door?"

"Oh. Because you were standing in front of it." Well that explained everything.

"Josie! Put the stethoscope down!" Her words came out as a growl and Josie dropped the device around her neck. "Now focus. Start from the beginning."

"Ok, I was making the brownies like you said, when your mom came in and we were talking. Then just as I put the brownies in the oven we hear this loud noise upstairs and we thought it was you so we went running out of the kitchen and swung the door open and it hit you smack in the face." Josie smacked herself in the face to demonstrate for Megan then said, "Ouch." Megan rolled her eyes.

"So we get upstairs and we hear Ted moaning so we open the bathroom door to find him butt naked flat on his back in the floor with all these marbles." She wrinkled her nose and said in barely a whisper, "Kinda kinky if you ask me, but hey, whatever works right."

Megan closed her eyes and tried to feel sorry for Ted but just couldn't after he'd yelled at her. So he bumped his head. Big deal. He already had a headache anyway. Her mother walked into the room carrying a pan of brownies and made a big fuss over Megan. Back off woman and hand over the damn brownies.

"Anyways, so Ted falls and he's screaming obscenities so your mom shoved a sock in his mouth and called 911." Megan's eyes widened and she looked at her mom.

"Well, that language is just uncalled for, Megan. I was not going to listen to it."

Megan thought '*Right On Mom*' and decided she should really appreciate her mother more.

"So anyways, we go downstairs and find you in the floor and I decided to bring you to the hospital and your mom waited for the ambulance to pick up Ted."

"Plus the brownies were still baking." Her mother pointed out.

"Right," Josie continued. "So then I get you here and they are watching you for a concussion."

"And Ted?" Megan asked because it was her duty as a wife even if he was scum.

"Well he's…he'll be able to go home tomorrow," her mother said.

"There keeping him for a bump to the head?"

"Well no he uh fell on a marble." Megan looked confused so her mother continued, "He sort of uh…landed on a marble." The confusion remained so she tried again. "Well honey he uh…well the marble uh…"

"He got a marble up his butt," Josie blurted. And Megan's mom kicked the door shut with her foot. "So they did a Marble-ectomy." Josie cracked up laughing and then Megan did too.

Her mother said, "It's not funny," in the most authoritative voice one can manage while choking back laughter.

They were still cracking up when a good looking man in a white coat named Dr. Rogers came in and stood way too close to Josie, then Megan figured out that she had his stethoscope around her neck and wondered if that's like the equivalent of wearing a boys letterman jacket in high school when you're dating. Josie put her hand on the Dr's behind and Megan's mom crossed herself. Josie moved fast.

"Mrs. Malone, your husband suffered a very unfortunate accident with a marble." While the tone of his voice was absolutely professional it was obvious he was using serious restraint to keep the laughter out of his voice. Megan tried to listen intently but lost the battle and cracked up laughing again. "He should be fine and we are going to keep him for the night to keep an eye on him but I'm very confident he will recover."

"Can he eat?" Josie asked.

"Sure, at this time eating would be encouraged so that…" Everyone had wrinkled their noses, not needing to hear the rest of it so Dr. Rogers finished with, "You know."

"Mrs. J., Maybe you should take him these brownies. You know comfort food?"

"No!" Megan growled holding the pan close to her.

"Yes!" Josie said prying it away from her and handing it to her mother.

"Josie dear, I'm sure there's enough for everyone."

"Mrs. J., there are more at home and Ted might need comfort during the night. He should have them really."

Her mother looked at Megan and then Josie and after a moment said, "Ok. I guess so." And she took them to Ted.

"Hey! Those were my damn brownies."

"Trust me; you don't want to eat those."

"Yes, I did." Megan caught Josie's expression and then said, "What did you do?"

"You'll love this," Josie sat down on the bed and smiled with excitement. Ok, remember how you said I could spit in them? Well I figured I do one better so I looked in your medicine cabinet and found a box of ex-lax and I melted it and threw it in the mix." Megan groaned.

Josie said, "Wait it gets better. So when I took the ex-lax out of the microwave I spilled it on my shirt so I went to the pantry to get some stain guard and that's when I found the pot."

"What pot?"

"Ted's pot, from the basement?" Megan remembered she'd hid it in the pantry where Ted would never find it but she'd forgotten to flush it.

"I really don't want to hear this, do I?"

"Of course you do. So anyway I had the pot and I was smelling it and feeling it." Megan gave her a stern look and Josie said, "I was curious Okay! And anyways I heard your mom coming in the door so I dumped the bag in the brownie mix. Then your mom came up and told me I was over stirring it and she put the mix in the pan and finished them. Lucky for Ted, the Ex-lax will help with the marble."

Lucky for Ted, Megan thought. Leave it to Josie to think of it that way.

"Oh my God," Megan said rubbing her face with her hands. "I am a terrible person. There is probably a special place for me in Hell. My life is such a mess."

"Oh Meg, you aren't a terrible person. I've done far worse," Josie said.

Megan said, "I don't want to know about it. I'm corrupt enough all by myself."

The door opened and Megan's dad walked in. "I would have been here sooner but I was busy with the cops." He rubbed his daughter's cheek and kissed her forehead.

"The cops?" Megan and Josie both shouted.

"Well the EMT's called them in because they thought it was a domestic dispute but they couldn't figure out if Ted knocked you out or if you dropped the marbles for Ted and then knocked yourself out trying to run away. Your Mom rode with Ted in the ambulance so I didn't really know what happened but I did tell them that you've been known to knock yourself out on occasion. I think they thought we were all out of our minds and then they smelled the Marijuana."

"Oh shit!" Josie said and looked at her watch. "Gee look at the time I'd better..."

"Sit down Josephine, before I call your father."

"Yes Mr. J." Josie sat back down as Megan's father continued.

"So we looked around and we couldn't find the dope and..."

"Because Mrs. J. brought it with her to the hospital," Josie said, and Megan's father sat down and popped a Rolaid in his mouth.

"Spill it girls," he said.

So Megan and Josie explained everything from dressing Megan up for passion to when she got knocked out with the door. Her dad let out a long sigh, then crossed himself and Megan felt like hell for driving her dad to religion.

"So the marbles were an accident?" he asked his daughter. She nodded.

"I swear Daddy."

"And Ted's cheating for sure?"

"Yes Daddy."

"And the dope wasn't yours?"

"No Daddy."

"Okay. Well I'd go up there and kick Ted's ass but he kind of did that himself, so I guess I'll go home and watch the game. You call me if you need anything Meg." He rose to go then stopped at the door and turned, "Meg, tell your mother nothing." Megan nodded and he added, "Because if you do she'll probably erect a cross in the front yard and invite the whole town over to pray and then I'll have to move in with you."

***

Megan and Josie made it home about noon. Megan was dead on her feet and Josie had a date with Dr. Rogers to rest up for so they decided to go in take a nap and try to meet the girls at the usual place at five. They were just about to climb the stairs when the doorbell rang. Josie answered the door and hollered for Megan. The cops. The pot. The domestic disturbance. Megan calculated her chances of escape and decided that with her luck she'd probably forget to open the door, run into it and knock herself out again. They'd take her back to the hospital and Ted was there. She'd take her chances with the cops. How bad could prison be? But when she reached the foyer, there were no cops there, just Tom. Looking as exotic and magnificent as ever.

"Hello Tom," she said and he looked at her face and frowned.

"Mrs. Malone." He stood on the porch for a minute until Megan's manners kicked in and she invited him in.

"So this is Tom huh?" Josie said nudging Megan who then handled the introductions. "I must say Tom, you are sexy as hell," Josie said and Megan bumped her with her hip hard enough to make Josie stumble.

"What brings you here?" Megan asked Tom.

"Well I called earlier to make sure you were feeling better and to let you know the ER bill was taken care of, but your Mother said you were in the hospital. So I went there and they said you were released."

"Oh yes, I uh had an accident. I'm fine though, really." He didn't look convinced.

"Megan." His eyes softened and Megan had to avert her eyes from his gaze, "Who did this to you? Was it your husband? Because if it was…"

"Oh no, Ted didn't do anything." Except cheat and yell. "Really it was an accident." Tom still didn't look convinced and Megan wondered just exactly how bad she looked. She hadn't even thought about a mirror.

"She knocked herself out again," Josie blurted.

Megan narrowed her eyes at her and said, "I did not. You and Mom knocked me out."

"Well it was your fault for being dumb enough to stand behind a door."

102

"You're talking to me about dumb? This coming from the cleavage queen with a pea size brain and a mouth the size of the Grand Canyon," Megan snapped.

"At least I have cleavage," Josie yelled.

"Yeah well as least I have an IQ over 15."

"Well your IQ isn't going to get you a passionate night of mind numbing sex."

"No, it'll get me more than one night because the guy will know I'm not as dumb as a box of rocks and flush my phone number." Josie fisted her hands.

Outside a car pulled up and Mickey introduced himself to Tom then leaned on the porch rail and settled in to enjoy the show. "Did it just start?" he asked as if he were settling in to watch a movie at the theatre. Tom just gave him a wry look.

"Did you just call me dumb?" Josie asked.

"You called me dumb first."

"Well, doesn't matter now, 'cause I'm gonna kick your ass." She stepped out of her shoes and handed them to Tom who either out of shock or disbelief took them. "We'll see how much your IQ helps in a street fight. Come on!"

Mickey who was leaning on the porch rail, his long legs stretched in front of him said to Tom, "We need popcorn. And chairs to watch the show." Tom looked at Mickey, a mix of amusement, intrigue and incredulity on his face.

"Take your best shot, Lolita!" Megan said and put her fisted hands up.

"I will. And I probably won't even have to knock you out. You usually do that all by yourself." A black SUV slowly rolled up to the curb in front of Megan's house.

"Alright! That's it! Let's rock," Megan said.

"Shouldn't you girls take it outside?" Mickey said.

"Shut Up!" They yelled back.

"Well, can we at least pop some popcorn?"

"Shut up," they yelled again.

Mickey grinned at Tom and said, "Ding Ding."

Megan and Josie were circling each other in the foyer while Tom was pleading with them both to calm down. Mickey was enjoying the show, when a man started walking up the sidewalk.

Josie lunged at Megan, who lost her footing and tried to duck. Tom threw himself in front of Megan, all the while trying to keep her from falling, but instead he too fell, landing on top of Megan. Megan lay there stunned with Tom on top of her, both trying to catch their breath.

"Get off of her! You're hurting her!" Josie screamed at Tom who was trying to get up when a hand grabbed the sleeve of his shirt and yanked him into a standing position. The yank was followed by a solid punch to the jaw which sent Tom floundering backwards a few steps holding his jaw, his face fierce with anger.

Mickey and Josie stood speechless and Megan lay flat on the floor staring at the two men facing off in her foyer. Life used to be so boring. Predictable. Why me?

"What, you didn't get enough hitting on her the other day? Came back to finish the job?" Tom stared at the man who was now talking to him in a strong deliberate tone, his face an inch from Tom's. "You want to hit someone. Try hitting me."

Megan jumped up from the floor and grabbed Jack's arm. "Hey!" she yelled, but he talked right over her. Aside from the anger in his eyes, he seemed in perfect control, his voice was low but stern, his body language menacing but calm.

"Man, I didn't touch her," Tom said assuming a fighting stance.

"Then how'd she get two black eyes huh? I saw her last night and aside from a lump on her head, she was fine." He tilted Megan's chin up to Tom and Megan batted his hand away. "Explain this!"

"Jack! Or Magnum or whatever your name is. He never touched me. Leave him alone," Megan said. Then she realized he'd said she had two black eyes. Holy cow! Why hadn't anyone told her? Jeez, Stacy was right. She was an accident waiting to happen. No wonder Ted was sleeping with Tiffany.

Jack turned to face Megan, his voice and eyes softer, "Megan, your mother said, some guy hit you."

"Well she lied," Jack looked like he wasn't buying any of it. "Tom is a nice guy."

Tom rubbed his jaw and Josie being very observant of a hunk in need, tried to lure him into the kitchen for an ice pack-and more than likely his phone number- but when he refused to go she went and got it for him. Mickey followed her into the kitchen, no doubt to make popcorn.

"Then how'd you get two black eyes."

"Josie and my mom knocked me out with the door." Jack raised a skeptical brow.

"And the lump on your head?"

"Freak accident at the gym." Megan could understand how ridiculous it all sounded because she wasn't sure she believed it herself.

"Well, Ethel was yelling at him to stop hurting you. Don't you see how it looked?"

She could see his point. What was the word he had used last night? Rescuing her.

And having walked up when he did, the situation could have been perceived that way. But what she didn't understand was what the hell was he doing here and why on earth did he consider it his job to rescue her. He was a burglar for Christ's sake.

A robber. A thief. A really rugged, handsome thief, now that she had actually seen him in the daylight but a criminal just the same.

"Ok. Look, I know how it looked." She looked at Tom who agreed that he might have done the same thing. "But this, Mr. Whatever Your Name Is, is none of your business. I am none of your business. Which reminds me, how did you find out where I live?" Josie brought Tom the ice pack and seductively held it to his jaw, pressing her cleavage into his arm.

"I'm a private investigator. Remember?"

"Right. That is what you say, although you've provided me no proof…" He fished out his wallet and handed it to her. He motioned for her to open it and when she did, she discovered from his various forms of identification, that he was in fact Jackson Westin, Private Investigator. So much for the prison tattoo defense the next time she had a temporary passionate thought about him.

"Okay, Jackson Westin, what are you doing here?" He motioned for her to step outside just as Mickey returned with the popcorn.

"What'd I miss?" Mickey asked.

Megan looped Mickey's arm and drug him and his popcorn outside with Jack following. Jack closed the door to the house and leaned his hip on the railing.

"I thought about what happened last night. And I wanted to talk to you about why I was there." He frowned and shook his head. "I can't tell you everything, but I put myself in your position and decided that there are some things I'd want to know if I were you. I thought maybe I could help you."

"Oh really? Well that's noble of you." She tilted her chin high and defiantly said, "But here's the deal, I didn't ask for your help. And after your little performance in there, I'm not sure I want it." Jack took a handful of popcorn and popped a piece in his mouth. Megan's gaze lingered on his mouth and those luscious lips and she snapped it up to his forehead, envisioning a big, tasteless tattoo across it. Looking in Jack's eyes-or some of his other features- was like staring directly at the sun. Dangerous as hell with a tendency to blur your concentration. It was so much easier when she'd thought he was a burglar.

"You might be in danger, Megan," he said sincerely.

"Yeah well, danger's my middle name. Right Mickey?"

"Absolutely Babe!" he said around a mouthful of popcorn.

"So I'd appreciate it if you'd leave." He reached out and touched her arm gently, like a friend might do. Her skin prickled at the touch of his warm calloused hand and she jerked away. She ran her fingers through her hair, and gave an exasperated sigh. "Look Mr. Westin, while I'm sure your intentions might be good, you gotta look at this from my perspective, I've never seen you before in my life, and then I catch you breaking into my husband's studio, which I'm sure is against the law. Then you con me into giving you information without keeping your end of the deal. Next you show up at my house uninvited and punch my friend in the face, which again is illegal..."

"Under the circumstances I'd do it again," Jack said, the muscle in his jaw jumping, his hazel eyes tender beneath eyelashes that should be illegal.

"...And now you want to help me, because you think I might be in danger. Now call me crazy, but I have a real hard time believing anything you say and frankly the only danger I see here is you." He frowned and opened his mouth to protest but stopped short. "So what I'd like for you to do, Mr. Westin, is kindly get in your car, and stay the hell away from me."

Jack stood there for a long minute surveying her face, his hands in his pockets. Eventually he pushed off from the railing and handed her a business card. "If you change your mind," he said. "Or if he –referring to Tom- wants to press charges." After one last searching look, he walked down the steps, through the yard and to his car. Megan breathed a sigh of relief and headed inside to deal with Tom and Josie.

Tom, bless his heart, had been a sweetheart about the whole thing. Megan offered him Jack's card in case he wanted to contact the authorities, but he declined saying he could see Jack's point. He asked Megan to come back to the gym and she declined. He then asked her to have dinner with him, and again she declined although she did ask for a rain check. He appeared to be a hell of a nice guy, and if he was sweet enough to ask her out while she had two black eyes and a red swollen face, he deserved dinner, just not right now. She needed to get rid of Ted first, and get the swelling out of her face and the lasagna out of her hair.

Next to deal with was Josie, which was usually pretty easy. Over the years, since they were kids really, Josie and Megan had been the best of friends and the worst of friends. But the friendship had always been strong and the fights were always short. Plus it helped that Josie had the attention span of squirrel and was easily redirected. Josie, who was prowling through Megan's closet, had forgotten what they were fighting over by the time Megan went upstairs to reconcile.

"Can I borrow this skirt and those shoes for my date tonight?" she asked Megan.

"Of course you can. We good?"

Josie wrapped her arms around Megan's neck, gave her a warm, friendly hug and said, "We're always good."

Megan stepped away, crawled in her bed fully dressed and said "Good, I'm going to sleep. Don't wake me up for at least 48 hours."

"What if your mother calls?"

"Give her Jack Westin's phone number." If anyone deserved the Divine Intervention Lecture it was him, for popping into her life and adding to the growing amount of drama and chaos that seemed to follow her around.

Amy Johnson

Chapter Ten

While Megan was sleeping- for the first time in thirty six hours- Jack sat in a smoky room, sipping tepid coffee and doing his best to listen to the yuppie looking young man who was talking. And he hadn't heard a word he said. Since last night, every thought he had was about Megan. And that's why he was now sitting in the Baptist Church at his first AA meeting in over four years. He'd been fine until last night when he'd felt the rush of feelings he still held for Megan. Now he wanted a drink, needed a drink.

At first he tried to tell himself that what he was feeling was sympathy for her and the firestorm she would surely struggle with in the months to come. He knew what it was like. He'd been there himself and it had been then that Jack Daniels and depression had become his only friends in the world.

Obviously Megan had had her suspicions, but as he knew first hand, nothing could prepare you for coming face to face with the concrete, intimate proof of the betrayal from someone you love. Although he couldn't see the look of sadness on her face when she stared into that picture of Ted and Tiffany, he knew exactly how she felt. And while confirming her suspicions he knew that until that moment she was probably clinging to the hope it wasn't true. He knew he had five years ago, when his world had crumbled and fell apart.

But when he'd touched her, and looked into her clear, blue eyes watered with tears, his heart had clenched in his chest and the only thing he wanted to do was rescue her. Rescue her from the pain, from Ted, and from herself.

When he'd first took this job, he'd felt guilty at the pang of pleasure that had seared through his body of finally nailing Ted. He'd tried before, right after Megan got married but Ted had appeared to be an altar boy; hardworking, devoted and completely faithful. Finally he conceded, figuring Ted had obviously grown up and that the night Jack had seen him with Lisa Mason in the back seat of her Buick less than a week before Ted's marriage was just one last fling. The infamous, last taste of freedom that many men went through.

For years after that night ten years ago, Jack had wondered if he should have told Megan. Would she have believed him? Would it have changed things? Would she have married Ted anyway? Would Jack have had a chance to tell her how he felt about her?

None of that really mattered now. He'd decided last night after lying awake for hours that he wouldn't repeat the mistake he made ten years ago, and that was why he'd gone to see her today. He'd decided he would come clean with her as much as he could, and offer her what help and support he could to bring her through it. He'd offer her friendship and if it turned into something else he'd be thrilled, but his motives weren't going to be selfish or based on his wants or needs.

And besides, it looked as if she needed to be rescued. Her entire life seemed to be a chaotic mess. Her mother had said some man had hit her, her husband was having an affair and bankrupting them, and then there was the guy from the gym- who Jack believed was the one abusing her- and she was now walking around with two black eyes. And then there's the issue Wild Turkey.

He remembered seeing her last night with her right temple swollen, pasta in her hair, clutching a bottle of whiskey. She was the poster child for instability. And now she was in danger. Quite possibly big danger, judging by the amount of trouble Ted was in with the worst kind of people. The kind of people who were not above making an adversary disappear only after punishing that person and everyone around them. Like Megan.

Jack swished around the last of the bitter coffee in his cup, wishing it was whiskey as another speaker stood to speak. For the last four years he considered passing a bar and not giving into the urge to go in and drink himself senseless as a triumph.

Tonight it felt like torture. Because tonight he felt like he was that invisible geek from high school still stupidly trying to fit in where he obviously didn't belong and wasn't wanted. Megan had made that very clear when she'd ordered him into his car and out of her life. He left and as she wanted, he wouldn't be back.

***

Megan awoke to a heavenly scent coming from downstairs. Coffee? She stretched and smiled, sitting up in bed. The clock on her night stand indicated it was 7:06 in big red letters. She'd been asleep six hours and could probably sleep six more. She sat up and ran her hand over Ted's pillow. He wasn't there of course and Megan wondered how it was going to feel to wake up alone from now on. She sighed and got out of bed just as she heard a bizarre sound coming from downstairs. She sat ramrod straight, her eyes wide, listening for another sound. A moment later she heard a whispering voice curse "Dammit". Ok was that a female whisper or a male whisper? And then she heard the noise again, followed by what sounded like glass breaking.

There was a burglar in the house. Or a private detective, as if there's a difference in the two. Jackson Westin! Maybe he wasn't done snooping around. She threw the covers back and got up, ready to read him the riot act then stopped at the door. What if it wasn't Jack? What if it was a real burglar? Who made coffee while robbing her blind? Nope, it was probably Jack. Or Josie, maybe she'd cancelled her date.

"Josie!" Megan whispered and no one answered which didn't surprise Megan. Josie didn't cancel dates with Doctors to hang out and drink coffee. And she knew it wasn't her mother because the voice had cursed, and not her dad because the Cowboys were playing. There could be a terrorist threat requiring worldwide evacuation, but if there was a Cowboys game on her Dad wouldn't move. She opened the closet and grabbed a golf club and went out the door, moving silently and slowly.

"Hey Girlfriend," Mickey hollered from in the floor where he was comfortably stretched out on a sleeping bag.

"Hey," Megan said weakly. "What's going on?" She was looking at what was left of her living room. All of her furniture had been pushed against the walls, and there were sleeping bags strewn about in the floor. The coffee table had been turned into a buffet with a delicious looking spread of brownies, popcorn, cookies, pretzels, beer and chocolate. The whole gang was there, wearing pajamas and looking at Megan excitedly.

"Pajama party babe," Mickey said, while blowing on Josie's toenails.

"Yeah, we're here to cheer you up," Stacy said.

111

"And make sure you don't knock yourself out again." Mickey pinched Josie.

"Plus, we didn't want you to be alone tonight," Ali started, "So, we're all here to take your mind off everything. We'll have an old fashioned P.J. party like we used to."

"OK." That one word was all she could manage. She felt her heart swell at the love inside that room.

"So we've got chick flicks, beer, snacks, makeup, manicure kits..." Ali began.

"But what about your date?" Megan asked Josie still touched that she'd canceled it on Megan's behalf. "You canceled it?"

"Uh, not exactly. I invited him to come over if he wanted to. I told him my best friend needed me, so if he wanted to see me he had to come and get a makeover and a manicure like the rest of us." That should have sent him running for the hills. But we were talking about Josie here. She had a way of making men do ridiculous things for her. Must be her cleavage. Or her sunny disposition. Definitely the cleavage Megan decided as she watched Josie slap Mickey on the side of his head for smudging the paint on her toenail. "He'll be here about nine," Josie reported.

"Well get your ass down here and join the party babe. We'll get drunk and talk about our last times," Mickey said and Megan realized she was still standing on the stairway looking like a moron. She joined Ali on the couch and grabbed a beer.

"Our last times?" Ali asked.

"Yeah, remember the last pajama party we had? We were what? Sixteen? And we snuck beer from Josie's dad and talked about who we lost our virginity to." Half of the gang winced at memories of their first times and most likely who they were with. "Yeah, I don't wanna relive mine either," he continued remembering his was with a girl. He shuddered, "So we'll talk about our last times instead. It'll be fun." Sure it'll be fun Megan thought, if she could remember her last time.

"Oh, I got this one," Josie began, "Remember, that guy from the club the other night, what was his name? Oh yeah Chad something. Anyways we went to his place and..."

"Can we talk about something else?" Megan asked. Pointing out her sexual repression to her was not going to cheer her up.

"Like what?" Stacy asked at the same time Josie was talking about 'ice cream on her nipples.'

"Anything else. I can't even remember my last time, much less compete with ice cream nipples and pineapple slices." Although Megan was curious about the pineapples slices.

"Well as long as we don't talk about Ted, I'm open to anything," Stacy said. "Let's just have some fun tonight and figure out what to do with him tomorrow."

"Actually I've already figured out what to do with him," Megan said and everyone except Josie looked at her with careful, but curious expressions on their faces.

"Did you decide to kill him?" Josie asked as everyone gaped at her, "Because I used to date a guy that can have that sort of thing done." Megan shook her head and tried to say no but Josie kept going. "I think he only charges like ten thousand dollars or something but most importantly he's like the greatest lay." Eye rolls came from everyone. "I mean killing people must be exciting because he can stay hard all night and he's very talented. The only drawback is he makes this weird throaty quack every time he thrusts. Sounds just like a duck. It's really annoying but if you wear ear plugs it probably won't bother you." For once everyone was speechless as Josie looked up thoughtfully remembering the sex. "Should I give him a call?"

"No!" Several voices shouted.

"Maybe I will anyway for like a consultation. Just in case, you know." She dug her black book out of her purse. "Anyone have any ear plugs I can borrow."

Ali shook herself, and turned to Megan. "She's nuts!" she said referring to Josie who was standing up thrusting her pelvis and making quacking sounds to a very interested Mickey. "So, what do you want to do about Ted?"

"I'm going to divorce him. I'm going to go see a lawyer tomorrow and kick him out when he gets out of the hospital."

"Have you thought about this? I mean really thought about it?" Stacy asked concerned. "Ten years is a long time Meg. You need to be sure."

Ali took Megan's hand. "Don't rush things Meg. Maybe take a little time to think about it."

"What's there to think about? He's bangin' the redhead, babe. And Megan's not happy. Time to say adios asshole," Mickey said putting cotton balls between his toes before putting his large feet in Stacy's lap. "What color?" she asked and he batted his eyes and smiled. "Right. Siren Red!" she said and retrieved the polish.

"He's right guys; I mean Ted's having sex with Tiffany and her silicone sisters. I don't want him here. She can have him. It's time I face it and move on with my life. There's someone out there for me, that'll love me and treat me right." I hope she added silently. At least she had Spot and the pups still.

"And rock your world 'til your head spins." Josie closed her black book and tossed it to Megan. "This should get you started. If they have three stars next to their name, that means they made me see stars. There's a legend in the back for deciphering the codes. K is for kiss, P is for props, S is for size, O is for oral ability, C is for creativity…etc. There are comments by the initials."

"Thanks." Megan muttered opening the book to a random page. Her eyes just about popped out of her head as the name Ted M. stared back at her. She looked at Josie through narrowed eyes and then glanced back at the page.

Ted M.: K- Yuk, S- made me laugh, O-lot to learn, overall rating- I'd turn lesbian before I'd let Ted go down under again.

Well at least she was accurate in her descriptions.

"Meg?" Stacy asked and Megan slammed the book shut.

"Hey, uh I need to make a phone call. But first, what do you guys say we turn this into a packing party."

"Huh?" Stacy asked.

"Yeah, we can go get some boxes and we'll move Ted's stuff out. I want him gone now! We'll put all of his stuff in one of those storage trucks and when he gets home I'll just hand him the keys."

"And tell him what?" Ali asked, "Hi Ted, Guess what? While you were in the hospital you moved?"

"Sounds good to me," Megan said flatly.

"You're sure you want to do this?"

"Yep." And she wanted to find a baseball bat and have a little talk with Josie.

"Ok, I'm in." Stacy said, although she seemed unsure about it.

"Me too." Ali said, "Let's get rid of him."

"I'm in too Babe, soon as my toenails dry."

"I just had a manicure, so I'm not sure yet." Josie said and then Megan said, "I'll let you break stuff." Maybe with your head she thought and then scolded herself for even thinking it. It could be a different Ted M. who was lousy in bed.

"Ok, I'm in then. Finally we get to have some fun. Should we call Tom?"

"Why, you need to add him to your black book? You afraid someone else might get to him first? Like me?" She regretted the words before she even got them out.

"Megan," Stacy said in a calming voice but Josie cut in. "Actually, I think you should. It wouldn't kill you to get laid. It'd probably do you some good, because I don't know if anyone else has noticed but you've been really bitchy lately. A little action might adjust your attitude, which will save me from having to do it. Hell, if Tom hadn't of stopped me earlier I would have already done it." She stood there defensively staring Megan down, no doubt thinking about finishing what they'd started earlier when Megan decided it wasn't worth it. She loved Josie too much.

"Josie, I'm sorry. That was uncalled for." Josie softened and plunked down on the couch downing the rest of her beer. "Let me make that phone call guys, and we'll get started."

"We'll start without you. Take your time," Stacy said.

Megan went into the kitchen with Ali following her. She shut the door and turned to Megan talking in a low tone. "What was that all about?"

"Nothing!" Megan searched the junk drawer looking for a phone number.

"That wasn't nothing. What's up?"

"Just typical Josie. Don't worry about it." Megan found the number and picked up the phone but paused before dialing.

"Meg, what did she do? If it's about what she said, forget about it. She's just Josie you know? She never thinks before she talks." Megan handed her the book open to the Ted M. page. Ali scanned it and snapped it shut. "Oh shit."

"Yeah! Oh shit. Obviously she never thinks before she does anything, including my husband."

"I had no idea," Ali said, her face a mix of shock and disgust. Josie had done a lot of things but this... "We need to talk to her."

115

"No. Just forget about. I don't care. It might not even be my Ted anyways, although the rating is accurate." Ali was shaking her head so Megan added, "I mean it. I can't lose my husband and my best friend in the same day. Just drop it."

Ali nodded and wrapped her arms around Megan. "We'll figure this all out Meg. Everything will be Ok, I promise." Megan nodded and asked Ali for some privacy so she could make the phone call. Megan stared at the card she held in her hand. Jack Westin, Private Investigator. She'd worked this out in her head when revenge and payback sounded so good. Right now she wasn't sure this was what she wanted, but she'd come this far so to hell with it. She dialed the first number on the card. No answer. That was probably a sign that this wasn't a good idea. She dialed the second number. After four rings she was just about to hang up, when Jack's husky voice answered with a curt "Yeah?" And her nipples became instantly hard at the sound of his voice. Ok maybe that was a sign. Wrong guy, but right idea. "Jack Westin?"

"Yeah, what?"

"This is uh…This is Megan Malone." That got his attention. He moved to the back of the room so that he wouldn't disturb the meeting.

"Okay." He said carefully knowing that if he were smart, he'd hang up immediately and forget she'd ever called. "What can I do for you?"

"Well first of all, I wanted to apologize to you for what happened earlier. Things were kind of haywire then. Anyway, Tom said he didn't want to press charges or anything so…"

"Thanks for letting me know. Have a good night." She cut him off before he could say goodbye and for a second he almost snapped his cell phone shut anyway. "Wait, Jack?"

"Yeah?"

"I also wanted to um, well remember your offer to help me?"

"Yeah." Hang up now his brain told him. This woman had threatened his sobriety.

"Is the offer still good? I mean, would you still be willing to help me out?"

"Depends. What do you want?" Her voice wavered when she asked and he didn't have the heart to hang up on her. He'd at least hear her out first.

"Oh, Okay. Well can you come by my house tonight?" She hadn't meant to say that. Damn. What the hell was wrong with her? Her nipples seemed pleased though. On the other end of the line Jack frowned. He was not going over there.

"For what?" He started to say 'You told me to never come back.'

"I wanted to discuss this with you face to face," when he didn't answer she added quickly, "I'll pay you for your time of course."

"Give me half an hour." He heard her sigh like she was relieved. "And Megan? You can keep your money."

"Oh Okay, Thank you Mr. Westin," Megan said to a dial tone. Jack was a jerk. He hadn't even said goodbye. She dropped the phone and went to start packing with everyone else.

"Where is everyone?" Megan asked Ali who had removed Ted's shelf with all his sports junk on it. She was handling everything with care, and Megan resisted the urge to try to learn juggling with Ted's bobbing doll collection.

"Mickey and Josie went to get boxes and tape. Stacy went for a beer run." Megan nodded and stood beside Ali grabbing a frame and a baseball from the second shelf. Ali sniffed the air and looked at Megan. Megan sniffed herself.

"I think I'm going to grab a shower right quick. Do you mind?" Megan asked.

"I'd mind if you didn't. You smell like lasagna. You're making me hungry."

***

Jack glanced at the clock on the wall in the smoky little room. 7:46. The meeting would be over in fourteen minutes. He sat back down, deciding he needed to stay until it was over. He tried to focus his attention on the woman who was now speaking, but his mind was busy analyzing that phone call from Megan. He assumed that since she'd invited him to her house that Ted wasn't there. Maybe she'd kicked him out or he'd left on his own. Maybe she had reconsidered her initial impression of him and had decided to let him help her. Or more probable she wanted to know what he'd found in Ted's studio.

He looked at the clock which had only ticked two minutes away. Shit, these things could go on forever. He remembered the tone of her voice. She sounded sad, but calm, almost apologetic. He also sensed a little uncertainty in her voice, like maybe she wasn't sure why she was calling him. Maybe she had felt some sort of connection with him.

117

Probably not. Odds were, she was oblivious to thinking about him as anything other than a low life, law breaking PI.

Then why had she called? She'd already confirmed Ted's infidelity. She seemed to have Tom, who would probably rush to help her if she needed him. Maybe she was worried about that comment he'd made about her being in danger. The clock showed ten more minutes to go when Jack finally gave up and slipped out the back door. He'd go to Megan's and find out what she wanted, but this time he'd listen only to his head and ignore his heart completely.

***

Megan sat in the closet floor, mindlessly throwing Ted's shoes into a box, while Mickey dumped the contents of Ted's chest of drawers into another box. Mickey was humming while he worked, obviously aware from Megan's silence that she needed some space. He'd tried to initiate small talk, but knowing her as well as he did, he could tell her heart wasn't in it. She couldn't get Josie and Ted out of her head. The fact that Ted had slept with Tiffany-and God knew who else- didn't really bother her anymore. She'd come to terms with that. But Ted and Josie? That was more than she could take. It was a double betrayal by the two people she'd loved unconditionally for a large portion of her life. She choked back a tear and when she looked up she saw Mickey staring at her, his brown eyes soft under a web of fake eyelashes and eye shadow.

"Come here," he said and opened his arms. She leaned into them and rested her head on his chest. "This'll pass Meg. I know it's hard right now but it'll get easier. Before long, you won't even miss Ted." He rubbed her back to soothe her.

"I already don't miss Ted. This has little to do with him." His hand stopped moving. He pushed her from him and searched her face.

"Aw Meg, you look like you've lost your best friend." A tear escaped her eyes and she leaned her head back on his shoulder and said between sobs, "I have."

"What do you mean? We're all your best friends and we're all here for you Babe."

"She slept with Ted, Mickey. She slept with him and she never told me. It never should have ever happened in the first place, but she's been lying to me the whole time."

He looked at her quizzically and said, "Tiffany?"

118

"No, Josie." He shook his head and she nodded, "It's in her book, look." She handed him the book and showed him the page.

"Megan, I know everyone she sleeps with, we share everything. This must be someone else. She'd never sleep with Ted. She hates Ted."

"Well how many Ted M.'s do you know?"

He seemed to consider it but apparently he still found it to be a coincidence because he said, "I still don't believe it. I mean Josie gets around, but even she has her limits."

"I don't know, Mickey, I'm beginning to wonder about that."

"Well, if it was your Ted, why would she give you the book?"

"Because she's clueless. Hell, she probably didn't even remember writing in it there. I mean, this book is full!" She flipped the pages for him to see. "I don't know how she can keep up."

"Oh, she doesn't have a problem keeping up. It's the men who can't keep up with her." He flipped through the book scanning the names. "You want me to talk to her?"

"OK, I guess, I mean I don't really want to know, but I if I don't know for sure I'll probably just obsess about until it drives me crazy."

"Don't worry about it, Babe. I'll find out." He stopped on a page and began grinning until a chuckle finally escaped.

"What?" she asked.

"I wanted to know what she said about me." Megan couldn't hide the shock on her face. He laughed, "Look I got three gold stars, and points in size and creativity. I'm the shit girlfriend." He high fived the air as Megan sat silent shaking her head.

"I can't believe you slept with her. When did that happen?"

"I didn't sleep with her, Michael did, and it happened one drunken night when I was confused." He laughed. "I wasn't confused anymore after that. She scared the shit out of me, I've sworn off women ever since."

"She's that bad?" Megan asked. He looked at her seriously. "No, she's that good. I mean that woman is very innovative and talented! And believe me she used every trick she had and probably invented a few on the spot."

Wow! Megan thought. Maybe her search for passion was over. All she needed to do was get it on with Josie. Mickey's look said he was reading her mind and he said, "Don't even think about it. She only plays with boys."

119

***

Megan jumped at the sound of the doorbell, for some reason nervous to see Jack. Or Tom. Or her mother. Or anybody for that matter. She looked at herself in the mirror, no makeup, air dried hair, two black eyes. Well, one thing was sure; she wouldn't have to worry about any spontaneous sex with anyone, including Josie. She made it down the stairs just in time to see Dr. Ross step into the foyer, still wearing his white lab coat and carrying a bottle of wine. He smiled at Megan and she gave a weak wave, her mind busy trying to figure out why she was disappointed not to see Jack standing there. Dr. Ross was being introduced to everyone by Josie, when Josie suddenly stopped and put her hands on her hips.

"Where is your stethoscope?" she demanded. He looked puzzled.

"It's uh at my office. I usually leave it there after my shift."

She narrowed her eyes and said, "Well I had plans for that thing. You are going to lose some serious points later for not bringing it." She blew her bangs out of her face and threw her hands in the air. "I can't believe it, a doctor who doesn't even bring his tools."

While Dr. Ross was standing there perplexed, Josie began to explain, "It's like this Doc, if you work in construction, then you would bring your tool belt and hard hat, cops bring handcuffs and batons, firemen bring helmets and their hoses. See how it works? I need variety, that's why I don't date bankers or stock brokers. What are they going to bring, laptops and mechanical pencils?" She paused and thought for a moment, as Stacy located the bottle of Tequila. "I did date a zoo keeper once and…"

Stacy took a swig of the Tequila, shook her head and went back to the kitchen to find a straw. Josie could drive even the most sensible of people to alcoholism.

While Josie was babbling on about God knows, with the ever attentive Dr. Ross at her side, Megan had stepped outside to assemble more boxes. Ted had a lot of stuff, more than she'd realized, and that wasn't counting what was in the basement. She assembled a box and flipped it upside down to reinforce it with duct tape just as Mrs. Everett stepped outside and turned on her porch light. Megan peeled a long strip of the tape off the roll and realized she hadn't brought anything to cut it with. If she went back inside to get scissors, Mrs. Everett would probably follow her in and then drop dead from a heart attack at the sight of a the six foot drag queen, or the couple who were probably playing doctor-literally- in her living room. If she stayed outside she'd have to talk to the nosy old women who would undoubtedly make a bee-line for the phone to spread the latest gossip. Gritting her teeth, she raised the tape to her mouth and began gnawing at the spot that needed to be cut. Now she had a reason not to talk to Mrs. Everett, because her mother always told her it's not polite to talk with a mouth full. She gave Mrs. Everett a quick wave with her free hand and went back to her task when she heard a familiar voice behind her. "Need some help?" Jack asked, coming up the sidewalk, pulling something metal from his pocket. Megan felt her stomach flip flop as every muscle in her body stood at full sexual attention. Megan nodded and Jack opened his pocket knife and snipped the tape for her just as Mrs. Everett made her way to the fence. Megan rolled her eyes and made a silent promise to herself to move far, far away as soon as she could. Megan assembled another box ignoring the woman, now standing less than fifteen feet away gawking at her. Jack had taken the role of head tape snipper, while standing there looking sexy as hell.

"Megan?" The nosy old bat called out. Megan gave another quick wave.

"Megan!"

This time her voice was almost a yell and Megan flat ignored her while Jack watched humorlessly. "Town gossip," Megan explained. Jack snipped another piece of tape, then cocked his head towards the old woman who was now coming around the fence to Megan's yard. "Shit!" Megan muttered and Jack smiled.

In the darkness of night with only, the porch light casting interesting slashes of light across Megan's face, Jack realized he was holding his breath. The site of her framed by the clear night sky and the twinkling stars had stolen that breath straight out of his lungs and he wondered what she'd do if he kissed her right then. He never should have come over because now he didn't want to leave until he answered that question.

"Megan! Did you hear me calling you?" Mrs. Everett asked.

"Yes, I did, Mrs. Everett, but I'm kind of busy. No time to talk," Megan concentrated on assembling the next box not making eye contact with the woman.

"Well ignoring your neighbors is rude, Megan." Her eyes landed on Jack accusingly, "Are you having a yard sale?"

121

"No."

"Spring Cleaning?"

"No."

"Don't tell me you're moving."

"Nope." Jack stretched out a strip of tape and ran it across the bottom, touching Megan's hand in the process. Her nerves jolted, her hand on fire.

"Well?" Mrs. Everett asked and Megan met her gaze with frustration. "You going to tell me what you're doing then?"

"I'm assembling these boxes," Megan snapped as Jack brushed his hips against her trying to get a better position on the box he was reinforcing. She closed her eyes as she felt the heat spread throughout her body and she hoped Jack hadn't noticed.

He had. Even in the darkness, he was completely aware of her reaction to his touch, so he did it again, just as Mrs. Everett took a step closer.

"Well I can see that you're assembling boxes, Megan. My ears may be going, but my eyes still work." Megan considered duct taping the woman's mouth shut. "My question was what are the boxes for?" Megan gave up. Everyone would know soon enough.

"Ted's stuff. He's moving out," The old bat didn't look shocked enough so Megan added, "Actually I'm kicking him out. He's in the hospital shitting marbles and when he gets out he and his twelve year old girlfriend are going to live in a U-Haul with the homeless people under the bridge." Mrs. Everett looked absolutely mortified and Megan smiled. Jack seemed to enjoy it too. Although Megan couldn't see his face, she could see his shoulders shaking from laughter. For once the old bat didn't have anything to say so Megan said, "You better be running along now, Mrs. Everett. I'm sure you have plenty of calls to make and lies to tell. Make sure you get the story straight, and don't forget to call my mother."

"I have no idea what you're talking about," Mrs. Everett said, her chin tilted high, her posture ramrod straight. Jack had moved and was standing directly behind Megan, close enough that she could feel the heat radiating off his body.

"What, are you resigning your role as Gossip Queen? Crowning someone else?"

"I do not gossip," she growled, "I was just being neighborly. And you are being extremely rude." Megan shrugged and the old woman continued, "You used to be such a nice girl, Megan. I don't know what happened to you. Why, I've heard all kinds of things about you lately and I found it all hard to believe…"

"Yeah well believe it. Believe it all. I'm tired of being a good girl. As a matter of fact I feel like being really naughty. Maybe even naughty enough to spray a nosy old bat with the water hose for not leaving me the hell alone and minding her own business." Mrs. Everett's hands were hanging at her sides fisted, her lips pursed.

"That's it Megan, I'm calling the prayer team…"

"Good. I'll give you some good gossip to forward to them." She turned to face Jack and stood on tip toes to plant a sloppy kiss on his lips. Once he got passed the shock, he responded by encircling her waist with his arms, his hands resting loosely on her hips.

She'd intended the kiss to be short and quick, basically just for shock value. But Jack opened his mouth and deepened the kiss, and Megan found herself responding back. His tongue raked across her teeth, then worked it's way expertly, gently around her tongue and for a moment she saw stars. He leaned into her, their pelvises touching, and she kissed him like he was the first drop of water after a seven year drought. Then she realized that that wasn't far from the truth. After allowing herself to enjoy the ecstasy for only a moment she broke the kiss. Jack showed his disappointment by seductively biting her on her bottom lip.

The look on Mrs. Everett's face was priceless, a delicious blend of shock, horror and disbelief.

"Who is that man and why is he kissing you? Oh my God! I'm calling your mother. And don't think I won't tell Ted." Megan could've cared less.

"You might want to take notes here, Mrs. Everett," Megan said, realizing Jack's hands were still wrapped around her from behind. "His name is Jack and I'm using him for sex. Mind blowing, earth shattering, hot, steamy, wild, monkey sex." Mrs. Everett's eyes were tiny, little slits as she glared at Megan. "And I'd suggest you find yourself a Jack, and do the same. It's very liberating." Megan threw her hands out and looked up at the night's sky. "I feel great. Just like a new woman." When she looked back down, Mrs. Everett was stalking across the yard, no doubt heading inside for a gossip telethon.

After she was gone and her porch light curtly extinguished, Megan stood deathly still, Jack's arms still encasing her, trying to process the consequences of what she'd just done. She'd acted purely on impulse, agitated with Mrs. Everett and everyone else. Everyone knew every little thing she did, and most of the time they added to and embellished their stories until they had something worth telling and when Megan would defend herself, the gossip was considered truth as if it were the Bible. She wanted to lash out and make a statement, and she had. Problem was, what kind of statement had she made to Jack?

And where on earth did he learn to kiss like that? Good God, he had magical lips. Lips that could probably perform much more magic on her. If only he wasn't a criminal. Her image of him behind bars was starting to fade, with lips like that; conjugal visits could be a possibility. Then he'd bitten her lip. Just a playful little nibble actually, but she'd never experienced that kind of pleasure from a kiss before and she wondered what else this man knew. If he wasn't a lowlife she'd be inclined to find out. Plus, Tom had asked her to dinner and he probably knew a few tricks as well and he wasn't a lowlife.

"Jack," she whispered and heard a vague "hmm?" from him. "I'm so sorry about that. I got caught up in the moment, and that…that woman has made my life a living hell for the last ten years and I just…" She stopped, realizing she was babbling and that his arms still held her. She stepped away and gathered some of the boxes they'd put together. He also picked up two boxes and she had just gestured him inside when Ali came to the porch carrying the phone, "Meg, your mom's on the phone and she's…well she's quoting the Bible and talking about the fires of hell." Megan took the phone, clicked the off button and walked in the house with Jack a step behind her. She should be packing her things, she thought, Moving was looking better and better. By the time her mother got a hold of her, even Jesus wouldn't be able to save her.

Jack sat at the kitchen table waiting for Megan. She'd asked him to have a seat, offered him a beer and told him she'd be right back. As he sat there, he thought about her and that kiss. God, he'd waited fourteen years for that kiss and it'd been worth every long, miserable second. Her mouth tasted like heaven and beer. Mostly heaven, though, he thought as he remembered the shyness of her tongue as she explored his mouth, until her moist lips finally parted and the kiss deepened to the level of hysteria. She drank him in hungrily, passionately, desperately, and as he responded she leaned her body into his and it was all he could do to remain standing. He wanted to throw her down in the grass and take her body beneath his and kiss her thoroughly, starting with those magnificent lips and not stopping until he'd bathed every inch of her body.

He recalled the dreamy look on her face as she broke the kiss and searched his eyes. Her lips were swollen from the kiss, her hair mussed from his hands, her body on fire beneath his arms. But it was her eyes that had given her away. He'd seen that erotic glaze in her crystal blue eyes, their lids half closed. The look that said she'd felt the same thing he had. The unquenchable desire, that connection between them.

The kiss may have been strictly for show, but it stung her too. He knew that not only by that look, but by the way she paused and searched his face and allowed herself to relish in the pleasure before turning to that nosy old woman. Yep, it'd taken him fourteen years to get that kiss and it was better than he ever dreamed it would be. And it also confirmed what he'd always known, that one kiss would never be enough.

125

Amy Johnson

Chapter Eleven

"So, the reason I asked you over, is because I want to offer you a job." Megan had joined Jack at the kitchen table, sitting directly across from him, her gaze focused on his hands peeling the label of his beer bottle, which appeared to still contain most of its contents. Hers on the other hand was empty.

"Okay," he said carefully, following her gaze to the bottle.

"As you've probably figured out, I'm going to divorce Ted. His belongings are being packed as we speak. Come Monday morning, I'm getting an attorney and that'll be that."

He nodded, and when she didn't continue he said, "So what do you want me to do?" She went to the refrigerator and pulled out another beer then took her seat again. Jack twisted the cap of the bottle and placed it front of her.

"Thank you," she took a long pull from the bottle, then continued, "Well, first I want to say, that I'm not the person you've seen the last couple days." Finally she met his gaze. "The real Megan is this predictable, boring good girl, who lives a simple, little life, and never strays out of the ordinary. That person would never snoop around in buildings at night, or drink whiskey, or kiss strangers on the front lawn, or disrespect old women." He nodded again and said nothing because he had no idea where she was going with any of this. "See I've lived by this set of rules my entire life, you know, behave, be quiet, do my part for society, make my mother happy. Problem is, I found out that living that way doesn't make me happy," she paused for another drink. "So, I've decided to do something about it."

"Divorcing Ted," he said and she nodded then said, "Yeah, but that's not all. See I want revenge. I want to do something so unlike myself, so…crazy, so exciting, so…freeing. Something that says, I'm Megan Malone, and this is my moment. Everybody else back off and stay the hell out of my way."

Jack was unsure where she was going with this, but he listened intently and let her speak. "I want to embrace life, so to speak," she finished, giving him that crooked smile, and for the first time since high school that sparkle in her eyes was back. She wanted to take a stand, enjoy life.

He could help her do that, especially if it had to do with getting another of those kisses that made his head spin and his knees go weak. "So how can I help you, Megan?" She looked at his hands again, as her scrubbed clean cheeks, took on a pink blush, and she smiled weakly.

"Well, see when I was in high school, I was this prim and proper shy girl that no one really noticed-" He couldn't hide the surprise in his face at the statement. It was so far from the truth. "-and when all of my friends were making out under the bleachers or going to parties, I was at home reading or going to Sunday School or doing whatever my mother said the proper girls did. I'd never even had a beer until I was twenty one years old." She laughed. "My whole life has been a rip. I met Ted,-The All American Boy, when I was seventeen, and married him at twenty, wearing a white dress because I'd earned it." He took his first sip of his beer then, and tried to hide his surprise. Being a good girl was one thing, but remaining a virgin until she was twenty was... "Anyway, we bought this house and I kept waiting for the fairytale to begin, but now it's ten years later and I'm still waiting. So I've decided the wait is over. I want to have some fun. It's my turn, wouldn't you say?" He nodded.

He spread his hands out on the wooden table and asked again, "And how can I help you with this?" He noticed that she was wringing her hands together and keeping her gaze in her lap. She was nervous. She looked like she was still in high school. He wrapped both hands around his beer to keep from touching her, but it took tremendous restraint. He wanted her bad.

"Ok," she said finally, meeting his gaze. "I don't want you to get the wrong idea here, like I'm trying to relive high school or anything, but here's what I want." She thought about Josie's black book and how much fun she probably had filling the pages. "I want you to help me locate some of the guys I went to high school with. You know the ones that all the girls wanted, the ones who had meaningless hot sex in the back seat of their dad's chargers, then never gave those girls the time of day the next day. The Casanovas I guess you could say."

Jack hadn't realized how hard he'd been holding on to that beer, his knuckles were white and the muscles in his forearms were sticking out. He let go of the beer and it spilled all over his lap, and it was a good thing but the sudden chill served as a well needed diversion from the anger and pain he felt spread through his chest. She wanted him to help her get laid? She had to be going somewhere else with all of this. He took a deep, steadying breath and tried to think of what to say, but instead he heard, "So you want me to help you get laid?" pop out of his mouth in a deep harsh voice. His words or his tone must have surprised her because she startled and stared at him through wide, blue eyes, acting as if he'd just socked her in the jaw.

"Well..., um I didn't exactly say it like that. I mean that sounds so...so harsh."

He tried an apologetic look but failed miserably. "But that is what you want right? You want me to find these guys and say 'Hey, remember this girl from high school? She wants to get naked and fuck your brains out in the backseat of a Charger. Would you like to make an appointment with her to do the nasty?'" He hadn't meant to use that sort of language or the angry tone, but dammit he was mad. She flinched at his use of the f-word and shrank back a little in her chair. He regretted it instantly, but there was little he could do about it and for some reason he just wasn't in an apologetic mood. "I think you'd better take a better look at my job description. I'm a Private Investigator. Not a Pimp." Her eyes began to water and he kicked himself for making her cry. "And I'm not interested in the job. Have a good night Mrs. Malone." He stood to leave but she pinned him in place with angry tearful eyes. She was even beautiful when she cried he noted, but she could cry herself a river and he'd just swim right on out the door. And out of her life.

She stood to and pointed a shaky finger at his chest, "You say it like I'm a whore. Some two bit floozy on a street corner. Well, I not. I just want one night, one amazing night." Her voice rose and she took a step closer, cornering him against the counter, "After ten years of being a loving, supportive, faithful wife, then being traded in for a younger model, with a bigger rack, I think I deserve a little fun. Is one night of meaningless animal sex too damn much to ask for?" He stared at her with an angry incredulous look. She couldn't be serious. She called a

129

private investigator, to help her find a worthy pity screw. Or revenge screw or whatever she wanted to call it. It was absurd. The whole damn idea was ridiculous.

"Maybe you should call your friend Tom. He seemed interested. I bet he'd be happy to screw you."

"I don't want Tom. I mean, I am interested in him and he asked me to dinner but..." her tears began faster and she fiercely wiped at her eyes. "It's just that I'm not sure I'm very good at that sort of thing. Sex, that is." Jack looked at her as if she'd just told him she had a vicious case of Rabies. "What I mean is I've only ever been with Ted and when I read in Josie's book how lousy he was in bed I thought well I must suck too. I mean, sure I've had sex but only with the same man for ten years, and I knew nothing when we started so if I learned from him and he's so bad, then I'm probably even worse. After one night with me, Tom or any other man for that matter would probably, run for the hills or suddenly decide to be gay." Jack said nothing because he couldn't believe the bullshit that was spewing from her mouth. He'd rather acquire a fatal case of Athlete's Foot on his crotch, than listen to this. But she was serious and she was crying harder, genuinely distraught by this. He pushed his way past her and put his hand on the door knob. He wanted to touch her, to take her in his arms and say anything to make her stop crying. Or to make love to her in the back seat of a charger until she screamed so loud the windows shattered. But he would do nothing, except get the hell out of there and drink her off his mind. Forever. His heart couldn't take this.

"Goodnight Mrs. Malone," he said before opening the door.

She put her hand on the door trying to stop him "Please Jack?" She pleaded with those angelic eyes and he averted his to his boots. "I just want you to find them, find out if their single, if they still live here. I don't want you to do anything else. I just want to feel like one of the special girls. The ones who got all the dates, the ones the boys noticed." He froze, too numb to move. If he'd left before that last comment he would have been fine. He was angry, heartbroken, frustrated and pissed as hell. He'd have been able to slam the door and stay that way. But when she'd said she just wanted to feel like those girls, to be noticed, his head shut down. He couldn't sort through the mix of emotions spiraling through him and he didn't want to. Pissed off was good. Angry was good. He could handle those and they'd keep his head on straight so he'd stay the hell away from Megan. But he knew there was more and that he'd spend a great deal of time, trying to sort through them, obsessing over them. One thing was sure. He had to get out of there. Soon, before he said or did something stupid.

"Goodbye Mrs. Malone," he said his brown eyes, staring directly into hers. "Good luck on your quest."

She followed him out, "Please think about it Jack," she called out to his departing back. He climbed into his truck, started the engine and had the truck in gear before he even shut the door. With his foot flat on the floor, he guided his truck down her street and to the nearest bar.

Megan's mother passed Jack on the sidewalk as she was walking up the driveway to Megan's house. Megan plastered smile on her face, and waved at her mom. Her mom was not smiling and was clutching her Rosary beads in her hand. Oh Boy! Megan was big trouble now. That thought brought a surge of excitement...

"Hello, Mom. It's an exceptionally beautiful night wouldn't you say?" Megan said in her perkiest, ain't I cute voice. In the background she heard a roar of laughter followed by 'Go Mickey, Go Mickey, It's your birthday.' The gang was in the living room and Megan was sure Mickey was doing his famous beer bottle balancing trick, where he balanced the bottle on his forehead, while simultaneously, downing the contents of another one all without using his hands. Either that or he was doing a strip tease. Either way, they were having a blast and Megan would have much rather been in there. Instead she was facing down a rather angry woman who was carrying a crucifix, Rosary beads and a Bible, all the essential equipment needed for bringing down the wrath of God on a rotten child. Outside thunder cracked and Megan prayed for lightening to strike and torch the kitchen. Her mother pushed past her and threw her purse on the counter.

"Mom, I..."

"Cut the crap, young lady." Oh boy, she said crap. She was pissed. "I don't know what the heck has gotten into you, but I've had enough. Being rude to sweet Mrs. Everett, kissing that...that man in your yard," the laugher erupted again, "having wild parties. I've had enough of it and so has your father. You are not going to ruin our good names. We are well respected in this town and..."

"Mom," Megan was on a roll tonight, no since stopping now, "Put a sock in it." Her Mother's face went white. "What I do has nothing to do with you. I am thirty. Didn't you get the memo? I am free to live my own life anyway I damn well please and if you don't like it then move. Or better yet, I'll move. I've been thinking about it for a while anyway." A few stubborn tears formed in the corners of her mother's stern blue eyes. "I'm divorcing Ted, and I'm going to kiss a few boys, and maybe even have sex with one of them. I'm going to get drunk if I want to, and if I feel like it, I'll run down the street naked shouting the f-word at the top of my lungs. Hell, I might even get arrested, I've never ridden in a cop car before and it might be kind of fun." Her Mother's face was a mix of anger, disgust, and horror. She was clutching her crucifix so tight Megan was afraid she'd break it. Her mother said nothing.

"Oh, and by the way, I write a smut column for a local woman's magazine and I've been doing it for years. It's called Meg's Moment and you might want to check it out. It's mostly sex and stuff, but I try to throw in a few baking tips and household remedies every now and again. Pretty good stuff if you ask me."

The kitchen door opened and then shut quickly, and Megan's mom said, "I need to sit down." Megan guided her to a chair and instantly felt like hell, for what she'd just said to her mother. The look on the woman's face made Megan's heart break. She was a horrible daughter. A rotten, human being. Her mother was fanning herself with her hand and fighting back tears.

"Mom," Megan began, "go home. Forget about what I said, I'm sorry. I love you very much. You are a wonderful mother and you did an awesome job raising me. I'm a horrible person and that is no reflection of you. You can blame daddy, or someone on his side of the family. Maybe I got a hold of some bad genes. I'll try to do better. Just go home and we'll start fresh tomorrow."

Her mother rose and Megan braced herself for a blow to the head with that infamous brown purse. But instead her mother wrapped her arms around Megan's neck and pulled her close. "Do you need money for a divorce lawyer?" she said and Megan about fainted. "Because if you're going to do it, I want to make sure you have a good attorney."

"I'm fine Mom, but thanks." Megan heard herself say through the lump in her throat. She loved her mother so much and from now on she was going to try harder to appreciate her. Even when she was nagging her to a premature death.

Her mother pulled away and held Megan's hands, her eyes soft and maternal. "Make sure you pick up some of those uh condom things at Rite-Aid, and have your teeth cleaned. No one likes to kiss a dirty mouth." Megan smiled and nodded. "Oh and don't forget to call for a ride if you have too much to drink. You may be a pain in the ass, kid, but you're my pain in the ass, and I'd like to have you around to send me to my early grave." She patted her daughter's cheek and gathered her things. Laughter erupted again and she said, "Go on Honey, You're missing all the fun."

"I love you Mom." Megan said feeling her heart swell in her chest.

I love you too, dear." She turned to leave then stopped, "Oh and Meg, don't leave "your phone off the hook again. I'll try to overlook everything else, but avoiding your mother is a carnal sin. Don't do it again."

Megan smiled, "Ok, Mom. I won't." Her Mother left and Megan got a beer, and went into the living room to join the party feeling like a totally new woman. Free and liberated and fun.

***

Jack sat on the creaky bar stool at Dude's, a low budget country western bar about a mile from Megan's. He'd been there ten minutes and the bartender had been ignoring him sitting there the whole time. Jack rapped on the wooden counter for about the fifth time when the gentleman, finally sauntered over, swiping a bar cloth over the surface as he came.

"Shot of Jack," he growled, "and keep 'em coming." The old man shook his head.

"Not at my bar, son," he said in his raspy nicotine voice.

"Come on, don't start this with me."

"Then leave." Jack hung his head and stared at the scarred surface of the bar as Frank worked his way to the other end of the bar. Jack knew Frank meant well, and maybe that's why he didn't just get up and go to another bar. He didn't really want to throw his sobriety down the drain, and he knew he'd hate himself for it tomorrow. He just didn't want to feel anything but numbness right now, because everything he felt either made him want to break something or cry. From the other end of the bar, Frank was watching Jack. He didn't look up but he could feel the man's stare penetrating him.

Megan wanted his help. She wanted to have fun. She wanted a few lessons in sex. All that was good and fine if she'd have wanted those things with him. But no, he was only supposed to be the gopher. Like the water boy in the football game. Just a mere enabling bystander, that she could toss aside once his job was done. He located the shelves on the wall, holding various bottles of liqueur. On the second shelf, shining like a beacon of light was his long lost friend, its black and white label, calling his name. He stared at the bottle half full of the glowing amber liquid and closed his eyes. He could almost taste the stout, smooth, sensation as the liquid rolled down his throat. He wanted that bottle, but he knew he wasn't going to get it. Not because of Frank, hell if he raised a big enough stink Frank'd probably cave and if he didn't, he could go somewhere else. Hell, there were a dozen convenience stores on his way home that sold it. Nope he wouldn't get it because he didn't want it. Sure, right now it sounded great, but he knew if he had one drink, he'd never stop and his sobriety was way more important. He'd come too far to throw it away. Even if it was for Megan, he'd do just about anything for that woman, except this.

He hung his head back down and inhaled the familiar scents of the bar; cigarette smoke, sweat, beer. He ran his fingers through his brown hair and cocked his head to the side and came face to face with a pair of the finest crafted breasts poking out of a shiny silver halter top. He glanced up at the owner of those breasts and found a pretty blonde headed woman, staring at him, her gleaming white smile dancing in her green eyes.

"Hi handsome, haven't seen you around here. How about you take me for a spin on that dance floor and I'll help you forget about all your problems."

"No thanks," he answered staring straight ahead at the blinking Budweiser sign, its light reflecting off the mirrored background.

She rubbed his forearm, and tried another dazzling smile. "C'mon, you look like you need some cheering up." He said nothing so she placed her hand on his thigh and parted her lips, "Just one dance?" He removed her hand, and frowned. She stiffened on her stool, rolled her eyes, and motioned Frank over. "Gimme another Frank", she said and after Frank sat her drink on the counter, she scooped it up, gave Jack a your-loss look and scampered away. Jack fished his wallet out of his pocket and threw a five on the counter to pay for her drink, just as Frank leaned his elbows on the bar opposite him.

"Must be one hell of a woman; get a man this upset and stupid enough to turn Audrey down. You could have taken her home tonight and had quite a time but I guess you know that already." Jack looked up into the man's tired, brown eyes, and the old man nodded, a knowing look in his eyes. He disappeared behind the bar and returned with a tall glass of Coke plopping it down in front of Jack.

Jack reached out and gently grasped the man's wrinkled hand. With a brief squeeze, he said, "Thanks, Dad."

The old man smiled and said, "Anytime, Son. Been there myself." Jack sipped his coke, and thought about his dad and the years he'd spent in the bottle when his mother had gotten sick. After his mother's death, they'd gone to AA and gotten sober together, been that way ever since. Jack polished off his Coke, shrugged his jacket on, and lifted a hand to his father. Frank nodded and waved at his son, proud that he'd come there, when the urge to drink had been so strong, knowing that his dad would be there to steer him straight.

***

Megan had joined her guests, plopped down her high school yearbooks and filled the gang in on what she asked Jack to do for her.

"Did you tell him why you wanted to find these guys," Stacy asked. Thanks to the Tequila, she was being really cool about the whole thing. Ordinarily she would have lectured Megan on taking a few years and dealing with the divorce, blah blah.

"Sort of," Megan said, "But really he figured it out. Told me I needed a pimp instead of a PI." Mickey raised one perfectly plucked eyebrow.

"Well is he going to do it? Find these guys?" he asked.

"Oh he'll do it," Megan said, "or I'll have his butt thrown in jail for breaking into Ted's studio." She thought about that kiss and what a shame it would be to have those lips locked up. "Plus I kissed him," from around the room, curious looks were being shot at her, "and he seemed to enjoy it."

She told them about old lady Everett and how she kissed Jack to shock the old woman, and how he told her to take a hike and then she filled them in on the conversation with her mom.

135

"Your mom said crap, condoms and ass all in the same night?" Ali said surprised. "Shit, the end of the world must be near."

"I just can't believe she told you to get your teeth cleaned, like she's giving you pointers to help you get some. Almost sounds like she wants you to have sex," Stacy said, having traded in Tequila for iced tea.

"I doubt that, but I guess when I do get some she wants to make sure that I don't spread tarter germs while I'm at it. You know my mom she always tends to the details." Megan smiled and opened her senior year book. "So, let's see who's hot, who's not and whose revenge sex worthy."

"Finally something I am can contribute to." Josie nestled up beside Megan and began scanning the head shots of the class of 1999. "Oh Ben Jacobs remember him? He used to have the mullet haircut, and a never ending collection of Metallica tee shirts. Remember he's the one who lip locked Mrs. Ferguson on the fifty yard line during the state championship."

Mickey nodded his head and said, "Yeah he got suspended but he said it was worth it because he got Mrs. F's phone number."

Ali added, "And he was labeled Best Butt in Parker Point."

"Ok," Megan said scrawling his name down, "he goes on the list. But if he's in jail I'm not doing him. Next." They continued their search, pausing to make fun of those who were style challenged or not genetically gifted. "How bout him?" Megan asked, pointing to a picture of Jody Collins.

Josie held up her pinky and said, "Been there, or at least I think it was there, it was too small for me to tell really." Stacy laughed and agreed with Josie. Guess she'd been there too.

"Find Eric Worley," Ali said, "I dated him my junior year. We didn't go all the way, but if kisses are any indication, then he's a definite ten in the bedroom."

"He's married," Stacy reported and Megan frowned, "his wife goes to my gym. Let's find Aaron Sharp, I know he's single and he was hot stuff back in the day."

They found Aaron smiling seductively, next to a girl with big hair, and a bony kid and a cowboy hat. "See? He was hot back then, still is. Remember he dated Felony Melanie back then- a name she'd been given for her habit of stealing her father's car-along with most of the cheerleading squad. He was the man back then." Megan remembered him. He used to hang around with Ted.

She looked at Josie for her input but Josie flipped her hand in the air and said, "He had a skater cut, I wasn't into skaters back then." Finally somebody Josie hadn't slept with, Megan added him to the list.

"Oh, Oh," Mickey said excitedly, "find Drake Colburn," everyone gave him a look that said 'duh', he shook his head rapidly, "No he's not gay, my sister used to date him. Well not really a date, just one time, but she still talks about that boy and his magical tongue to this day. Just think how much better he'd be now that he's had some time to perfect his skills. Megan scrawled his name down.

"And don't forget Chase Kilborne," Ali said and there was a collective sigh followed by the word "Awww" from everyone in the room. Chase was Mr. Popularity. His nickname was Killer because it was rumored that he'd once killed a girl by giving her a fatal orgasm. He was the one all the girls wanted to play spin the bottle with, just so that they could say they'd kissed him.

"Yeah, Chase is a definite yes!" Ali said, "I think there's like a shrine to him somewhere in the school, like the Vietnam memorial, only it has the names of the women he left heart broken and extremely satisfied." She shivered and smiled at the memory. Mickey pounced like flies on a cow patty.

"You little slut! You and Chase?" Ali's smile widened and she said sweetly, "A lady never tells."

"I'll take that as a yes," Mickey said. "He live up to his reputation?"

"Yep. Twice," Ali said.

Josie said, "Twice? Damn, you must've swung off the chandelier in a whip cream bikini to make it to repeat offender status. He never slept with the same girl twice." Dr. Ross seemed to be fantasizing about Josie and a big tub of whipped cream.

"Ok, so Chase goes to the top of the list," Megan said underlining his name three times. She also made a mental note to check Josie's black book for his rating.

"And don't forget Clint Waters," Stacy said. "He was so fine, but he didn't get around much." She flipped through the W's until she found him. "He was kind of shy, but the girls he did sleep with started a support group when he moved. He's back now, recently divorced and looking like sex on a stick." Everyone surveyed Stacy's face and Megan checked to make sure her tea wasn't spiked. "Hell if I wasn't married to Scott, I'd have him on a plate with a side of mashed potatoes." Megan reminded herself to stash Stacy's keys.

"Ok, Clint Waters, AKA Sex on a Stick, just took the #2 spot," Megan said. "Now what about Derek James? What did everyone used to call him?"

"Motor mouth," Josie supplied, "he used to do this thing with his lips that would leave you so breathless you'd need CPR to revive you." She began demonstrating the task while Mickey tried to mirror her actions and Dr. Ross paid close attention. "But you don't want him on the list," Megan had already written his name down and she paused, "he's let himself go, beer gut, scraggly hair, trailer park. Guess now his nick name is Motor butt, what with all the beer farts and all."

Megan scratched his name off as Ali and Stacy let out "Eeyuww" shrieks and Dr. Ross laughed.

"Oh, let's find Van Castillo. He was major backseat material," Ali said and Josie and Mickey both shouted "Gay," at the same time.

"Hey, what about Travis McPhillips? Remember him, Wranglers, boots, belt buckle and Stetson hat," Josie said, "he used to tilt his cowboy hat, give that devilish grin, and wink at you with a look that said buckle up. We did it on the mechanical bull in his dad's old warehouse and let me tell you, I definitely got more than an 8 second ride. Shit, I can't even watch a rodeo on T.V without my nipples getting hard." She shivered. "If you do him, make sure you have plenty of singles." Megan looked at her confused. "One dollar bills. He invented the Stetson Strip Tease; it's kind of his trademark." Megan quickly added his name, underling it twice and drew dollar signs next to it. A strip tease and a mechanical bull? Looks like Travis just tied Chase for first place.

By around mid-night, the party was winding down. Megan had her list of fantasy sex candidates, Mickey had a full drag makeover, Stacy had an empty bottle of Tequila, Josie had plans to play doctor, and Ali called Bill for phone sex. All in all, it had been an exciting night.

Megan went outside and let the dogs in, cuddling them close before filling their bowls with dog food and went in the living room to check on Spot. His water was still clear, so apparently nobody had emptied their beer in his bowl in an attempt to get him drunk, although there was a beer cap floating like a little fish raft at the top of the bowl. She dumped some food in his bowl, blew him a kiss and went upstairs to brush her teeth. Josie came in the bathroom a moment later.

"Meg, you mind if I split?" Josie was going through Megan's lipsticks, opening each one, extending it all the way out and then closing them. "I think everybody else is staying."

"No, go ahead. You had plans tonight anyway. Have fun."

"He's pretty great huh?" Uh oh, Josie never looked at guys as being great. She looked at them like they were lunch and once the hunger was gone so were they.

"Yeah, he seems sweet." So sweet, he didn't stand a chance next to Josie.

"I really like him."

"Josie, you just said the L word. You like this guy?"

She smiled and looked up thoughtfully, "I did huh? Wow. I must really be drunk, but yeah he's…different from other guys. He's more…"

"Conservative? Law abiding? Disease Free?"

Josie seemed to ponder each attribute and said, "He's just…I don't know, but he's something. Anyways, we're going to go to his place. He has his Doctor's bag there. We're going to play Gynecologist," Josie gave Megan a quick peck on the cheek, threw her bag over her shoulder and took off. Megan turned back to the mirror shaking her head. She gave her teeth one last final scrubbing, in honor of her mother, spit and rinsed and crawled into her bed.

Amy Johnson

Chapter Twelve

Saturday was a beautiful morning. The sky was overcast with a slight breeze, the leaves falling off the trees in slow motion. It was something you'd see on a post card, autumn morning, serene and quiet. Megan was snug in her bed, the covers pulled up to her chin, Bitty and Bug possessively on either side of her. If the damn phone would quit ringing she'd be in heaven. She rolled to glance at the clock on the night stand, the big red letters telling her it was 6:30. What kind of person called at 6:30 on a Saturday? Her mother. Or Ted. She let the machine pick it up; she could call her mother back and Ted...well never mind Ted. If Ted was so lonely, he could call Tiffany Triple D.

The phone rang again. She put her pillow over her head and hummed the Star Spangled Banner. It stopped as the machine got it and then almost instantly it rang again. She crossed her eyes and sang 'I'm a Little Tea Pot'. It continued to ring. She was just about to get up and get the damn thing when Mickey filled her door way carrying the cordless. He fell face down on her bed, his feet hanging off about a foot, and handed her the phone. "It's for you," he mumbled and instantly fell back asleep.

"Who is it?" She asked and got a grunt and a snore for an answer. She tapped his shoulder and asked again, and he batted her hand away and put the pillow over his head. "Mickey?" she whispered, and he keeping the pillow over his head, he reached one hand out and pushed her off the bed. She hit the floor with a thud, and retrieved the phone from where it had fallen under the bed.

"Hello?" She said and was greeted with Jack's sexy voice, perky as hell.

"Rise and shine boss."

141

"Boss? This mean you're going to take the job?" she asked standing up and taking the phone with her to the bathroom. Her black eyes were now purple and she had bed head. Well at least she was still beautiful on the inside right?

"I have a few conditions, but if you agree, yeah I'll take it. What was that noise, you fall out of bed?"

"No, I have a drag queen in my bed."

"You're an interesting woman Megan Malone." She could hear him smiling. No one in their right mind smiled before eight o'clock in the morning.

"So I've heard. What are these conditions?"

"Well first it's going to cost you." She'd figured that much.

"Alright. What else?"

"How many guys we looking for?" He tried to keep his tone light even though he was grinding his teeth so hard he had shards of enamel on his tongue.

"About eight or ten give or take." Unless he found Chase or Sex on A Stick first.

"Well, I work by myself, and this is a big job, so if you want these guys found, before Haley's Comet comes back, I'm going to need some help."

"Okay," Megan said carefully. What was she supposed to do, run an ad in the newspaper? 'Wanted, PI assistant to help find high school sex legends for lonely, bored, inexperienced divorcee.' Yeah, that would set well with her mother. "So?"

"So, the only way I'm going to do this is if you help me." She was already protesting when he said, "You probably want to check these guys out first anyway. Kind of window shop 'em, before you decide to make a purchase. We'll start today. Be ready at 0700 hours." Dammit Jack, it was too early for math.

"I can't I have to uh…" Wash her hair? Scrub the tile grout? Electrocute herself?

"Work. I have to work today. Yep, really busy day at work."

"You work? Doesn't matter, look I'm putting other cases on hold for you," he lied. "Call in sick today, I'll be there at 0700 if you want me to do it. If not that's fine too," He tried to feel guilty about doing this to her, but couldn't.

"You have to do it. If you don't, I'll have you thrown in jail. You burglarized Ted's studio and I witnessed it..."

He'd thought of that already. "No I burglarized his brother's studio, and you can't prove it. First of all I didn't steal anything and secondly I wore gloves. And you were drunk by the way; the police will think you were hallucinating."

"My mother saw you. They'd believe her," Megan argued.

"Maybe, but do you think your mother is going to want all the neighbors to know that she had to rescue her drunk daughter from humping a burglar? That would be front page news in Parker Point. It would be quite scandalous."

He had a point. "Well, still you can't blackmail me into doing this with you," She snapped, furious at herself for not thinking this through more carefully.

"Why not?" She was feisty as hell at 6:30 in the morning, Jack thought. Now if she could just redirect that energy into so something sinful with him... "Isn't that what you're doing to me? Blackmailing me? That's illegal too, Megan."

He had another point. She hadn't thought of that. "So what am I supposed to do?"

"Who's first on your list?" he asked smiling. This was going to be fun.

"Chase Kilborne, Travis McPhillips or Clint Waters,"

Good he knew Chase. "I'll get started running those names. Be ready at 7:00 and bring your list."

"Yeah, sure." Shit. How had this happened? This wasn't the way it was supposed to work. He was supposed to find them and what? Bring them to her? Like a pimp? Maybe his plan was better. Window shopping he'd called it. Then she could approach them where it wasn't so obvious. Maybe keep her reputation from going from zero to slut in six seconds. "But first I have to go rent a truck. Mickey and Dr. Ross are going to load it with Ted's stuff this morning. He's supposed to get out of the hospital today and I want him gone." Maybe, she added silently. Ten years was a long time and the way her life had been the past couple days, her monotone, miserable marriage to a pot smoking, cradle robber wasn't looking as bad as it had yesterday. Of course that was before she'd been kissed so well she forgot her first name and made her list of tutors to help her with the horizontal mambo.

"Okay, I'll take you to get the truck. Be ready in half an hour." Jack said then cut the connection.

***

Jack arrived about forty five minutes later, dressed in black and looking like a rugged GQ reject. His dark Levi, button fly, jeans fit snug and he wore a black tee shirt that fit tight enough, to make Megan squeeze her knees together. His thick, black hair was wet and looked finger combed, and he hadn't shaved since she'd seen him last night, so his jaw and chin were slightly stubbled which gave him a rustic Bruce Willis kind of look. He looked dangerous and sexually lethal and when Megan opened the door and came face to face with those almond shaped brown eyes for a moment she was dizzy. He smiled and she held her breath. Either he hadn't ever looked this...dashing and...lustful or she'd never really looked at him before, because the man standing in front of her was spectacular. Or maybe it was just all the beer from last night. Either way, today was going to be dangerous. And Exciting.

"You ready?" he asked, but Megan hadn't heard him. She'd been staring at his lips from the moment he parted them to speak. He asked again, "Megan, you ready to go?"

"Yep, sure, let me get my purse." She grabbed her purse from the coat rack, and took a moment to catch her breath. Either she was going to have to swear off beer forever, or do something to tame her hormones. When she was getting squishy over a thug, a guy that was probably voted most likely to end up in orange overalls and a jail cell, it was definitely time to make a drastic change.

But the funny thing was Jack didn't seem like a criminal. Aside from the fact that he unlawfully entered Ted's Studio- which for all Megan knew was something PIs did all the time- there was no indication that he was a bum. No tacky, jailhouse tattoos protruding from his shirt sleeves, or house arrest devices on his ankles. Hell for all she knew he could be an upstanding fine citizen that volunteered in nursing homes and charity events. She turned around to see him melting her with those eyes. Maybe she'd been wrong about him. Maybe she'd try to change that.

"Ok, let's go," she whispered, so she wouldn't wake everyone up.

They made it down the driveway and he opened the passenger door on his Jeep for her, and once she was inside, he shut the door. Well if he was a criminal, at least he had good manners. Her mother would like that.

"So how big a truck we need?" he asked, in his usual all business tone.

"Whatever a hundred bucks will get us." He looked at her and grinned. "See we always agreed to only spend a hundred dollars on each other for our anniversaries, and since next week will be our tenth, I figure I'll give him his freedom for a gift. And since I can't put a price on freedom, I'll splurge the hundred on a truck." She laughed and he kept his eyes on the road to avoid looking at her. Lead with your head, not your heart he told himself. She continued, "Anything that doesn't fit in the truck, I'll throw in the yard and have a yard sale. I mean after all, he gets Tiffany Triple D, I might as well make a buck or two."

"Tiffany Triple D?" he asked just so she'd keep talking and he could hear her voice.

"Yeah, that's what I call his infant girlfriend because of her...," she held her hands out cupping an enormous imaginary chest. "Did you know she's only nineteen?"

"Yeah, but she looks older."

"I guess," she said wanting that subject to drop. "So how long have you been a private investigator?"

"About four years. Actually I used to help my grandpa before he died, I kind of inherited his clients and I like the work, so I guess you could say I picked up where he left off."

"He was a PI here?" Megan had obviously lived a sheltered life. She thought PIs were only in big cities or on T.V. screens.

"Yep, for thirty-five years. He mostly worked for lawyers and consulted for the law enforcement agencies, but there's always the occasional cheating spouse or suspicious fathers. What about you? What do you do?"

She blinked; no one knew she worked, "I maintain the household. Ted never let me have a job, so I don't have one yet. I plan to get one though."

"On the phone, you said you had to work today." She had? Shit. She could lie but he's a private investigator, he could find out anyway.

"Oh that," she waved a hand as if to minimize it, "Promise you won't laugh?" He looked at her and smiled, then nodded his head. "I write a sex column." His eyebrows rose and he did he best to hide his

145

smile, "Well it's more of a relationship advice column, but there's a fair amount of smut involved. People send in questions, and then my editor emails the good ones to me. Then I write the column and email it to my editor and that's it. I don't even have to leave the house."

"And Ted doesn't know?"

"Nope, no one knew except for the girls until last night. I told my mom but I doubt she believed me. She thinks I'm taking drugs or going crazy." The crazy part was not far from the truth.

"So let me get this straight," Jack said. "You write a sex column, but you believe you lack experience in the area, and that's why you want to find these guys from high school?" He pulled into the U-Haul parking lot and killed the engine, turning his body sideways to face her. She was fidgeting with her hands again obviously embarrassed or nervous about the conversation.

"I know it sounds silly," she said seeing the irony in it, "but it's easy to fix other people's problems. From the outside looking in it's always easier. Plus, I always consult with the girls first. We meet every Thursday night and discuss the topics." He seemed to be completely focused on her and she liked that. It had been a long time since someone actually listened to her with that type of intensity. Either that or he was mesmerized by the spectrum of colors on her face from her bruises and black eyes. "And the sex questions are easy. Josie knows everything about anything wild or kinky, Mickey consults on the homosexual stuff, Ali's a newlywed, so she pretty much handles the romance junk and Stacy...well she's no help in that department. Mickey says she's Asexual, which to him means boring."

"Sounds very interesting," he said opening his door.

"It is," She said, but not interesting enough.

***

It was almost nine when they got back to the house and everyone was still sleeping except for Ali, who was making omelets and coffee. Josie had called and let them know that she and Dr. Ross were on their way to start loading the truck. Mickey came stumbling down the stairs in a slinky purple night gown that hit him mid-thigh, and purple fuzzy slippers. His hair standing on end, he was missing a fake eyelash, and his cheek was red from sleeping on it. He looked like a used Q-tip, with feet. "Coffee," was all he said before disappearing into the kitchen.

"He's not a morning person," Megan explained to Jack.

"Guess not," Jack said because he didn't know what else to say.

"Let me get Stacy up and we can have coffee and get the boxes outside."

"I'll back the truck up to the house," Jack said flipping the keys in his hand, he turned to leave when a breathless Josie came barreling in the front door with Dr. Ross right behind her. "Sorry we're late," she said, "we had an uh busy morning."

By the smiles on her and the good doctor's faces that was the understatement of the century. "All we need is coffee and we'll be ready." She made for the kitchen and stopped. "Oh Meg, Jon called in today..."

"Jon?" Meg asked and Josie looked at her like she'd just eaten a canary.

She grabbed Dr. Ross's shoulder, "Jon, Dr. Jon Ross," Megan nodded, "So anyway he called the hospital to check on his patients this morning and get this, seems Ted has developed some, uh, digestion problems. Seems he's got a mega case of the shits." Megan's eyes grew wide, her mouth hung open, "Yeah, and that's not the worst part of it, he's got like a major case of the munchies too, eating everything in sight."

"Imagine that," Megan said flatly, guiltily.

"I requested he stay another day so I can keep an eye on things. Plus he still hasn't passed the marble yet." Dr. Ross added.

"Keep him as long as you like," Megan said, "And I mean that literally."

Megan went upstairs to the guest room to wake Stacy, and found her lying sideways on the bed, face up, her eyes open. She looked like hell's cousin.

"Stace, rise and shine. It's too pretty a day to be in bed," Megan said cheerfully.

Stacy threw her the finger. "Go away. I can't move. If I do, my head'll fall off and tequila will spew out."

"Ok Stace, but you'd probably feel better if you had some coffee. And Ali's making omelets. Yum." Megan rubbed her stomach and when Stacy rolled her head to look at her she crossed her eyes and stuck her tongue out. "Plus you're gonna miss all the fun. We're getting rid of Ted today. You don't want to miss that."

"Sure I do, take pictures and I'll look at them once I can see in single vision."

"C'mon Stace, if you stay in bed you just gonna feel like crap all day. And you gotta hear the latest gossip on Ted." She grabbed Stacy's arm and tugged. She didn't budge.

"Did he die?"

"No, but he probably wishes he was dead."

"Then come get me when he dies," Stacy said, putting a pillow over her head.

"Okay, fine. Be a part pooper." Megan snatched the pillow and turned on the ceiling fan. It started spinning and within seconds so did Stacy's stomach. She came out of that bed like it was on fire and made a mad dash to the bathroom. Megan smiled. The ole ceiling fan trick worked every time.

By ten thirty everything was loaded except the boxes that were stacked up neatly near the top of the stairs. Ted's stuff from their bedroom.

"That all that's left?" Dr. Ross asked and Megan nodded.

He and Jack started up the stairs to get them when Josie grabbed Jon's hand and said, "Save your energy."

She then stomped up the stairs, rolled up her sleeves and with one violent push she sent the first box sailing down the stairs. Megan's mouth dropped open and she felt a warm masculine hand lift her chin to close it. Jack. She knew it was Jack, because her insides went squishy. "Josie," she said, but was quieted when two more boxes came flying down.

"No sense wasting your energy baby, you're going to need that later." Baby? Megan couldn't figure out what scared her more. Josie throwing boxes down the stairs or her calling Dr. Ross baby. And that was after she'd spent the night with him. Any other guy, Josie called asshole or jackass. But baby? Dr. Ross must've pulled out all the stops. And then some.

"What the hell is all that noise?" Stacy demanded, after spending the last hour and a half paying homage to the tequila Gods. Once she saw the source of the noise she said, "Oh," and hefted two boxes down the stairs, before going into the guest room and slamming the door shut. So much for reliable, sensible Stacy.

***

148

After the last of Ted's stuff was loaded, Jack slammed the door of the U-Haul down, and dusted his hands.

"Now what?" he asked, "Anything else we need to do." He looked at his watch as if he had a schedule to keep. He sort of did really. He was going to give Megan one week. He'd pretend to look for her list of guys, while he seduced her into wanting him so bad she's sell her soul for just one night. Then at the last moment, when the mood was set, the time was right, and she was eating out of his hands, he'd zip up and walk away, not even giving her a taste. Two could play the game of revenge and she had just met her match. And while the game was in motion he planned to make it hell on her, making her do the most ridiculous things he could think of. Nothing mean or dangerous of course, just a few things to make it fun.

"Now I feed you," Megan said grabbing his hand and hauling him inside the house. He felt his body burn up from her heat, and kicked himself in the chin to compensate. So she scored the first point, she'd caught him off guard his head said. His heart said, yeah right, you're toast.

Megan ordered pizza and the whole gang was crammed in the kitchen chowing down when the backdoor opened and Megan's mom poked her head in carrying a plastic bag from Rite-Aid. She settled her gaze on Jack and said, "Good you're here too." Jack scooted his chair a good foot from Megan's and plastered an innocent look on his face, keeping his eyes on her purse.

"Don't worry I'm not going to hit you," she said, "unless you get her pregnant." Megan let her head fall face first on the table and asked God for a meteorite to come through the roof and land directly on her head leaving nothing but Megan bits for her mother to sweep up. As usual God was on the other line and didn't take her call. Meanwhile, her mother was digging through the plastic bag. Jack just sat there going for innocent, but looking more like sex against the wall.

"Ma'am I have no intentions of…" he began but her mother interrupted him.

"Well I didn't intend to get pregnant either but that didn't stop me. So I…"

Megan's head shot up., What, now she illegitimate? "I thought I was planned," she said.

Her mother said, "You were honey, after you were conceived."

149

Everyone gaped at Mrs. J in shock and Mickey came up and wrapped a long hairy arm around her neck and said, "Mother Teresa, you got knocked up. That's so cool."

She removed his arm. "Shut up Michael," she told him then turned back to Jack. "Now I've taken the liberty of picking up a few things for you. What size are you?" She realized what she'd said then blushed bright red. Jack sat still an incredulous smile on his face, "What I meant to say is," she pulled out several boxes of condoms and squinted to read the sizes on the box. Megan dropped her head with a thud. "Do you take a small, medium, large or Magnum?" Megan banged her head. Had her mother just said Magnum? Holy shit!

"Mom!" she shouted, "You've got the wrong idea, me and Jack are just…"

"Megan, I know when someone's got it, and you've got it bad. Now be quiet while I talk to your boyfriend." Megan contemplated suffocating herself with the plastic bag. "Now young man, I know boys like to boast, but you have to be honest with me here. If you get one that's too small it'll break and Megan's father will have to shoot you if you don't marry her." Jack opened his mouth to protest and she waved him off. "And if you get one that's say a Magnum and it's too big, it'll fall off and you'll be running from that shot gun again. So be honest and if you want me to, I'll bend down so you can whisper it in my ear." She winked. "It'll be just between us." Dr. Ross had noticed that he and Josie were still holding hands and he jerked his away. He did not want to be next.

Jack didn't look like he wanted to be first but he said in as a kind a voice he could muster, "I'm not sure what size I am, I've never measured him, it."

Megan had decided that if her mother asked him to whip it out and determine what size he wore by trying a few on, she'd have to kill her mother. She wouldn't like it, but it would have to be done. Thankfully her mother had other ideas. She opened the box labeled medium and held the condom in the air. "What do you think, too big, too small?" Jack shook his head. She opened another box.

"Mom!" Megan yelled this time getting up from the table and taking all four of the boxes. She threw them all on the counter where Mickey picked up the Magnum and stuffed it under his shirt. "We don't need condoms! We are not having sex!" Yet she added silently, looking at

Jack sitting there radiating passion and head board thumping sex. Maybe she should hang on to those condoms just in case.

"Well not right now you're not. I can see that," her mother said, "But later on might be a different story." Megan gave up.

"Fine, leave the rubbers and I promise to have him try them on if the need arises."

"It better rise." Josie said and Megan threw a spatula at her. "Well I'm just stating the obvious." Jack shifted in his chair, feeling the most uncomfortable he ever could. If Megan's mother was worried about birth control she could relax. After this conversation if the occasion did ever arise he wasn't sure he'd be able to get it up without envisioning her mother in the room with them. Then whatever came up would definitely go back down in a hurry.

"Okay, but make sure you get a tight fit."

The room erupted with laughter and Megan slapped herself in the forehead. "Mother!" she said.

Her mother looked at her clueless. "What?" she asked.

"Nothing Mother," Megan gathered her mom's purse and put it on the woman's shoulder turning her towards the door. "Thanks for stopping by. Sorry you couldn't stay long. See you later."

"Wait, I'm not done," her mother protested.

"Yes you are," Megan nudged her mother with her hip. "Go away, run along."

"Let her finish," Ali said, "If she can top that, I'm calling Fox and getting her her own sitcom. Maybe call Jerry Springer or Howard Stern?"

"Yeah, what else you got, Mrs. J?" Josie asked. "French ticklers? Pecker rings? Battery operated fun guns?" Megan covered her face with her hands. Jack assessed the exits. Megan's mom blushed and looked like she'd been hit with a Cadillac.

"Where's the tequila?" Stacy asked.

"You were saying, Mrs. J?" Mickey said grinning from ear to ear.

"Well, Megan I needed to tell you that I made you an appointment with the OBGYN, you're going to need to get on the pill."

"I can write her a prescription for that." Dr. Ross said and her mother marked that off her list.

"I also made you an appointment to get your teeth cleaned." She explained the logic and suggested Jack do the same. "And I found this Victoria's secret catalog mixed in with your father's 'Field and Streams'.

I highlighted some classy items." Megan took the catalog without looking at it and threw it on the counter. "And I brought this for the dogs," She pulled out a video tape labeled 'Lassie Reruns'.

"You used to love this when you were little. You probably watched it a hundred times. Anyhow, I thought it could keep the pups' busy while you two…uh…you know." She walked over and pinched Jack on the cheek. "You two have fun now."

Jack sat there, a perplexed, incredulous look on his face. He would have said something if he'd known what the hell to say.

"Mom, get out," she tried to put all of her mother's sexual aids in the bag but the bottom fell out and everything hit the floor. "We're not having sex, I'm not buying Victoria's secret, my teeth are clean, I'm on the pill, and the dogs aren't allowed to watch T.V." She took her mother's key ring and fumbled with it. "And I am taking back my house key. You are not allowed to come over here anymore. You have lost you freaking mind and-."

"But the door was wide open, I didn't use my key," her mother said. "She's right Meg, the door was…"

"Mickey! Shut up! Go play with your Magnums!" She finally got her key removed and flung the keys at her mother.

"Go to church mom. Bake something or sanitize something. Just go."

"But I was only trying to be supportive," her mother said, her eyes soft. "You're my only child and I just want you to be happy. If he makes you happy then…"

She looked from Jack to Megan admiringly and said with excitement, "Oh you two are going to make such beautiful babies." Megan opened the door and pushed her mother through it, "You kids have fun now. Stay out of trouble. Josie you hang on to that one, he looks like a good one. Stacy…" Megan slammed the door and bolted both locks. She stood with her back against the door, her arms spread out as if she were holding it up. "Not a word from any of you," she growled and grabbed Jack's arm and drug him out the front door. Jack reluctantly went, laughing the whole way.

"Should we put on Lassie?" Ali hollered just before the door shut so hard it knocked stucco off the outside of the house.

"I'm so sorry Jack. She's nuts, a certifiable loony toon! I wasn't sure until today but there's no question now." Megan laughed out of hysteria, "I think she's smoking pot or abusing Metamucil. I'm going to talk to my father about getting her some help. She…" Jack put his hand on her knee and gave it a light squeeze.

"Meg," he said trying his best not to laugh because she was serious but the whole damn thing was just hilarious. "Meg, it's fine. She just loves you. Maybe this is her way of being helpful." Megan narrowed her eyes and gave him her best What-Are-You-Freaking-Nuts-Monkey-Boy look. "Really, it's no big deal." It was a big deal. Her mother was trying to help her get laid. She almost told Jack how ridiculous that sounded until she realized that was what he was doing. Helping her get laid. She buried her hands in her head and started to cry.

Lead with your head, Jack reminded himself. "Don't cry Meg. It's not that bad."

"It's not that bad? Ha! I'm thirty years old, with two black eyes, a swollen nose, a big, honking, yellow knot on my forehead, and the haircut from hell. As if that isn't enough, I had a transvestite in my bed this morning, my husband is a lying, cheating, cradle robbing, bastard, who at some point slept with my best friend." Jack scooted over to the middle of the seat, and stopped listening to his head and wrapped his arms around her. Big mistake! From inside, four faces were pressed to the window. "My last orgasm-with a partner- was…hell I can't remember when! I frequently knock myself out for entertainment purposes, I have little boobs, big feet, squishy panties, nosy neighbors and demon possessed fish. God hates me!" Jack held her tighter "I have frequent flyer miles at the hospital. I fed my husband marijuana Ex-lax brownies and shoved a marble up his butt." Jack pulled away to look at her and she was serious. And crying. Big, sad, alligator tears that made his heart swell. "My mother is a holy rolling, Catholic Dr. Ruth, complete with condoms and Rosary beads. I write about relationships and sex, both of which I suck at and I hired a Private Investigator to pimp me out." Jack burst out laughing and she pushed him away and swatted his shoulder. "And now you're laughing at me. Could things get any worse?"

At that precise moment Josie rapped on the window and after Jack pushed the button on his side to lower it, she threw the box of Magnum sized condoms in the window. "Here, use two and call me in the morning." She had Dr. Ross's stethoscope around her neck and she added, "Doctor's orders." Megan rolled the window up and thought about throwing herself under the tires of a fast moving semi.

"At least she got the size right," Jack said.

"She always does Magnum."

***

Megan glanced at her list as Jack was driving her home. She had ten names on it to begin with, and they'd already determined that four of them weren't still in Parker Point. That left the following: Chase Kilborne with his fatal orgasms and whipped cream bikinis. Clint Waters, AKA Sex on A Stick. Travis McPhillips, and mechanical bulls, Stetson Strip Teases and one dollar bills. Ben Jacobs, rebel without a cause with the best butt in Parker Point. Drake Colburn and his magic tongue. Aaron Sharp, fetish for felonious women.

What a motley group. If she could take a little from each of them and stuff it all in one man, she'd be set.

They'd spent the rest of the day- after getting rid of Ted- working on finding the 'popular boys' on her list. When she'd asked Jack how long this would take he'd said, "You only get me for a week." Good. A week was all she could stand.

What pissed her off was that she thought she was getting played. When she'd formulated hiring Jack in her mind, she thought she would give him a list of names and he would sit behind a computer and find out if they were married and if they still lived in Parker Point. That should narrow the list down, then all he had to do is find out where they hung out or worked and she would handle the rest.

Like, say Chase was handsome and single and working in an auto body shop. She could just rear end a stop sign and take her car in for an estimate, then to get it fixed, then go back to pick it up, maybe build up some sexual rapport and then bada bing. But no, Jack said it wasn't that easy. They had to locate them, scout them out, and perform surveillance. It sounded absurd, but what did she know, he was the private detective.

But why would he be playing her? The only motive she could come up with was that he was making her participate so she'd realize how stupid the whole thing was and call it off. He'd mentioned Tom several times telling her that the smart thing to do would be to go to dinner with him and see where it went. Then if they ended up under the sheets she could just follow Tom's lead and experiment until she got it right.

She'd said, "In theory that might work, but what if I'm really bad."

"The worst piece of ass I had was still good," he'd told her. "Men don't worry about things like that. There's no such thing as bad sex." Yeah that's because men always get to finish with a touchdown. Their contribution was simple.

She glanced over at Jack to see him still looking dark and handsome and incredibly hot in a criminal kind of way and she couldn't help but wonder what kind of contribution he'd make. Then she quashed that thought because Jack obviously wasn't interested in contributing anything. Aside from this morning when he'd held her during her mini-breakdown, he'd kept his distance from her and made very little conversation. When she'd asked him about his past, he'd dodged every question only revealing that he'd been married once but was now divorced and that he'd served his time in the Navy. She didn't know where he was from, how old he was, if he had children, nothing. Jack was the mystery man and apparently he liked it that way.

He glanced over and caught her staring at him and she snapped her head in the other direction. That's all she needed was to give him ideas. She had enough of those on her own. They pulled up to her driveway and he turned to face her, his eyes dark in the moonlight.

"So," she said, "I'll see you Monday."

"Right. Be ready about eight o'clock. We'll scout out Chase, then later that night we'll go after Bronco Billy."

"Who?" she asked and he said, "Travis. The rodeo strip tease guy."

"Oh." She wanted to invite him in but couldn't come up with a good reason. She sat staring at her house. Her empty, dark house. Her lonely house.

"So, I guess I'll go on in then," she managed, trying to work up the nerve to tell him she was afraid of the boogie man.

"Have a good night," he said and he leaned across to open her door from the inside. His hand brushed against her breast and she felt that hot skin all the way through her tee shirt.

"So," she said, trying to dilute the silence until she could figure out something else to say. She settled for, "It was fun."

"Sure was," he said and Megan thought, Oh hell I'm just going to have to come right out with it and ask him to walk me in. If he'd been a damn gentleman to begin with he would have thought of it first. She stared at her house and made no attempt to move.

155

She was driving Jack crazy. All day he'd done his best to lead with his head and keep his distance. It was hard as hell especially given the fact that she was wearing those snug jeans, that tight red tank top and that ridiculous red ball cap. Top that off with a couple black eyes and she was irresistible. She looked like a blonde raccoon in a Santa Suit and he wanted to tell her he'd been a naughty boy all year so she could spank him.

He'd caught her staring at him several times and when he'd look her way she'd advert her eyes and her cheeks would flush with color. Her mother was right! She had it for him. Problem was she just didn't know it. Yet. Now watching her sit there with that weary look on her face, he saw her take a large sigh, her chest rising and falling with the breath and he found himself staring at her neck, admiring the curve and angles. He wanted to plant tender kisses there and move up to her mouth and take it and…No, that was no good. He knew from experience that one kiss wouldn't be enough and he'd just be torturing himself when she sent him home or started talking about that damn list again.

That list. What the hell had she been thinking when she came up with that brilliant plan.

Come on Jack take the hint. "Well, I'm beat, I guess I'll…"

"Megan," he said and she thought Thank God. "Unless you're going home with me, you need to get out of my truck," he said, because he was thinking with his head, but his heart was saying, walk her in and comfort her and his hormones were saying take her now in the truck.

She was scowling at him. Asshole! Couldn't he figure out that she was scared to enter her big empty house alone? Maybe she could call Mickey and ask him to stay over, he had no life. He'd be happy to do it. But first she had to go into that empty house.

"Ok Jack, see ya," She pushed the door open and took her time getting out of the truck. She shut the door and he waved and she stood there staring at her house. This was ridiculous, she told herself. This was a good neighborhood, she'd lived here ten years and she'd never been scared before. But before she had Ted to protect her. And before Ted was her father. Oh the hell with it. She'd been praying for a disaster for days and nothing had happened. Probably nothing would. Plus if anything did the old hag next door would be all over it. She didn't miss much. She started up the sidewalk, leaves crunching underneath her when she felt something touch her arm and she screamed at the top of her lungs and swung her elbow around catching Jack square in the ribs.

"Ouch," he growled.

"Sorry, I thought you were the boogie man," she said, not sorry because he should have walked her in anyway. "What are you doing out of your truck?"

"Making sure you get inside in one piece. Making sure you don't knock yourself out." He smiled then and she elbowed him in the ribs again.

"You can go now," she said. "I'll be fine." She didn't look fine in the truck staring at that house. She'd looked scared, of what he didn't know.

"I better be getting hazard pay, if you keep hitting me like that," he said rubbing the spot she just hit. Megan ignored him, furious with men in general.

"Keep it up and you'll need Workers Comp," she snapped, not sure why she was so angry with him. He hadn't really done anything. Maybe that was the problem.

She was fumbling with her keys in the dark when he said, "Give them to me," and she kept fumbling trying to guide the key in the hole by feel when he took them out of her hand. "I work well in the dark," he said and Megan decided not to think about just how well. He opened the door and stepped aside for her to go in first. She flipped on the light and he followed her in shutting the door behind him.

Megan immediately went to let the pups in to feed them and out of habit she hit the play message on the answering machine on her way to the backdoor.

She had seven messages: Two from her mother probably calling to confirm Jack's size, a dinner invitation from Tom- which made Jack scowl at the machine-, one from Josie saying she was spending the night with Jon, call if she needed her, one from Ted, call me Meg,-fat chance she said to herself, and the last two were from unknown callers, Malone we want our money and we're getting impatient, and the second was the same person, "You have a pretty little wife, we'd hate to have to hurt her."

What? What money? Pretty little wife? Hurt her?

Megan replayed the messages as Jack loomed over her in the kitchen.

157

Danger? Jack had told her that day he'd come by and ended up punching Tom, that she might be in danger. And now she was here alone. She swallowed, wide eyed and scared and Jack felt like hell. He should have told her. He should have come clean about the trouble Ted had gotten into.

She played the messages again her blood running cold.

"You know anything about that?" Jack asked her and she shook her head nervously.

"What did you mean when you said before that I might be in danger? What's going on?" She was staring at the machine as if it were ticking time bomb.

"Megan, Ted has done some shady dealings with some very bad people. From what I've been able to tell, he owes quite a bit of money to these guys and he wasn't planning on paying."

"What kind of people?" She asked recalling the expensive new watch Ted had come home with and the restoration of the Jaguar in the garage. "The studio is booming," he told her when she asked how they could afford those things. "Business is great." She felt like an idiot now for believing him.

Jack crossed the short distance separating them and although the hunger to touch her was overwhelming, he crossed his arms over his chest to keep from it. "Do you know the name Madrino?" She nodded. She knew of them. They were a couple years ahead of her in high school but everybody knew them. They used to wear these cheap knock offs of brand name Italian suits, pinky rings and slicked back hair dos. They told everyone that they were related to these big mob guys in New York but everyone knew it was a crock. They were a bunch of loser wanna-be's with big talk and nothing to back it up. They claimed to be in this gang called the 'The Junior Mafia' but they looked more like The Mario Brothers. Everyone would laugh at them and they'd threaten to call their infamous Uncle Vito. They got picked on more than the nerds and geeks. Megan laughed remembering the Madrino brothers and Jack frowned.

"I know the name," she said. "We used to laugh at them all the time."

"Well people don't laugh at them anymore. They're dangerous. And stupid." Jack said and Megan's laugh faded.

"So what does that have to do with Ted?"

"The Madrino's run a lot of drugs. Pot and Ecstasy mainly, although they've been known to dabble with cocaine on occasion." Jack's eyes were intense and serious, but Megan still found the whole thing ridiculous. These guys were losers; they probably couldn't deal a deck of cards much less drugs.

"So Ted bought drugs from them? That could be. I found a bag of pot in his darkroom. How much money could he owe them? Isn't pot pretty cheap?" So Ted owed the chumps for a bag of dope. Big whoop. Let them sic Uncle Vito on him for a dime bag. She laughed again as she imagined some fictitious mob guy dressed to the nines with an assault rifle and a couple of muscle guys showing up at her door step looking for Ted and the twenty bucks he owed them for a bag of dope. It sounded like a corny movie, comical and outrageous.

"From what I can tell, he owes them close to a hundred," Jack said, his expression still grim and serious. Megan laughed and pulled her checkbook from her purse.

"A hundred bucks?" They'd threatened to hurt her over a hundred bucks. Sounds like the Madrino boys hadn't changed. Idle, outrageous threats over basically nothing. She wrote the dollar amount on the check. She'd pay them just so they'd quit calling. She signed her name to the check laughing as Jack stared at her with disbelief.

"A hundred bucks," she said again sighing at the absurdity.

"Grand," Jack said. "He owes about a hundred grand." Megan's pen stopped still poised and she met Jack's eyes, her expression a mix of confusion and shock.

"A hundred grand?" she shouted. "Like, as in five zeros?"

"Yep," Jack said relieved she was finally getting it. "And that's not the worst part," he said and Megan closed her checkbook and stepped away from the counter. Uncle Vito suddenly seemed more of a real threat, maybe even with a real Italian suit and real guns.

"So?" she said her voice coming out more cheerful than she expected. "What's the worst part? Uncle Vito gonna come knee cap Ted?" Serves the bastard right she thought. Hell this might not be so bad, they could kick Ted's ass and maybe she could watch. Maybe they could kick the marbles out of him.

"Tiffany," Jack said, and Megan snapped her head up to meet his gaze suddenly interested, "See Tiffany is Sal Madrino's girl. He hired me to keep tabs on her. I didn't know anything about the drugs at the time."

Megan suddenly felt the need to sit down and she gripped the counter for leverage. Jack took her hand and guided her to a chair then took another chair and sat it directly in front of her, so close that their knees were touching.

Ok Ted was in trouble. What did that have to do with her? People don't laugh at them anymore. They're dangerous. And stupid. Shit.

"Go on," she told Jack.

"Apparently, Ted was looking for a way to make some quick cash so he approached the Madrino brothers about doing some business. I'm pretty sure it was Tiffany's idea or she at least introduced them. Anyhow they did a few small deals that Ted made good on, so when he wanted to up the ante they were happy to oblige." Jack was sitting so close to her that he could smell her subtle perfume, and he yearned to reach out and stroke her hand, but he didn't dare. If he let his heart get involved this time he'd probably end up back in the bottle. Or if she let him touch her and taste her and…he'd always wonder if it was because she was scared and vulnerable. He wanted her to want him. Bad.

"So, what happened then? And what does all of this have to do with me?" Megan asked in a detached tone. So Ted was a drug dealer. It didn't surprise her although a week ago it would have. She never would have thought he was a cheater either. Hell, if Jack told her Ted had been the mystery shooter on the grassy knoll, she'd probably believe that too.

"So they made a larger deal, and Ted moved the stuff. I think he stashed the money in his office, although I'm not sure and then it vanished. When the Madrino brothers came asking for their money, Ted gave them excuse after excuse. Guess they're tired of excuses." Jack noticed the change of color in her face but couldn't decipher her expression. To his surprise she cracked up with laughter. He frowned.

"What?" he asked and she struggled to speak between laughs.

"Nothing, it's just that you look so serious and these guys…well they're a joke. You should have seen them when they were kids," she said and he thought I did, I grew up about four blocks from them. "I mean they were losers with a capital L. Always talking about their mob connections and crazy uncles. It was all such B.S. Hell, they graduated way before me and we were still laughing at them after they were gone. These guys are harmless. All talk."

Had she never read a newspaper? "Megan, Sal served six years for rape and he was guilty of a lot more." Her smile disappeared. "And

Angelo has been in out of jail for everything from possession to attempted murder, not to mention his acquittal on a murder charge." Her body stiffened and he saw the color of her eyes change from a clear, playful blue to dark, blue fear. He put his hands on her knees as a steadying comfort.

"But this has nothing to do with me. Why would they hurt me?" She cried her voice small, her mind still trying to grip the reality.

"To get to Ted. To get their money back," Jack said, wanting to take her in his arms.

"So we call the cops," she said, "and then I'm going to see Ted. And he better be glad he's in the damn hospital because when I get through with him, he's going to have a lot more than a marble up his butt. I'm gonna kill him. Save the Madrino brothers the trouble."

"Megan," Jack began but stopped when a car pulled into to the driveway, the lights casting a glow on the kitchen wall. Jack moved to the window and saw a Taxi sitting in the drive with an elderly woman getting out of the back passenger side door. Megan standing behind Jack peered out and went to the back door.

"That's my granny. What on earth is she doing here?" Megan said noticing the small suitcase the petite woman was carrying. "Granny?" She called out, holding the door open as the little old lady climbed the two steps and walked in.

"Where's the can? It's been a long ride. I gotta pee worse than a dog in heat gotta sniff butts." Megan pointed her to the downstairs bathroom even though the plumbing often got clogged, doubting her grandmother could make it up the stairs to the other bathroom. "You know when you get old, nothing works right. My bladder's shrunk to about the size of a jelly bean. I'm thinking bout getting me some of those Depends diapers. I got a cute little meals on wheels boy who I wouldn't mind changing my diaper." Megan blushed bright red and Jack bit back a laugh. "I'm always telling him older women make better lovers. Why just the other day I was telling him about how me and your grandfather used to…" Her voice trailed off as she shut the door to the bathroom and Megan covered her forehead with her hand and picked up the phone to call her mother and when no one answered she cradled the phone and sat down. Grandma Lou came out of the bathroom and undressed Jack with her eyes.

"Why, aren't you a cutie patootie," she said as flirtatiously as a seventy five year old woman dressed in polyester and smelling like moth balls could. She pinched his cheek and smiled. "Much handsomer than that stick in the mud Ted. Now move your cute little tush and get my bags from the cab." Jack looked at Megan and caught the dreadful expression on her face.

"Yes ma'am," he said and opened the door when Megan's hand caught his arm and stopped him.

"What bags Granny?"

"Oh, forgot to tell you. I'm moving in," then to Jack, "Hurry up sweet thang, the meters running." Megan felt like throwing up. Grandma Lou was a handful and Megan was already up to her ears in shit. She didn't need this. Jack opened the door wider and Megan's grasp on his arm tightened.

"What do you mean you're moving in? What happened this time?" Megan inquired dreading the answer. Granny was hell on wheels and apparently another nursing home had kicked her out.

"I got kicked out of Peaceful Meadows. Never liked the damn place anyway. Bunch of prudes. I keep telling them blondes have more fun but they're just a bunch of party poopers."

"Granny you're not blonde." Her grandmother removed her scarf from her head and Megan took a step back. Not only was her grandmother a platinum blonde, but her hair was cut in a punk rocker spike with streaks of hot pink glittering brightly.

"Granny!" Megan said but her grandmother was busy flirting with Jack, who was complimenting her on her hair.

"Why thank you, hot stuff," Granny said. "Now get my bags and pay the cabbie will you?" Megan released Jack's hand and he went out the door. "And be careful with that little bag. It has my crystal ball and medicine in it." She winked at Megan and Megan forced a small smile. Jack returned carrying three bags a huge grin on his face. Megan wanted to slap him. Or jump him. Either would be satisfying about now.

"OK Granny, why did you get kicked out this time?" Granny ignored Megan and sat at the table, ordering Jack to do the same.

He sat down and she grabbed his hand turning it palm up. "OK young man let's see what you've got." Jack was patient giving that dangerous grin while Megan explained to Jack that her grandmother thought she was a palm reader. Granny narrowed her stern eyes at Megan and pursed her lips.

"I am a palm reader, been doing it sixty years. Never been wrong either." She went back to Jack's calloused palm leaving Megan pacing the floor.

"Granny, why did you get kicked out?" Megan said and her grandmother raised a hand with neon green fingernails to quiet her. Megan gave up for the moment and fed the dogs. When there was a fine male specimen in the room or a palm to be read, Granny had a one track mind.

"I see darkness here," Granny indicated running a long finger across Jack's hand. "Lot's of secrets and pain." She looked at Jack and he nodded still smiling that devilish grin.

"Granny," Megan said and her grandmother once again raised her hand and ignored her. "But here, oh my son, I see love." Jack glanced at Megan with a heat in his eyes that made Megan's stomach flip. She involuntarily held his gaze, feeling the electricity from it penetrate her. "And babies, lots of brown eyed babies." Megan turned from Jack's intoxicating gaze and went to feed Spot.

When she returned to the kitchen her grandmother was setting up her crystal ball as Jack sat watching the old woman with a humorous expression.

"Granny," Megan said, moving the crystal ball from her grandmother's reach. "Tell me why you got kicked out of the retirement home or I'm calling Mom." Her grandmother slapped her hand and chuckled, a rebellious look in her eye.

"Go ahead. She won't answer the phone."

"What?" Megan asked hoping she hadn't heard her grandmother correctly.

"That sourpuss Lydia, from the home already called her. She told her to send me here." She paused and surveyed the kitchen. "Got anything to feed an old woman?" So her mother was home and not taking her calls? Oh hell!

"Ok for the last time Granny, what did you do?" Megan asked through narrowed eyes as Jack settled in comfortably to watch, his brown eyes dancing, his mouth tipped up into a sultry smile.

"I was just having a little fun."

"Granny!" Megan planted her hands on her hips.

"It was nothing really."

"Granny!" Megan leaned forward to challenge her grandmother's menacing grin.

"Oh alright, it all started because one of those hateful Bingo broads called us the blue haired club during Bingo and it really yanked our chains."

"So?" Megan said raising an eyebrow.

"So, on Thursday when sweet cheeks came to visit I had him do our hair." She ran her finger through it and grinned. "Then he did our nails and toenails."

"Sweet cheeks?" Jack asked amused.

"Mickey," Megan informed him. "Granny calls him sweet cheeks because he used to have chubby cheeks and she used to squeeze them."

"Not true Megan," Granny argued. "I call him that because he has a nice set of buns. Too bad he's gay. I'd like to show him a trick or two. Anyway, he did our hair and told us we looked bitchin' so we told the Bingo hag our table was to be referred to from now on as the Bodacious Bithcin' Babes."

She flashed Jack a big smile and he said, "You Go Granny."

Megan shot him a look that could've singed his eyebrows. "Don't encourage her."

"So," Granny continued, "they kicked us out of the bingo Hall. Said we can't use that kind of language. The prudes!"

"Uh huh," Megan said reminding herself to bitch slap Mickey.

"And you know how I like to gamble."

"Uh huh," Megan said.

"So we formed our own club." She gave a dramatic pause. "We went to Mildred's room and planned us a poker night."

"So they kicked you out for playing poker?" Jack asked, "That's kind of overkill."

"Just wait, I'm sure it gets better," Megan said knowing that mischievous tone in her grandmother's voice. She prompted Granny, "So?"

"So we had Ester's grandson smuggle us in some booze and smokes. Can you believe that idiot brought us Mad Dog 20 20 and generic smokes?" Megan grimaced. Well at least Granny wasn't smoking dope. Yet. "And we spread the word about the big game." Megan rolled

164

her eyes and sat down as her grandmother continued, "So I stood at door to collect the cover charge and frisk people as they came in and…"

"Frisk them for what?" Megan asked not wanting to know the answer.

"Nothing really I just always wanted to do that. You know like in the cop shows. Plus I'm an old woman, frisking old men was the highlight of my day. You know, see who can still get it up?" Jack laughed while Megan was mortified. Her grandmother got kicked out of a nursing home for playing with old men and she had orgasms on massage tables. Her mother was going to have a stroke.

"Ok, so you sexually harassed a few old men. That's not so bad. I'll take you back and you can say sorry and you'll be back in your room by bedtime."

"It gets better," Granny said. "Or worse if you're poor Frankie."

Great! "Go on," Megan mumbled.

"So we're playing poker and after me and Mildred cleaned Sam and Harry out of their Social Security checks we got bored so we decided to make it interesting."

"Oh hell," Megan growled, "I hate interesting." Her grandmother smiled and Megan knew from the twinkle in her eyes that whatever was coming next was bad.

"So we decided up the stakes and play strip poker. We was doing pretty good too till Olivia dropped her top and Frankie had a heart attack."

Megan dropped her head on the table and waved her hand in the air for Granny to go on. It couldn't get much worse could it? It's not like the last time Granny got kicked out for showing up to the line dancing class wearing only a cowboy hat, an arm sling and smile.

"So," Granny continued, "We buzzed Pork Chop the four hundred pound nurse to roll Frankie out so someone else could take his spot at the table. Next thing I know Herb and Otis are fighting over Frankie's chips and a fight breaks out."

"Of course," Megan mumbled.

"Then Frankie starts yelling at them to leave his chips alone and I look around for Mildred and find her dancing topless on her hospital bed throwing back the last of her forty ounce." Jack winced at the mental picture Granny was providing. "Once Frankie got an eyeful of Mildred's quarter pounders he clutched his heart again and keeled over."

"Wait a minute, quarter pounders?" Megan asked and Granny and Jack both laughed.

"Her boobies Megan. Get with the program," Granny said and all Megan could do was picture Mildred Myers- her first grade teacher- flashing her hamburger style boobs at her and asking her if she'd like mayonnaise or mustard. "Should I go on?" Granny asked.

"I'm dying to hear it," Jack said and Megan thought about drop kicking him out of his chair just because he was there and she was frustrated and he was enjoying himself way too much.

"So when the dweeb nurse gets there, Frank is sprawled out face down in the floor, Herb and Otis are throwing poker chips at each other fighting over Frankie's winnings, and Mildred is giving Benny a lap dance." Megan pounded her head again, this time hard, and thought about standing under a tree in a lightning storm. "Old Mildred," Granny continued with a wistful look, "she's a hot little thing. Shoot when they dragged her off that bed she had dollar bills sticking out of her panty hose. Think she made about twenty bucks, but won't know for sure till they get all the poker chips out of her stockings." Granny pulled Megan's head up by her hair and said, "You listening to me?" Megan nodded and Granny went on. "Good thing Nazi Nurse grabbed her by the waist and drug her down, because she was just about to kick old Crazy Howie's shriveled up butt cause he put a five spot in her waist band and was digging in her panty hose to make change." Granny smiled and Jack broke out in a roar of laughter. "Men just don't have respect for strippers no more."

"It's a damn shame what the world's coming to," Jack agreed.

"So in one night, Granny," Megan began trying to process everything, "you turned a Christian Nursing Home into a scene from a sleazy Vegas Casino complete with a dead guy and eighty year old strippers."

"Mildred's only seventy-four, Megan, and Frankie was going to die anyway. Might as well croak staring at a nice pair of jugs…"

"OK Granny, that's it. You can't stay here. My life is a mess and you're crazy. I'm going over to Mom's and I'll kick the door down if I have to. Be ready to go. Mom will be here to pick you up in a few minutes."

"I guess you're not having sex yet," Granny said winking at Jack. "Maybe you should grab him and go upstairs. Loosen you up a little.

You're just like you're mother, uptight and repressed." Megan let out a screech and threw her hands in the air.

"I have plenty of sex Granny and..."

"Not according to your mother, she says you been kissing this good looking guy though." She turned back to Jack, "That you?" He nodded and she said, "You sure look like fun. If Megan don't jump you soon, give Granny a call. I'll tuck you in bed and show you how we used to do it in the forties."

"I'll keep that in mind, cutie," Jack said and Megan grabbed him by the arm and drug him outside.

"Jack, keep an eye on her. I'm going to run to my Mom's and make her come get her." Jack grinned and Megan slapped his shoulder. "This is not funny."

"Oh I don't know, seems pretty damn funny to me. Now I know where you get all your spunk from." Jack noticed that Megan was still grasping his arm and he wrapped his other arm around her waist. Her body stilled and for a moment she relaxed into him.

"Don't let her out of your sight," Megan warned.

"We'll be fine," Jack said brushing his lips against her temple.

"And don't let her by the phone. The last nursing home she was in kicked her out for prank calling the mayor." Megan felt Jack laugh against her forehead and she didn't want to move. He was a lot easier to resist when he was pond scum.

"Don't worry, I'll keep her busy," Jack said trailing his lips down her cheek.

"Don't let her frisk you," Megan said enjoying his sensual teasing kisses.

"You jealous?" Megan broke the embrace eyes wide.

"No, of course not."

"Just checking," Jack answered missing her heat immensely. "Go on, if we get bored we'll play strip dominos or Spin the Bottle." Megan smiled and Jack couldn't resist her anymore. To hell with his head, his heart was right. He never had a chance. He was a goner. Big time. And he didn't care.

"OK, I'll be back. Fifteen minutes tops."

"Be careful," Jack said as she turned to go. Then, abruptly, he grabbed her arm and she spun back around "One more thing, Megan."

"What?" she said and before she realized what was going on Jack had her in a tight embrace, his hands holding her tightly at the hips, his warmth and touch leaving her almost breathless.

"This," he whispered before lowering his head and claiming her mouth with his. His touch electrified her and she parted her lips and he captured her tongue with a fierceness that buckled her knees. She pulled back a little but he drew her closer, hungrily commandeering her mouth until she gave up and deepened the kiss, mingling her tongue with his. She heard his approval by the low groan that came from his throat and when she wrapped her arms around him letting them caress his muscular back she felt him jump, releasing a short burst of air and she smiled inside. She'd done that to him and it felt awesome. His hand lingered to her round butt and she too released a breath she realized she'd been holding. His now obvious erection brushed her stomach startling her and she was thankful the kiss was interrupted by her grandmother's voice stating that she needed her medicine.

Jack broke the sultry kiss and rested his head on her forehead gazing into her eyes with a hungry, unquenchable lust.

"I've waited fifteen years to do that," he said in a low satisfied voice and if Granny hadn't been shouting at them Megan might have questioned the meaning of those words. Megan stepped back and touched her swollen kiss-stung lips.

"The shot glasses are over the refrigerator," she told Jack as she started down the driveway.

"Shot glasses?" He asked, wanting her back in his arms immediately.

"Yeah," Megan said, "Her medicine is moonshine. It's probably in her red bag. I'll be right back. Have fun." Mrs. Everett's porch light shut off and Megan grinned. Let the old bat get her kicks.

Jack watched her depart admiring the view of her firm little bottom, with just enough jiggle to make any man's hormones sizzle and when she slowly turned her head back and gave him that smile he thought he'd died and gone to heaven.

Megan enjoyed the two block jog to her mother's. She needed it to cool her off from Jack's sizzling heat and get her brain back to the problem at hand. Granny.

Her mother would know what to do about Granny and then Megan could figure out what to do with Jack. And how many times. In how many positions.

And where the hell had that come from? Jack was a rebel, a PI who bordered criminal level. He probably had a rap sheet, a couple of illegitimate children, bad credit and trailer house.

But he was gorgeous and funny and the walking picture of up against the wall, forbidden, heart stopping sex. Hell the passion in that kiss alone had surpassed anything she'd felt in the last half of her marriage. And despite her logical, analytical mind that was telling her he was bad news, she wanted more of him. If that one, short kiss was any indication of what Jack Westin could do to a woman then…

Heart racing wildly and hormones overflowing she opened the back door of her parents' house and let the screen slam shut. She saw the glow of the T.V. from the living room, Jeopardy on the screen, her dad in his chair.

"Hi Daddy," she called out and got a quick wave which was all anyone ever got from him when Jeopardy was on. She hollered for her mother and found her folding clothes in the bedroom. She looked at Megan with a knowing smile and a guilty twinkle in her eye. Megan planted her hands on her hips and narrowed her eyes.

"Mom, you have to go get her,"

"No." Her mother shook out a sheet and said, "Grab an end, dear."

"What do you mean no?" Megan grabbed the end of the sheet and helped her fold it. "She's driving me crazy."

"Short trip," her mother muttered and Megan grunted and took the sheet to finish folding it.

"Go get her. She's already read Jack's palm and she coming on to him Mom. Like sexually." She shuddered. "It's… gross."

Her mother was smiling. "Yeah, she does that." She tossed another sheet at Megan. Raising her eyebrows she said, "You jealous?"

Megan bit back a slew of curses that would have made a sailor blush. "Jealous? Are you kidding me? Of course I'm not jealous. Jeez Mom!"

"Then what's the problem?"

"The problem? Gee let's see, maybe the fact that she's like eighty." Megan finished folding the sheet and handed it to her mother not amused with the humorous look on her mother's face. "Grandmas aren't

169

supposed to have sex. I mean they shouldn't even think about it. But no, my Granny is about to jump my..." Megan stopped. Her what? What exactly was Jack? He wasn't her boyfriend that was for damn sure. Of course after that kiss...

"Boyfriend? Lover?" Her mother asked in a teasing tone.

"No!" But even Megan wasn't convinced considering she'd answered the question too quickly with too much of a defensive tone. "Jack is strictly a friend." Her mother laughed and raised her brows in a mocking gesture. "I swear Mom, he's just my friend, but I'm not here to talk about Jack. Granny is the problem. She's got to go. You have to go get her."

"No. You're her favorite grandchild. It would make her happy to spend time with you. Plus with Ted gone you might get lonely."

I'd rather be lonely with Jack. "Mom, I'm her only grandchild and she hates me. Just ask her. By now she's probably on the phone with that Nazi Nurse begging to go back to the home."

"Or sitting in your boyfriends lap." Megan's eyes widened with shock. Her mother was definitely losing it. "You'd better run home. Granny moves fast. She might be ruining him for all other women as we speak." The mental picture Megan got in her head was enough to kill every glorious raging hormone from Jack's kiss. Suddenly her mother's motive was clear. Damn devious woman.

"Mother! You're just doing this to punish me."

"Spending time with your grandmother is punishment?" All teasing and humor had left her voice and she was frowning at Megan obviously disappointed.

"Well no but...you're just using this situation to your advantage." Megan's mother put her hands on her hips and glared at her daughter. "You're sticking me with her so she can baby-sit and tell you everything I do. You just don't want me to have sex or anything and you know I can't with her around."

Her mother looked at her incredulous. "So I send a sex crazed senior citizen, who after a couple shots of moonshine will be oblivious to the world to keep an eye on you. Get real Megan, you're grandmother probably gets more than you do."

"EEYEEW!" Megan shrieked and her father yelled, "Keep it down, it's Double Jeopardy."

170

"Ok, so maybe she's not there to chaperone me, but she can't stay. It's not safe. I'm in grave danger." Her mother rolled her eyes. "I'm serious mom, people are after me. They could show up anytime."

"I believe they're already there. Mrs. Everett called before you got here and she said you were kissing your friend on the back porch."

"Not Jack! Drug dealers. They could be coming to kill me. I'd hate for Granny to be shot in the cross fire." Her mother threw her another sheet. God, how many sheets could one person have?

"Drug dealers," her mother said, "You should have just stuck to the sex story. At least that I could believe."

Sex with Jack. Megan shivered and felt her hormones kick back up. "I'm serious Mom. Ted owes the Madrino brother's a hundred thousand dollars and they said if he doesn't pay they'll hurt me. They could hurt Granny. You have to go get her."

Her mother was laughing so hard she had to sit down. "The Madrino brothers? I'm supposed to believe that?" Megan banged her head on the door frame. "Those yahoos can't spell gun much less shoot one. Don't worry Meg, Granny can take them both. She'll protect you. Go home to Granny, Megan. Better hurry before she convinces Jack to play Twister in the buff."

"Mother!" Megan yelled.

Her father yelled "Put a sock in it, will you?" Megan slammed the door and turned back to her mother who was shaking her head and snickering.

"Go home, Meg. You and Granny have a lot in common; boys, booze, and bad behavior. Monday morning I'll collect her things from the nursing home and see if I can find another one that'll take her but for now she's all yours. Have fun." Megan opened her mouth to protest but her mother opened the door and pushed past her laughing. Megan gave up and went to plead with her father. She was Daddy's princess. He never told her no. Course Jeopardy was on so it'd be a miracle if he even paid attention to her.

"Daddy, you have to help me," she said plunking down on the couch.

"What is the Louisiana Purchase?" her father said eyes glued to the tube.

"You have to tell mom to go get Granny. She's driving me crazy."

"Who is Aaron Burr," her father said to the T.V. then to Megan he said, "No."

No? Daddy never said, No. Was everyone nuts today or just Megan. "Dad, are you even listening to me? I have real problems. I need help."

"What is General Electric," her father said then to Megan, "That's nice, dear."

Ok, to hell with niceties. "Daddy I just came by to tell you that I am really a nude dancer and my stage name is Nikki Nipples. I'm madly in love with a circus midget and we plan on going on the road and making and marketing sex tapes for the vertically challenged all the while setting up my portable pole and G-string in nursing homes across the country in hopes of giving old men heart attacks to save the country the growing expense of Medicare to take care of the old farts." Jeopardy went to commercial and her father muted the sound. He replaced the remote control carefully and looked at Megan with that stern Dad look.

"Final Jeopardy starts in less than two minutes Ms. Nipples. Make it quick."

Megan smiled. He'd heard every word she said. "Tell mom to go get Granny."

"No."

"Why not?" Megan asked frustrated, throwing her hands in the air.

"Because she doesn't want to. Plus she's happy. She's been whistling all day."

Mom get lucky? "I noticed that? Why is she so happy and...relaxed." Final Jeopardy came back on and after the question was read, her father answered.

"What is Prozac?" Megan read the question and said, "No Daddy the answer is 'Who is Olivia Newton John'."

"Zoloft," he repeated, "That's why you're mother is so happy. She saw the crazy doctor today. Leave her alone."

"Mom takes Zoloft?" She frowned. She'd actually driven her mother crazy. Damn. "When did this happen?"

"Dumb Ass," her father said to the bucktoothed dweeb who'd missed the Final Jeopardy question. He changed the channel and turned to Megan, "Mom says your divorcing Ted and kissing some tough guy. Mrs. Everett has us on speed dial. Close your curtains, use that duct tape you've got to tape your Granny's mouth shut, hit her moonshine bottle and you and your tough guy have a little fun. Not too much fun though.

I'd hate to have to kill him while there's a game on." He frowned at the T.V. and checked his watch. "Monday we'll take care of Granny, and you can have your house back to yourself. Go home honey, the ball game is coming on." And with one click of the remote, the T.V. was blaring and her father was back in his ball game trance. Megan stood and brushed the knees of her pants.

"Daddy," she tried on last time giving him her best pitiful puppy dog look.

"No," he growled, then thought to add, "Be careful going home. Don't knock yourself out." Megan grimaced, gave her mother one last pleading look and walked home, thoughts of Granny, Jack, and moonshine dancing in her mind.

Amy Johnson

Chapter Thirteen

Back at Megan's things appeared to be quiet. Too quiet. The dogs weren't outside which either meant Jack or Granny had let them in, they'd been kidnapped by the Madrino brothers or they'd ran away. She entered her yard through the back gate and automatically Mrs. Everett's porch light went on. The old bat was always on alert, neighborhood watch would be proud. Megan gave the old woman her best scowl and bite me gesture and stood ear pressed against the backdoor before going in. She heard Granny hooting and hollering and figured things were probably normal or about as normal as it gets when you are housing a geriatric delinquent under your roof. While she was listening at the door a pair of headlights clicked on and a car screeched from the curb about a block from Mrs. Everett's house. *Damn teenagers*, Megan thought.

Since it looked like rain and Megan was not fond of sleeping outside in the cold she slowly opened the door. The dogs just about knocked her over to get back outside and once the dust settled Megan saw Granny and Jack crouched against the wall, a stack of cash in a pile, and Granny rolling dice. Jack saw Megan, and rushed to her side.

"Glad you're back, I'm down eighty bucks," he said breathlessly.

"Well you've still got your shirt. That's more than I expected," she said kicking herself for being disappointed about the status of his shirt.

"That woman is evil," he said.

Granny said, "Damn right I am. Evil and eighty bucks richer."

"She casts spells you know," Megan said nonchalantly. "She's been threatening to use her powers to make my dad impotent for years. 'Course if she really wanted to piss him off, cursing the T.V. would be the way to go."

175

Jack laughed and Granny yelled out, "Get your sweet little butt over here and roll the damn dice. I ain't done with you yet." Jack pulled the lining out of his pockets to indicate he was out of cash. Granny smiled and eyed him from head to toe. "Guess will just have to make this interesting." Jack froze.

Oh, boy. "I hate interesting," Jack said.

Megan said, "Hey, that's my line."

"C'mon pretty boy, Granny needs a little action," Granny said and Jack threw Megan a look that unmistakably said 'help'.

"Granny, take a couple shots of shine and go to bed."

"Already had my moon medicine," Granny said slipping Megan a side glance. "So you talked to your mother?"

"Yep," Megan answered.

"You stuck with me?"

"Yep."

Granny nodded and threw the dice one last time.

"Well don't worry Meg; I'll be on my best behavior." Her best was about equivalent to three time convicted felons. "You and Jack go have some fun," she smiled a witchy smile at Jack, "I'll just hit the crapper and go on to bed."

Megan was still standing in the kitchen and she became vaguely aware of Jack's hand caressing her back, starting at the nape of her neck and lingering down to her waist. It felt…comfortable and relaxing. Her stomach did that flip flop thing again and she found herself staring into Jack's caramel brown eyes. Their gazes locked for a long silent moment before Megan surprised them both by standing tip toed and brushing her lips against his in a gentle, inviting kiss. His hand stopped moving and he sucked in a shallow breath.

"Get a room," Granny shouted, then standing up and collecting her winnings she said, "I can take a hint. I'm off to bed." She winked at Megan then said, "Don't worry, I won't tell your mother. I'll wear ear plugs and keep my door shut."

Jack looked at Megan waiting for her to set Granny straight and when she didn't, he suddenly felt very uncomfortable. It looked like someone had pitched a tent in his Levis and after fifteen years of lusting after this woman, one touch would probably do him in meaning her eighty year old grandmother probably had more stamina in the sack right now than he did.

"Where are the dogs' leashes?" he suddenly asked.

"In the pantry," Megan answered, "Why?" Jack dropped his gaze to the arousal in his pants and Megan gulped. Oh Damn. His smile was liquid fire.

"I need to take a walk," he explained. Megan nodded. "I figured I'd take the dogs for a quick, brisk walk in the cold rain.

"I'll get those leashes," she said grabbing his shirt at his abdomen and gently tugging it out of his pants. It didn't help. He had an erection about the size of the Sears Tower that no amount of cotton fabric could hide. Granny's lips curved in a knowing smile and she left the kitchen snickering. Megan found the leashes and handed them to Jack then bent down to grab Granny's suitcases.

"I'll get those," Jack said as he threw the leashes over his shoulder and picked up the suitcases then followed Megan out of the kitchen to get Granny settled in. They'd just crossed the front window in the living room when the sound of glass shattering, followed by screeching tires and a loud thunk stopped them dead in their tracks. Jack dove for Megan.

Granny came running out of the bathroom, her neon pink hot pants at her ankles. The Sears Tower disappeared. "What the hell was that?" Granny asked tugging her pants up. Jack had thrown Megan to the ground and protectively plastered himself to her, balancing his weight on his elbows. "Oh," Granny said when she took site of Jack and Megan. "Don't worry, I didn't see a thing. Well except for that rocket in his pocket earlier." Jack stood and extended a hand to Megan. Granny glanced at his crotch and grabbed a long candle from the mantle. Using the candle as a mock microphone she said in a mechanical voice, "Houston we have a problem. Our pocket launcher has refused to launch. All systems failed. Requesting back up…and Viagra. I repeat…"

"It's a brick," Jack said ignoring Granny's analysis of his lost arousal. Crossing the room in two quick strides he retrieved the brick which had a yellow piece of paper rubber banded around it and frowned. Megan came to stand beside him and cocked her head to read the print. Granny was hitting her moonshine, excitement dancing in her eyes.

"It's from the Madrino's," Jack said. "Guess they saw the U-Haul parked out front and thought Ted was skipping town without settling their debt."

"What debt?" Granny asked snatching the note from Jack. She squinted her eyes and angled the paper where she could read it. *Running is not wise Malone. We will find you.* "Who's running? Who's going to find him?"

"Nothing Granny," Megan said enjoying the warmth from Jacks arm around her shoulder. Funny how casual and comfortable his touch had become. "Just some drug dealers that Ted owes a hundred thousand dollars to." Granny's eyes grew wide and her smile was pure mischief. Megan rolled her eyes and leaned her head on Jacks broad shoulder. "Granny, it's nothing to get excited about. In fact I'm calling mom to come get you right now."

"Uh huh, I'm staying. This is where the action's at." She shifted her false teeth around as she often did when in deep thought. "Think we'll get a drive by. Or maybe one of them grenade things thrown in the window. Maybe we should stock up on some ammo. You know so we can return fire. I've always wanted to pump someone full of lead." Megan went to get the phone while her grandmother rattled on. Granny really had to go now before she got online and ordered up a Sherman tank and scud missiles. Jack took the phone from Megan and stepped in the kitchen to call the police.

"Turn the lights off and stay away from the windows," he told Megan before shutting the door. Megan sat with her back against the wall holding the brick in one hand and the note in the other. Granny was beside her still mumbling on about assault weapons and bombs and Megan thought about clocking Granny with the brick to shut her up. 'Course that would only piss her off and she'd probably cast an anti-orgasm spell on her. A couple days ago Megan would have welcomed that, but that was before she met Jack.

Much later that night, after talking to the police and finally getting Granny settled down, Megan put on boxer shorts, and a tank top and was brushing her teeth before calling it a night. Her mother still wasn't answering the phone and Granny had refused get in Megan's car to be transported there. She was now asleep snoring like a drunken lumberjack in the spare room.

Jack had taken on a bodyguard-security role and insisted on covering the broken window and changing the locks on the doors. Megan argued about the locks even when Jack pointed out that Ted had already lost two keys to his studio-the one he stole and the one Megan stole- so there was no telling if he'd lost any house keys. What finally sold her on the argument was when he pointed out that her mother wouldn't be able to drop in unexpectedly and since she was still steamed at her mom for not answering the damn phone, she finally agreed.

He'd refused to leave the house to get the supplies instead he called his buddy Steve to make a Wal-Mart run. Together he and Steve covered the broken window with plywood and changed the locks as well as installed a motion light in the driveway. Steve had been happy to do it and took only a beer for payment, refusing Megan's money.

Jack had also declined her offer to pay for supplies and labor saying he was happy to do it. Megan melted. It wasn't exactly what he said that made her melt it was how he said it; the lustful concern in his eyes, the soft caress of his thumb on her cheek. Either he was just one hell of a nice guy, or he wanted in her jeans. Nevertheless, she was touched.

Granny, on the other hand, had been hell on wheels. Being around her was like being on an episode of 'Kids Say The Darndest Things' only featuring intoxicated elderly free spirits in hot pants with bad dye jobs. She had asked Steve to show her his drill, pinched Jack on the butt and told the boys jokes so obscene they both blushed. Megan rolled her eyes so many times she had to hit the side of her head to knock them back to their original position. Finally she gave up and told Steve that the old woman was a drunken retired stripper who had broken out of the loony bin and was holding Megan hostage. He laughed and made a date with Granny for dinner. The idiot. He had no idea what he was getting himself into.

Ted had called six times, and each time Megan answered the phone, spewed a curt 'Drop Dead' and clicked off, except for the one time when Granny answered and read him the riot act, not forgetting to rave on about Jack and his rocket launcher.

Megan was rinsing and spitting when she heard footsteps on the stairs and when she turned she saw Jack's lean, muscular, build framing the doorway. His dark hair was littered with saw dust, brown eyes glittering with lust and his lips were curved in a tired, rugged smile. He looked dark and dangerous and dazzling. And she looked like hell; baggy sleep attire, no makeup, and disheveled hair from running her fingers through it nervously. Not to mention the toothpaste flavored drool running down her chin.

"Hi," he said in a lazy drawl. She wiped her face and stood before him. He held out two keys. "The locks are changed and the plywood should last until Monday. We'll get someone over to fix the window then."

"Thank You," she said and meant it.

Uncomfortable silence lingered for a few full minutes.

"I'm sorry about my grandmother," Megan said feeling the need to apologize. "She's...eccentric and...Well there's no need to sugar coat it. She's a fruit loop, crazy as they come."

"I like her." He would. "Steve likes her too. He's looking forward to that date."

Megan frowned. "About that, she probably won't even remember it. He should forget about it too. He was only being nice."

Jack smiled. Megan locked her knees together. "Oh, I don't think anything about that woman is forgettable. She'll get that date."

"Steve might get more than just a date." Like a lap dance or God forbid, more.

"He's never met a woman he couldn't handle." Jack assured her.

"He's never met Granny."

"True." Megan, being scared and lonely and vulnerable, or just plain horny, crossed her hands around Jack's waist and laying her head on his chest gave him a slow, sensual hug. Jack froze, arms stiffly at his side, but when Megan gave him a gentle squeeze he lightly hugged her back.

She felt so damn good in his arms it made him dizzy. She was soft and lush and warm. He could smell her flowery scented shampoo, wintergreen toothpaste and the fabric softener on her clothes. Her hair was a mess, her eyes were heavy and her cheeks were tinged a light pink–probably from scrubbing her face-and the outline of her nipples were clearly visible in her thin cotton top. She looked like she'd just rolled out of bed after a long night of making love. Be still my heart.

He dipped his head to take in her scent one last time before breaking the embrace and running one long finger the length of her face, her lips parted and she leaned into him. He took a step back. She reached for his hands and, frowning, he quickly shoved them in his pockets. She searched his eyes and he looked at the floor not wanting her to see the need, the lust in his eyes. It took every ounce of control he had not to throw her on that bed and bury himself inside her. But he didn't because, as much as he wanted her, he didn't want her because she was vulnerable or scared. He wanted her to want him because she wanted him. Not for any other reason. She stood tip toed and kissed his cheek. A thank you kiss. A friend kiss.

"Do you have a blanket?" he blurted and she frowned. "I'm going to sleep in my truck in case anything happens."

Megan stepped back. She'd all but written a sexual invitation on her forehead in big, black, magic marker and he wanted to sleep in his truck? "Sure, but you can sleep on the couch if you like. Or I can bunk with Granny and you can sleep here." She nodded to the bed and Jack's jaw locked. "Or we can…"

"I'll take that blanket," he said and she opened the closet to get one.

"Really Jack it's getting cold at night and you're welcome to…"

"I'll be fine," he answered hoarsely. Megan handed him the blanket.

"Okay," she whispered, "Would you like a pair of sweats or…"

"No thanks, I'll be fine." He looked at that big comfortable bed. He imagined Megan looking tired and satisfied and lazily sprawled across the rumpled sheets, her head resting on his chest, their bare legs intertwined. Megan underneath him her eyelids heavy from erotic… "Goodnight Megan," he finally said before taking the stairs as if the house were on fire. He might have to stick a water hose down his pants and blast the burning desire there but he'd do that before he'd take advantage of her. Pausing at the foot of the stairs, he gave her bedroom door one last glance before hearing it click shut.

***

Sunday morning was cold, windy and overcast. Megan slipped out of bed after a restless night of tossing, turning and thinking about Jack. She paused outside the guest room door and heard Granny snoring in a loud steady whistle. Stretching, she headed down to the kitchen to make coffee and breakfast. She'd feed Jack, apologize for being an ass, get rid of Granny and then hopefully spend the rest of the afternoon in his arms.

And then there was Ted. He would likely be released from the hospital today and he probably wasn't going to be happy when he found out that he was now homeless. Of course he could go stay with Tiffany Triple D or maybe the Madrino's had a nice big trunk they could stuff him in. None the less he was history whether he liked it or not.

Setting the coffee maker to run she began pulling ingredients from the fridge when the phone rang. She looked up at the ceiling and prayed it was her mother calling to discuss Granny. No such luck.

"Megan, it's Ted."

181

"And?" She started the bacon cooking, more interested in clogging her arteries than talking to the idiot.

"Where have you been? I've been worried sick. I've been calling constantly." The jerk actually sounded concerned.

"Why would you be worried Ted? You up to no good?"

"No...but..." Megan smiled, he was stammering. Good.

"Afraid your girlfriend might stop by? Or maybe the Madrino's looking for their money? Or maybe your brother wanting the deed to the studio that you so discreetly sold him," she heard him coughing and wondered if it would be too much to ask for him to contract the plague. "Am I missing anyone? Anyone else you've slept with or pissed off."

"Megan, I know I have a lot of explaining to do but..."

"Save it," she said looking out the window. Jack was still there on guard duty. She smiled and felt a tingling sensation burn through her body. "Why did you call?"

"I need a ride." Ted said flatly. So did Megan, but probably not the same kind.

"Call Tiffany," she retorted.

"I already did..." he stopped as if he'd just caught what he said. "She's uh unavailable."

"Call a cab," Megan growled.

Ted snorted. "A cab? Are you kidding me? I'm in a freaking hospital gown. I need clothes too."

Megan laughed. "So have the cab drop you off at Wal-Mart, you can buy clothes there."

"I don't have any money!" he shouted.

"Me either, seems my husband spent all his on a red-headed whore and drugs."

"Megan!" His voice was so loud and thick it vibrated the phone.

Megan began making static sounds and said, "Sorry Ted, phones all static. Gotta go." She hung up the phone with Ted in mid scream.

The phone rang again and she unplugged it not feeling one bit sorry for Ted. After getting eggs and toast going she filled Ted's thermos with coffee and sat it on a cookie sheet that she draped with a doily. She'd prefer to take Jack breakfast in bed but since he'd slept in his truck, breakfast in a Jeep would have to do. Maybe she could serve him dinner in bed. Hell, maybe she'd be dinner.

After loading the tray with food she ran upstairs to dash on a little makeup and grab her robe.

Jack saw the backdoor open and he closed his eyes to play possum. He'd spent the night watching the house, mainly her window, and kicking himself for choosing the truck instead of her warm bed. With her in it, warm and cuddly and naked. She approached his window and rapped lightly. He ignored her. She tried the door handle and found it locked. She knocked again softly and called his name. He concentrated on ignoring her but then she pounded on the window making him jump and he opened his eyes and lowered the window a bit.

"Good you're awake," she smiled and he knew he didn't stand a chance. "I made breakfast. Want to come inside?"

Yes! "No, I'm fine. I'll just take some coffee if you've got it."

"I thought we could talk over breakfast," she said holding up the thermos. Maybe she could lure him out of truck with it. Either that or she could open that robe.

"C'mon Jack, Its cold out here and you can't be comfortable."

"I'd rather stay put."

She opened the thermos and, with her eyes half closed and a wicked smile, inhaled the scent. It looked like she was having an orgasm. Jack gripped the stirring wheel.

"It's really good," She said huskily.

No shit! "Thanks." He rolled down the window to take the thermos and she hit the switch to unlock the door. He stared at her while she opened the door.

"Scoot over," she said. He didn't budge. She crawled over him, grazing her butt over his thighs and his mind went to mush. What the hell was he doing? He wanted her, she wanted him. Game over!

"If you won't come out, I'll just come in," she said once she got settled. The food was on the hood but she handed him the thermos. "Now, if I hop out to get the tray are you going to lock me out?"

He was more tempted to lock her in. "No," he said, then after a moment, "I'll go inside and eat."

"Good, because I'm freezing." He opened the door and got out and she crawled back across the seat to follow. He took her hand to help her out and she pulled him close to her and bit his bottom lip. His lips parted and she filled his mouth with an intoxicating kiss, tasting and teasing until the kiss erupted to an orgasmic level. He needed that water hose quick. He was about to come and he'd barely touched her. How embarrassing would that be? She leaned into him and felt him hard and stiff against her thigh and she smiled against his lips. To hell with subtlety, he'd take her right there. He couldn't wait any longer. Parting the robe he reached in and cupped her soft breast through her tank top, her nipple was taut and hard and when he ran his thumb over it she moaned and tugged him closer.

"Megan," he whispered, "we should probably go in…"

"Shut up Jack."

"But if we don't go inside your neighbor's are going to get one hell of a show."

"Shut up Jack."

"I mean it; I've waited a long time for this. I won't be able to control myself."

"Shut up Jack!" Megan and Jack both jumped because this time it wasn't Megan's voice telling him to shut up. He felt a warm breath at the nape of his neck and a hand on his butt and looked at Megan who had both hands in his hair.

"Granny!" Megan shouted after opening her eyes and seeing Granny standing behind Jack her hand cupping Jack's luscious butt. "Go in the house!"

"No, the fun is out here," Jack turned his head and Granny said, "I'm next."

Jack stood there frozen, his hand still in Megan's robe. He felt like he was fifteen again being busted with a girl in his daddy's truck. He slowly removed his hand from her breast and placing one hand under her knees and the other behind her back he scooped her up and hauled her up the driveway towards the house. Granny was hot on his heels carrying the tray of food.

"Granny has got to go," Megan muttered into Jack's chest.

"Damn right she does. She's hell on a hard on."

"I heard that," Granny said. "I can't help it if your firecracker has a weak fuse."

"There is nothing wrong with my firecracker except that ever since I saw Megan again at Ted's studio I've been walking around halfcocked, on fire and ready to burst." Megan looked at him confused. It didn't make any sense. He'd said since he'd seen her again. And the other night he said he waited fifteen years. She had never met him before that night. What the hell was he talking about?

"Sounds like a case of the crabs to me," Granny retorted.

"Granny!" Megan shouted and then to Jack she said, "Just ignore her she's crazy. She's obviously lost it."

Granny snorted. "I haven't lost anything. He's the one who keeps losing it."

"Enough!" Megan said to the two of them. It was just a little weird arguing with her grandmother over Jack's hard on. If Mrs. Everett found out she'd have Jerry Springer on speed dial. Talk about your dysfunctional family sex triangles.

Jack sat her down on her feet in the kitchen and Granny shut the door pouting.

"All I'm saying Megan is maybe lover boy has got a dud down..." Megan was ignoring Granny and Jack was taking the old woman in stride. He'd stifle a chuckle here and there and seemed to focus most of his attention staring at Megan with that intoxicating animal sex look in his eye.

Damn oh damn! Granny has definitely got to go. Quick!

"Oh look we got company. This oughta be good. Should we pop some corn or just go straight for the liquor." Megan made it to the window just in time to see Ted getting out of a Taxi cab, his hospital gown blowing with the wind. He was mooning the entire neighborhood. Mrs. Everett probably had her camera in one hand and the phone in the other. Jerry Springer show recruiters were probably on their way.

Oh hell!

"How do you want to handle this?" Jack asked her, pressing his body close to hers from behind. His arms circled her waist in a possessive hold and his breath against her ear was causing yet another pair of her panties to turn to squish. How was she going to give Ted the boot when all she could think about was knocking boots with Jack? Double Hell!

Granny's eyes lit up. Her voice giddy she said, "He's naked. Hot damn, got me a naked boy coming in."

"Let's lock the doors and pretend we're not home," Megan said knowing that wouldn't work. She'd have to face Ted sometime. Might as well be now when she was running on hormones and lust. And Jack, who

God bless him, was sporting the mother of all boners. And rubbing it against her back. Oh damn, double damn!

Taking a deep breath she grabbed the U-Haul keys from the counter and went to the front door to meet Ted the cradle robbing dickhead.

"My key won't work," he said still holding his key in the newly changed lock.

"Hi Ted," she handed him the U-Haul keys. "Try these they'll work." He looked at her dumbfounded, taking in Granny and Jack's smug faces.

"Megan?" he said looking pathetic, confused and stupid in his thin cotton gown.

"Oh, I forgot to tell you. While you were in the hospital you moved. Your stuff is in that truck and we'll go through the rest later after I talk to a lawyer. I'm filing for divorce. Have a nice day." She went to shut the door and he stopped it with his fist. Jack took a step forward and Megan pushed him back.

"Megan, I don't want a divorce." His voice was weak, his eyes wide and sad. "I don't understand."

"You cheated on me," she said and he began shaking his head. "I found pot in the basement and you owe the Italian Wannabe's a butt load of money and you sold the studio. And you slept with Josie!" Ted winced. "What's not to understand? You screwed up. Now get out."

"Wait!" he said and Megan frowned and opened the door about an inch for him.

"Two minutes Ted, then I'm slamming this door."

"Ok," he sighed, "Tiffany is over. I don't know what I was thinking. I just…we just…and she was so…" He locked eyes with Jack. "Who's he?"

"Jack. Now you're wasting time here, Ted. Spit it out." Megan said impatiently.

"I called Tiffany in the hospital and told her it was over. That's done."

Megan could have cared less. "So call her back. You're homeless now; you can probably pitch a tent in her cleavage." Jacked grinned and put his hands on Megan's shoulders. Ted narrowed his eyes at Jack and took a step closer to Meg.

"I can't call her back. She's gone. Disappeared. Plus she hates me."

"Imagine that. Well, she must be smarter than me because it took me ten years to get to that point." Ted looked like hell so she asked, "Why does she hate you?"

"Because she told me she was pregnant and I told her to get lost." Megan's blood boiled and she slapped Ted across the face. Then did it again. Ten years she'd spent with him wanting kids, his kids and he knocked up that red headed bimbo. Ted was rubbing his stinging cheek and shaking his head. "No, Megan, wait! It's not mine. The kid isn't mine."

"Go to hell, Ted. You better be glad I don't have a gun right now. They'd be scraping your nuts off the siding if I did. I swear to…"

"Mabel's grandson has a gun. He's a felon. Want me to call him?" Granny said. Megan ignored her and stared at Ted with pure hatred. Insert knife in heart and twist. This was the final freaking insult. Jack pulled her to him and she buried her head in his chest soaking his black tee shirt with violent angry tears.

Ted was still rambling on. "Megan there's no way that kid is mine. I swear."

"You were sleeping with her right?" she wailed, "You do know where babies come from don't you? Insert dick, shoot sperm and presto. It not rocket science."

"Hear me out Meg, the…kid…is…not…mine." She slapped him again.

"Granny, feel free to make that phone call now." Granny giggled and disappeared into the kitchen. Jack tried to pull Megan into him but she pushed away. This was between her and Ted. And, if he pissed her off again, Mabel's grandson.

"Megan, I'll take DNA tests to prove it." Megan refused to look at him and he blurted, "I had a Vasectomy five years ago. There I said it. So there's nothing to worry about. Tiffany's history and it'll never happen again." Ted reached out a hand to stroke her cheek that was against Jack's chest again and she batted his hand away. Granny returned with a rolling pin and a set of pliers.

"You had a what? Five years ago. You bastard!" She nailed him with the rolling pin square on the side of his head. He stumbled back a bit and before he got his footing she hit him again. "You promised me kids and this stupid freaking fairytale and now you tell me this."

"Here let's crack his nuts." Granny said holding out the pliers and Megan waved a hand at Ted's gonads. "Be my guest, Granny." Ted let the back of his gown go and brought both hands to cover the nuts in question. Granny narrowed her eyes and squeezed the pliers in a menacing manner. Jack winced and Ted shifted on his feet trying to avoid the jaws of hell, nipping at his scrotum.

"Your stuff is in that truck. Get in it and disappear. I don't ever want to see you again." She popped him again, this time dead on his forehead. "I'm keeping the pups and Spot and you are not getting visitation. So stay the hell away." Megan said through clenched teeth.

"Yeah, or Jack's gonna kick your ass," Granny said, "Right Jack?"

"Right wild woman," Jack answered smiling with teeth bared. Hell, he wanted to kill him just for making Megan cry. Her heart was breaking and he felt every crack mirrored in his own. How on earth he was going to make everything alright he didn't know. He just knew he'd do it. Whatever it took. This hopefully involved kicking Ted's ass then getting Megan naked.

"And make sure you settle your little drug deal. They are threatening me, calling, throwing bricks in the window." Ted closed his eyes and seemed genuinely sorry.

"Megan, I tried to warn you. You wouldn't answer the phone. I'll take care of them somehow. I had the money. It just…disappeared." Like Tiffany Jack thought. Hmmm. "They're going to kill me if I don't pay them. I don't know what I'm going to do." Megan took a double take. Ted was crying? Good! She hit him again.

"Sell the Jag. Sell your soul. Whatever. Just pay them and leave me alone."

"Megan…" He grabbed her shoulder and spun her around. Jack grabbed his arm and they stood there, eyes locked, tempers rising, both in a strong hold of strength and wills.

"Don't touch her!" Jack growled in a low, deadly rumble, his eyes almost black. Ted let go and Jack released his hand and pulled Megan out of the way. Granny used that exact moment to strike, clutching the pliers hard one time and striking flesh. Ted let out a piercing cry and knelt forward his hands cupping his groin and with one swift move- which was impressive for a retired fortune teller with the libido of a sixteen year old and a moonshine habit- she caught the top of his head with her foot and kicked him hard enough to knock him off the steps.

She wiped her hands together and slammed the door. "So who's hungry?" she asked heading to the kitchen. "I for one am starved. I don't know what it is but the two F's always just take it out of you." When Jack and Megan just stared at her with blank expressions she elaborated, "The Two F's. You know, fighting and fuc.."

"We got it Granny. Jeez!" Megan gave Jack an apologetic look but he was busy caressing her back and spreading gentle kisses down her throat. Megan's world had just fallen apart and Jack was horny and Granny was hungry. Megan bit her bottom lip afraid she might start crying. Jack pulled her closer and Megan noticed he was still aroused. Big time! She laughed. At least she'd gotten the fighting out of the way. That only left the...

Amy Johnson

Chapter Fourteen

Jack was on cloud nine. He finally had Megan Johnson in his arms and he'd watched Ted Malone get his ass kicked by a girl and a little old lady. Talk about your testosterone depleting moments. Ted had stalked around on the front porch for about an hour after Megan gave him the boot but he finally climbed into his U-Haul and drove away after having drawn a gathering of gawking neighbors eyeing him in his backless gown and having his crotch sniffed by a Boxer pup from down the street. He looked like hell; unshaven, loss of weight, rolling pin shaped bruises on his head. Jack laughed. Megan had worked him over but good. And Jack felt great about it. She needed to get it out somehow. Of course lying beneath him naked experiencing the most mind blowing orgasm of her life would do just fine too, but that could come later.

Megan seemed a little shaky at first but she was coming around. She'd checked the window at least fifty times to see if Ted had left yet after Granny performed the Nut Cracker and kicked him out and she'd paced at least a country mile or two in the kitchen. She wasn't sympathetic or sorry. Just hurt. Terribly hurt. Obviously she wanted kids and Ted's betrayal-his secret Vasectomy-had done a number on her. Jack reassured her that the whole kids thing was still a possibility as she was only thirty years old and it was probably better she and Ted hadn't procreated because then there would be innocent children involved in this whole mess. That seemed to comfort her. That and the fact that she had him to lean on.

And didn't that feel good. Megan in his arms all soft and warm and lush. Her little cupcake breast crushed against his chest, her arms tightly around his neck, their hips rocking slowly. Jack might have to install a water spigot in his crotch to cool him off but it'd be worth it. She was

191

coming to him freely, welcoming his touch and. although he tried to get his mind on Algebra or The Law of Inertia to distract himself, it seemed his dick had a mind of its own. And it was always on Megan. She'd noticed it too. She'd leaned into him and even laughed about his constant state of erect arousal. She wanted him and that only made him hotter.

"Jack?" Megan's voice pulled him out of his thoughts and he turned to see her dressed in a pair of men's boxers, a tank top, freshly showered, her hair a curly mess on her head. Her eyes burned through him like electricity, full of innocence and...desire?

He tried to speak but his mouth went dry. He cleared his throat. "Yeah?"

"I'm uh kind of tired." She hesitated. "I was uh wondering if you might uh lay down with me and hold me. I could kind of use some company right now."

Oh Mama! "Sure," was all he could spit out. He was shocked and pleased and harder than a nine iron. She could have asked him to assassinate the president and he wouldn't have thought twice. She walked up to him and took his hand, leading him to the stairs. Oh Mama Oh Mama Oh Mama!

Up the stairs and into the bedroom. Oh Yeah!

To the unmade king size bed. Holy Shit! And then reached in a dresser drawer and pulled out a pair of purple shorts with neon green flames on them and tossed them to him. "Those might be more comfortable than your jeans." Whatever you say babe! I'll wear a tutu and cluck like a chicken if that gets you hot.

He said, "Thanks," instead and dropped his jeans. Megan turned her back to give him privacy and he yanked those puppies up and was beside her in an instant. The shorts were so tight he looked like the Incredible Hulk shedding his skin but he didn't care. She turned around and threw her head back in laughter.

"What?" he asked as if he didn't know. If anything they worked to his advantage putting his entire package on display like a buffet at IHOP. Now if Megan would only hop on him...

Her laughter roared. "Nothing, it's just...I mean...Let me put it this way. Mickey never did those shorts justice."

"Mickey?" Purple and Green flames. Flaming! Oh hell!

"Yeah, those are Mickey's. I uh borrowed them from him once and never returned them." Jack's eyes went ridiculously wide and he was staring at his crotch deciding he'd boldly gone where no other man should ever go. Into another man's shorts. He looked at the window and waved.

Megan followed his gaze, "Who are you waving at?"

"My hard on. I think it just took a permanent vacation." To his departing anatomy he said, "Nice knowing you big guy. Come back soon. You hear?"

She laughed again, giving him that crooked smile and those sparkling eyes and he surrendered. So what if he was wearing a drag queen's hand me down shorts that were so tight his boys couldn't breathe with flames shooting down his crotch. Could have been worse. Could have been Mickey's G-String.

She lay on the bed and patted the quilt beside her. His soldier came back to full attention and he was beside her in two strides. He lay down beside her and she cuddled, nestling her head on his chest and he froze breathless. She grinned and took his hand and slipped it behind her neck and snuggled closer. His jaw locked.

"Relax, Jack. I don't bite." She said her breath warm against the cotton of his tee shirt.

"I might," he said once he caught his breath. He wrapped her tight in his arms and when she pressed closer, their legs intertwining, skin smoldering to the touch, he bit her on the ear lobe. Just a nibble, a teeny weeny taste. Then he silently recited the alphabet backwards to get some blood back in his brain.

***

Megan woke up in Jack's arms to the sound of a car alarm going off. Jack was wide awake, staring at the ceiling, either oblivious to the shrieking sound or just ignoring it. She looked at the clock and realized she'd gotten over two hours of much needed sleep after a night of fantasizing about Jack. And now he was here, in her bed, warm, hard and unbelievably sexy.

The damn car alarm was still going off. What's the point of having one if you're just going to ignore it when it goes off like that and wakes the whole freaking neighborhood? What a moron. Whoever that car belonged to, they deserved for it to be stolen, with them stuffed in the trunk.

Someone knocked on the door.

"Who is it?" Megan asked.

193

"Me," a loud deep voice bellowed. Jack tensed a bit, Ted?

"Come in, you got some 'splainin to do." The door swung open and Mickey towered in the doorway, a cocky grin on his face. He nodded at Jack.

"Magnum," Mickey said, then to Megan he said, "Whose Jeep is that parked out front?"

"It's mine," Jack said, "Why?"

"It's got a shovel sticking out the front window, babe. Didn't you hear the alarm?" Yeah he'd heard it but he'd have had to leave the bed of a half naked woman to deal with it. The man had priorities. Jack stood quickly looking for his shoes. "Nice shorts, I used to have a pair just like them," he shot Megan a look mixed with pride and a little you-go-girl.

"They look better on him," Megan pointed out.

"Remember I got points for size," Mickey reminded her, then when he turned his attention back to Jack, "Does that truck come standard with a shovel or was that an add on?" Jack didn't see the humor in it as he bolted to the door and down the stairs. Megan threw the sheet off and followed with Mickey right behind her.

"So, how'd he score?" Mickey whispered.

"He didn't, we just cuddled." Mickey frowned at the lack of juicy details, "But he kisses great. Oh and he bit me."

"Where?"

"The ear lobe." She was flushed pink and smiling like she'd just had an orgasm that had required firefighters to hose her down. Mickey rolled his eyes.

"Heteros are so boring," he said.

Once outside, Jack disabled the alarm and removed the shovel. On the spade of the shovel, written in big, black letters were the words: Pay up or we shoot the dogs.

"The Madrino's?" Megan asked feeling extremely guilty about Jack's truck and fighting angry about those assholes threatening her dogs. Jack didn't answer her but, but she knew she was right.

"Those low down, SOB's. They touch my dogs and I swear to God, I'll kill them with my bare hands." Megan was screaming and sobbing and Mickey put his arms around her as Jack took out his cell phone to call the cops. "What kind of person threatens innocent dogs? Why can't they just kill Ted and get it over with? I could live with that, but not my pups."

"Don't worry Meg; we'll keep the pups safe," Mickey said.

"Oh my God, Granny! Where's granny? She must have been kidnapped otherwise she wouldn't be missing the action."

"Granny's fine, she went to the adult shop with Josie," Mickey answered and the look on Megan's face said she was clueless. She really had led a sheltered life. "The adult shop as in erotica, sex toys..."

"I got it," Megan said reminding herself to strangle both Mickey and Josie in her spare time. They were seriously corrupting her grandma. Like that was possible.

When Jack was off the phone, Megan said, "Jack, I'm so sorry. I'll pay for the window. This is all my fault." She covered her face with her hands and Jack took both of her hands in his and kissed the back of first one and then the other.

"It's not your fault, Meg. Don't worry about it." More kisses. "I have insurance to cover the window. I'm more worried about you and the dogs...," He looked around then said, "...and your grandmother. Where is she?"

"Porn shop," Mickey reported and Jack shook his head stifling back laughter.

"You think they'll hurt my dogs?" Megan asked, "because if they do, I'll...uh...well I'll do something and it'll make a marble up the butt look like a picnic."

Jack laughed. He was irresistible when he laughed. "We can take the dogs to Steve's place until this is over." Megan was shaking her head. "Or do you have any ideas? Your parents?"

"They're still avoiding me. Mom's on Zoloft and Dad is probably glued to the set. It's Sunday, football you know."

"Okay I'll call Steve."

"No wait, Mickey can take them, right Mickey?"

"Uh..."Mickey tried to protest but Megan cut him off.

"You got my granny kicked out of the nursing home and now I'm stuck with her so you are taking the dogs." He opened his mouth to protest again and she put a finger to his chest and said, "You're lucky you only have to put up with two sweet puppies. I'm stuck with Granny."

"Granny's buying porn. I've got popcorn. I'd rather take her."

Megan and Mickey argued until Mickey finally caved and they went to get the pups along with all the doggie gear Mickey would need to care for them. As they were loading the pups the cops showed up to respond to Jack's call.

"Nice threads, Westin," said a young cop named Weaver. Jack looked down at his flaming shorts, grinned at Megan and went back in the house to put on something a little more masculine.

***

That afternoon Megan and Jack sat at the kitchen table dining on Dairy Queen. Granny was on her 'date' with Steve, where she was undoubtedly trying to molest him at the Bingo hall. Mickey had taken the pups to his house and promised not to dye their coats hot pink. Spot had been fed and was now swimming fishy laps around his bowl. Josie had stayed to chat for a while after dropping Granny off. Seemed that she and the good doctor had been pretty hot and heavy the past couple days. She said his bedside manner was incredible. Since she said it with a lick of her lip, Megan was pretty sure she didn't mean medically. Nonetheless, Megan got the impression that Josie may have met her match. Hope Dr. Ross could keep up.

Megan had finally talked to her mother and was assured that first thing in the morning, her mom would scout out old folks homes for Granny. When Megan mentioned the brick and shovel incidents hoping to convince her mother that it wasn't safe for Granny to be at Megan's, her mother simply laughed and told her to either quit making up stories, or make up better stories next time. Megan finally gave up figuring that if worst came to worse she could drink all granny's moonshine while Granny chased the bad guys around with pliers.

Ted was another bit of unfinished business. He'd stalked around the yard for a while then knocked on the door endlessly until he finally gave up and sped away in the U-Haul. He'd called and left message after message begging for forgiveness and wanting to come home. Megan finally disconnected the answering machine and unplugged the phone again. The house was now quiet.

She took a bite of BBQ brisket and stared at Jack who was effectively stuffing his face directly across from her. He'd stopped by his place when they'd gone on the food run to grab an extra change of clothes, shower and shave. He looked delicious in his Semper Fi tee shirt and snug Jeans, his hair still damp and his dimpled chin now smooth. If he were on the menu at Dairy Queen the place would be swarming with women all the time, each ordering a BBQ plate with a side of Jack for desert. That made Megan wonder why he was still single. What was wrong with him?

"Jack."

"Mmmm?" he said through a mouthful of potato salad.

"How come you're not married?" Jack wiped his mouth on a napkin and took a long drink of his soda.

"I'm not married because I'm divorced," he said and Megan thought, *No shit!*

"Yeah, I surmised that, but why did you get divorced and how come you're not with someone now?" He frowned and sculpted his mound of potato salad into what looked like a volcano. "What I mean is, well you are so good looking, and you seem to have great inner qualities. I'm just wondering why some woman hasn't snatched you up yet." He took a bite of the volcano.

"Maybe I haven't allowed myself to be snatched. I'm waiting for the right woman."

"But what if she never comes along? You just going to be alone?" Megan asked wondering if there really is 'a right one' for anybody. She thought Ted was hers and look where that got her.

"She already has." He locked gazes with her and his eyes were full of a heat she'd never seen before. It was scary and down right sexy at the same time. She contemplated making herself an ice pack. "She just doesn't know it yet."

She raised a brow and tried to hide her disappointment that he'd already picked out Ms. Right. "What do you mean she doesn't know it yet? Have you told her?"

"No," he said pinning her in place with his eyes.

"Then you have to tell her. If she's the one, you can't let her get away without at least telling her how you feel."

He frowned and rubbed his jaw. "It's a long story."

Megan looked at her watch. "I've got plenty of time. Let's hear it."

He hesitated, his eyes studying her face. "When I was fifteen, I went to school one day and there she was, dressed in her cheerleading outfit, sucking down a milkshake and laughing with her friends. She was like a fantasy, gorgeous, sweet, popular. But the thing was, she didn't know it. She was shy and reserved and that only made her more desirable." Jack paused and Megan thought what a putz. He was still pining over some cheerleading slut from high school. Loser.

197

"The first time I saw her I knew she was the one," he continued, "There she was leaning on a brick pillar, pom poms in hand. She tilted her head up, swung her long brown hair off her shoulder, and laughed at something someone said and then she looked directly at me with eyes bluer than the sky and smiled a sweet crooked smile and I melted on the spot. I'm talking total evaporation. It was love at first sight. I was toast."

Ok change that to mega loser. "So? Did you ever tell her? Ask her out?"

Jack shook his head. "I wasn't in her league. I was a scrawny dork. She dated jocks and the cool guys. She deserved someone better than me." His eyes flashed something that looked a lot like hurt and Megan mentally changed his status back to just plain old loser. She took his hand and he flinched then relaxed into her grasp. Poor guy, she felt the same way in school. Josie was always the hot one and Megan was just the average, smart girl that everyone asked out after Josie shot them down. Not that Josie shot many of them down.

"Jack, I can't imagine you as scrawny. And even if you were, it was the other way around. If she couldn't see beyond the packaging to what was inside, she didn't deserve you." He raised her hand to his mouth and lightly kissed her knuckles. "I'm telling you Jack, high school was awkward for everyone. Me for instance, I was totally invisible, completely average." Jack tried to hide his surprise at that statement. She couldn't possibly not know how beautiful she was and still is. "I hung out with Josie, so I just looked like the schoolie side kick. The straight A, honor society geek with no curves and a best friend that looked like a walking Barbie Boll. If it weren't for Josie, no one would have ever even known I was alive. And even then, I think they just dated me to try their chances at Josie. She was the real prize."

What was she crazy? Jack laughed. "Megan, I appreciate the support, but I find it hard to believe you were anything but beautiful. You may not of known it but I'd bet the bank everyone else noticed." I sure as hell did.

"Your sweet," Megan said then changed the subject. "So what happened to this girl? Have you tried to find her?"

"Last I heard she married some blockhead idiot who had no idea what he had and he broke her heart. I believe she's divorcing him." Megan took her hand back from Jack and felt her heart shrink in disappointment. Little Miss Pom Poms was back on the market and Jack was obviously still in love with her. He'd go after her and this bimbo would be a fool to let him get away. Megan forced a cheery smile.

"Well that's perfect, for you anyway. All you have to do is find her, win her heart, confess your love, and live happily ever after." She tried to sound perky but her voice came out more like a robots. She didn't want the cheerleader heart stealer to have happily ever after with Jack. She didn't know if she wanted it either, but she sure didn't want some shallow, stuck up snob to have him. He deserved better.

"Lucky for you, you're a private detective. Finding people is what you do."

I already found you. "Yeah lucky for me," Jack said in a distant voice. After a moment he took a swig of his tea, wiped his mouth and said, "Megan I need to talk to you."

At the same time she said, "I want to talk to you, Jack."

"Go ahead," they both said in clumsy unison.

Jack grinned and gestured for Megan to go ahead. She folded her hands together on the table, took a deep breath and began, "Jack, first I want to say thank you for everything you've done," she gave a shy smile, "including dealing with Granny and putting up with my mother. I swear my dad is normal. Kind of. Anyway, you have been wonderful and I don't know how I could possibly repay you." I can think of a number of ways, Jack thought but decided to keep that quiet for now. "Also, I owe you a major apology." Megan frowned and met his eyes, her eyes electric blue and full of sincerity and truth. "When I called you that day and uh asked you to help me locate those guys, I uh well I had no right to blackmail you the way I did." Jack nodded and smiled and Megan shook her head and continued, "I also have to apologize for thinking of you as a lowlife. I acted shallow and stupid and now that I've gotten to know you, I see what a wonderful person you are and well I'm sorry I didn't see it sooner. I wasn't looking and I'm so sorry for misjudging you." He took her hand, his eyes molten chocolate and burning a hole through her.

"Megan, you don't owe me any apologies."

She was shaking her head. "Yes, I do. I have been behaving like an idiot…"

"Megan…"

"- and I promise I'll make it up to you…" Ok that sounded promising.

"Megan, I'm the one…"

"-because I really value our friendship." Ouch! The f word. Not good. Not sure how to proceed, Jack simply nodded and said nothing. He had planned to tell her how she had been the girl that had stolen his heart so long ago and that she still held it but the whole friend thing shook him. He knew that they were a whole lot more than friends, or at least he hoped she didn't swap tongues and share erotic cuddling with her other friends, but he wasn't sure if she was dumping him—before she ever picked him up—or if she was too shy to pick him up, or if she was too confused to know what she wanted, which was really frustrating the hell out of him. In fact his eyes were probably crossed as he tried to mull this over and figure out what he wanted to do.

"So," she said after waiting for Jack to say something. "I think we should talk about your rate." He raised his hand to protest but she cut him off. "And I need to pay you and Steve for securing my house." Again he tried to jump in, but now she was digging in her pocket. "And here's your eighty bucks back plus ten for the cab fare Granny had you pay."

"Megan..." She pushed the money towards him and nodded.

"Just take it Jack. And tell me what I owe for thus far into our little investigation."

Ok, this was not going the way she wanted it. She'd gotten through the 'I'm Sorrys' but she didn't have the guts for the 'Now Take Me' part. Adele was right, she was a wuss.

And Jack wasn't helping any. He just sat there and nodded. If she didn't know better she would have thought he was incapable of even a monosyllable thought. He reminded her of Ted's bobbing head collection of stupid sports guys. If he nodded one more time and his head didn't fall off, she was tempted to just knock it off and get it over with.

"About our 'little investigation'," Jack said, "I think we should ca..."

"Jack, before you go any further, I want to talk to you about the list. So far we've only found four guys on it which still leaves four more." And to be honest with you, I was really looking forward to finding the other guys on the list..."

Oh hell! That stupid list. That was what this whole thing was about? Once again he'd let his heart get in the way and once again she'd burned him down. The kisses, the hold me crap. More of her manipulative, mixed signal bullshit. As much as he wanted to interpret it some other way, it just wasn't possible. The truth had hit him again like a brick freaking wall, only this time he was listening. He could take the hint. He'd finish the job. He'd find these geezers. Or not them actually but some inbred hillbilly stand in that made Jethro Clampett look like a freaking Don Juan and then when she found out that the green grass on the other side was actually growing above a septic tank, she'd settle for him. And he'd give it to her long and hard, leaving her the moment she went to sleep with never so much as a backwards glance. He'd get Megan Johnson out of his system and then he'd move the hell on.

Good God she was still babbling but he hadn't heard a word she'd said.

"…here I was searching for something when all along it may have been right underneath my nose. So If it's OK with you I'd just as soon pay up and cancel the rest of the job." All Jack heard of this plea was 'the job' and his scowl was downright rude and scary. She looked at him with misty blue eyes full of confusion and he snorted.

He stood abruptly. "Look Megan, I have somewhere I need to be. Call Mickey or Ali or someone to come stay with you so I can go." Oh hell here come the tears.

"But Jack, I want you to…"

"I'll pick you up tomorrow morning and we'll finish our little investigation."

"But I don't understand, I said I wanted to…"

"Be ready at nine." He opened the back door and with his back turned to her he said, "I'll be in my truck until someone gets here to stay with you. If you have any trouble tonight call the cops. Lock your doors." He left letting the door slam behind him. Megan was at the backdoor following after him but he made it to his truck and slammed the door just before he heard her say, "Jack I want you." He snorted. Yeah, she wanted him alright. To serve as a guard dog, to find her old flames from high school so she could get it on in the back seat of a charger, to rev up his hormones and then shoot them back down once she got her cheap little thrill, but mostly she wanted to break his heart. Over and over again.

Amy Johnson

Chapter Fifteen

Megan and Jack spent the next week, searching for the guys on the list. Jack had insisted she go with him every day and he made her life miserable the whole time. Just as miserable as she was making him. They had just finished scouting the Great Chase Kilborne who was not so great anymore.

"Drive," Megan yelled when she got to the truck and Jack put the truck in gear slowly idling into first gear, holding his side from laughing so hard. Megan did not seem to find the situation as funny because she had retrieved her water bottle from the cup holder and was pounding him in the shoulder with it. Needless to say, Chase Kilborne, and his fatal orgasm were now history.

"Jack?" Megan asked once she could find her voice again. "You want to get something to eat. Maybe try that new Italian place?"

Jack seemed to hesitate. "Can't," he finally said.

"Can't or don't want to?"

Jack kept his eyes on the road. "Both." Megan looked defeated and even though Jack had willed himself not to care about her feelings, his heart just wasn't in it so he added, "I need to be somewhere at 7:00. It's important."

"Business?"

He hesitated again and Megan concluded from his silence that there was probably someone else in Jack's life. She was angry because if that was the case he had led her on, but disappointed at the same time because she was afraid she was falling for Jack Westin and…

"It's a family matter," he finally said and she chose to believe him although before she marked him as her territory she was going to find out. As soon as he dropped her off, she was going to tail him and make

203

sure. She nodded slowly and let the subject drop. After all, what business was it of hers anyway?

"Jack?" Megan asked after a long silence.

"Mmmm?"

"Do you think after your appointment tonight you could stop by? There something I want to…"

Jack was calculating an answer when he was saved by his ringing cell phone. "Yo," he said into the phone followed by, "Have you called the police? Call them now! Are you Ok? Where are they now? I'm on my way?" Megan was ramrod straight, eyes wide, awaiting a response.

"That was Granny," he said while making a U-turn and accelerating his speed. Megan's face went pale white and her heart about leaped out of her chest.

"Don't panic Meg, she's fine," he pushed up the console separating them and pulled her from the passenger seat to the middle right beside him. Draping his arm protectively around her he squeezed her tight and explained, "Apparently the Madrino brothers showed up and she, according to her, knocked them out and tied them up."

"Oh my God! Why was she even still there? She was supposed to be at Mickey's place until Mom found her a new retirement home." Megan was shaking with a combination of anger and fear and Jack whispered, "I don't know, honey," while applying soothing kisses to the top of her head. "But everything will be OK."

***

When they arrived at Megan's house, a squad car was already there and as Jack jumped out of the truck and helped Megan out a car skidded to a stop just behind them, and Josie, Dr. Ross and Ali got out quickly.

"We heard it on the scanner," Josie explained to a perplexed Megan and Jack. The entire group made it to the door and Jack burst out laughing as soon as he entered the kitchen.

Sprawled out on the floor was Angelo Madrino, obviously unconscious, his arms and legs duct taped sloppily. Beside him was Sal Madrino, also duct taped, including his mouth, his eyes wide focused unflinchingly at his crotch, where Granny held a steaming hot pot of coffee half a foot above it. In her other hand was a small electronic devise that Jack recognized as a stun gun or a Taser. Granny wore only a robe, curlers in her hair and green gunk on her face.

"I juiced the big guy, and kicked the little on in the nuts," she was explaining, while the two uniformed officers were trying to get her to surrender the coffee pot. They would make a move for it and she would jerk it back and the hot coffee would slosh around and Sal Madrino would try to move to miss it, all the while squealing like a baby.

Jack made a mental note. Do not piss off the Johnson women.

"What happened?" Megan asked pretty sure she had it figured out. "And what are you doing here? You are supposed to be at Mickey's." Jack took the coffee pot away from Granny and Granny pressed her foot to Sal's crotch to emphasize she still had control of the situation.

"Well I was at Mickey's and then I remembered my date with Steve. He's taking me to the Bingo Hall again tonight and then maybe out for a night cap." Her expression became wistful. "Such a sweet boy that Steve."

"Granny, focus." The officers took out their notebooks, and everyone else listened amused, intrigued, and, probably for Sal, a little uncomfortable.

"Yeah, Ok. So I told Mickey to drop me off here so I could get all prettied up you know for my big date."

Josie clapped her hands. "Granny's getting her groove back."

Ali snorted. "Granny never lost it."

Megan shot them both looks to shut them up.

"So I showered, shaved my legs," Jack and Dr. Ross exchanged amused looks, "and had just put my mask on when I heard these two yahoos come through the pantry window. So I hid in the kitchen under the table and when the big guy came by, I zapped him in the butt." She started laughing as did most of the crowd. "Big lug went down like a ton of bricks. Then the short guy came to check on his buddy and I tried to zap him too, but my zapper didn't have enough juice left so he pulled me out from under the table by my hair and when he saw I was just a helpless little oh lady he let go of me. He asked me if I was OK, and I nodded then asked him for a hug because I was just so scared."

"Wait a minute ma'am," the young cop asked, "You asked a burglar for a hug."

"Well I didn't think, 'Come closer so I can knee you in the nuts' would work."

The officer tried to hide his laughter, Jack didn't. "You went for that you idiot?" Jack said, and Sal shook his head, but then quickly changed it to a nod when Granny applied a little force with her foot to his lower region.

"So continue from the hug," the older, balding, officer instructed.

"So he hesitated for a minute and then I turned on the charm." Several eyes were rolling, "And then when he came close enough I kneed him in the gonads and while he was nursing those I clobbered him with my crystal ball." She gave a devious grin baring her false teeth. "I predict pain and a boyfriend named Bubba in his near future."

"And then you called me?" Jack asked.

"Nope, first I taped up the little guy and then plugged in my zapper, just in case I needed it again. Then I taped up the fat guy best I could, put on some coffee and ate a bagel." She turned to Megan. "You have really got to go grocery shopping, dear. I just about starved to death."

"Then you called me?"

"No not yet. First, I had a good long talk with the little guy and told him if he ever messed with my granddaughter again, I'd hunt him down and give him something in common with John Wayne Bobbit. You know the guy whose wife cut off his thingy." Everyone nodded through their laughter and she continued, "Then I gave him a wedgie, just because he messed up my plans for my date and then I called you."

"You go Granny," Josie said and she and Granny did some secret diva handshake.

"Yeah, I must say you kick butt, Granny," Ali said and gave Granny a high five.

Megan said nothing. She crossed the room and embraced the old woman and began to cry. Granny started laughing and made a show of flexing her wrinkled muscles.

"Where did you get a stun gun?" Megan asked her.

Granny smiled and said, "EBay. I would have gotten a grenade or something like that but I guess you have to have a permit or something and Mickey wouldn't help me get one."

Thank God for that, Megan thought. At least he used his brain once this century.

"Well I hate to be a party pooper, but I gotta get ready for my date." She bowed for her audience, gave Jack a quick peck on the cheek, admired the young officers behind and went upstairs.

Jack talked with the officers and told them about Ted, the drugs, the money, all the previous mishaps with the Madrino's. Dr. Ross offered to check out the Madrino brothers before the police carted them off while the officers questioned Megan on Ted's whereabouts to which she told them the truth, that she had no clue. After the officers, the burglars and Granny and Steve had left, Megan, Jack, Ali, Josie and Dr. Ross sat at the kitchen table and discussed the evening's events over beer and iced tea for Jack.

"I think you should load up your stuff and stay at my place for a while," Ali told Megan and Megan shook her head.

"No need," Megan said, "I have my own bodyguard."

"Granny?" Josie asked and Megan pointed to Jack. "Oh," Josie said, "I see."

"No it's not like that. He chooses to sleep in his truck at the curb or in my driveway." She locked eyes with Jack before going on, "No matter what I do I can't coerce him to come inside."

Jack stood abruptly and surveyed the group. "Anyone hungry, I could go for a steak myself."

"You got a grill?" Dr. Ross asked Megan and she nodded. "Okay, how bout us boys, go get the grub and you girls, well just do what you do. We'll cook and ya'll can clean."

"Sounds good," Ali said.

Megan nodded and Josie said, "I don't know about the cleaning part but everything else sounds fine."

Jack pulled Megan aside and then took her outside with him while Dr. Ross was kissing Josie goodbye. He leaned her up against the side of the house and looked her dead in the eye and spoke in a deliberate, delicious voice. "I'm staying here tonight, inside, without coercion and you and I are going to have a long talk." She nodded. "I'll be back in a few minutes. You go inside, lock the door and do not open it, until I get back. Got that?"

"Yeah."

"I'll have my cell phone with me. You call if you need me."

"Okay," she said taken aback by his sudden serious tone. He then dipped his head and kissed her with a passion that made her aware of nothing but Jack, his strong musky masculine scent, his thigh pressing between hers, his hands on her back and in her hair. When he broke the kiss, he rested his head on her shoulder and muttered, "My God, Megan," just as Dr. Ross stepped outside. Jack held her hand for a moment, turned it palm up and kissed it in the center and then left without another word.

Megan stood stunned for a moment then regained her strength and went inside, locking the door behind her as instructed.

*****

Jack sat in the passenger seat while Dr. Ross drove Josie's car to the store. He kept up the small talk with Jon, but his mind was focused on Megan and the talk he planned to have with her. He was just going to come out with it and find out what the hell she wanted from him. She was sending all the right signals and if he could just drop his guard he'd have been able to read them loud and clear, but he'd been wrong before and he didn't were to get hurt or take advantage of her.

He was going to tell her about how he'd duped her on their search and then confess the way he felt about her—the way he'd always felt—and see how she reacted. If she didn't feel the same or didn't wish to explore things between them, he'd resign from their business arrangement and leave without looking back. If things went differently, then he'd be a very happy man and he'd spend the rest of the night making her a very happy woman. Then they could see where it went from there. He knew one thing, the games were over and all bets were off. It was time to come clean.

*****

Megan had replayed the last couple day's events to the girls who listened excitedly at the humorous situations she and Jack had gotten into. She'd told them about Chase and Aaron and the ridiculous lengths she'd agreed to go to find the bums.

"Know what I think?" Ali asked while taking a sip of her beer. "I think Jack is leading you on a wild goose chase."

Megan blinked. She'd had the same thought. "Why would he do that though?" Megan asked.

Josie patted her hand. "Because he's in love with you silly." Megan and Ali both froze. Josie never said the L-O-V-E- word.

Josie nodded and tilted her head up, a wistful sparkle in her brown eyes. "I know, I know, I never say the L-word. I never really believed in it until now." When the shock subsided smiles emerged.

"You and Jon?" Ali asked and Josie nodded barely able to control her excitement.

Good for them. "Have you told him you love him?"

"Not yet, and he hasn't told me, but we both know its there."

"Take it slow," Ali advised, then remembered she was talking to Josie, "Well, you know what I mean."

Josie nodded. "But enough about us, let's talk Jack and Megan."

"Jack and Megan is too confusing," Megan said, "How bout we talk politics or religion, something a little less complicated." Ali gave her a wry look.

"Megan, it's not that complicated. I've seen the way you two look at each other. There's enough electricity between you too to light up The Empire State Building on Christmas. You're just in denial."

"I'm not, he is. I know I want him. I just don't know if it's more than lust."

Josie raised her eyebrows. "Only one way to find out."

Megan looked miserable. "I know, but I'm not sure he's interested. I mean I've done everything but say 'Do me big daddy' and he hasn't gotten the hint yet. He sends all these messed up signals. One day he's all over me, then the next he ignores me like I don't exist." She took a long pull of Jack's ice tea. She'd abandoned her beer earlier. "Take today for instance, he pretty much ignored me all day. And don't think I didn't try to get his attention. Before Granny called I had asked him to come over tonight because I wanted to...you know get to know him better, but before I could get the words out he said no, he had an appointment. I asked about after that and he still said no, and we both know he would have been here tonight patrolling my driveway anyway. Then just before he and Jon left to go to the store, he freaking kissed me like there was no tomorrow. I just don't get it."

"Maybe you're sending mixed signals too. Maybe you guys just need to tune your radios to the same station." Ali suggested.

"Like how? I mean what do I say?"

"How about 'Do me big daddy.' I think that'll get the point across," Josie said.

"I can't say that." Megan put her head in her hands, "After that fiasco with Ted my self-esteem is on the floor. What if he shoots me down like Ted did."

"He wouldn't," Josie said.

At the same time Ali said, "Then you'd know."

"You know what? You guys are right. I'm just going to go for it. I know what I want."

"Go get it!" Josie hollered.

"And get some for me. Bill's been on a job for a week straight," Ali said.

"I can help," Josie said. "Here's what we'll do."

Chapter Sixteen

Josie called the boys and told them there'd been a change of plans. Instead of throwing steaks on the grill, the girls were going out. She explained the plans to Jon, who being love struck himself was happy to fulfill his part of the plan. Josie, Megan and Ali had headed over to 'Makeover Headquarters' AKA, Josie's apartment, where the magic would begin.

"It's not going to work, guys. I should just stick to my original plan," Megan said, while Josie and Ali were selecting the perfect outfit for the evening's plan.

"And that would be?" Ali asked, rummaging through Josie's shoes and paying no attention to Megan.

"I uh, well I don't actually have a plan yet, but…"

"Exactly," Josie said, "This'll work Meg, trust me. Nothing gets a man's attention like giving him a little competition."

"But I think Jack may be a little dense when it comes to things like this. I mean he hasn't figured it out yet," Megan answered, while Ali held a slinky black dress to the front of Megan's body. Ali nodded appreciatively and Josie smiled. Megan crossed her eyes because as usual, they weren't listening to a damn word she said.

"Oh he's figured it out. He probably just hasn't figured you out yet," Josie said.

"Maybe he's scared," Ali observed. "You said he's divorced right? Maybe he's a little gun shy when it comes to love. I know I was after my first marriage."

"Maybe," Megan said, "That could be my problem too. Ted did a number on me."

211

"You know, I went to a therapist after my divorce. It really helped me. Maybe you should consider it."

"You guys want to call Dr. Phil or are we going to go get Megan's prince?" Josie asked, shoving Megan into a chair and fussing with her hair. "Megan doesn't need counseling, what she needs is a little sexual healing in the form of Jack Westin."

"Okay, fine! Let's do this. But if it doesn't work, I'm going home and sticking my head in the oven." Ali chuckled and Josie grinned. If things went well tonight, Megan wouldn't even make it near an oven for at least a week.

After a quick forty-five minute full body restoration, Megan was ready. Josie and Ali stood admiring there handy work while Megan fidgeted in her seat anxious to see a mirror.

"Gorgeous," Ali said.

"Sinful," Josie agreed.

"Dazzling," Ali said.

"With just a splash of sex," Josie decided.

"Guaranteed to bring any man to his knees," Ali said.

"Or his elbows," Josie said.

"Enough already! Just give me the damn mirror!" Megan shouted and Josie spun Megan around to the full length mirror in the bathroom. Megan froze. She looked magnificent. Stunning. Sexy enough to render a man unconscious with just a look. She glanced at Josie and Ali in the mirror, both of which were admiring their work and smiling, their eyes dancing with pride and mischief. She turned around and hugged them both, trying frantically not to cry and ruin her beautifully applied make up.

"I'd do you," Josie said and Megan laughed.

"You'd do anybody," Ali retorted and smiled at Josie.

"Good," Megan said. "Remember you said that. If Jack doesn't get the point, I may take you up on that."

***

Jack was pissed. Megan was running from him. After he'd told her he wanted to talk to her, to drown this tension between them, she'd apparently decided to bolt. It was probably just as well. He'd much rather it happen now, than later when he'd been in too far to get out.

So why was he so angry? And hurt?

212

Because although he may be able to walk away, he'd be leaving his heart behind.

"Want to get a drink somewhere?" Jon asked. Poor schmuck. At least Jack wasn't the only one have a shitty night. Josie had dumped Jon and he looked as though he might faint.

"Thanks, man, but I don't drink," Jack replied.

"That's too bad, I could sure use some company about now," Jon covered his face with his left hand and made low sobbing sounds.

Oh hell! "Don't cry man," Jack said giving Jon a sympathetic pat on the shoulder. "It'll be alright."

Jon began to sob louder. "No it won't. She dumped me," he cried, "She said she doesn't know what she wants."

"What do you want?"

Jon let out a desperate cry and sniffled. "I want her."

"Then you got to go after her." Jack sighed and his voice dropped to almost a whisper. "If you don't, you'll regret it the rest of your life."

"But I don't know what to say," Jon said through a smile he concealed with his hand. This match making stuff wasn't too bad. Plus Josie had promised to reward him handsomely for his performance.

"Do you love her?" Jack asked.

"Yes."

"Have you told her how you feel?"

"No."

"Then that's what you've got to do. You've got to go to her and wrap her in your arms and look her dead in the eye and tell her how you feel. You've got to lay your heart on the line, put your cards on the table, go for broke and make her understand that she is forever on your mind and in your heart." Jon snuck a look at Jack who was staring out his window, his eyes misty, his expression miserable. Perfect!

"Are you sure? I mean is that what you would do?"

No, I'm a hardheaded coward. "Absolutely!" Jack said.

Jon took a moment pretending to gain his composure. "OK, you want me to drop you at Megan's?" Jack didn't say anything. "You're truck is there right?"

"Yeah, but I just want to go home."

"But what about your truck?"

"Its fine there," Jack said. "I've got my bike at the house, and I could use a ride about now."

*****

Jon dropped Jack off and called Josie.

"I, my dear, am one hell of an actor," he told her.

"So he's a miserable mess?"

"Yep."

"He gonna come sweep her off her feet?"

"That'd be my guess."

"Well, well Dr. Ross, how can I ever repay you?" Josie purred.

"I've got a few ideas."

"Mmmm, I can't wait to hear about them."

"There will be little talking involved. I plan to make you pay up with action."

"Then you'd better get your ass over here, so I can start immediately," Josie said.

Jon killed the engine in her car. "I'm already here. Come outside and make your first payment," Jon said and hung up just as Josie walked out the door of the bar.

Megan and Ali sat at the bar inside the 'Longhorn' sipping their drinks and watching the drunken crowd of dancers stumble on the dance floor. Several cowboys had asked Megan to dance, all of which she'd sweetly turned down and the hunk of a bartender was frequently giving her the eye.

It had already been an hour and Jack was nowhere in sight.

"I'm really kind of proud of her," Ali was saying and Megan had to think a minute about what they were talking about. Her mind was certainly somewhere else.

"Josie?" Megan asked and Ali nodded. "Yeah me too," she said.

"She's finally in love," Ali said, "And with such a great guy."

"I told her it would happen someday," Megan said with a forced smile.

"Don't worry hon, you're prince is on his way too."

The bartender had obviously been eavesdropping. He strutted his stuff over to Megan, tilted his cowboy hat, winked and smiled which would have made most women go weak in the knees upon impact and said, "Have you ever heard the story of the 'Cowboy Prince'?"

Megan shook her head and Ali muttered "Oh Brother!"

The bartender was not deterred. "Tell you what," he continued, "you come home with me tonight, and I'll tell you all about it, in surround sound, with special bonus features."

Ali snorted. "You sound like an advertisement for a DVD."

"And what would these bonus features be?" Megan asked in a bored tone.

"Whatever you want pretty lady. I aim to please."

"Let me guess, satisfaction guaranteed?" Ali retorted.

"Of course," 'Mr. I'm full of myself' said. "And I'm not above retelling the story all night long over and over until every little detail is right." He traced his finger along Megan's delicate collarbone and licked his lips. "And I promise not to stop until you are completely, 100%, satisfied."

"Oh?" Megan said not even tempted, her body filled with desire for Jack.

"Oh yeah," he said, his voice a low rumble.

"Travis, quit molesting the ladies and bring me a beer," a raspy voice hollered out.

Travis grinned at Megan and said, "I'll be back."

Megan sat stunned. Travis? As in Travis McPhillips? As in rodeo, strip tease and sex on a mechanical bull. Well hell's bells. She'd finally found Bronco Billy, the last guy on her list and she could have cared less. He was gorgeous, and sexy and probably lived up to every last bit of his delicious reputation, and in her eyes, he didn't hold a candle to Jack.

***

"Where is she?" Jack growled before Josie even said hello. He'd called Megan's house, her cell, her mother's, Mickey's and if Josie didn't know where she was he was going to scream.

"Huh, uh, hang on a second." Josie shifted underneath Jon and tried to catch her breath. Jon groaned, then settled back against her and began moving ridiculously slow making her eyes glaze over and her body shutter. She momentarily forgot about Jack.

"Josie!" he yelled. "Where the hell is she?" She grabbed Jon's behind and halted him to a stop. Her body protested immediately.

"Oh uh, where is who?"

Jack slammed his fist onto the table. "Megan! Where is Megan? And don't play games with me dammit. Tell me now!"

She resisted the urge to say Megan who? "Oh Megan, she's with Ali."

Jack gritted his teeth, "Okay where is Ali?"

She resisted the urge to say with Megan. "Ok Jack, but you didn't hear this from me. Ok?" Jon began moving slowly again and Josie gasped.

"Ok," he snapped ready to explode.

"Last time I saw them they were at the 'Longhorn'. Megan was sitting at the bar talking to Travis McPhillips, who was working his charm on your girl. Oh my God!" Josie purred and Jack crunched his eyebrows together and held the phone out and looked at it curiously.

"What?"

"Oh sorry, I wasn't talking to you. Anyway if I were you I'd hurry up and get down there before Travis shows her how to ride his bull." John hit the right spot and Josie shattered. "Oh God! Oh God! Oh God!"

"I hope to hell you're in the middle of prayer, Josie," Jack snapped. "Because if you're doing what I think you're doing, you're messing up. Jon loves you and he's looking for you right now so he can tell you." Josie smiled and cut the connection. She looked into Jon's heavenly eyes for a long minute, cupped his jaw and while riding one of the greatest waves of orgasm she'd ever experienced she said, "I love you."

Jon lost it then too and it was at least a full minute before he had recovered enough to say, "I love you too."

***

Jack grabbed his keys and helmet and got on his bike in less than a minute. 'The Longhorn' was about ten minutes away. He'd make it in five.

Freaking Travis McPhillips. She must have figured out where he worked and her and the girls set out on the mission together. What if she wasn't there now? What if she and Travis were...?

He accelerated and almost took out a street sign trying to navigate the turn.

He tried to slow down his thinking. Megan wouldn't just go home with any guy. Not this quickly. She might give him her number or take his and then go on a date or something and then maybe...

But what if she was drinking and Travis was mixing her drinks way to strong so that he could get her too drunk to say no. Ok, Jack would have to kill him then.

He sighed with a little relief as something suddenly occurred to him. Ali was there. Surely she'd keep a watchful eye on her friend. She was too responsible and level headed to let anything happen.

But what if she was drunk too? Oh hell! Jack screeched around the last corner and skidded to a stop just in front of the main entrance to the bar. Several people were standing around eyeing him suspiciously but he abandoned the bike, swung the door open and like a man on a mission went to find his girl. At first glance she was nowhere. He surveyed the bar. Travis wasn't there either. "Shit," he growled and ran his hand roughly through his hair.

That's when he spotted Ali leaving the ladies room. He fell into step with her and grabbed her arm. "Where is she?" he asked then noticed Ali staring at his hand grasping her arm. He let go abruptly. Ali pointed to Megan.

Relief washed all through Jack and he was just about to head that way when Ali stopped him by grabbing his arm. She came up on her tip toes to brush an unruly strand of hair out of his face and patted his cheek.

"Good luck," she said and Jack wondered if he had his feelings written across his forehead.

"I hope I won't need it," Jack replied and set off to the pool room.

"You won't," Ali added and stepped on the dance floor.

***

Megan was shooting pool with two guys. One was short and stocky with unremarkable features and the other was tall, a little on the heavy side, with a handle bar mustache and a belt buckle the size of California.

Jack spotted Megan before she saw him and he lost all the air in his body. She looked beyond sexy. Beyond fabulous or beautiful or any other adjectives he could come up with. Her hair was softly tousled into a simple, stylish shag. Her makeup was light but flawless. Her little black dress hung off of her delicate shoulders, and flowed just above her knees. And those legs. God help him, those legs were bare and toned and led the way straight to heaven. He made the mistake of letting his eyes drop to her feet. The curve of her elegant feet, with brightly painted toenails, encased into those elegant shoes set his body on fire. Those feet were going to be over his shoulders while he backed her up against that pool table right here in front of God and everybody if he didn't calm himself down. He stepped into the room.

"Where's your partner?" the big guy was saying, "It's her shot."

"She went to the bathroom," Jack said watching Megan turn at the sound of his voice. "I'll take her shot."

"I don't know," the little guy said and Jack laid a fifty on the table and picked up a cue.

"Chicken?" he asked, teeth bared and the little guy took a step back.

"We ain't playing for money," the big guy said and Jack frowned.

"Stripes or solids?" he asked Megan and she muttered quietly stripes. Jack eyed the table. If Megan was stripes them she was getting the pants beaten off of her. Or in this case the dress. "What are we playing for?" he asked never taking his eyes off Megan.

"Just for fun. Maybe for her phone number," the little prick said.

"How bout this," Jack said. "You and your partner there take that fifty and have a few drinks on me." They both looked skeptical and didn't budge. "Or, I can always just run the table, get the lady's phone number and then kick your asses before I take her home with me." Jack stood seriously still, his eyes liquid fire, the pool stick in one hand. Both guys stared at Megan.

"What's it gonna be boys?" Jack asked and Megan nodded for them both to leave.

"You sure ma'am?" the big guy inquired and Megan looked at Jack, her eyes lighting up and she said, "Yep. Scoot." They left the room and then the little guy came back in, ducked down a little, grabbed the fifty and left quickly.

***

Jack racked the balls. "We're going to play a little game," he said.

"What are the stakes?" she asked, selecting a stick and chalking the end of it.

"My heart," he said and Megan's own heart swelled in her chest. She didn't respond because she didn't know what to say. "Here's the deal, for every ball I make you have to answer a question of my choosing. I'll do the same for you. You can end the game at any time by pocketing the eight ball, but I must warn you if you do that, you forfeit and I win." Their eyes locked "And I will make you pay."

"What's the price?"

"That's still to be determined, although I will tell you that it might be a good idea to clear your schedule for a couple weeks."

"You're toast," she said accepting the challenge.

No shit. His eyes glittered. "We'll see." He handed her the cue to break and she motioned for him to go ahead. He broke and sent the balls spinning. He sunk the two and the six balls. He met Megan's eyes and grinned. Leaning his cue on the table he backed her up against the table and put his hands on the table on either side of her.

"Two balls, two questions," he said. She nodded and gulped. His face was nose to nose with hers and he looked like sweet sin. His eyes were the color of hot cocoa and they were staring clear through to her soul.

"Shoot," she said coolly.

He grinned. "Do you know how fantastic you look tonight?" he asked his mouth beside her ear, his hot breath setting her on fire.

"Um, I don't know," she whispered. "How bout you tell me."

"I would if I could find the words," he murmured and ran his hand down her back starting at the nape of her neck and ending well below her bottom.

"Next question."

"Can I kiss those delicious lush lips?" He brushed his lips lightly against hers, then pulled back waiting for her answer.

"So this is like an interactive game, huh?" she asked and he nodded smiling. She answered his question by positioning both of her hands on his butt and licking his bottom lip. He responded hungrily and hoisted her up on the pool table to gain better access to her mouth. Just when the kiss was reaching levels that made her body shake and tremble he released her and retrieved her stick for her. "Your shot."

"Huh?" she asked dazed and a little frustrated. "Oh," she grabbed her cue and took a shot. She missed. Jack chuckled and lined up his own shot. He sunk the four and cornered Megan against the paneled wall.

"One question," she told him.

He pressed his body into hers and lowered his head close to hers, his eyes hot with sex and desire through silky long lashes. "Do you have any idea how crazy I am about you?" Before she could answer the question he had captured her mouth again. She wrapped her arms around him and he traced the curve of one breast with his hand, caressing softly and then more aggressively when he found her nipple. She forgot to breathe and leaned into him and he smiled against her lips and pushed back from the wall.

Do you know how bad you're driving me crazy? She thought.

"Your shot," he said again and she grunted and took the damn stick. She shot and big surprise she missed again. She looked up at Jack who was holding his stick, smiling as innocent as a choir boy, as if he hadn't just made love to her mouth and assaulted her nipple. It was his fault she couldn't sink a ball to save her life.

"You give up yet?" he asked, thoroughly pleased with the state of frustration he had driven her to. She looked so damn cute with her swollen lips and flushed skin he almost wanted to sink the eight ball and take her on the green velvet of the table. Almost.

"In your dreams," she replied hotly as he lined up a shot.

"Good to know," he said sinking the five and the one.

Megan winced and muttered, "Shit," as he closed in on her. He separated her legs with his thigh and pressed an impressive erection into her belly.

"I get two questions," he said. "You ready?" She pressed her hand to the strained zipper of his jeans, closed her eyes and licked her lips. Jack closed his eyes and felt the air leave his lungs and couldn't get the air back to his brain to formulate his questions. Megan massaged him and he braced his hands on the wall.

"I've been ready Jack." You blind idiot!

"Huh?" he said too dizzy to think. She dropped her hand.

"Two questions, Magnum. You wanna ask or do you forfeit?"

"Oh, I'm asking." He ran his tongue down her neck and slid a hand under her dress. "First question, am I making you hot?" She moved against his hand and he smiled obviously pleased with her answer. Just the feel of him touching her—anywhere or everywhere— drove her insane and he knew it. He was deliberately touching and teasing her skin in the gentlest way yet his kisses were hungry, full of lust and explosive. He was teetering on the edge of control and taking her with him.

"Next question," she purred. He slid his finger inside the elastic of her panties.

"Do you want me to stop?"

"No," she whispered just before he buried his head in her breasts and gently bit her nipple. The material of the dress was hardly any barrier and his hot wet tongue, along with his magic hands were sending her out of control. She grabbed on to him for support and when she felt the first delicious wave of release coming he stopped and pulled away, grinning like the devil. He handed her her stick and opened his mouth to speak.

"I know, I know, you evil bastard. My freaking shot!" She grabbed the stick, found the damn eight ball and shot. And missed. "Dammit!" she growled and decided enough of this. She stood directly behind him, thankful this section of the room was pretty closed in and private and shimmied her panties off. When she was done Jack was just lining up his shot and gloating. "One more ball and…," he said.

"You think you'll make it," she asked and he chuckled.

"Positive, babe." He brought back his cue and paused.

"You're pretty sure of yourself aren't you big guy?"

"Absolutely." He brought the cue forward at the same time Megan threw her black, silk thong panties on the table and he faltered causing the cue to tear the felt on the table. "Hey, that's not fair," he protested with little commitment.

She chalked her cue. "All's fair in love and war babe," she said before she lined up the twelve ball and sank it. Jack stood frozen leaning on the table staring at her panties. She walked up behind him, put her lips to his ear and said "I get one question. You ready?" He nodded. She positioned herself in front of him, pulled his body toward hers, ground her hips into him and said in a low husky voice, "You ready to get out of here?" Jack stood statue still for a moment, then reached around her for the eight ball, cupped it in his hand, sunk the damn thing in the pocket, then scooped her up, stuck her panties in his pocket and turned to exit the pool area just in time to see Ali, Josie, and Jon try to scramble out of sight. When they realized they'd been busted eavesdropping and watching, they stopped running and began clapping, unable to contain their smiles.

"That was so romantic," Ali said.

"It's about damn time," Josie added.

Jon handed Jack two rubbers he'd bought in the men's room, "Take two of these, and don't call me in the morning," he said.

***

Jack carried Megan to his Harley and plunked her down on the seat. He got on so quick he realized he'd left his helmet and keys inside.

"I'll be right back," he said and nearly ran Ali over. She was standing just inside the door dangling his keys and helmet before him. "Thanks," he said hurriedly and bolted back out the door. He sat down on the motorcycle and handed Megan the helmet.

"My place or yours?" he asked, then said, "Never mind, mine's closer and Granny isn't there." He cranked up the bike, Megan wrapped her arms around him and they were in his garage in less than ten minutes.

He parked the bike and was about to get off when Megan stopped him. She climbed off the back of the bike and then climbed back on in front of him, straddling his thighs. Before he could say a word she had her mouth over his, teasing his tongue with hers while she went to work on the fly of his jeans. His arms found their way around her waist and he greedily grasped at her dress bunching the sleek material up around her hips. "Oh yeah," he said when his hand finally found her sex, wet, swollen and waiting for him. He slid a finger in and Megan closed her eyes, allowing a desperate moan to escape from her throat. His mouth was sweet and his finger felt divine, but it wasn't enough. She wanted him inside her immediately. He found a rhythm that was driving her insane, and she wrestled with his jeans and then his boxers to get his sex free. He offered no help as he had both hands occupied and he was savoring every touch, feel and taste.

Megan let out a disgusted grunt. "A little help here Jack?" she growled.

"Uh uh," he mumbled. "I'm busy."

Oh, no you don't. No more teasing. "Jack, I want you now!"

"Be patient, I'm enjoying the foreplay."

"We already did that at the bar."

"More is better."

She lifted herself up long enough to free him from underneath her and wrapped both hands around his rod, giving it a good hard yank. He opened his eyes and stared directly into hers which were electric blue flames. "Jack, have you ever seen the movie 'The Fast and The Furious'?" He nodded confused. "Well right now it is time to get fast and get furious and do it in a hurry. I want you hard and fast inside me right now or I am going to scream."

"Damn right you're gonna scream," he countered.

"You're all talk," she said breathlessly when actually she was on the verge of screaming from what he was doing to her with his hands. How in the hell can he be so patient? she wondered. Well to hell with that. She wasn't going to wait another second. She grabbed the condom from his shirt pocket and ripped it open with her teeth, while Jack was delivering slow sweet kisses to her breast. She rolled the condom down his length and grabbed Jack's face in her hands, locked eyes with him and shouted. "Shut up and do…"

He was inside her before she got her demand out. And, oh my God, he felt so good. He gripped her hips and began moving her up and down on him hard and fast and oh God, she felt like she was losing control. Hell she was losing control and it was fantastic and phenomenal because this was Jack and her body belonged to him now and she never wanted this moment to end and oh my God he was moving faster and filling her so completely she thought she was going to break in two. His mouth found hers with this unruly greed and lust and when she couldn't take any more she screamed his name and began to shatter in his arms. He moved faster and harder and deeper and when she reached the peak of the awesome relief, he thrust in her one last time and he fell apart beneath her.

They clung lifelessly to each other for what seemed like an eternity, then Jack found his voice and said, "Told you I'd make you scream," in a cocky sex filled drawl.

"I faked it," Megan replied coolly.

Grinning, Jack said, "Liar."

"Guess you'll have to try harder next time," she said with mischief in her voice.

"No time like the present," Jack said getting off the motorcycle and helping Megan down.

"Be careful. Don't fall," he told her noting the weakness in her knees.

"I think I already fell," she said which sent a sensation through Jack that made his own knees go weak.

***

Jack's house was a small but tidy bachelor's pad, with the usual male essentials; simple functional furniture, big screen T.V., a home entertainment center elaborate enough to make Radio Shack's mouth water, and minimal décor. There was definitely not a woman's touch in the place, but everything about the house screamed Jack. Megan stood looking around, taking everything in, but obviously Jack had seen it all before and didn't care to reminisce with his furnishings. He tugged her hand and pulled her into him, his hands everywhere.

"Oh my God, you have fish!" she said with obvious excitement, spotting a large aquarium. He didn't seem like a fish kind of guy. Spot would be so pleased.

"Yeah, I got a bed too. Wanna see it?"

"And I love that sculpture. Where'd you get it?"

Jack nipped at her ear then trailed kisses down her neck. "Pier One. Same place I got my bed. Let me show it to you."

"Is that a gun?" she asked pointing to a dark shadowed object on his entertainment center. Did he need a gun in his line of work? Did people shoot at him?

"Yep and if you don't let me show you my bed soon, I may have to shoot myself with it." She laughed and he let out a low masculine grunt and picked her up by her hips and shuffled her into his bedroom, kicking the door open with his foot.

"You have entirely too much clothing on," he said sliding the only article of clothing she was wearing down her shoulders where it pooled at her feet. He left her only long enough to flip on the light and then he pushed her on the bed and lowered himself on top of her, balancing his weight on his elbows. He began allowing his hands to explore her pale smooth skin and she tensed. He stopped.

"What's wrong?" She flicked her eyes away from him.

"I um, I'm uncomfortable with the light on." She nervously licked her lips. "Can we turn it off?"

"Why?" he muttered.

"Because I probably look a lot better in the dark."

"What are you crazy? You are sexy as hell." He delivered sweet kisses to her belly. "In any light."

"No I'm not. I have chunky thighs, and…" she squeezed her love handles, "…and these. And that's not to mention my lovely A cups."

He closed his eyes and sighed. How could she not see how beautiful she was? She was perfect, a feast for his eyes, he couldn't take them off of her.

"Megan," he said sincerely, "You are by far the sexiest woman I've ever seen." He kissed the inside of first one thigh, then the other. "I love these," he growled then moved on to her love handles, "and these," then to her small but perfectly rounded breasts, "and especially these."

"You do?"

He stroked her backside. "And your ass is world class, babe," he kissed her forehead, "and you have the bluest bedroom eyes that make me melt."

"Really?" she asked breathlessly, his kind words and low urgent tone curling her toes. One look in those smoky brown eyes and her body was on fire.

"Hell yes," he said and he took her hand and held it to his crotch. "See? I'm already aching for you again babe." She seemed to be relaxing. "If you want the light off I'll turn it off, but I want you to know that I would be in heaven just laying here looking at you all night."

She almost cried. How could she not fall for him? "Oh Jack," she whispered nestling herself in his strong capable arms. "That's very sweet."

"It's also very true."

She stroked his forearm and smiled. "There's only one problem though."

"Oh?"

"Now you are wearing entirely too much clothing," she complained. She grasped the hem of his tee shirt and with his help yanked it over his head. Her gaze settled on his broad chest, covered in course spirals of black hair. His biceps were shaped to muscled perfection, from hard work instead of hours at the gym. She lowered her gaze down his abdomen to the inviting trail of dark, thick hair that led to promise and satisfaction and Jack hard and full insider her. Oh Yeah! Unable to resist she ran a finger along that trail, her touch so tender, so light, Jack's skin prickled with sensation and he stilled her hand with his.

"Megan," he ground out, "Let's slow down. I don't want another 'Brace Yourself' replay from the garage."

"Did you hear me complain?" She looped her finger in the waistband of his jeans and took pleasure in the way his breath caught and his eyes slid closed. He stopped her and now held both of her hands. Oh damn!

"Now what are you going to do?" he teased transferring both of her hands to one of his in a firm grip giving his free hand the opportunity to explore her lush body.

"I'm gonna lie here and let you make me scream," she purred, her voice thick.

"That a girl."

"Then I'm gonna make you scream." Oh Mama! He liked the sound of that.

His mind was racing, and his hormones weren't doing much better. He wanted to go slow and savor every inch, but he wanted to go so fast he was dizzy. It had been less than a half hour since the last time he'd had her and he was still so hungry he was about to burst. Fifteen years of want and need could do embarrassing things to a man's stamina. He could've tried to silently recite the table of elements from chemistry, if he'd actually paid attention to them. The only element he could even come up with right now was s-e-x and he was pretty sure that didn't qualify. Chemistry would have been a lot more enjoyable if it had.

"Jack," Megan growled her voice full of frustration. Good at least he wasn't the only one. He tightened his grasp on her hands and lowered his body even closer to hers pinning her in place, his naked chest against hers, the sensation incredible.

"What?"

"I'm dying to get you out of those jeans." She tried to wrestle her hands free.

His hold held firm. "I'm dying to get out of them," he said.

"So what are you waiting for?" Ok, it was a simple question right? Except he wasn't sure why he was waiting either. In the living room he couldn't wait to get her in his bed, naked and beneath him. Now he had exactly that and he was…hesitating?

Maybe it was because he wasn't sure this was real. Maybe it was some wicked dream that would dissipate before he got his pants off. He bent his head and caught Megan's mouth. Ok it wasn't a dream. She was kissing back, with a fierce, hot passion that was turning his brain to mud.

He broke the kiss and gazed into her eyes, the blue barely visible under the erotic curtain of her heavy lids and thick smoky lashes. Her lips were still parted, her skin flushed with arousal, her hair mussed from their previous session of lovemaking in the garage.

It came to him. The reason he'd been holding back. True, he wanted to take her in every way imaginable, hard, fast, slow, in every position known to man. But he also wanted to tempt and tease, seduce and savor, bring her to the depths of orgasm she'd never experienced before until she screamed his name loud enough to crumble the drywall and rattle the windows. He wanted to taste every smooth, seductive inch of her inside and out. He wanted to feel her body spasm beneath him, around him, while he was inside her. He wanted to hold her, caress her, soothe her, thrust into her like there was no tomorrow. He wanted to love her. Not shag, screw, mount, tag, lay. No, he wanted to make love to her.

He gave her a wicked grin that relayed everything he wanted to do to her. She licked her lips and parted her legs. His eyes crossed and his blood boiled. Slowly, he used his free hand to work his jeans down his hips, and then kicked them off his legs. All that remained were his snug, white boxers. Grabbing the waistband he pulled them free and repeated the procedure of kicking out of them. His sex rested on her stomach, throbbing, stretching, twitching with need. Megan's smile was a mix of anticipation, excitement, and desire.

"You are so beautiful, Megan. I've wanted you since the first time I laid eyes on you." He delivered heavenly kisses down the curve of her throat, her collarbone. She pressed against him, all soft, lush, warm woman. He nearly imploded.

"Yeah?" she breathed. "Now that you've got me, what are you going to do to me?"

Now that you've got me. The words almost did him in. "Anything you want."

She smiled a lazy crooked smile. "Sounds promising."

She smothered his response with a thirsty kiss, violently claiming his mouth as hers. Her mouth was hot and sweet and with every thrust and suck of her tongue it was as if she was drinking him in trying to get her fill. His free hand was exploring the sweet, feminine folds of her now swollen sex. She was on fire and wet and welcoming his touch. He penetrated her with his finger, using his thumb to gently stoke her clitoris, never breaking the kiss. Her body began to shake, tremble. Low, rumbling moans fought their way out of her mouth. When she was almost there, hanging on by a thread, squirming and shaking from his touch, he stopped and began working his way down her body with his tongue. She tried to free her hands. Again he tightened his grip.

"Hold still, woman or I'll handcuff you," he said teasingly.

"You have handcuffs?" And damned if she didn't sound intrigued. What a woman! He tilted his head up and gave her a predatory grin.

"Maybe later," he told her not wanting to let go of her long enough to get them. "Right now I'm busy."

"Uh Jack, My shoes?" He looked at her feet in those sexy, black, stilettos and bit his tongue. "Leave 'em on. They'll look good on my shoulders," he replied.

He turned his attention–and his tongue-to her breasts, licking, tasting then slowly, softly captured each rosy nipple with his teeth, sending her writhing beneath him. He dragged his tongue down to her naval, admiring the slight slope and curve. He planted tender kisses to each hipbone, the inside of each thigh. She violently tried to free her hands, her high heels dug into the mattress. She closed her eyes, moved her head from side to side, moaned sweet sexual sounds and parted her long, toned legs further.

And the gates of heaven opened.

He kissed her there, dragging his tongue along every hot, wet fold of pink flesh. She cried out, and her breath came faster, shorter. He took her cue and allowed his tongue to explore her more thoroughly, rougher while he used his hand to taunt and tease her breasts, her nipples. Licking, lapping, milking her, savoring her scent, her taste, the smooth, slick texture of her sex.

A scream escaped her mouth –"Oh God, Oh Jack, Oh my…" and she fell apart, her body shaking, her legs trembling. He rested his head on her belly and stared up at her face, her head tilted back, eyes closed, lips parted. She looked like sex personified and it was without a doubt the sexiest thing he'd ever seen. He could spend the rest of his life looking at her just like this and it wouldn't be enough.

He snatched the condom from beside her—luckily he'd had enough blood left in his brain to think to remove it from his shirt pocket and have it handy— and ripped the silver packet open with his teeth, covered himself and brought his body back over hers.

He looked into those gorgeous, sated, blue eyes and entered her slowly, not wanting to hurt her. Her muscles clamped down hard around his cock, accepting him, inviting him. His body was smoldering. He released one of her hands catching it with his free hand and pinned them both on either side of her head. She arched her hips up to meet his thrusts, taking him deeper, further until he became a part of her. He found a comfortable rhythm and they rocked together, their heartbeats pounding, their flesh glistened with sweat, their bodies a perfect fit.

Megan wrapped her legs around his waist and he felt her shoes bucking against his back. He came to his knees, still inside her, bringing her up with him, released her hands and patted his shoulders. "Right here. Let's see 'em."

She obediently complied with that fantasy and placed her delicate feet encased in those elegant high heels on his shoulders and he wrapped his hands around her small, pretty ankles.

"God, Megan you feel so good," he breathed. She began to shake again and rocked her hips rapidly speeding up their rhythm. With every thrust, her muscles contracted around him, squeezing him, milking him. He fought for control.

She screamed, her voice penetrating the sex filled air and she lost it again, her body convulsing wildly, a smile curving her lips, her eyes heavy lidded and erotic.

They locked eyes as she rode the waves of her release and purred, in between strained breaths, "Jack, — I've — wanted you — for — so long."

She wanted him. That was it. He gripped her ankles, slammed into her hard one last time, jerked his head back and as his own release shook his body he too screamed her name in a low, thick rumble, just before he collapsed on top of her breathless, satisfied, the happiest man on earth.

She ran her fingers through his hair massaging his scalp, which lay on her chest, listening to her rapid heartbeat.

"Told you I'd make you scream," she said. "Now about those handcuffs…"

Amy Johnson

Chapter Seventeen

Holy Mary Mother of God! If she hadn't felt so boneless and thoroughly satisfied, she'd of danced a jig. Jack was incredible. In ten years of marriage to Ted, the minute man, she'd never felt so alive, so elated so...passionate. In the first couple years of her their marriage Ted had been a generous if not fantastic lover. Nothing as heart stopping as one night with Jack but still he held his own. But as the time passed, Ted became selfish in bed and when they did have sex, it was quick, boring and all about him. Wam bam thank you ma'am, now go to sleep and don't touch me. So different from Jack with his hot demanding hands, his undivided attention to her needs, his intent on driving her insane until she came so hard she just about passed out, all the while penetrating her with those ashen brown eyes full of...love.?

And what the hell was she thinking. In her current state of affairs, love was the last thing she needed. She wasn't even divorced yet, her husband's girlfriend was pregnant and the paternity was at best questionable, she had a pair of knucklehead drug dealers hounding her, her mother was on Zoloft, her father was oblivious to everything but his remote control, and her Granny was dating when she wasn't busy getting expelled from nursing homes. Talk about dysfunction.

If Jack were a smart man, he'd run like hell and never look back.

She tilted her head up to glance at Jack, his face hard planes in the dim light, his smoldering eyes closed with sleep, his broad chest heaving slowly in a slow, steady rhythm. She had her head on his chest and both of his arms embraced her in a sensual, protective hold.

She felt something for him. It was definitely deeper than lust of infatuation, but love? Oh, who was she kidding? She was hooked, line and sinkered. Toast. Not that she would ever admit it. Maybe she could keep things light, sexual…casual.

Nope that would probably never do. Jack didn't seem like a casual kind of guy and in all honesty Megan knew she wasn't either. She could never open her legs for a man without opening her heart first.

And that's what she'd done with Jack, although she didn't know it at first. It had been building, growing and now looking back she couldn't see how she'd missed it.

It scared the hell out of her.

It was too fast, too strong and too damn confusing. It was an emotional overload that sent her head spinning. She caressed Jack's chest, her touch light as a gentle breeze. He caught his breath and shifted a little and she noticed his heavy erection pressing against her thigh.

She wanted him again.

He obviously wanted her.

He'd taken her three more times last night and although he never broke out the handcuffs, promising he would later, she hadn't missed them. Jack Westin didn't need props, he was incredible without them.

She was so sore, she was afraid she couldn't move, yet the anticipation and excitement of him inside her, filling her so completely masked her physical discomfort. She reached for him and took his length in her hand. His muscles tightened but he didn't wake. Slowly, she lowered her head past his belly and near his sex, her hair tickling the skin on his hard abdomen. He shivered.

Teasingly she licked him and delivered sweet, hot kisses to his already throbbing erection. His body jerked and his eyes shot open. After a second he tangled his hand in her hair.

"Megan."

"Shhh, I want to satisfy you," she whispered and he began to slowly circle her back with one hand and loosened the grip on her hair with the other one.

She continued what she was doing, with the lightest touch and if possible his erection grew. She heard a low groan come from his throat and reverberate throughout the room. She smiled and experimented, tasting him, taunting him, taking him.

***

"I'm satisfied," he managed.

232

Jack was on the edge of losing control. He'd fallen asleep with Megan in his arms, on his mind and in his dreams. And awoken to her…down there doing things to him that should be downright illegal. It's not like this was his first experience with oral sex. He'd had plenty, but this was Megan and her touch completely set him on fire. Not that he was complaining, he just wasn't used to his dreams coming true.

This one certainly had.

"Just tell me what to do, Jack," she said her voice a little uncertain, thick with eagerness and emotion.

"Umm, you're doing fine," he ground out through clenched teeth, feeling more than touched that she was so worried about his needs.

"But I want to please you," she whispered and Jack felt his heart expand. Hearing those words almost did him in. He pulled her up to him and kissed her silly. He'd meant for the kiss to be gentle and reassuring but around Megan he couldn't keep his self-control and almost before it started the kiss was rough, and hungry, and bordering on the line of insanity. He broke the kiss panting.

"Sweetheart, I woke up with you in my bed, your tongue on my cock. I'd say I'm pleased."

She frowned. "I know but I've never, um, done that before and I wasn't sure I was doing it right." The emotion in her eyes broke his heart. "I wanted it to feel good."

He laughed. He knew it was the wrong moment but he couldn't stifle it. "It felt good, babe. Better than good. Earth shattering."

She smiled. His heart exploded. "Really?" she asked.

He took her then, pinning her beneath him, kissing her crooked mouth, caressing her breast, spreading her legs with his thigh. Before any logic reached his brain he was inside her and she felt so good, so tight and wet and accepting. He froze. He wasn't wearing a condom. Never before had he ever lost his head like this and practiced unprotected sex.

Never had he been so in love with a woman that he lost control from just her touch, the pouty set of her lips in a smile, or the tenderness in her eyes.

Never before had he made love to Megan Johnson.

Megan stilled beneath him aware of his uneasiness. "What's wrong?"

Hell if he knew. "I forgot a condom," he said truthfully. Her eyes widened and he quickly added, "I just lost my head Megan. I didn't even think about it. All I could think about was you and your touch and how much I love making love to you and…" She wiggled under him forcing him deeper inside her. "And oh my God, you feel so wonderful without the barrier of a condom…" She moved again and his thought process disintegrated. "Quit moving, woman I'm trying to think here."

"I was just trying to get comfortable." She said.

Alarm rocked through him. He'd taken her relentlessly all night. "Are you sore? Did I hurt you?" The thought of hurting her just about killed him.

He remained completely still. "No," she said but he wasn't buying. She gave a wary smile, "a little maybe, but it feels…wonderful anyway." He narrowed his eyes at her. She should have told him. She'd been so intent in bringing him pleasure that she hadn't even thought of herself. His heart ached. Seeing his expression change, she added hastily, "I don't want you to stop, though. I want you to make love to me."

He debated. She was hurting and that was more than he could take. He wasn't wearing protection and they were taking a big risk there. And she felt so damn soft and warm and sweet and the feel of his naked flesh against hers was beyond description. He resented the need for a condom and damn it he didn't want to leave her body.

Not now. Not ever.

He was a selfish bastard he decided.

At a total loss he asked her, "Tell me what you want me to do sweetheart? We can stop, if you're too raw or wary of our lack of protection."

"I'm fine, Jack. I trust you. I know you won't hurt me." Seeing the concern on his face she added quickly. "Really, it's OK."

Jack closed his eyes. "I'll be careful, baby." Slowly, very slowly, he pulled almost completely out and eased back in. She arched her hips and he nestled his head in her bosom giving her taut nipples the attention they deserved. He suckled and nipped, as he tenderly thrust into her. She responded with her body and ran her hands along his back, his shoulders.

Slowly sliding into her slick wetness when they were both ultrasensitive was blurring his brain, his release begging to come out. But he fought to hold control wanting her to get there too.

As if on cue, her breaths became short and rapid, her fingernails digging into his shoulders, sweet moans escaping her throat. He kissed her throat, her temples, her forehead and then as her body began to shake he landed his gaze on her tightly closed eyes.

"Open your eyes sweetheart. I want to see you," he ordered softly and when she did he plunged into her so deep he felt her womb and he hoped she was almost there because he couldn't hold back much longer. She trembled, dug her teeth into her bottom lip and then she exploded beneath him, her body writhing, her soft moans transforming into a scream. He stared into those heavenly blue eyes now dark and dilated from the adrenaline of her release and he felt tears sting his own eyes, his heart swell with pride and contentment. She smiled and released a lazy sigh of pleasure.

"I never dreamed I could feel this good," she said. "so happy, so satisfied, so…full. I love the way you love me, Jack. Promise me you'll never stop."

He didn't intend to.

Hearing those words, along with the lump in his throat and the feel of him inside her, her body clamping down on him, he thrust three more times, before he couldn't hold back any longer. With a low, deep groan, he spent himself on her stomach and because his entire body had turned to Jell-O, both emotionally and physically, he collapsed beside her, too drained to move. She absently raked her fingers across his chest and down his abdomen, in light, loving strokes.

He fought hard to keep the words of love from tumbling out of his mouth. It was too soon and she had to be emotionally and physically drained.

He was able to stand without falling flat on his face and he went into the adjoined bathroom and warmed a washrag to clean her with. From the mirror over the sink he caught her reflection, sprawled out gloriously naked in his bed, looking like a bent angel, with a satisfied glow.

His angel. Whether she knew it yet or not.

Returning to the bed, he gently bathed her stomach, her inner thighs. She stared down at him with big, blue eyes that melted his heart, turned his bones to putty. He took the rag back to the bathroom and tossed it in the hamper, then shook two Advil from the bottle and got a glass of water. When he returned to the bed, Megan was already dozing.

He smiled. She had to be beat and she looked so peaceful he almost didn't want to disturb her. He was also worried about her being in pain. Because of him and his lack of restraint.

He ran the side of his thumb across her forehead. She opened her eyes, stretched and smiled. His heart fluttered. "Here, sweetheart. Take these."

She sat up and reached for the glass. "What is it?"

"Advil, honey. You're going to be really sore. I don't want you to be uncomfortable." She frowned but popped the pills in her mouth and took a long thirsty gulp of water. Jack felt like a bastard. "I'm sorry Megan. I didn't mean to hurt you. I…"

She waved her hand in her air. "Jack, I woke you up remember? You have nothing to be sorry about." He frowned and she added reassuringly, "I'm fine anyway. I just had a gorgeous man make love to me all night long in the sweetest and most satisfying ways. I feel alive and content and too damn happy to move. If I'm a little sore tomorrow, it'll be worth it because right now I feel like the luckiest girl alive." She socked him in the shoulder. "So quit fretting and hold me damn it."

Smiling, he lay beside her and circled his arms around her waist, spooning her from behind. She thought he was gorgeous. She thought she was lucky. She had it backwards. He was the lucky one and he hoped his luck never ran out.

***

Megan's house was empty when she arrived home the next morning. Jack brought her home, did a quick walk through of the house and, satisfied that everything was Ok, he headed off to his office to return his calls and get some paperwork done. He'd be by around lunchtime. At first he'd insisted on her spending the beautiful Wednesday morning in bed at his house but she had been anxious to get home. With the Madrino's in jail for now, Ted gone, and Granny at Mickey's, she felt safe being home and was looking forward to some alone time to think about Ted, Jack and how things had gone from boring to bedlam in just under two weeks.

Plus she wanted to bring the pups' home, she missed them like crazy. Spot needed a little quality time and her column was due tomorrow.

She smiled thinking about the email that spurred everything. Passion or comfort. She'd experienced both now and her mind was definitely made up. Passion won in a heartbeat. Now the question is does it fade and if so can, you keep it alive with a balanced level of comfort. Something that would stand the test of time.

Sitting at her computer she buzzed through her column, choosing to tackle the topic of first impressions. She'd judged Jack right from the start and if she hadn't come to her senses she'd have missed out on last night. And this morning.

Her phone rang and she picked it up on the third ring. It was her mother.

"Megan Diane, where in the heck have you been young lady?" Megan rolled her eyes and considered changing her phone number. "I phoned for hours last night, and came by to check on you but you weren't home. You need to give me my key back for emergencies like this." Like hell, Megan thought.

"Mom, it wasn't an emergency, I'm fine."

"And what about your poor grandmother. She was probably worried sick."

"I doubt it, Mom. She had a date."

Her mother choked. "She had a what?"

"I'll let her tell you about it," Megan said then tried to end the conversation by saying, "She's at Mickey's, Mom, why don't you call her and ask her all about it."

Her mother was a determined woman. "So where were you? And why didn't you call me. You're father barely slept a wink for worry that you might have been abducted or worse." Yeah right, her father could sleep through a drive by shooting. "Stacy and Mickey had no idea where you were, Ali said she wasn't sure where you were but you were fine and Josie, well Josie said you'd kill her if she told me, but she did say you were right where you wanted to be doing things that needed to be done. What exactly did she mean by that?"

Megan laughed at Josie's elusive accuracy. "Did she tell you she was in love?"

"What?" her mother seemed stumped for a moment but quickly recovered. "Answer my question Megan."

Megan felt rebellious. "No," she said.

"Did you say no?" Her mother sounded shocked. She was probably contemplating strangling Megan with her rosary beads.

"Yep, that's what I said."

"OK, I'm on my way over. You will not disrespect me like that over the phone. What happened to the sweet little girl I raised?" Megan growled. Here comes the guilt trip delivered in full catholic fashion. "You know I was in labor for fifteen hours with you and this was before they had all those fancy drugs. And you were a colicky baby Megan; I didn't sleep for two years…"

"Maybe you should catch up on that right now, Mom."

"…I never missed a dance recital, school play, T-ball game, or anything else that was important to you." Her voice cracked and Megan winced. "And I've spent my entire life giving you everything a mother could and for this you tell me no. No, you can't answer one simple…"

"Mom, I was with Jack, Ok?"

The sniffling stopped. Carefully her mother asked, "All night?"

"Yep."

"What were you doing?"

"Do you really want the details?"

There was a long silence and Megan figured her mother was preparing a sermon or overdosing on Zoloft. She finally found her voice and said, "No, I suppose I don't. You're safe and I guess that's all that's important."

"Thanks, Mom."

"But what about Ted? He's not going to like this, Megan. He's been calling here nonstop trying to convince us to talk some sense in you."

"Tell him to eat shit. That's what Granny tells him."

Her mother sucked in air loudly. "I will not tell him that."

"Fine, then I will. And what he likes or dislikes is no longer any of my concern. I've already filed for divorce. I'm moving on with my life. I think that's fair since he moved on with his a long time ago."

"I suppose you're right. I just hope you know what you're doing."

She did. She was doing Jack. And it was incredible. "I do, Mom and look, I've got to go. I have to get my column finished for tomorrow's deadline. Gotta go. Love you."

"If you want to hang up, just say so. Don't lie to me about that stupid column."

Megan crossed her eyes and stuck her tongue out at the phone. "Sure thing Ma, take care." Before her mother could protest she clicked off and the phone rang again almost instantly. She debated answering figuring it might be her mother again, but it could be Jack. She already missed him. She answered the phone just in case. This time it was Stacy.

"We need to talk," Stacy said almost immediately.

"About?"

"You, Jack, Ted, Josie and her Dr. Ross. Lot's of things really. We just need to catch up," Stacy said her voice sounding tight.

"Is everything Okay? You sound weird." Stacy never sounded weird. Usually she just sounded bored.

"Yeah, you gonna be home? I need to round everyone up."

Alarmed, Megan said weakly, "Okay."

"I'll be by in a few." And without further explanation Stacy clicked off leaving Megan sitting there with her imagination running wild. If it had been anybody else, she wouldn't have been worried. But it was Stacy and even sputtering drunk, Stacy was the most sensible person she knew. Something was up. Something big.

Megan tried to shrug it off and called her grandmother to trade date stories. This time, she'd bet she could one up her granny. Granny probably didn't get any.

Granny was just telling her how all the old ladies at the Bingo Hall were ogling at her man when Megan's call waiting beeped. Putting Granny on hold she answered and was greeted by Jack's husky baritone on the other end.

"Are you Okay?" he demanded as soon as she said hello.

OK this was getting weird. "I'm fine, why wouldn't I be?"

"Megan, I want you to get out of the house. Go to Mrs. Everett's until I get there. I'm on my way." He sounded stressed, angry... concerned.

"No, I hate that woman," More than a little angry herself she asked, "What the hell's wrong with everyone today anyway. First my mother, and then Stacy, and now you. For God's sake I'm thirty years old and I am perfectly capable of..."

"Just get out of the house Megan!" His tone was loud and sharp and Megan flinched at his rudeness.

"Look Jack, I'll have you know..." She heard a dial tone before she got finished with her verbal butt chewing. Figuring she'd had enough insanity for the day she went to deal with Spot who might be a pain in the butt, but at least he was consistent about it. He was hiding in his treasure box when she tapped on the tank. He strutted out, stuck his fishy chin in the air and flipped her the fin. Megan blinked. Okay maybe she was the insane one imagining things because there was no way a fish could… She heard a key in the back door and jumped.

It was Jack and he looked enraged, worried and irresistible. In a few quick, deliberate strides he had her in his arms lifting her off her feet. After a brief but nipple hardening kiss, he sat her at the bottom of the stairs and began looking out the window scanning the street and the yard. What the hell?

As if he'd read her mind he said, "Stacy called me and she said you might be in danger. Apparently she overheard something at a bar." Megan had never known Stacy to go to a bar. Maybe this tequila thing was getting out of hand. While Megan was pondering this and Jack was searching for the boogie man, Stacy barreled in the door with Mickey, Ali and Josie close behind.

"We dropped Granny off at your Mom's," Stacy quickly explained then to Jack she said, "See anything?"

Jack frowned, "Not yet, but we aren't taking any chances. She can pack a few things and she's going home with me."

Megan blinked. "Am not!" she protested.

Mickey, who was strictly Michael today, chimed in, his voice deep and manly, "That's probably a good idea. I'll help her pack."

"I'll gather Spot's things," Josie added and disappeared into the kitchen.

Ali was next to speak, always the voice of reason, "But first I think we need to notify the police even if we're not completely sure of what's going on."

"Good idea," Stacy said.

"What is going on?" Megan asked and was ignored by everyone.

"And she probably needs to call her mother so she doesn't worry," Mickey said. "We didn't really give Granny any real explanation as to what was going on."

Josie laughed. "That's just because she would've wanted a piece of the action."

Megan stood up and addressed the group. "What action?"

Jack nudged her to go upstairs. "Haven't you been paying attention sweetheart? Get packing. We need to get of here."

"No!" She shouted and everyone stopped what they were doing and stared at her. "I'm not going anywhere or doing anything until I know exactly what the hell is going on." She plunked down on the couch and crossed her arms over her chest for emphasis. Chin high and eyes narrowed she growled, "Now who wants to tell me?"

Jack looked at Stacy who was looking at the ceiling. Mickey stood suitcase in hand, eyeing Josie who has stuffing Spot's fish food in her bra for transport.

"Well?" Megan prompted and Stacy shifted her weight and frowned.

Oh hell. This was going to be worse than bad.

"Okay here goes." Stacy sat beside Megan on the couch and took her hand. Jack also came to Megan's side sitting beside her, cuddling her close to him, one strong arm possessively around her shoulder.

"I was at Dino's," Stacy began, "and Ted came in and sat at the bar a couple stools down from me. He looked like hell. I'm pretty sure he hasn't showered or shaved in at least a week. He's lost weight too. Anyways, he kept looking around like he was nervous or something when finally, his uh…that girl came in and he joined her at a table."

"Tiffany," Megan supplied flatly and Stacy nodded.

"So I hear them talking and your name comes up. I was curious and the table behind them was empty and since the bartender was hitting on me constantly I moved to the empty table."

"Was the bartender Todd?" Josie asked.

"I think so why," Stacy said momentarily distracted.

"I dated him. He has this weird fetish about…" Stacy raised her hand to stop Josie.

"Not now Josie," she said, then turned back to Megan. "So I'm eavesdropping and I hear them talking about how Ted needs a lot of money to pay off those dug dealer guys and how Ted has this plan to get the money.

"It seems Ted knows all about you're little pool table bar scene with Romeo over there." She gestured at Jack who smiled. "And from the sounds of it he wasn't too happy about it."

Megan jumped in to protest. "So what! He cheated first. And anyway I've already filed for divorce, we're separated."

"I hear you," Stacy said. "But that's not the issue."

"Then what is the issue?" Megan asked her impatience growing.

"Well, they were talking and Ted says that everything he owns is already in hock and these Madrino guys are going to kill him if he

241

doesn't pay up, so he tells the redheaded winch that he has a plan to get the money and have enough for them to get out of the country and get married and all that."

"I wish them well. So what's the plan?" Megan wanted to know. She felt Jack tighten his embrace a little and she leaned into him just to feel his warmth. He felt so solid and strong and protective. She momentarily remembered that solid frame on top of her, inside her, driving her into sweet mindless oblivion…

Stacy looked around the room nervously and wrung her hands together.

"Come on Stace, spit it out," Ali prompted.

Stacy went pale and licked her lips. "Well, um they said…well they want to…uh their going to…"

Megan was getting irritated, "What? They want to what? Get married? Start selling Tupperware? Start an escort service? What?"

Josie got to the point as usual. "They're going to kill you."

Megan's mouth dropped open and she directed her gaze back to Stacy who was nodding her head with tears streaming down her face. Ali immediately went to her side and offered support.

"That's what they said Megan," Stacy said her voice strained. "Ted said that he'd talked to someone about taking care of you."

Megan was flabbergasted. "But what would killing me accomplish?"

"For the insurance money," Jack said and she turned to face him.

Her face was pure confusion and disbelief. "What?" she said in barely more than a whisper.

Stacy continued, "Meg, he told Tiffany that he had a life insurance policy worth a half a million on you. He said you both took them out years ago." Megan nodded. They had done that about five years ago. It seemed like the responsible thing to do. Hell it had been her idea. She reached for Jack's hand and interlaced their fingers. He kissed her temple and brushed a stray hair behind her ear.

"So they plan to kill me, pay the Madrino's and then run off together for a happy ever after?"

"Almost," Mickey said taking over for Stacy who was crying all over Ali's fuzzy, purple sweater. Megan thought it was a really cute sweater. When her ex-husband was done making attempts on her life, she'd be sure to compliment Ali on it. "Actually Ted had given the whole thing a little more thought. He was gonna have Billy bump you off for the insurance money. You got that right." He held up his index finger and smiled. "But he didn't plan on paying the Madrino's. This is the genius of it. He knows they've threatened you and knowing you, he figured you would have reported it."

"Which we did. We wanted to leave a paper trail," Jack said catching on to Ted's intentions. He was really going to have to kill Ted he decided.

"Exactly," Mickey said, "And since the cops know it, once you were dead he was going to pin it on the Madrino brothers…"

"And play the grieving widower until the check came in," Jack finished for him.

"Right again," Mickey said.

"And to make sure that things went as planned, Tiffany was supposed to call the Madrino's and schedule a meeting to settle Ted's debt at the same time you were wacked so that they wouldn't have an alibi." Stacy said. "She'd swear she was with Ted at the office where he was doing a shoot in front of an entire JV football team as witnesses."

"Pretty tidy," Mickey commented.

"Not tidy enough," Jack said.

"Wait a minute, this is absurd," Megan said. "Ted wouldn't kill me." She took in the faces of everyone in the room. "Would he?"

"He's hit rock bottom, Meg," Ali said. "People do desperate things when they think they've run out of options."

Megan felt the warm tears trickle down her cheeks. "But he's not a murderer."

Josie snorted. "You didn't know he was a drunk, a drug dealer or a cheater either."

She had a point.

Jack wiped away her tears with the side of his hand and his eyes grew intimately soft and protective. "We won't take any chances honey. Let's get you packed and out of here."

Megan ignored him. Another thought had crossed her mind. "How come he didn't recognize you? He's known you since like kindergarten. He would have seen you at the bar."

Stacy shrugged. "He was pretty drunk and I was um wearing a disguise."

Josie's brown eyes glittered. "Well my, my, Little Miss Goody Two Shoes out getting some strange?"

Stacy burned her with an outraged glare. "No! I just don't want Scott knowing I was at the bar."

"Why not?" Mickey asked. "You're over twenty one, it's not a crime."

"Because, uh…well it's not important right now."

Megan's suspicions were confirmed. "The hell it isn't. How often do you go to the bar? And why do you feel the need to hide it?" Stacy leaned back into Ali and began sobbing loudly.

Jack's voice was understanding and calm, "Because she's an alcoholic." Stacy nodded without removing her head from Ali's chest. "And she's ashamed of herself and worried about what everyone will think about her. She wears the disguise, not only to hide her addiction from everyone else, but also to hide from herself and whatever she's running from."

Megan's heart ached for her friend. She had no idea what to say so she settled for, "It's okay, Stace. We'll get you help and we'll support you all the way. Right guys?" Everyone nodded, their expressions sincere.

Megan's safety was Jack's first priority. "But first we need to get you out of here," he told Megan.

She shook her head and stared at him with stubborn blue eyes. "No, I can't leave right now. I can't leave Spot and I have to finish my column and my mom…"

Jack was the one shaking his head now. "Sweetheart, Spot can go with us, and you can write your column there too. And call your mom."

"I'll talk to Mrs. J," Josie said. "I'll let her know what's going on so you won't have to listen to her lecture." Oh boy.

"And Granny can stay with me till things settle down," Mickey said then smiled thoughtfully, "You know, I really like having her around. She's teaching me how to have cybersex with her online friends."

Megan fried him with a stern glare. "Don't encourage her, Mickey." Mickey laughed and Jack proceeded to argue with Megan about going home with him while Mickey enlightened Josie on the basics of internet sex and Ali soothed Stacy and offered support with battling her addiction. Megan was pacing in front of the window facing off with Jack and everyone was still bickering ten minutes later when the window—

that had just been replaced Monday— suddenly shattered and a flaming bottle with a rag stuffed in it, came smashing through landing on the floor about a foot from the coffee table. A second later the bottle exploded with a deafening boom. For a brief second everyone froze, except Jack who had thrown Megan to the ground then grabbed the couch cushions to try to stomp out the fire that was now spreading from the carpet to the recliner. Mickey quickly joined Jack in an effort to help stop the fire.

Josie was screaming, Stacy was calling 911, Megan was bleeding on the floor and Ali had run to the kitchen.

A moment later, Ali returned with the fire extinguisher Megan kept under the kitchen sink and put out the flames, drenching Jack and Mickey in the white, foamy solution. Jack immediately rushed to Megan and began frantically assessing her injuries, from flying glass, and being thrown to the floor. She had blood coming from her head, her face and her arms and legs. After being assured that help was on the way, he carefully scooped her up and carried her into the kitchen where he sat her on the counter and ran some warm water.

Damn it, there was so much blood he couldn't see where she was cut or how deep or anything. It was just everywhere. He tried a few deep, calming breaths, but the panic wouldn't subside. She wasn't fatally injured, he knew that, she was talking and responding to his words and touch. He felt her hands running across his skin and realized she was checking him for injuries. His heart hit the floor.

"I'm fine baby, hold still. I need to get this piece of glass out," he told her while he carefully removed a shard of glass that was embedded in her right shoulder.

With his rage barely contained, his emotions overflowing and shaky hands he removed seven shards of glass from Megan's arms and legs while Ali and Stacy used the first aid supplies from Jack's truck to tentatively dress the wounds. Mickey was dealing with Josie who had also taken some glass to various parts of her body while she cried frantically on the phone with Dr. Ross who was already in his car and on the way.

Other than quiet soothing words to Megan and a brief check to make sure everyone was alright Jack was deathly quiet, with thoughts of killing Ted with his bare hands dancing in his head. Once most of the blood had been cleaned up and he was sure Megan was going to be okay, he fought to relax his muscles and calm down. He lost the battle as the smell of blood, salty tears and fear of losing the woman he loved crept upon him and by the time the first sounds of sirens were ringing in his ears he was crying and shaking with anger and rage.

Four uniforms came barreling through the door along with two firemen, Dr. Ross, old lady Everett and Megan's father.

Megan's father rushed to his daughter giving her a quick once over and with tears brimming his weathered eyes, hugged her gently so he wouldn't hurt her.

"Are you okay?" he asked her and when she nodded he said, his voice booming "What the hell happened?" Jack told him the short version and then his boom went to a roar when he said, "I'll kill the son of a bitch!"

"You'll have to stand in line," Jack told him "Because if I find him first he's a dead man." Megan seemed in a daze probably from the shock but everything seemed to hit home when she looked into her father's eyes filled with tears. She began crying again and tightened her grip on her father with one hand and Jack with the other. After a moment she noticed someone was missing.

"Where's Mom?"

"She took Granny to tour a new old folk's home. They weren't there when Ms. Everett called and I didn't take the time to call them. Hell, I didn't even take time to put on shoes."

Megan glanced at her father's chubby bare feet and smiled. Cupping both her dad's cheek and Jack's she said, "My heroes," then in a shaky voice she added, "I love you."

Jack was thankful for the lump that had risen in his throat because if it hadn't he would have told her he loved her too and he wasn't sure she her words had been aimed at them both. But he did love her and as soon as things settled down he planned to tell her and show her in every way imaginable. But first things first, and top of the list was getting her medical attention, getting her safe and keeping her safe. In his house, in his bed and in his heart was his preferable way to achieve that. "Will you stay with her?" he asked her dad and when he nodded, Jack kissed her cheek and said, "I'm going to talk to these guys honey. I'll be right back."

Jon relieved Mickey and took Josie in his arms as the firemen got out their equipment and began administering first aid, while the police began asking questions and scribbling in their notebooks.

Jack and Stacy relayed everything to the police starting with the incidents that had previously been reported, the scene in the bar and ending with the firebomb through the window a few minutes ago. They finished their statements and while Stacy called her husband, Jack went to find Megan. He found her sitting on the counter with Dr. Ross examining the back of her head. She was fit to be tied and angry as hell poking a finger in some poor EMT's face and yelling at him while her father yelled at her. Jack smiled. She was the perfect mix of sugar and spice. Sweet and sass. Heaven and hell. His bent angel.

"You are going to the hospital," her father shouted. "The guy says you need stitches."

"For the last time, I-AM-FINE!" she shouted back. Then to the EMT; "Find Jack! He's hurt too. He was bleeding and there was glass every…" Jack walked toward her and her father gave a sigh of relief.

"Here, you handle her," He told Jack. Shaking his head he said, "She always has been a stubborn little shit. Gets it from her grandmother."

"I'm right here, Meg, and I'm fine. I think most of the blood on me is from you."

Jack met Dr. Ross's gaze, "How bad is it?"

"Bad enough to be properly cleaned and stitched up. It's deep. She needs to go."

Jack kissed Megan softly. His forehead against hers, he said, "You've got to go to the hospital honey." And after minimal protest she agreed to go. "And then you're moving in with me." She rubbed noses with Jack and brushed her lips against his.

"You gonna nurse me back to health?" she whispered. "Kiss all my boo-boos?"

"With pleasure, baby." Jack replied and her father decided that if Jack could make his daughter glow with happiness like that he wouldn't beat him to death for sleeping with her. He still wouldn't like it, but he wouldn't kill him over it.

Jon had returned to Josie where he was professionally kissing every injury she had while Mickey and Ali were taking their turns being bandaged. Stacy was sitting with Megan's dad who was rubbing her back and trying to comfort her.

It had been a long day.

"Oh Dear God," Mrs. Johnson screamed announcing her presence as she and Granny crammed into the already crowded room. "What in God's name has happened?" Megan looked around the small kitchen and laughed. It looked like a make shift emergency room with the walking wounded scattered about. Granny was checking out the men in uniforms butts while her mother was in hysterics, crucifix in one hand and performing the cross with the other. "There's blood everywhere and…" she glanced at her husband with a perplexed look. "Where on earth are your shoes?" then her gaze fell on Jack who had his lips nuzzled in Megan's throat. "And why are you kissing my daughter? And why is she covered with blood?" then on to Jon and Josie, "Oh dear, God, one of your boobs is swollen." And those were her last words before she fainted.

"Another one bites the dust," Granny said and broke out the moonshine.

Jon rushed to Mrs. Johnson's aid while Josie patted her boob and rolling her eyes, she said, "duh," and removed the can of fish food from her bra.

Chapter Eighteen

Late that night, Megan lay stretched out next to Jack on his couch watching Jay Leno, his body hard and strong behind hers, his hand curving around her hip. She'd been to the hospital, got her head stitched and was now flying high on some kick ass pain killers. Her mother had been treated and released and was now in the habit of calling every ten minutes to check on her. Her father was watching TV and yelling at Granny who was having an online date with a retired Hell's Angel from Ohio. Life was as dysfunctional as ever.

Josie was at Jon's and would probably be moved in by the end of the week and Ali and Mickey were having a Julia Roberts marathon at her house. Stacy was no doubt having a long talk with Scott about her problem with alcohol.

"Jack, I'm worried about Stacy," Megan said.

Jack stroked her hip. "Me too."

"She needs help. We have to make sure she gets it."

"We can be there for her, but she has to do it on her own." Jack sighed, "It won't work unless she wants it."

"You know a lot about this?" Megan asked.

He rolled to his back and positioned her on top of him. His brown eyes conflicted with pride and shame, he said, "I've been sober for about five years now. It was the hardest thing I ever did, but it was also the smartest thing. It takes time and patience and lots of dedication, but I have faith in Stacy and like me, she'll get through this." Megan was speechless, shocked. Then she remembered never seeing Jack drink, and his concerned looks when she did, which lately had been way too much. And the meetings at 7:00.

"Did you go to AA?"

"Yep," Jack laughed. "Actually that's where I was when you called me with that ridiculous list hunt. I left there and went to your house where you were having a party."

Megan winced. "I'm a horrible person. I drug you out of an AA meeting and offered you alcohol. Remind me not to not to sponsor Stacy."

Jack kissed her chin, then her lips. "You didn't know, babe. Plus I already told Stacy I'd sponsor her, but she has to call me. I won't pressure her into it. It has to be her choice." If she hadn't already been falling for him, she would have then. He was the most patient, compassionate person she'd ever met. He'd known Stacy less than two weeks and already he was willing to share her pain and assist her to recovery.

Megan kissed him sweet and tenderly along his jaw. "Is it hard?" she asked. Jack was confused and she realized that around Jack that was a loaded question. "Recovery I mean. It is difficult?"

He seemed disappointed for only a moment. Propping his arm behind his head he said, "Yeah, it is. Its real tough, but I had my dad to lean on, so I was lucky."

"But I thought your dad owns a bar?"

"He does but he's also a recovering alcoholic. We did it together. It was my mother's dying wish." Megan's heart broke for him. "See my dad and I never saw eye to eye on much. When I got old enough, I started spending the summers with my uncle, who was also a pretty heavy drinker, so I got exposed to it a lot. Then my mom got sick and my dad really hid in the bottle. By the time she was bad, I was getting out of an awful marriage, and my dad and I both were in pretty deep." He paused for a moment and stared straight at the ceiling. "So the day before my mom died she called me and my father in the room and told us that the only thing she wanted from us before she died was for us to get sober and work on our relationship because after she was gone we would be all each other had." Megan didn't bother to wipe the tear that fell down her face. "We promised and the next day she died. We went to a meeting that night."

Megan didn't know what to say so she just held him tight, admiring his strength and courage. She'd had a storybook childhood and little tragedy until recently. Her heart ached for him and his father.

And Stacy and the journey she was just beginning.

The phone rang and Jack reached behind him to get it. She heard her mother's voice coming through loud and clear and she folded her hands in prayer and tucked them under her chin, tilting her head to the side and closing her eyes. Jack smiled and said, "Yeah she's still asleep. She's fine. I won't let anything happen to her. You should get some sleep now, you had a tough day. Okay then, have a good night."

Jack clicked the phone off. "That is one persistent lady."

"We Johnson woman tend to be. We are used to getting what we want."

Jack smoothed her bangs out of her face. "And what is it you want Ms. Johnson?"

She smiled the smile that started it all. "I've already got it. I want you."

Jack sat up and carefully cradled her in his arms. "Good, get used to it. Because you're mine." Her heart fluttered and her belly did that whole flip flop thing.

"Then take me to bed," she purred and Jack stood and carried her to the bedroom and laid her on the bed. He leaned over her, not putting any of his weight on her because she so banged up, and kissed her lovingly and gently, just a sensual, soul kiss, then after disrobing he joined her. Megan nestled into him and feeling his arousal she reached for him but he stilled her hand.

"Honey, I almost lost you today. You're cut up, stitched up, bruised up and probably still very sore. I was a selfish bastard last night and…

"Jack."

"…and I refuse to be tonight. I can make love to you tomorrow and the night after that, and the night after that, and the night after that and the night…"

"Jack."

"…and I know I am irresistible and it will be damn near impossible for you to keep your hands off of me but if I have to handcuff you…"

"Handcuffs?"

"…don't think I won't. You will just have to be happy with me holding you all night. Feel free to dream about me and if you must you have my permission to indulge yourself in a wet dream if it gets you by but…"

"Jack!"

"…there will be no ride on the love train tonight. Sorry to disappoint ladies, but as promised Jack will return to his regularly scheduled love making tomorrow at a time to be later announced. So stay tuned and…"

"I was only going to say goodnight."

"Liar."

Megan smiled and fell asleep indulging in her first real wet dream starring the dreamy and delicious Jack Westin.

***

Megan's head was pounding when she woke up in perfect tune to the phone that was ringing off the hook. She ignored it and reached for Jack but he was gone, leaving behind a tantalizing impression in the sheets of where he had laid. She heard the shower turn off and then Jack's hurried footsteps into the bedroom to quiet the ringing phone so it wouldn't wake her up.

Too late. If the phone hadn't done it, the site of him standing blissfully naked two feet in front of her would have. Hell, that delicious site would be enough to wake any woman from the dead.

"Hi," he said and smiled, leaned down to kiss her.

"Hi yourself," she managed her heart thudding wildly in her chest.

The phone rang again and they both stared at it.

"If we don't answer it, she'll just come over," Megan informed him and after giving the matter a moment's thought Jack snatched up the phone, winking at Megan, and touching her in places that sent her body into overdrive. Megan was so turned on. *Foreplay while talking to her mother on the phone, definitely a carnal sin*, she thought, *but quite possibly one worth experiencing the wrath of hell for.* She grabbed Jack's arm and dragged him down on to the bed with her, teasing and taunting his amazing erection with her fingers. He shivered and tried to bat her away and she found that she enjoyed the challenge. She moved her tongue seductively down his neck and to one flat copper nipple, buried in a mass of chest hair. She gently sank her teeth in and pulled and Jack shot straight out of the bed, almost knocking her to the floor. His demeanor went from teasing and seducing to serious and concerned in a spilt second. He stood, naked as a jay bird, running his fingers through his hair nervously pacing the room. He hung up the phone and tossed it on the bed, then sat silently as if trying to get his bearings together.

"What?' she asked and he took her hand, his eyes a stormy brown. He opened his mouth to speak but no words were able to come out. "Just tell me, Jack. I'm a big girl. What's the matter? Is it my Mom? Granny?" her voice broke, "Stacy?"

Jack looked at their hands interlaced together. "Ted," he said and Megan couldn't control the relief that consumed her body. The cops had found Ted. Good, she had a few things she wanted to say to him.

"What about him?" she asked feeling a little control surface.

"He's dead." Okay that was the last thing she expected. Her face went pale, her legs suddenly numb, she asked, "What do you mean dead? As in heart stopped, not breathing?" Jack nodded and pulled her into his arms.

"How?" she breathed not able to control her emotions, and not bothering to understand them either. She didn't want Ted, she didn't love him and had filed for divorce and would have been content never seeing the snake again. But dead? Never. She would have never wished that on him. Jack held her tighter and she figured he was probably fighting with a few emotions of his own.

"I don't know, sweetheart. That was the police and they want us at the station for questioning. I guess we'll get those answers there."

She forced herself to calm down. "Okay," she said, "we probably should get dressed then." She got up and began rifling through her bag and wrestling on her clothes. Jack too got dressed and they were on their way out the door when the phone rang again. This time they ignored it and trekked to Jack's truck.

***

Megan and Jack were immediately separated as soon as they arrived at the police station. Megan glanced around the room at the busy hum of the city's finest bustling around. There was the sound of fingers drumming on key boards, phones ringing, radios crackling and heavy hurried footsteps. An elderly man dressed in a crisp suit, with a head full of salt and pepper hair, smiled at Megan and offered her a Styrofoam cup of thick black sludge. She accepted the coffee and thanked him.

"Mrs. Malone, I'm Sgt. Wagner. I just have a few questions for you dear." Megan nodded and admired the honest gray coloring of his eyes. For a man of his age—which she guessed was around mid-sixties— he was still quite handsome.

"Let's start at the beginning," he said.

***

By the end of her interrogation, Megan was exhausted. She was scared, confused, angry and pretty much brain dead. Ted being dead didn't make sense, the questions Sgt. Wagner had asked her didn't make sense and now she was left all alone waiting to be questioned some more. About murder. Of her cheating, drug dealing husband.

Megan was now sitting in a small room with four chairs, a scarred wooden table and a window covering one wall. She'd seen enough cop shows to know that it was a two way mirror. She resisted the urge to cross her eyes and stick her tongue out. Of course that might help with her defense if she had to use an insanity defense.

***

Finally, an officer came in and collected her and she was led down a long hall, decorated with photographs of officers both past and present in various situations. She was led through a door into a spacious office, where Jack sat along with a man who looked like he was a ruthless all business kind of guy, Sgt. Wagner, another man who she assumed was Wagner's partner and her father. Jack immediately sent her a look that said shut-up-and-listen. She nodded and looked back at her father who didn't seem the least bit worried. He had probably taped Jeopardy Megan decided and there weren't any games on in the morning so he was probably safe. Jack lightly patted her thigh as he introduced her to her attorney. "Megan, this is Donald Templeton, you're father and I have retained him to represent you."

I don't need an attorney! She wanted to say but instead she simply nodded.

The Chief was next to speak, his voice deep, but gentle, his eyes almost as black as night under Grouch Marks style eye brows. "Mrs. Malone, first of all I want you to know that I'm very sorry about your husband," he paused and folded his beefy hands, resting them on his desk. "Let me take a moment to bring you up to date. Your husband was found dead in his studio this morning by our officers who had gone there to question him about the incidents of last night and his association with the men who were responsible for the previous incidents at your home."

She nodded, unable to speak. Jack found her arm and lightly caressed it giving her silent support and comfort.

"We have confirmed your alibi and collaborated your statement as well as those of Mr. Westin and your father's with the previous reports and the events of last night." Megan nodded again, feeling like one of Ted's ridiculous bobbing doll figures and the Chief frowned.

"However, there are a lot of things that are pointing to you in an unfavorable manner."

"Like what?" Megan asked, surprised her voice still worked.

The Chief consulted a file on his desk and diverted his gaze to the attorney. "Let's just take this slowly Mrs. Malone. From what I understand, you found out your husband was having an affair and according to one of Mr. Malone's associates, you became violent and split his lip during a fit of rage."

One of Ted's associates? Tiffany. She was the only one Ted associated with.

Megan opened her mouth to explain but her lawyer quieted her.

"And then Mrs. Malone, there was that unfortunate marble incident and your husband's repeated accusation to the hospital staff that you were trying to kill him, first by poisoning him and then by uh the marble thing." He stifled a laugh and raised his hand. "But you must believe me, Mrs. Malone; I'm inclined to disregard anything he said in the hospital as he was apparently not in his right mind. I understand he was under the influence of some mighty strong pain medication and understandably so. I would imagine his condition was quite painful."

"And then there's the matter of the assault on your doorstep while he was in his hospital gown. According to him, you beat him with a rolling pin while your grandmother uh took a set of pliers to his uh genital region."

Had Ted called the cops on her? How the hell did they know all this?

The Chief answered that question without her asking him to do so. "We picked your husband up for indecent exposure as several neighbors had called and reported a man streaking through the area and he told us what happened, but refused to press charges. We figured he'd suffered enough and didn't charge him. My guys were rolling on the floor with laughter and making new commitments to remain faithful to their wives for fear of a woman scorned." The chief gave a hearty laugh and Megan felt some of the tension leave her knotted shoulders. Her father was smiling too. But Jack remained stone cold serious so Megan stiffened.

"And we can't ignore the fact that Mr. Malone was shot in his studio with no sign of forced entry and he didn't try to defend himself which leads me to believe that he was shot by someone he knew." Well duh, Chief. Our tax dollars pay for these observations that could easily be made by a kindergartener. "And we do have a witness that described a woman fitting your description leaving the scene, in a car described as the one you drive."

"But I was with..." Megan was stopped again by her attorney's hand tugging her arms gently.

"Mr. Westin," the Chief finished for her. "I know that, but there is the matter of the gun." Megan gulped. Okay whoever she'd pissed off hadn't taken it lightly.

"The gun," the Chief continued, "which we believe to be the one that killed Mr. Malone was found under the front seat of your car along with a lengthy letter from the deceased addressed to you," he paused and studied her face. "So what we're going to need to do is..."

Mr. Templeton spoke on Megan's behalf. "You have our complete cooperation. My client will be happy to comply with the necessary fingerprinting and ballistic tests needed to eliminate her as a suspect and clear her name."

The Chief smiled. "Just like that?"

"Yes sir," Mr. Templeton said, "I believe my client to be innocent and I'm sure she would like to get this whole ordeal behind her as quickly as possible."

"Ok, then Sgt. Wagner, get this young lady printed and then turn her over to ballistics." He turned back to Megan and spoke in an almost paternal tone, "Mrs. Malone, I want you to know that I truly believe you are being framed. I appreciate your cooperation on this matter and hope you the best. Again, I'm very sorry for your loss." With that she was escorted by Sgt. Wagner and her attorney out of the room. Jack and her father both smiled at her then, and at that moment she knew everything was going to be okay.

Jack was waiting for her when she was finished and released to go home. She had been told to stay in town and she gave them Jack's number and address so that she could be reached. Jack rose from the rickety chair in the lobby and took her arm as he escorted her to the door. Once they were in the truck, she had no idea what to say, so she simply, laid her hand on top of his on the console and rubbed it. He looked up and she said, "Hi." So it was lame, she was drained and she had no idea what the appropriate thing to say to your sort of boyfriend would be after he'd just spent hours at the police station helping you out of being suspected for murder.

"Hi, yourself," he replied which was equally lame. At least they were consistent. He rubbed her cheek with the side of his hand. "You Okay?"

Sure peachy! "I guess, just a little overwhelmed I think."

He laced her fingers around his. Through eyes full of love and sincerity he said, "Just takes time sweetheart. I'm here for you."

"I know." She smiled at him although it didn't come close to touching her eyes. "Thank you."

"Anytime, baby."

***

Back at Jack's she made the appropriate phone calls to Ted's parents and business clients. His mother had been so distraught Megan's heart ached for her. Although Megan had always gotten along with her in-laws, they'd never been close. Ted's parents had moved to Wyoming a year after Megan and Ted had married and aside from the occasional visit or phone call, they didn't speak much and Megan got the impression it had quite a bit to do with her. They hadn't much cared for Megan from the get go and nothing she ever did would have made her good enough for their son. Anthony, Ted's brother had once told her that Ted could have married Queen Elizabeth and that still wouldn't have been good enough. He said he'd quit trying to please his parents years ago and suggested she do the same.

Megan had chosen to avoid discussing the circumstances of Ted's death or who was responsible. Jack had said she had nothing to worry about because she was innocent, he knew it and she did too. Still the police thing had shaken her up a bit, and truth be told, her faith in the justice system wasn't all that great. Just look at the Madrino's. Jack said they'd both been in a lot of trouble and they were still free. Free to sell drugs and possibly kill her late husband.

Jack came back into the room carrying ham and cheese sandwiches, chips and sodas. He sat a paper plate in front of her and opened her coke can.

"Thanks," she said not touching the food.

"You need to eat, Megan." He was right she did need to eat. She couldn't remember the last time she'd had anything to eat. She'd been

257

too busy making love with Jack and being firebombed to worry about trivial things such as food.

"My mom is coming to pick me up in a while," she said, "We've got to go to the funeral home and make some arrangements."

"You need help?" Jack would just as soon toss Ted in a hefty bag and toss him on the curb for garbage pickup but he didn't think that would set well with Megan.

"No, I think we can handle it. It shouldn't be too hard, since he wanted to be cremated. I told his mom, I'd have it done and then Fed-Ex her his ashes but she insists on a small ceremony here with his friends. I started to tell her he didn't have any friends but figured it wouldn't do any good. She's hell bent on being here for his funeral."

"Maybe she just needs closure. Really that's the purpose of funerals. It gives the family a chance to say goodbye and remember their loved ones."

Megan nodded and fought back tears. Jack rubbed her back and said, "Go ahead and cry honey. You need to. It helps, trust me. I cried for days when my mother died and its part of the healing process."

Megan sniffled and shook her head. "It's not that. I'm not crying because Ted's dead. I mean don't get me wrong. I hated him, but I am sad that his life ended so soon and in such a tragic way."

Jack hauled her into his arms. "Then what's wrong?"

"I'm going to hell, that's what." Jack searched her face comically. "Yep, first class straight to hell."

No more pain pills for this little bent angel. "Why?" Jack asked.

"Because I just found out that my husband of ten years is dead, violently murdered in his studio, and all I can think about is you and how good it feels when you touch me, how my heart flitters when you're around and how heavenly it feels when you make love to me." Jack hid his smile and stroked her hair lightly. "It's like I just want to get him in the ground and get back in bed with you. It's horrible." For Ted maybe, Jack thought. It wasn't half bad for Jack.

He went for the standard response. "You're just under a lot of stress right now, baby."

"I guess. I think maybe my marriage has been over for a long time and I was just realizing it. And he's done so much to me in the last couple weeks, I'm just still too angry to grieve for him."

"That could be it."

"Well I'm going to get dressed. I have an idiot to bury and my mom will be here shortly." She broke the embrace and kissed Jack sweetly on the lips and made a beeline for the shower.

***

"$600 bucks for an urn?" Josie shouted. "These prices are ridiculous. I say we just stuff him in a zip-lock bag."

"I got an empty shoe box we can put him in. It could be like a miniature coffin and it only cost me nine bucks." Granny offered helpfully.

"Shhh!" Mrs. Johnson said outraged by their disrespect of the dead. "We're buying an urn and that's final. Now shut up! This is hard enough on Megan as it is." She squeezed her daughter's shoulder offering support.

"Just tag him and bag him," Megan told the funeral director, a man in his seventies whose clothing suggested he never quite emerged completely from the fifties.

The man gave her his best used car smile. "Might I show you something from our catalog? We have some very lovely…"

"Look, my husband was a liar, a cheater, a drug addict and dealer, and basically the lowest piece of scum I've ever had the misfortune of knowing. I'm not mourning his death, in fact I've already moved on and by this time tonight I'll probably be hitting the sheets with my new flavor of the week." Her mother had to sit down. "If I had my choice I'd skewer the bastard and toss him on the grill, but I'm sure the police frown on that kind of behavior and probably I would need a license for such things. So really all I need from you is for you to sell me the cheapest, crappiest, low budget urn you've got and make me a hell of a deal on barbequing the idiot so I can write you a check and get the hell out of here."

"Preach on sister!" Granny hollered.

"Why me God?" Mrs. Johnson asked.

"Funeral shopping is the shit!" Josie commented.

The old man pursed his lips and opened a catalog showing Megan the bottom of the barrel in urns. "This one right here will run you a hundred and fifty dollars, plus tax and shipping of course."

Megan dug her check book out. "Sold!"

"One fifty!" Josie shouted. "Don't you have one that's been dropped or something for say around twenty bucks? We could super glue it back together. Ted would never know."

"I feel the fires of hell burning the soles of my feet now," Mrs. Johnson cried.

"Oh can it, you big wuss!" Granny hollered and then moving like a cat she walked over to the display of expensive urns and with a wicked gleam in her eyes she innocently knocked one off with the tip of her finger. It hit the floor with a clatter sending pieces of glazed glass everywhere. "Oh will you look at that," she said with all the innocence of a catholic school girl. "I think it's a sign from God."

"Yeah that you're going to hell!" Mrs. Carrigan blurted.

Megan stood shell shocked and then started laughing hysterically.

"Okay, we're gonna need a dust pan, a zip lock bag, and some super glue," Josie said. "What do we owe you?"

Jack was laughing so hard he had iced tea spewing out his nose. "I can't believe your grandmother did that!"

"Believe it. I thought the old man was going to drop dead on the spot. He was utterly mortified."

"But you got the urn and everything arranged?"

"Yep, I ordered the one for a hundred and fifty bucks, scheduled his service and got the hell out of there," Megan said, around a mouthful of popcorn.

"And your mom? How's she holding up? She hasn't called yet."

"I think she's disowned me. She hit me with her purse and wouldn't stop until I promised her I wouldn't have sex with you tonight out of respect for Ted."

"That's only right I guess." Jack said remembering the infamous brown purse beating he'd gotten at his first encounter with Megan's mother.

"Well, since it's already past eleven, if we started a little foreplay now, we could probably be all the way up to the good stuff by mid-night. 'Course my mother would probably kill me and bury me in the super glued urn if she ever found out."

Jack smiled and brushed his lips against her ear. "Mmmm. My lips are sealed."

And at 12:01, the fireworks started only to be interrupted by the phone ringing.

Megan belted it off the nightstand.

"I'm changing my number," Jack said.

"It won't do any good. She knows where you live."

"Then let's move to Somalia."

***

Two weeks later, Megan sat nestled next to Jack on his leather couch. Bitty and Bugs, her four legged children sat at Jack's feet looking like starving Ethiopian puppies hoping he'd accidentally drop a Cheeto. Spot was flirting with a rather eccentric blowfish in Jack's aquarium, strutting his little fishy butt as he swam circles around his bowl. They were like a dysfunctional Dr. Doolittle family. All they needed was a smart mouthed bird and a stuck up cat and they'd be in business.

Later Jack took her to his bedroom and made mind blowing love to her yet again and she woke in his strong arms completely sated and wanting even more of him.

Whoa Mama! Holy cow! Talk about your mind blowing, headboard thumping, hot, steamy, wild animal sex. Megan smiled in spite of herself. She'd had sex before with Ted of course, even good sex from time to time, but this...this was blissful hysteria. Passionate, wild, no holds barred brain freezing pleasure. She should be asleep, God knows she was tired. Jack had passed out over and hour ago and after the workout they'd just had she wouldn't be surprised if he slept for the next two days straight.

Her stomach growled and she thought about cheesecake. Sex and cheesecake. No great sex and strawberry deluxe cheesecake. Now that is living the American dream. Carefully, Megan untangled her legs from Jack's and lifted his hand from her shoulder. She was just about to lift her head from his arm when he mumbled something in his sleep and snuggled her close.

She grinned. He'd said her name. He was dreaming about her. He mumbled something else and she froze.

What did he say?

It sounded like he said...

Surely he didn't say...

261

Shit! He said it again. Suddenly all thoughts of cheesecake were gone. Her hunger had turned into nausea as she replayed his words in her head, then he said it again.

Double, triple shit.

"Marry me, Megan." Those three little words were unmistakably clear even in his slurred, sex drugged sleep. "Marry me, Megan."

Chapter Nineteen

Marry me, Megan. What was he crazy? She had to get out of there. Now! Before he woke up and said those three ridiculous words in a conscious state of mind.

Sure she cared about him, she knew she loved him, but enough for marriage? Hell no! No way! Not now. Maybe not ever. So what if he was the sweetest, most sensitive and decent man she knew. So what if sex with him was off the charts. So what if the last couple weeks of her life had been the happiest she'd ever known. All of that was all good and fine but not a reason to marry him. Certainly not now after they'd known each other for a month. Hell, Ted was barely in the ground. The last thing on her mind should be marriage.

She stole a long, dreamy look at Jack. His eyes were closed, his jaw was stubbled and his hair stuck up in every direction. He was the essence of masculine perfection, gorgeous and content. He made her feel like a woman, a beautiful woman, in and out of the bedroom. He made her laugh one minute and had her mad as hell the next. He made love to her with a ferocious passion that curled her toes and made her heart hammer in her chest so hard she sometimes feared it would pop out. He held her when she cried and cracked corny jokes to cheer her up. But most of all he made her feel alive.

He loved her; she knew that, even though he hadn't told her. He liked her family, her friends, her pets. He was helping Stacy through AA and he accepted Mickey openly. He was a fantastic person, there was no denying that. But did that make him marriage material?

She shivered and slinked out of bed.

'Mrs. Megan Westin.' 'Mrs. Jackson Westin.' Okay so maybe it rolled nicely off her tongue, but so did Megan Malone and what had that gotten her?

She slipped out of his room quietly and headed for the front door before she realized she was naked. Clothes, she needed clothes. Her clothes were in Jack's room. With Jack, who was sleeping, and wanted to marry her. Involuntarily she shivered again and decided she'd risk going home naked before she'd wake him up and hash things out tonight. She needed space and time to think about things.

The laundry room. There were clothes in there and she'd take dirty clothes over a marriage proposal any day. She entered the laundry room and opened the dryer door. "Thank you Jesus." She pulled out of pair of Jack's sweats and a Harley Davidson tee shirt that had seen better days and wrestled them on, foregoing her underwear and gathered up her purse and Spot. She ran them to the car then went back for the dogs, who were curled up at the foot of the bed, snoring in sync with Jack. She whispered their names and Bitty raised his head. She motioned for him to come on and he stood, circled the bed and lay back down beside Jack where Megan had laid minutes earlier. Bugs, who was crashed out on the floor on Jack's side of the bed ignored her. "Traitors," Megan accused and slipped back out of Jack's room. She'd collect the dogs tomorrow. She could deal with Jack tomorrow. Tonight she just needed to get the hell out of there. Quick!

***

Jack awoke to the sensation of something warm and wet licking his chin. He smiled and decided to play possum so maybe she'd end up licking her way down his body below his belt. He remembered the first time she'd done that and the incredible feeling that had filled his entire body. Waking up with Megan in his bed was one thing; her naked in his bed was another, but her naked in his bed with her tongue on his…well that was beyond words.

She was panting Jack noticed and again he smiled. She wanted him bad. She was impatient and he decided not to make her wait a moment longer. Still keeping his eyes closed he reached for her and his hands came in contact with…hair? Lots of it! He stiffened and opened his eyes quickly, coming face to face with an excited, overweight, dog licking him like he had a pork chop strapped to his head. He patted the dog and surveyed the room. Megan wasn't in there but her clothes were still there, her shoes in front of the closet. Maybe she was in the shower, although he didn't hear water running. Maybe she was in the kitchen grabbing a bite to eat or at the computer working on her column.

Stretching lazily, he rose and pulled on a pair of boxers, and strolled into the living room calling her name. She didn't answer. Shit! Maybe she'd stepped out for something. He stumbled into the kitchen and put out some food for the pups— Megan had stocked his house as well as hers with puppy food. Remembering the fish, he went to the bookcase— where Spot lived during their visits— to feed him too, but Spot was gone. Jack eyed the coat rack and discovered Megan's purse was gone too. What the hell? If she'd just stepped out she would have taken her purse, but not the fish. He looked around the kitchen counter, the table. No notes or at least there wasn't one in any of the obvious places. Had she left without telling him? Without taking the dogs? That seemed very unlike her. He picked up the phone, listened for a dial tone and dialed.

***

Megan had abandoned sleep for cheesecake. After defrosting her favorite, Strawberry Chocolate Swirl, she poured herself a large glass of milk and not bothering to even slice the cake because she'd end up eating the whole damn thing anyway she dug in. Spot eyed her longingly for a bite so she crumbled a little crust and tossed it in his bowl. He darted to the top, ate the now soggy substance and didn't seem impressed. Fish were hard as hell to please.

The ringing phone startled her and she let the machine pick it up. She couldn't imagine anyone on the other end that she cared to talk to. Her mother would be calling to lecture, her father usually just showed up if he had something to say, and she didn't have the energy to deal with Granny. Josie would be with Dr. Ross this early in the morning probably engaging in a quickie before they both had to go to work. Bill was home so Ali was busy being blissfully married, Mickey never got up before ten and Stacy was with Scott on a much needed get-a-way.

That only left Jack, which Megan knew he was the caller. He hadn't left a message but Megan knew it was him anyway because her heart flip-flopped and her nipples hardened. Damn, he'd gotten under her skin with that dark honey voice, those chocolate bedroom eyes, those experienced capable hands, those full, full lips and devilish grin. And that's not mentioning the way he made sweet mindless love to her every night until she was so sated she wanted to smile and scream at the same time. And now he wanted to go and screw everything up by asking her to marry him.

If he even remembered asking her. He'd been asleep when he said it and suddenly Megan kicked herself for not thinking about that. Maybe he was just talking gibberish in his sleep and had no clue what the hell he was saying. Maybe if she didn't say anything about it and he didn't remember it she could pretend it hadn't happened.

Nope that wouldn't work. She heard him say it and if he was thinking about it subconsciously he'd bring it up sooner or later. It was inevitable that she'd have to deal with it.

The phone rang again and again she made no attempt to get up and grab it. And here she thought the Johnson women were persistent. Jack could definitely give them a run for the money.

"What do you think Spot?" she asked the unconcerned fish. "Think mommy should answer that?"

Spot retreated to his treasure chest. "You're no help," she told the fish.

The machine picked up and this time she heard Jack's strong, thick voice. "Megan, pick up." A long pause passed then he said, "Pick up or I'm coming over." Another pause then in a softer tone, "Come on, honey what's wrong? Pick up."

The rest of his message was cut short by the beep on the machine. She settled her gaze on the half eaten cheesecake, her appetite now gone.

Just a month ago her life was predictable, boring, safe. Now Ted was dead, she'd had bricks thrown at her, her house firebombed, been a murder suspect, had multiple orgasms and a man who she loved very much who wanted to marry her.

"Ain't life a bitch," she told her fish and started up the stairs to take a shower and try to deal with millions of thoughts swimming around in her aching head.

***

Where in the hell was she? He'd called her house and got the machine, she wasn't at her parents and Mickey and Josie hadn't heard from her. He tried her house again from his cell phone as he drove the short distance to her house. Shit, still no answer. Logically he knew she was safe; he'd had a long talk with the Madrino's and was certain they wouldn't mess with her anymore, plus they were on their best behavior awaiting trial for their previous indiscretions. And everyone else loved

Megan, the woman had no enemies. Maybe something had happened to her grandmother, although he figured her mother would have said something if that were the case.

"Oh hell," he muttered to himself. It was as obvious as the nose on his face. Everything finally hit her. Ted's murder, their relationship. She hadn't taken the time to mourn, Jack knew that because he'd worried about it and now it had probably all hit home and she was probably feeling guilty and ashamed. Hell, she'd been making love with him the night Ted was murdered and she'd been on her knees so to speak when the call had come in from the police. He felt like a real bastard so he couldn't imagine how she was feeling.

He tapped the hard velvet box in his pocket. He'd been carrying it around for the past week waiting for the right time to ask her but suddenly he figured that that time was a ways off still. He removed the box from his pocket and tucked it in the glove box. He'd ask her and she'd say yes. Eventually. She had to because the thought of not waking up with her every morning for the rest of his life was something he simply couldn't do. He loved her, had for fifteen years, and letting her go was something he just couldn't do. Not now. Not ever. He'd be patient but he wouldn't give up.

***

Megan was blow drying her hair when she heard the doorbell ringing followed by loud, determined banging on the door. Jack. No doubt about it. She finger combed her damp hair and was halfway down the staircase when she heard his key hit the door. She tilted her chin, squared her shoulders and tried to prepare herself. The door swung open and Jack yelled her name, surveying the dark house.

"Right here," she said in a low voice and Jack startled and squinted to adjust his eyes to the darkness of the room.

He put his hands in his pockets and stayed where he was standing. "Are you okay?" he asked in a controlled, calm voice.

Shit, he sounded hurt. "Fine, why?"

"You didn't leave a note," he said quietly.

Crap, he'd been worried about her. "I didn't want to wake you."

Jack flipped on the light to get a better look at her. She'd obviously just showered, and she didn't look as if she'd been crying. That was a good sign. But still she looked like hell. Something was wrong.

267

"What's wrong?" he asked finally taking a step toward her. Megan wanted to fold herself into his strong arms and just forget what he'd said during his sleep.

She forced a smile. He didn't buy it for a second. "Nothing. I was just a little homesick I guess."

"You're lying." It was a statement not a question and she scowled at him. He read her too well, knew her too well.

"No, I'm not. I had things to do." He crossed his arms over his chest and narrowed his eyes. "Really I have lots of stuff to do. Plus I missed my dogs."

His jaw twitched and he frowned. "Megan, the dogs are at my house," he said through clenched teeth. Shit, she'd forgotten she left them there. That was the problem with Jack she couldn't think straight around him. "Now care to tell me what's wrong? Why I woke up to a dog fondling me and no sign of you. No explanation, note, nothing."

She fidgeted with her hands and kept her gaze adverted to the floor. "Nothing's going on, Jack. I just needed some space. To...think."

He sat then beside her at the bottom of the stairs. "What do you need to think about? Am I crowding you? Is this about Ted?" He tipped her chin up forcing her to make eye contact. "Or is this about us?" The look on her beautiful face answered his question and he felt like he'd been punched in the gut.

She didn't say anything so he said, "So it's about us then." Maybe he'd rushed her, not given her the time to grieve. But he'd backed off after Ted's death and she'd sought him out. He'd told himself to give her some time, some space, but when he was around her the voices in his head were drowned out by the love in his heart, the passion in his groin. "Talk to me Megan. What'd I do?"

Her eyes widened with shock. "Nothing! You didn't do anything?"

"Then what's the deal?"

"I just...I just need some time to sort things out." He'd give her time but first he wanted to know exactly what she needed to sort out.

"What things?" he asked quietly.

"Just us, you know where we're going. What happens next?" He thought about the ring in the glove box and considered excusing himself to go get it. The storm in her stunning blue eyes told him that was a bad idea.

"What do you want to happen next?" he asked carefully, scared to push her too far but even more scared not to push at all.

She hugged her knees to her chest. Not a good sign. "I don't know, Jack. That's what I've been trying to figure out." A tear escaped and ran down her cheek twisting Jack's guts. Tenderly he wiped it away and rubbed her cheek.

"Do I get any say in this?" he asked. She lowered her head and hid her eyes.

"What do you want, Jack?"

"I want you, Megan," he finally said. "That's all I want. Just you, for as long as you'll have me." Oh Damn, oh damn, oh damn. His voice poured over her like warm honey.

She met his gaze then. "Why?"

"Because I love you."

"No you don't." Although she knew it was coming, hearing the words cut her deep. She knew he loved her. Hell, she loved him, but she didn't want to get married and she knew telling him that was going to hurt him. "Take it back."

"I won't," he shook his head and hauled her into his lap. "Hell, I can't. I've loved you since the day I met you." He kissed her forehead, her lips. "It's always been you, babe. Only you." She pulled away a little.

"Why?"

"Why not?" She stared at him her expression unreadable. "Does love have to have a reason, Megan? It doesn't work that way. My heart chose you and I'm not about to argue with it. My body, heart and head are in total agreement. They all want you."

She was quiet so long Jack was tempted to check her pulse to see if she was still breathing. She looked at the floor and began to speak then stopped.

"I don't want to get married," she blurted finally.

Shit. Jack frowned and eased back against the staircase. "Who said anything about marriage?" he asked calmly.

Megan seemed surprised for a moment, surveying him wearily. "You did."

He did? "I did?" Maybe she'd found the ring or read his mind.

"Yeah, last night when you were sleeping." Jack sucked in a deep breath and blew it out slowly. "You were talking in your sleep and you said, 'Marry me, Megan' a couple of times."

"And that spooked you?" Jack asked already knowing the answer.

"Hell, yes it spooked me, Jack." Her eyes swam with tears and her throat felt like it was slowly closing, leaving her struggling for breath. She didn't want to hurt him, but even more she didn't want to lie to him. "I mean, I'm pretty much a mess, Jack. First I find out all this stuff about Ted, I decide to divorce him and end up having to bury him instead. I'm thirty years old and I have to start my life all over again. I'm confused and scared and just when I think I've got a handle on things, you have to go and ask me to marry you." Jack looked lost and sad and Megan's heart ached for him, but she'd said what needed to be said. They'd vowed to be honest with each other and no matter how badly it hurt either of them; she intended to keep that promise. Jack was silent, his gaze on his feet.

"You could say something here," she told him.

"Like what, Megan?"

"Like you didn't mean it, or that you have some sleeping disorder that makes you say crazy things, or that you just suffered from a single moment of temporary insanity." He shook his head and frowned. "Or you could just take it back."

Jack stood, leaned against the wall and crossed his arms over his chest. He wanted to grab her in a fireman's hold, haul her up those stairs and make love to her. Show her how much he wanted her, needed her, loved her. Instead he resisted the urge to reach out to her and ignored the hand she'd laid on his forearm.

"I won't take it back, Megan. It would've come up at one time or another. I love you, always have and that's not likely to change." He attempted a smile and failed. Shaking his head he continued, "Hell, I've even been carrying a ring around with me for the past week, just waiting for the right time. Guess my subconscious got ahead of me." He barked a dry laugh. "I'm sorry Megan, but I can't, won't take it back." She didn't say anything and Jack couldn't bear the silence that was ringing in his ears. "I should go. You know where to find me if you need me. The dogs are in my backyard. Feel free to get them whenever you want. I'll be gone most of the day." He touched two fingers to his lips for a sensual kiss then gently touched them to her lips. After a moment he turned and left without another word. Megan wanted to run after him, but her legs wouldn't move. Her head hurt, her heart ached, and her eyes stung from the tears she'd held back. As soon as she heard his car door slam she let them flow and cried. And cried. And cried.

***

Jack left Megan's and drove around resisting the miserable urge to find a bottle, crawl inside it, and never come out. He felt like he'd been sucker punched in the heart. She didn't love him. He'd given her ample opportunity to tell him if she did but she never took the bait. He knew asking her to marry him would be tricky. She had trust issues thanks to Ted, and was scared of getting burned once again by love. What she didn't understand was he wasn't Ted and she shouldn't make him pay for the mistakes Ted had made.

Jack stopped at a red light and glanced out his window at the neon sign that read 'The Longhorn'. Now that had been one hell of a night. Visions of Megan bending over that pool table attempting shots, her backed up against the wall while he drove her crazy with his hands…his mouth…his fingers. Then they were in his garage on his bike and she straddled him and he saw stars. And that bed. The things they'd done in that bed. He closed his eyes and remembered the way she felt, tasted, the way she bit her lip when she climaxed, the ways she arched her hips to him to take him deeper…deeper…until he thought he would explode…

A horn was blaring. "Move it asshole," some guy was yelling from the car behind him. Jack shook himself out of his little reverie and noticed the light had turned green. Jack accelerated and drove around for what seemed like forever and ended up in the parking lot of 'The Longhorn' once again. If he went in, he'd piss away five years of sobriety and probably waste the rest of his life brooding on it. He checked his watch. Ten-thirty. Too early for a meeting or at least any he knew of. He could go to work, but he wouldn't get a damn thing done. He dug for his cell phone and punched in Stacy's number.

Twenty minutes later she met him at Denny's, a worried look on her face, her brown eyes somber. They got the small talk out of the way and then Jack told her word for word what had happened with Megan. Stacy leaned back in the booth and sighed.

"Well, I know she loves you, Jack. I'm sure of that. Maybe it's like you said and she needs some time to adjust. I mean she's endured some pretty major changes in her life over the past month."

Jack's gaze never left his coffee cup. "Maybe."

"She'll come around, Jack, just give her some time."

He'd given her fifteen years. "That's what I'm doing."

"I could talk to her," Stacy suggested.

"Nah, thanks anyway though."

"Maybe you just need to go after her, be persuasive, not take no for an answer."

Jack shook his head. "Nope I won't chase her. She knows what I want and when she comes around, if she comes around, it has to be completely her decision. It will have to be because she loves me. Because she wants me. Not the other way around."

They sat in silence for a moment then Stacy said quietly, "Jack."

"Yeah?"

"Thank you. I couldn't do this without you."

Jack smiled and thought of the irony of the situation. He'd been helping her with her sobriety and now he was leaning on her to keep him sober. His mother had told him once that God put certain people in your life for a reason. She was obviously right about that because if he hadn't been sponsoring Stacy, if he wouldn't have been ashamed of himself for letting her down he'd have been shit faced drunk right now. "Anytime," he said and truly meant it.

***

It had been over a week since that dreadful night at Jack's when she'd snuck out of his house like the coward that she was. Aside from his urgent visit the next day she hadn't heard from him or seen him at all. It was as if he'd just walked away without looking back. She chided herself for feeling sorry for herself; she'd done it to herself. Jack had been up front about what he wanted. He'd told her he loved her and that he always would and she believed him. She was the one who had run and she regretted it now.

Jack was doing okay; she'd checked on him through Stacy who was going to meetings with him a couple times a week. Stacy also reported that he'd literally poured himself into his work, taking on extra cases and working long hours. Stacy had also cautioned her about losing Jack.

"If you love him, Megan, you'd better tell him so," Stacy had said. "So what if marriage scares you, you don't have to get hitched right away. What would really suck is losing him forever."

That would suck Megan agreed. In fact it would be downright unbearable but Jack wanted all or nothing and Megan wasn't ready to give it all to him.

Stacy had had an answer for that too. "Megan, he just wants you. Sure he wants his ring on your finger but he won't rush that. He'll wait until you're ready."

Damn Stacy was always so sensible. She made everything seem so darn simple when in reality it was a huge complicated mess.

"Just call him, Megan," Stacy had urged. "He misses you and I know you miss him. Remember he's not Ted and quit making him pay for Ted's mistakes."

And that was when it began to make sense for Megan. She'd been so wrapped up in all the chaos in her life that she hadn't dealt with her anger toward Ted and as long as she was carrying that around she was denying herself the right to love and trust again. She had lost Ted, but that had been Ted's fault. She wouldn't let Ted keep her from being happy by losing Jack too. That's when she cried. For Ted, for herself, for the loss of her marriage and for Ted's death.

She was mad at Josie too for sleeping with Ted. Although she hadn't confirmed it, she knew it in her heart so she called Josie and asked her about it and Josie didn't deny it. She had slept with Ted about a year before Megan and Ted started dating. She never told Megan because Ted had asked her not to and she didn't think it was relevant since it was before Megan and Ted were together. Megan dropped it and forgave Josie. She loved her too much not to and forgiving her was much easier than carrying around the hurt.

Next, she did what she should have done a week ago. She picked up the phone and called Jack. She got his voicemail and left a heartfelt message. "Jack, its Megan. I'm an idiot and I'm sorry. Please call me. I miss you."

The last thing on her list was to completely get rid of Ted. She'd packed most of his belongings and loaded them into the U-Haul which his brother had finally picked up and taken care of. But there were still little pieces of Ted all over the place and she couldn't move on until they too were gone. She started in the basement, packing up all his processing equipment and various collections of junk he'd kept. Mickey had helped her get all of that stuff out and disposed of, some of it going to his parents, some to charity and a small portion—his baseball cards and autographed sports stuff—she set aside for Tiffany's baby. If the baby was in fact Ted's, and she had no reason to believe otherwise despite Ted's supposed vasectomy, it deserved something of its fathers.

She was going through the bookcase when she found their old yearbooks. She pulled one out—hers judging from the notes from friends— and thumbed through it. There was a photo of the entire football team with Ted looking impossibly young, smiling that heart stopping smile that had made the butterflies go crazy in her stomach. She ran her thumb over his face in the photo and sighed. Who would have thought things would've ended up this way?

Flipping through the pages she found a photo of her, Josie, Stacy, Mickey and Ali. They were nothing but a blur of big hair, blue eye shadow and leg warmers; the notation said 'Friends Forever'. She smiled. Now that was one statement that had certainly held true. They'd been inseparable then and now they were each other's life lines. Her eyes filled with tears as she realized just how much she'd been blessed.

She turned to the last page in her yearbook and was startled when a familiar name jumped out at her. She wiped her eyes and stared at the signature, so sure her eyes were deceiving her. They weren't. She read the caption.

"The first time I saw you, you stole my heart and it will be yours forever. You were standing there in your cheerleading uniform, chatting with your friends and you looked my way and smiled. I melted inside and I knew at that moment I was yours. Of course I've only been able to love you from afar; after all you're Ted's girl. But my mother always said, 'When it's true love, set it free. If it comes back, it was meant to be. I guess only time will tell, but until then, I'll spend my time loving you. Always, J.J. Westin."

Megan hastily turned the pages until she found the W's. There smiling back at her was a much younger, much scrawnier, much geekier version of Jack smiling shyly at the camera, those big brown eyes glittering.

"Oh my God," Megan muttered. Suddenly things fell into place. She remembered Jack, that shy kid who was always around but no one ever really noticed him He was quiet and awkward, too skinny for his frame and the butt of way too many jokes from the cool kids and the jocks. Megan had actually felt sorry for him because he seemed so…sweet. She had always been nice to him but in hindsight she realized she'd ignored him like everyone else had. Well she wouldn't ignore him anymore.

She remembered the story he'd told her about his long lost love, that bitch cheerleader who still held his heart. She chuckled. She'd actually been jealous of herself. She was his cheerleader, his girl and she wanted to be his wife.

On the back porch when he'd kissed her he'd said he'd waited fifteen years for that. She hadn't understood then, but she did now and she couldn't imagine waiting fifteen minutes to be in his arms much less fifteen years.

She thought fast and developed a plan. If it was his cheerleader he wanted...

***

Jack got home late and checked his voicemail. His father had called, a salesman offering close out savings on siding for his house, and the last message was from Megan. Jack froze his heart thudding in his chest. He replayed the message and listened to it again. She said she'd been an idiot. She missed him. That sounded promising.

He eyed the clock. It was well past midnight; he'd been surveilling a store for the last six hours, watching the night stockers who were being accused of walking off with merchandise during the night shift. She was probably asleep and he didn't want to wake her. First thing in the morning he'd call her or maybe better yet he'd drop by. For now, about the most he could do was drop into bed and fall into a deep, dead to the world sleep. Maybe tomorrow night Megan would be beside him.

***

Megan ran to her mother's and rifled around in her old room until she found what she was looking for. Her mother stood sleepily leaning in the door jam.

"It's past midnight, Megan. What on earth are you doing?"

Megan hurried past her mother, stopping briefly to peck her on the cheek. "I'm getting married, mom. See you later."

Her mother crossed herself, "Dear lord, why me? And why not at a decent hour?"

Next stop was Josie's. Josie answered the door yawning, wrapped up in a sheet. Dr. Ross called out to see who was there from the bedroom.

"I need a favor Jos," she said and once she had what she needed she left as abruptly as she'd barged in, dragging Dr. Ross and Josie with her both bewildered.

An hour later she watched as Josie picked the lock.

"I don't think I've ever been so turned on," Jon said. "My woman is a criminal. A run of the mill thief in the night." Josie had the door open in less than a minute.

"Hot damn," Jon continued. "You gotta admire skill like that." He took Josie's hand and kissed it. "Will you marry me, Josie?" Josie blinked. "You know I love you and hell woman, I'd save a hell of a lot of money if I ever needed a locksmith."

"Well gee, when you put it that way, how can I say no." Josie answered then folded herself into his arms. "Let's go home and I'll be the naughty burglar."

"I'll be the, hardnosed, horny cop," Jon said and before Megan could thank them they were gone, Jon carrying his future bride down the sidewalk into the night.

Must be a full moon tonight, Megan thought.

Megan moved like a cat through the house and paused at the open door to Jack's bedroom. He was asleep on his side, clutching her pillow against his chest. His handsome features were dangerous and dramatic in the moonlit room, his face smoothed out in a peaceful sleep. She almost didn't want to wake him. Almost.

"Give me an I!" she shouted and Jack's eyes shot open. Immediately he squinted trying to focus. He looked completely surprised. Megan stood at the foot of his bed in her cheerleading outfit, pom poms and all, her hair long and brown, her face free of makeup except for a light splash of lip gloss. She looked just as she had fifteen years ago; the first time he'd seen her.

If this is a dream do not wake me up!

"Give me an L!" She shook her hips and swung her pom poms.

"Give me an O!" Jack was sitting straight up now, the sheet carelessly crumpled around his waist, allowing her to gaze at his broad chest, hard abdomen. Oh yeah!

"Give me a V!" She kicked one foot out in front of her, amazed at how well she remembered the moves. Jack was speechless and she liked that. She had plenty she needed to say.

"Give me an E!" Jack reached for her and she allowed him to cop a quick feel.

"Give me a U!" She shouted as he hauled her down on top of him so that she was straddling him. He ran his fingers through her long brown hair amazed. Then the wig fell off in his hand.

In a low sultry voice she said, "What does that spell? I love you, Jack."

He took her mouth then devouring her, drinking her in, staking his claim to her. She broke the kiss and whispered low in his ear. "I hear you've got a thing for cheerleaders." She ran her tongue down the contours of his neck.

"Only one," he responded.

"Yeah?" she unleashed that crooked smile on him. "You like the uniform?"

He was already tugging at it trying to get it off. "I like it better off." His grin was wicked, wild and purely Jack.

He made love to her slow and sweet and for the first time in her life she felt complete, content and truly happy. He tightened his hold on her and with his breath warm on her temple he said, "Don't ever leave me again."

"I won't," she rolled her head to stare into his mesmerizing gaze. "You set me free and I came back. So I guess this means we're meant to be."

"Damn right we are, babe." He traced his finger down her cheek, over her jawline.

"So what happens next?" she asked holding her breath. Jack reached into his nightstand and pulled out a small silver box. "Marry me, Megan?"

Amy Johnson

About the Author

Amy Johnson lives in New Mexico with her husband, children and 4 dogs. She is currently working on her next book which is a sequel to Meg's Moment. She enjoys writing, reading and crafting.

Author's photo taken by Leslie Bailey Photography.

www.ingramcontent.com/pod-product-compliance
Lightning Source LLC
Chambersburg PA
CBHW021953170626
46808CB00001B/131